To Marcia,
Enjoy.
Gloria

The Blue Rose

By

Gloria Alden

D1529126

Published by

Copyright 2012 Gloria Alden

Cover Design by Kristen Fritch

www.fritchieart.com

Dedication

To my son, John, who died too soon

To my parents, who instilled in me a love of reading

To my brother, Jerry, who shared my growing up years.

To my granddaughter, Megan, a little angel in Heaven

Acknowledgements

My sister, Elaine, started me on the path to writing mysteries years ago. I had thought about it for a long time, but procrastinated. Then one evening, Elaine set up a meeting with our sister, Suzanne, and we brainstormed a plot and characters. That's what I needed. Once I started, those characters and the plot took off on a life of their own.

I was helped down this long road when I joined Sisters in Crime, and even more so when I joined their subgroup, the Guppies. I wouldn't have a book out if it weren't for them. They are the greatest support group an unpublished or published mystery writer could have.

It is through the Guppies that I got my fantastic critique partners, Ann Godridge and Mary Willite. They have edited and encouraged me every step of the way.

My local Trumbull Writers Group has been a source of help and support for years, especially Laura Byrnes, who has been a great editor and supporter.

I'm grateful for my granddaughter, Kristen Fritch, who designed my cover.

I also need to thank my family; my children, Joe, who willingly posed as the dead body for my cover, Susan and Mary; my siblings, Elaine, Suzanne, Catherine and Phillip; and for my extended family; sister-in-law, Joanne, brother-in-law, Bill, daughter-in-law, Pam, and son-in-law, Mike; my grandchildren, Samantha, Emilie, Jacob, Chad, Steve and Kristen.

The Cast of Characters

Catherine Jewell - a part-time botanist at Elmwood Gardens and owner of Roses in Thyme.

John MacDougal - Police chief of Portage Falls and co-owner of Carriage House Books

Martha MacDougal – John's mother owner of The Elms, a bed & breakfast and co-owner of Carriage House Books

Augustus Chatterton III – The wealthy head of the board of directors of Elmwood Gardens

Ed Flavian – former head gardener of Elmwood Gardens who Chatterton fired

Violet Flavian – Ed's wife, hostess at Elmwood's Wisteria Tea Room and part time worker at Roses in Thyme

Millie Mullens – cook for the Wisteria Tea Room with a nose for gossip

Greg Robert Burns – a former monk now head gardener at Elmwood Gardens

Tyler Birchfield – The new manager of Elmwood Gardens who admits he hated Chatterton

Vera Chatterton – Chatterton's wife, a cold aloof woman

Alicia Chatterton   - Chatterton's daughter, estranged from her dad, but not several young men

Brad Chatterton - the missing son

Olga Yamikoff - mysterious Russian emigrant recently hired at Elmwood Gardens

Tony Montecalvo - John's young sidekick, a real chick magnet

Joe Salcone -   Full time policeman working nights

Rev. Bill Johnson - Minister of Trinity Evangelical Fellowship Church; part time policeman

Pete Domenici - Another part time policeman

Susy Fisher - The flaky secretary and dispatcher for the police department

Josh MacDougal - John's sixteen year old son

Alma Porcase - elderly recluse who supplements her income by rummaging in dumpsters and garbage cans

Father O'Shawnessy - Elderly pastor of Our Lady of the Roses Catholic Church

Maggie Fiest - Catherine's neighbor and friend

Winifred Partridge - a former math teacher now mayor and groundskeeper of Portage Falls

Tom Rockwell - college student working for Elmwood Gardens with an interest in Alicia Chatterton

Christy Taylor - Teenage part time worker at Roses in Thyme

Chapter One

"Morning has broken, like the first morning. Blackbirds have spoken like the first bird," Catherine Jewell warbled off key. Once a music teacher had told her to only move her lips without making a sound during a fifth grade concert. She'd been self-conscious about singing for a long time after that, but couldn't help singing when she was happy or when she heard a song she liked. Today she was singing along with Cat Stevens in nonexistent traffic as she drove to Elmwood Gardens. She turned the volume a little louder than suited this early morning hour to help drown out the ominous sounds coming from under the hood of her old truck. A white cat suddenly streaked across the road in front of her. Sucking in a sharp breath, she slammed on the brakes causing the truck's worn tires to emit a loud shriek. With relief she saw the flick of a white tail as the cat slipped under the chain link fence by the road. "That was a close one," she muttered. She'd hate to be responsible for a dead cat even if it wasn't a black one, she thought, then scolded herself. Since when had she become superstitious?

As her heart settled down, Catherine wondered if her stalled truck would start. Offering up a silent prayer to St. Joseph, she turned the key while carefully pumping the gas pedal so it wouldn't flood. "Please start," she said as the truck complained and made a few weak attempts to comply. She glanced at her watch and frowned. She didn't have time for this today and certainly couldn't afford a tow

11

truck right now, either. Finally, with a cough of resignation, the engine roared. Putting the truck into gear, she drove a few hundred yards before making a smooth turn onto the paved and curved drive leading to the entrance of Elmwood Gardens. A line of yard-armed security lights went off in unison as dawn lit the eastern horizon pushing a faint pink radiance through the light mist. A cherry picker was parked in the visitor's parking lot with several workers drinking coffee beside it. They turned to watch her as she pulled up to massive wrought iron gates and carded them. The gates swung open and she drove through before they closed behind her.

Catherine drove past the old carriage house that held The Terra Cotta Gift Shoppe and Visitor Center. The glint on bone china tea cups glowed in dozens of small windows. She took her time driving away from the entrance facilities to take in the panorama of the gardens. She liked to inspect the gardens in the early morning when they were so peaceful and quiet before the work crews pulled into the back lot at seven. To the east, bulb gardens and perennial beds with boxwood edges descended in levels down to Japanese water gardens and the lily pond from which much of this mist arose each summer night. Even now the mist floated upward, following an unseen gradient.

On the lawns in front of the visitor center, two large yellow and white tents with pennants flying seemed to float in the mist. Visions of huge decorated horses charging, their armor clad riders intent on unhorsing their opponents with long lances, filled her mind. She could almost hear the clash of lance against armor and crowds cheering. Catherine's smile disappeared and her eyes saddened as she thought of how Ellie, her daughter, would have loved it. She'd started calling herself Lady Eleanor of Aquitaine the summer before she'd died.

Ahead stood the foreboding Chatterton Manor, a massive cut sandstone building with Georgian chimneys projecting clenched fists into the early dawn. Much of the house was hidden from view by enormous white oaks, copper beeches and other old trees, but in her mind's eye she saw the elaborate trophy house built as an opulent display of one man's wealth, Augustus Chatterton, the First, grandfather of the current Augustus Chatterton. When she'd first driven up this drive more than a year ago to apply for the job of part time botanist, she'd been enchanted by the spreading lawns, large trees, many gardens and the mansion and wondered what it'd be like to be rich enough to own a place like this. Of course, now it was a public garden and hadn't been owned by any one person for quite some time. Soon after starting her job at Elmwood, she realized even if she were rich enough to own an estate like this, she wouldn't be as happy as she was now with the freedom to enjoy the gardens and grounds and few of the responsibilities that went with it. She wouldn't want to give up her business, either. She'd worked hard to build up Roses in Thyme, a small garden center on the outskirts of Portage Falls. If she was careful, she hoped to soon show a reasonable profit, too.

Reaching the manor house, she pulled into a spot beside the head gardener's truck, a truck even older than hers, parked next to his small stone cottage. She glanced at the cottage as she slid out of her pickup. He was probably up and out already. Clipboard in hand, she headed for the rose garden and the topiary garden.

Catherine entered the rose garden through a great cedar latticed arch crested with crimson roses. The first beds held hybrid teas each more beautiful than the ones preceding it. She stooped to smell a musky 'Midas Touch,' its golden blooms little suns in the gray morning. Walking between the rows of English roses, her eyes wandered over them checking for black spot. These damp mists created trouble for roses in this temperate climate, but they were luscious in their vibrant colors; their leaves perfect with no yellowed dead leaves marring the mulch beneath. Greg Robert Burns certainly was meticulous in keeping the gardens groomed, she thought. He was as good as Ed had been. She bit her bottom lip. Still, it was too soon to relax the vigil. This is early in the season for black spot even without spraying, but it could happen like it did last year.

Leaving the large rose garden, she went into the Blue Garden next. She'd checked it thoroughly the day before in preparation for today's reception that will introduce 'The Augustus Chatterton' rose, so she only gave it a cursory glance. Before going on to the Topiary Garden, she slipped down a partially hidden walkway to look at the White Garden. Surrounded by stone walls, it was one of her favorite places, quiet and tranquil. Standing at the top of the short flight of stone steps leading down, a smile touched the corners of her mouth and her shoulders relaxed as she felt its magic wash over her. White blooms in the mist had a surreal quality this morning. Earlier maps of Elmwood Gardens, had called it the Secret Garden because its entrance was camouflaged by a narrow path through tall rhododendrons. It'd been planned that way by the original creator of the gardens, Lela Chatterton, as a special retreat. Unless a visitor happened on it by chance, or read the maps carefully, most people missed this spot entirely on their tour.

Catherine surveyed the little pool and flowers below. A pillar of white clematis at the other end of the garden was shaped like a human form this misty morning. Blinking as one of the white shapes in the garden moved, she focused on what caught her eye then realized it was the head gardener's white cat. She wondered if it was the cat she'd almost hit. It crouched, belly low to the ground, a soft mouse clutched in its claws. Catherine turned away. She was resigned to the laws of nature, but didn't like observing its brutal side. Leaving the cat to its meal, she left the garden and entered the topiary garden through an opening in a tall hedge bordering the Blue Garden. Catching sight of a shadow melding into the topiary of an old bent gnome, she halted. Was someone there or was it a trick of early morning shadows that made the gnome seem to move? She shrugged, walked over and checked behind it. No one was there. Still she glanced uneasily at the topiaries nearby as she walked to the juniper dragon to check for the white juniper scale she'd seen last week. She looked closely pleased to notice the sticky drenched bark. Yep, insecticide. Great! It wouldn't do to have the favored topiary die.

Hearing voices in the perennial garden beyond, Catherine walked to the entrance and looked in. Augustus Chatterton, the head of the Board of Directors of Elmwood Gardens, was talking to Greg Robert Burns, the head gardener. Chatterton glanced up and saw her.

"Come over here. You need to see this." His voice matched the scowl on his face.

Catherine raised her chin as she walked over. She wouldn't be intimidated. She wouldn't be intimidated, she thought over and over. If only her heart would believe it.

"See that?" Chatterton pointed at a clump of irises behind a bed of pansies.

Catherine looked closely where he was pointing and noticed what had upset him. A few thin lines of yellow were running down the leaves of several irises. "Iris borers," she said

"Oh, iris borers," he said sarcastically. "And it took me to find them? Neither you nor Greg Robert saw them before this?"

Catherine looked at Greg Robert standing slightly behind Augustus Chatterton. He winked at her and his lips twitched up slightly.

"No, I didn't. Signs of them can appear overnight."

"So you're trying to tell me that all of a sudden on the night before my big reception, iris borers just happened to show up and make the irises look damaged? Maybe the board will need to rethink both of your contracts when they're up for renewal." He wheeled around and stormed off down the walk towards his home on the other side of the gardens.

"Dammit!" Catherine said when Chatterton was out of hearing.

"Oh, my! Such strong language from our Ms. Jewell," Greg Robert said.

She turned to look at him, saw his grin and returned it. "Do you think we need to look for new jobs?"

He shook his head. "I doubt it, and you're right, you know. You can't know iris borers are there until those little streaks appear. Don't let him get to you."

"You're right. It's just that I'm feeling a bit on edge today."

"What's wrong?"

She shrugged as she started towards the Wisteria Tea Room and coffee, and he fell in step beside her. "I don't know. I wish I didn't have to go to Chatterton's reception this afternoon. The whole thing is just . . ." She scowled and shook her hands as if to shoo away flies.

"I understand. You could just make an appearance and leave early." He studied her face when she didn't answer and asked gently, "What else is wrong?"

Her shoulders slumped, "It's my truck. I took her to Fortunati Ford 'cause she keeps stalling. The mechanic told me to prepare for the funeral."

"He said that?"

"Not exactly, but when he gave me an estimate of all that needs done, he might as well have. He said the engine was old and tired. It needs to be rebuilt or replaced. Oh, and the choke's bad. That's why she keeps stalling." She paused and took a deep breath. "The shocks and exhaust system are shot, too." She sighed. "He didn't say it, but I know I'm driving an environmental hazard."

Greg Robert looked at her in sympathy. "Guess you'll

16

have to trade it in."

"I can't afford it." Loath to seem like a whiner, she added "Oh, it'll work out. I've got St. Joseph on the job."

He gave her a mock frown. "He was a good carpenter, but a mechanic?"

"I'm sure he could be. Anyway, I think he's a caring saint for helpless females."

He snorted. "Helpless? You? Never!"

"Well, there are a few things beyond my skills. Like mechanics."

"I think what you need right now is coffee and one of Millie's cinnamon rolls."

She grinned at him. "That's where I was heading. Are you going, too?"

"I'll be there shortly. I have to pick up a flat of violas for the tables first," he said heading down a different path.

Catherine picked up speed as she headed for the manor house tea room. The domed Victorian conservatory beyond was beginning to glint as the first rays hit the horizon. She'd checked it out thoroughly yesterday, too. She paused for a moment at a stone alcove tucked into a hedge of rhododendrons near steps leading to the tea room terrace. A statue of Saint Fiacre, patron saint of gardeners, rested there with spade in hand. Last fall Greg Robert had put the statue there replacing a statue of Buddha. She'd never heard of this saint before, but now she felt a special affection for him. You couldn't have too many saints to call on for help, she thought, even though the scientist in her taunted this childlike faith. Today Saint Fiacre seemed melancholy. She traced the plaque at the base of the statue lightly with her fingers.

Glorious Saint Fiacre,
Thou canst do beautiful things;
Send a breeze of roses to calm
This feverish life of ours.

17

If only he could. Some days there seemed to be too many problems. How could she afford a newer truck if Chatterton didn't renew her contract? She shook her head, and climbed the terrace steps. When she opened the door labeled private to the staff dining room, the intoxicating smell of coffee combined with the yeasty smell of fresh cinnamon rolls greeted her. She paused a moment and inhaled deeply, a look of bliss on her face before she went in and sat down. Glancing around, she spied Millie's pert auburn head popping up from behind the counter.

"The usual for you?" Millie's voice, raspy from too many years of smoking, greeted Catherine as she headed for the coffee maker before hearing Catherine's answer.

"I'm more than ready."

Putting her elbow on the table and propping her chin on her fist, Catherine watched as Millie poured her coffee and placed a cinnamon roll on a plate. Millie looked like a young girl from the neck down. She wondered how old Millie was. Probably in her sixties, she thought and hoped she'd be that spry when she was her age, but it was hard to imagine being that old, although it was getting easier with each birthday, she acknowledged. As Millie approached, Catherine smiled into the myopic blue eyes magnified by thick lenses in blue, tortoise shell glasses perched on a pointed nose. She made Catherine think of a friendly sparrow. As Millie set the coffee and a roll before her, Catherine rubbed the tip of her own nose.

"Thank you." She turned her attention to the welcome cup of coffee, inhaling its rich aroma. It was a rare day when she had time for coffee at home before coming to the gardens.

"Where do you want these?" Greg Robert backed into the room holding a heavy box of violas in clay pots.

Millie's eyes widened as she smiled. "Lovely! On the terrace. I want to put one on each table."

18

He followed her through the swinging doors into the elegant Wisteria Tea Room to its separate terrace. In contrast the staff dining room was small and furnished with a hodge podge of tables and chairs, the wood scarred and marred by years of use.

"Hey, Catherine. Feeling better now that you've had some coffee?" he asked when he returned.

She smiled and nodded.

"Good!" He beamed and helped himself to a cup of coffee from the carafe before coming over to sprawl on a wooden chair across from Catherine. His muscular body was more suited for hard work than sitting at ease.

"You ready for the big day?" she asked.

He rolled his eyes heavenward. "Is Chatterton for real? I can't believe he's gone to such lengths."

"I agree," She took a bite of her cinnamon roll. She'd felt this way even before he'd reamed her out earlier.

His brows drew together. "Something's not quite right. But I can't exactly put my finger on it."

Catherine wiped syrup from the corner of her mouth. "Is it all the money he's spending?" She'd heard Greg Robert had been a monk before coming to Elmwood Gardens and wondered why he left the monastery to become head gardener here. She supposed a man who'd once vowed to follow a life of poverty would be uncomfortable with such a lavish display of wealth. She also wondered how such a good looking man could have embraced the life of a monk. But what did she really know about monks? She had to admit, though, his almost shoulder length brown hair along with his beard, looked like they'd go with a monk's habit. His mouth usually held a gentle amused smile. And his voice. She could listen to him reading even from an auto mechanic's book for hours. But it was his brown eyes she liked the most; eyes that reminded her of other brown eyes just as warm, just as kind. David's eyes.

19

He stirred his coffee a while without answering, then breathed out a deep breath. "True, but it's more than that. I can't picture him propagating a rose like 'The Augustus Chatterton.' Have you ever looked at his nails?"

"No. Why?"

"You ever see a gardener with manicured nails?" He picked up her hand, looked at it and smiled. "See what I mean?"

She colored and hid her hands, chipped nails and all, in her lap and out of sight.

He laughed. "Vanity, vanity."

Not vanity, she thought, not vanity anymore. She brought her hands back and picked up her cup of coffee.

Millie came back into the room. "Can I get you anything, Greg Robert?"

"I'll have one of those delicious rolls like the elegant Catherine is devouring."

Catherine raised her eyebrows at the word elegant, and her lips twitched. That was not the word to describe someone with chipped nails, someone usually in jeans or shorts, who kept her blond hair cut short and simple for convenience, and usually didn't bother with any makeup except for a quick dab of lipstick once a day if she thought about it.

Millie stood for a moment, head cocked. "There's something I've always wanted to ask you. Why do you go by both names? It's unusual, but kinda nice, too."

"My mother was from Scotland and such a great lover of Robert Burns, that I'm not sure she didn't marry my father because of his last name." He smiled. "My dad wanted me named Greg after him, but Mom had her way, too. She gave me the middle name of Robert and insisted on calling me by the full name of Greg Robert. I got used to it, and as a teenager I rather liked being unusual in a small way."

"It is rather lyrical. Greg Robert Burns." Catherine

smiled before giving him a severe look. "That reminds me. Your cat, Bonnie Charlie, had a wee mousie in the White Garden. I almost lost my appetite."

He laughed. "I'll have to speak to that cat of mine and ask him to confine his hunting to the dark hours of the night."

"Are you going to the reception this afternoon?" Millie looked at Catherine.

She grimaced. "Yeah."

"Violet's going, too." A wistful look appeared on Millie's face.

"She called last night and asked if I'd pick her up."

Violet was hostess in the Tea Room, and Millie was the cook. They were friends, about the same age, Catherine guessed. Violet also worked part time at Roses in Thyme for her when she was free.

"More coffee, Catherine?" Millie asked.

"No, I've got to get back and open the shop." She put money by her plate and stood up.

"See ya, Catherine, and don't worry about Chatterton," Greg Robert said as she headed for the door.

She gave him a smile and a wave as she left. Fortunately her truck started at the first turn of the key as if it'd never caused any trouble before. As she drove back down the drive, she noticed workers fastening lattice to tent poles, setting up tables, and placing potted plants and small trees on parquet floors under the tents. Although curious about what the final results would look like, she still wished she could skip this event. Earlier it was because she was uncomfortable with large fancy affairs, and now she hated the thought of facing Chatterton after what he'd said. She knew she should let it go, but she couldn't. At least not yet. Even more she didn't want to see what she felt was the undeserved acclaim Augustus Chatterton would be receiving today.

Chapter Two

Augustus Chatterton headed towards home. Although the day promised to be a good one with the faint mists clearing, he was still frowning and grumbling under his breath. Going through a gap in the hemlock hedge, he strode towards a modern redwood and stone home tucked into the hillside. It looked like a natural part of the landscape. Unaware of the sounds of birds or the sweet fragrance of an early June day, he thought only about Elmwood Gardens and Chatterton Manor, his ancestral home that he still felt by rights should be his. If it was too late to reclaim his heritage, at least he would be able to restore the name of Chatterton through the rose he was introducing today. That is if everything went well.

A ringing brought Chatterton out of his reverie. He checked the number on his cell phone before answering. "Yes?" He listened for a few moments as his eyebrows drew closer together. "Check Osborne's Funeral Home. See if they have a limo available. Hell of a time for you to develop car problems. That English group has already been delayed a day, and I want them picked up at the airport at once, and I don't care how you do it. Just get them here."

He should have known better than to trust Arnie's Taxi and Limo Service. Incompetent people seemed to fill his life, he thought.

Entering the house, he went in search of his wife.

"Vera! Where are you? Vera!"

He found her in the dining room plucking dead flowers from an arrangement on the sideboard and dropping them into a bag she held.

"Why didn't you answer me?" He scowled.

"I don't shout," she said, without turning around.

He stared at her. Her tall willowy build and pale skin made her look fragile, but that was deceiving, he knew, as well as anyone who was her opponent on the tennis court. But that was on the tennis court. At home she was a different person. Long ago he'd given up playing tennis with her. He noticed she wore a new dress. Blue. She looked good in blue. Her perfectly coiffed blond hair was impeccable, as usual. With her refined good looks, he had to admit she was the perfect wife for a man of his stature, in spite of the fact she annoyed him in little ways. While she rarely argued with him, there was often a measuring look in her pale blue eyes, a look that intimated she was biding her time. Had that look increased of late? He wondered, but then discarded the thought. This wasn't a day to dwell on it.

"Did the caterer call?" he asked.

"Yes."

"Well?" He bit out when she didn't go on.

"He couldn't get enough lobster tails and wanted to substitute poached salmon steaks," she said still without looking at him.

"Why didn't you call me?" He enunciated each word.

"I thought you were in the shower." Except for crushing the dead flowers with a bit more vigor, she showed no sign she was aware of his anger.

"What did you tell him?"

She spoke through thinned lips. "Whatever he thought best would be fine."

The cords on his neck stood out. He turned and went into the hall, and muttered a string of swear words as he punched in numbers on the phone.

"You've known about this for two months! Two months!" Chatterton shouted. "I would have thought with the money I'm paying you, everything would have gone smoothly and perfectly. I'll have to settle for the salmon, but don't ever use my name for a reference." Snapping his phone shut, he gritted his teeth as he went back into the library. "If I ran my businesses the way he does, I wouldn't be the success I am today."

"With my money," Vera murmured.

"What did you say?"

She drew in a deep breath before answering him. "Nothing." She ground a wilted rose in her fist and dropped it into the bag with the others.

Walking over to the French doors, he looked out over manicured lawns.

"Did Bradley come back yet?"

"No."

"That kid! I'll make him pay if he messes up my day." Chatterton wondered where Bradley was. Probably staying with one of his deadbeat friends. A rock band! Shit! His son was lucky he didn't deck him last night before he ran out. Was this going to be a generational thing? Was his son going to turn out like his grandparents living in some fantasy world of music and art?"

He said over his shoulder, "As soon as I shower and change, I'm walking back over to the gardens to make sure everything is going as planned. I'll see you there later and for once try to smile and act like you're enjoying yourself, won't you?"

As he went up the stairs to his room, he started to smile as he thought how the name of Chatterton would become as renowned as that of David Austin's when he introduced to the gardening world at Elmwood Gardens, his rightful home, the first and only true blue rose, 'The Augustus Chatterton.'

He didn't look back to see his wife watching him or the hatred on her face which added the color and life to her eyes and face that had been missing before.

Chapter Three

Catherine noticed Christy's bike parked near the front door when she returned from Elmwood Gardens. Glancing at her watch, she realized she was ten minutes late getting back. As she unlocked the door to Roses in Thyme, she was glad no customers had shown up yet.

She went outside to tables filled with perennials where Christy was watering foxgloves and watched the girl for a while before announcing herself. She was fond of this shy teenage girl with long brown hair falling into her eyes. Acne marred a face showing promise of a quiet beauty someday. She remembered her own teenage years when she'd been plagued with acne, too. How insecure it'd made her feel. She wondered if Ellie would've developed acne. Probably. It seemed to run in families. Catherine's brothers had it, too.

"Hi, Christy, "You're early this morning."

She looked up with a smile. "Ricky and Allie were being annoying this morning. It's more peaceful here."

Catherine grinned at her. "At least until the customers start coming."

"It's still more peaceful unless they bring kids like my brother and sister." She rolled her eyes.

Catherine thought of the two kids who'd raced through her nursery yesterday knocking over plants while playing hide 'n seek in the greenhouse and moving plants to hide behind. Fortunately most kids weren't like them.

"When you're done here, bring up more hostas from the back. Quite a few sold yesterday, and we need to fill the empty spots. Check to see which ones we need. I know we need some 'Frances Williams', but I'm not sure what else.

Christy put down her watering can. "I'll get them now and finish watering later."

Watching her walk away, Catherine was glad she'd hired Christy to work for her on weekends during the school year and some weekdays now that school was out. She was lucky to have Violet Flavian to help, too. Violet didn't know much about plants, but she was very sociable and loved visiting with people. Since there were signs up by each cultivar telling its needs, blooming time and other information necessary to a potential buyer, Violet's lack of knowledge wasn't a detriment.

Catherine headed to the herb greenhouse to work. She combined two half trays of pineapple sage into one and moved down the tables doing the same with the different basils, thymes and other herbs. Although she was glad so many herbs and perennials were selling, she preferred seeing the tables full to overflowing with a wealth of greenery and flowers. Can't have your cake and eat it, too, she mentally chided herself. She loved working in this section of the greenhouse with its pungent and pleasant aroma. Next year, if she could manage it, she'd add a greenhouse just for herbs. She tried not to think about the set back a newer truck would be to those plans. There were so many unexpected expenses with a new business. She hoped when she became better established, she wouldn't always be juggling to pay bills. Thank goodness I have the part time position of botanist at Elmwood Gardens, she thought, and then remembered Chatterton's threat. Even though Greg Robert thought it was an empty threat, Catherine wasn't sure. Since he'd fired Ed Flavian, an excellent head gardener, she wouldn't be surprised if he did the same with her. She felt depressed thinking about it. Well, she wouldn't go down without a fight, she decided.

Glancing at her watch, she decided she'd have time to repot some lupines. She'd just started when a car came in.

Wiping soil coated hands on her apron, she headed to the sales area in time to see Chatterton's daughter, Alicia, swinging long bare legs from her red Porsche, then stand still a moment to let a breeze toss her dark hair. Catherine watched as she threaded her way into the shop, swinging her hips as much as her thin body would allow before stooping to pick up dropped keys, showing much of what she didn't wear under her thin yellow sundress. It was a mating game played to perfection for the young man following her, another in a long series of young men, Catherine figured, chosen to stoke her self-esteem. She shrugged. She didn't really know enough about her to make judgments. It could just be exuberant youth. She put on a helpful salesperson face as she took off her apron and tossed it aside before going into her shop.

Catherine watched Alicia lift a potted miniature polyanthus rose to her nose before closing her eyes to sniff seductively. As Catherine brushed potting soil from the counter and cast it into the trash, she felt like an overgrown hollyhock past its prime next to the lovely Alicia, who seemed to have bewitched the man with her. Even though Catherine was no longer in the game, she felt a little put out that she'd been relegated to the anonymity of a dull middle-aged nonentity by the young couple in front of her. For crying out loud I'm only forty not ninety, she thought.

"He wants to buy me a rose for my balcony. Isn't he sweet?" Alicia murmured glancing from the corner of her eye at the dark haired young man. She set the potted rose on the counter, "I can't have it in this old pot. I'd like it repotted in that terra cotta jardinière." She pointed a manicured finger across the room.

The young man retrieved the pot, and Catherine took it to the potting area in the back of the shop. After repotting it, she put protective wrapping around it before returning it to Alicia.

Alicia murmured a thank you then turned to the young

man. "I really must drop you off and hurry, Sweetie. Daddy would never forgive me if I were late for this extravaganza he's planned. Such a bore." She rolled her eyes and left the shop, swinging those long legs back into the low slung car and peeling out of the gravel parking lot before her friend had his door completely closed.

As Alicia pulled out, scattering gravel behind her, she barely missed Maggie Fiest, Catherine's neighbor, coming in on a bicycle. The woman braked, turned and glared at the retreating car.

"That girl's going to kill someone someday," Maggie complained as she turned and walked her bike to the shop. Pulling her helmet off, she finger combed her brown hair.

Catherine smiled at her. "What brings you here this morning?"

"I wasn't sure you'd still be here."

"For a short while yet, but I've got to get ready soon. Anything special or did you just want to chat."

"A little of both," Maggie said. "I want to fill in a bare spot in the back of the border next to Anderson's pasture where my buddleia didn't make it. I'm thinking pink. Something that'll make a nice contrast with the Russian sage and artemesia."

"That's pretty sunny there. How about phlox? I've some lovely pink cultivars still left."

"Sounds good. What was the Chatterton girl doing here?" Maggie asked as they walked back to the perennial area. "She doesn't seem the type to be interested in gardening."

"No. She bought a miniature rose, or rather she had the guy with her buy it."

"I heard rumors she and her father haven't been getting along. She doesn't work for him anymore. Was that his idea or hers?"

"I don't know. People at the gardens speculate about the Chatterton family a lot, but I don't think anyone knows much about them. Mrs. Chatterton almost never comes around, and you never see her with her husband. We never see the son, either. Alicia comes around a lot, but it's not because she's interested in flowers."

Maggie smiled. They both knew what Alicia was really interested in. "I saw the new woman hired for the gift shop at Elmwood in the post office yesterday. She's certainly one striking woman! I've always wished I could wear my hair back in a French chignon like that and look classy, but my face is too thin."

"Well, I can't give you her life story," Catherine told her curious friend with a smile, "but her name is Olga Yamikoff. She told me she's from Russia originally, but didn't say more, and I hated to pry."

Catherine glanced at her watch and realized she needed to get moving if she was going to make it to the Chatterton reception. "Just get some phlox, my treat. I've got to get ready."

"No, I can't do that. I'll get Christy to write them up. You just scat. I'll catch you later to find out all the details of your big afternoon."

Catherine hurried past tables of potted perennials, the yard between her house and shop and into the house only stopping a moment to pet the tabby cat sleeping on the porch.

After a quick shower, she stood at her closet door wondering what to wear to the reception. She pawed through clothes hanging there and finally settled on a simple green dress. She'd bought it at Goodwill to wear to the small dinner her family had for her when she'd graduated from college a few years ago. It still looked nice. She went to her jewelry box and picked out an antique jade pin circled with tiny amethysts, a sixteenth birthday gift from her grandmother. A short while later, she grabbed purse and keys and hurried out, offering a little prayer of thanks when her truck started at the first try.

She headed for Violet and Ed Flavian's home less than a mile away in a development of small ranch houses built on slabs about thirty years ago. Each house was a duplicate of the others differentiated only by color and landscaping. It suited Violet, but Catherine felt sorry for Ed. He needed more land for gardening.

She pulled into the neat cement driveway of the gray house with mauve shutters. It's a wonder Violet doesn't have her house painted purple, Catherine thought. Probably the neighbors would've taken up a petition. She smiled. She really does take this lavender, violet, purple fetish of hers too far, in her opinion. She guessed it was Violet's statement in life.

Violet had the door open before Catherine was half way up the walk. She was a tall, sturdy woman with white hair tinted a soft lavender to match the color she always wore.

"I called. Christy said you'd just left so I was watchin' for you. I saw you pull off Main Street. I'm so glad you agreed to come and get me. Ed wants the truck today, and my car's being repaired. Fuel pump or somethin'. Hope it doesn't cost too much. I really didn't want Ed to take me," Violet chattered on as Catherine stepped inside, "Actually," she added in almost a whisper, "I don't want him anywhere near there. He says he's goin' just to see what kind of obscene doin's Chatterton's puttin' on. I think he just wants to go to bug him, though."

"Is Ed around?"

"He's in his room or out back in the garden." Violet shrugged.

"I'll go out and say hi." Catherine headed for the back of the house.

As she went her eyes were drawn to all the knick knacks and collectables Violet had accumulated. Against soft violet walls were three curio cabinets in this small living room. Combined with overstuffed furniture in a floral pattern of shades of lavender matching the Victorian style drapes over lace curtains, were end tables and a coffee table, all displaying various items.

It'd be a cleaning person's nightmare, Catherine thought, although she couldn't imagine Violet trusting her collectables to anyone else's hands.

In one curio cabinet were bells of all kinds and shapes. Another held a popular brand of cute children memorabilia. Catherine couldn't remember what they were called. A third cabinet held her collection of Chinese art. Behind the sofa, the wall was covered with collector plates. Other walls held smaller wall cabinets with collections of thimbles, little spoons and miniatures.

From previous visits, Catherine knew a third bedroom held her clown and doll collections, and in her bedroom was delftware on her dressers and in another curio cabinet. In the kitchen a built in cabinet held her china cat collection. This amused Catherine as Violet couldn't tolerate live cats. "Sneaky creatures," she always said.

Catherine mentally shook her head. She must be the delight of every mail order catalog company out there. It was obvious she'd never had children or grandchildren.

Ed's room, like the man himself, was a complete antithesis of Violet. Catherine often wondered why they'd ever married let alone lived together for forty-five years. He'd built his room onto the back of the house. Large windows with small panes looked over a pleasant garden. They'd lived here since the house was built thirty years ago so hedges and trees he'd planted were mature, and the gardens carefully nurtured and weed free. She sighed and wondered if she'd ever manage to have a garden like his.

The walls were paneled in old barn wood, and below the large windows were tables holding pots and jars of saved seed and a few small gardening tools. Under the tables were bins with potting soil. Even though Ed had a shed at the back of the garden, he did much of his work here, especially when the weather was rainy or cold. On the other side of the room was a shabby braided rug on the slate floor. A well-worn recliner in faded brown had a darker spot on the back where Ed rested his head and read. A table by the chair held a lamp. Catherine smiled at the table's clutter of papers, magazines, books, a coffee cup, and Ed's reading glasses. Bookcases built of the same barn wood as the walls were full to overflowing with gardening and science books and National Geographics. Indeed everything in the room was aged if not exactly antique, even the coat rack by the back door holding jackets and coats with rubber boots under it. A pot-bellied stove stood in a corner to add winter warmth to the room. She preferred this cluttered room in its simplicity to the rest of the house which was Violet's domain.

She spied Ed going into the tool shed and went to join him. He was short, sturdily built and walked slightly bent. Red suspenders held up baggy pants permanently stained at the knees. His uncombed gray hair still had quite a bit of black in it. Indeed, she thought with amusement, it looks like he trims it with gardening shears.

Shaving was something Ed seemed to do only when he thought of it, or maybe when Violet nagged him enough about it, although Catherine suspected the lack of shaving was as much to annoy Violet as forgetfulness.

She breathed in the smell of roses along the path. Ed's garden was small, but every inch well planned to make maximum use of the space available. At the end of a bed of roses, were several unusual white ones. Catherine stopped to examine them. They seemed to almost have a blush of blue. She frowned, puzzled. Maybe it was the light.

From the shed she heard Ed mumbling. "Where'n the hell is it?" Ed, like many solitary people, often talked to himself.

"Ed," she called out, and the mumbling stopped. He appeared scowling, chewing on the stub of an unlit cigar.

He was trying to quit smoking. His face lightened when he saw Catherine, and his deep blue eyes smiled under hooded lids.

"Don't you look nice," he greeted her after taking the cigar out of his mouth.

"Thanks. I don't get dressed up much so I feel kind of strange." She smiled. "I don't see much of you anymore. I miss you."

His face darkened, and he shoved the cigar stub back into his mouth. "That bastard tries to run me off the grounds every time he sees me there," he grumbled around the cigar, "Can't keep me away, though. They're my gardens more than his. I worked there almost forty years. What does he know about gardening anyway? Anything he knows comes from picking my brain before I caught on to him. I have a path from the back of my shed leading through the back of Anderson's farm right to the gardens," he added with a sly look. "What's he gonna do anyway? Call Chief MacDougal? Call the sheriff? They gonna throw an old guy in jail for trespassing? Bah!" He took the cigar out of his mouth and spit on the ground.

"This rose is unusual." Catherine changed the subject. She wasn't unsympathetic, but she'd heard his complaints often. She agreed he'd been wronged, but she couldn't do anything but listen. Maybe she could come up with a little extra money each month so she could hire him to help her design and put a garden in behind her house. Her eyes lit up with excitement at the thought, but then she thought of her truck and guessed it wouldn't be this year.

"Catherine! Yoo hoo!" Violet trilled, "We're gonna be late."

"Coming," Catherine answered then turned back to Ed. "It's a type of English rose, isn't it? It almost looks as if it has a bluish tint to it."

Ed stood looking at the rose, chewing on his cigar. "I had to start all over."

33

She looked at him puzzled.

"Catherine," Violet called again.

"You'd better go," Ed said then with a wink he added, "She'll probably be out here and drag you away physically in a minute. You know how much she's looking forward to being the belle of the ball."

Catherine smiled. "I don't think Chatterton would like it if I was late, not that he'd notice somebody unimportant like me missing, unless there's that odd question he needed to ask." It would be one more thing to hold against me, she thought, but didn't tell Ed about what he'd said this morning. She was still too upset over the injustice of his comment to discuss it.

She hurried back through Ed's garden to meet Violet, whose only gardening lay in the artificial; flowers in material, flowers in pictures and flowers on china.

"Let's go," Violet said as she repositioned her loose fitting, lavender, polyester blazer over her lavender flowered nylon dress. Catherine noted talcum powder on one sleeve and thought of powdery mildew. Perhaps because Ed was passionately involved with his garden, Violet felt slighted, and her obsessive collecting could be an escape mechanism. Catherine couldn't imagine being in a relationship like Ed and Violet's of hostile indifference, a contradiction in terms, or was it? Better to endure alone what fate decreed. She thought of her own marriage. She realized she was lucky, at least for the twelve years she was married. Not everyone was fortunate enough to have had someone like David.

"Let me get my purse." Violet bustled down a narrow aisle in her clogged living room.

"I'll go out and start the truck," Catherine replied relieved to get out of the stifling atmosphere of too much; too much violet color, too much stuff.

Chapter Four

The music of Schumann's Piano Concerto in A Minor filled the sunlit small apartment. Tyler Birchfield, manager of Elmwood Gardens, paused for a moment while getting dressed to listen to a favorite movement. His long slender fingers moved seemingly of their own accord as he played the music in his mind. When the movement was over, he finished dressing. Giving a final adjustment to his tie without looking at his lean face in the mirror, he turned away and went to the closet for his sport jacket. He noticed it was too large on him now, but it would have to do. Looking his best wasn't important to him anymore. He glanced at his watch, and decided he had enough time to listen to the rest of the CD. As the music played on, he moved to the window in his living area and looked across the lawns of Elmwood Gardens to where the big yellow and white striped tents had been set up. His apartment on the third floor of Chatterton Manor House offered an excellent view of the whole extravaganza. His face registered not only his distaste for such a display, but twisted into a look of bitterness when he spotted Mr. Chatterton on his way across the lawns towards the working area of the gardens.

Ahhh, Alicia, you've got to go," Tom Rockwell, a tanned young man in jeans and T-shirt said. "I've got work to do. I need to get this stone walk finished before this evening. Besides, you're going to get me in trouble coming around like this."

"Come on, Tom. Just another kiss," Alicia Chatterton begged as she wrapped her arms around his neck. Her thick dark hair smelled fresh, and her short, yellow, form fitting dress revealing all her young curves made it hard to resist her.

"You're going to get me fired," he said between kisses, "and you know how much I need this job."

"My dad certainly won't be in the compost area today," she murmured against his lips, loving the sweaty taste and smell of him. "He's much too busy getting ready to become 'The Great Chatterton.'"

She was wrong. Her father, red-faced and furious grabbed her by the arm and flung her away from the young man. She staggered and caught herself and faced him with a mixture of defiance and fear.

"Slut!" he ground out between clenched teeth. "Tramp! Playing around with a low-class gardener who'll never be anything. Go home and change your clothes."

Alicia screamed, "I hate you," before she turned and ran. Angry tears streamed down her face.

Chatterton turned to the pale and stoic young gardener, who refused to show anger. "You're fired! And don't even try to get a reference from this place." He wheeled around and followed his daughter.

With a large straw bag decorated with bunches of silk violets firmly on her lap, Violet rambled on and on. Catherine was a competent driver so the chatter washed over her much as the sound of a babbling brook would, or the chattering of a flock of sparrows to be more precise.

She interspersed an occasional "Hmmm" and "Uh huh," but Violet didn't seem to even need that. Just a live body, Catherine thought. And maybe not even a live body.

"You know how that old goat's gonna' be today." Violet said.

Catherine smiled at Violet's reference to Chatterton as an old goat. He was at least ten years younger than Violet. Not that any derogatory term for him would be far off the mark. She liked those days best at Elmwood when he wasn't there and dreaded seeing him today.

"I hear there are even people comin' in from The Royal National Rose Society of England," Violet rattled on, "as well as representatives from The American Rose Society, Jackson Perkins, Wayside Gardens, and lots of other big name nurseries, and reporters from all the gardening magazines." Violet gave a little wiggle at the thought of all those people she might rub elbows with.

"I'm sure glad Mrs. Feldstein invited me," she said. "Poor Millie. I know she wishes she could've come, but, well you know, she wouldn't fit in with this crowd."

Catherine rolled her eyes slightly. She couldn't help it, although she did refrain from making an acerbic reply.

"Can you believe all this hoopla the old goat is puttin' on? The tents alone must have cost him a fortune, let alone hirin' that fancy caterin' firm. He thinks nothin' local is good enough. Hmph! Had to go all the way to Cleveland to get one. Can you imagine how much that cost? And whose fool idea was it for all the waitresses and servers and cooks to be done up like somethin' out of the Middle Ages, I'd like to know."

She grumbled, but Catherine knew that for all her seeming indignation, Violet was excited and pleased to be attending this afternoon's gala when Mr. Chatterton would introduce his new rose. She'd certainly worked hard enough to get an invitation from Mrs. Feldstein.

"'A Rose for Camelot,' he's callin' this shindig." Violet's words flowed on. "Just because his grandmother was one of those uppity-up English ladies, or so I heard, he thinks he's some kind of lord or somethin'.""

"The rose's ancestry is from English roses," Catherine said.

"As if he really knows anythin' about roses. He's just a wicked phony, he is." Violet muttered and then lapsed into momentary silence.

Catherine understood Violet's anger over Chatterton's firing of her husband, Ed, but Violet's resentment and anger sometimes seemed overdone, especially since Violet and Ed didn't seem to have a good marriage. If Violet felt so strongly about Ed's being let go, why was she attending this event? Catherine mentally shrugged. The excitement and what Violet considered being a prestigious event to brag about was probably too much for her to resist. Principles sometimes can only be adhered to when there's no temptation.

"I sure hope Ed was jokin' when he said he was gonna' show up," Violet worried. "I don't know why he'd even want to set foot on the place after what they done to him. Firin' him after all those years at the gardens! Why he was responsible for much of the design of the gardens. Believe me, it wasn't all that much when he started there. What do those directors really know about gardenin'? Why Ed's forgot more than they'll ever know. He ain't much to look at, but he sure does know about plants. They was all happy enough with Ed until Chatterton took over. Tryin' to say he's gettin' senile. Why, he's always been a strange duck. Believe me, I know."

Catherine was glad to turn into the long drive leading to the gardens. A sign at the entrance pronounced the gardens closed to the public today.

"And roses," Violet went on, "It's as if roses was his babies. There ain't nothin' he don't know about roses. He more than tripled the rose gardens since he's been there. Why he was working on a . . . ." Violet stopped suddenly. "Look at all them banners!" she said her mouth open in

38

awe.

They both stared amazed at the dozens of pennants leading the way to the gardens with even more festooning each light pole in the parking lot. The pale yellow banners with a blue cabbage rose emblem blowing softly in the breeze left no doubt in Catherine's mind that today was much more than an ordinary reception.

"They were just starting to put them up when I left this morning," Catherine said.

"It ain't right! It just ain't right! The cost of those pennants alone sure would feed a lot of people," Violet said.

Catherine nodded in agreement. Her earlier feeling of unquiet returned. She was strongly tempted to drop Violet off, turn around and leave. Instead, mindful of her duty to her employers, she parked her truck and accompanied Violet to the entrance of Elmwood Gardens.

Chapter Five

Catherine and Violet entered through the front entrance after a guard checked their identification and approved them. It wasn't to start for half an hour yet, but Chatterton wanted any employees invited to be early in case there were last minute things needed done.

They walked across the lobby toward large glass doors leading to the gardens. A tall willowy woman, her dark hair in a classic French twist, stood with her back to them looking out. In her black dress, she made a dark silhouette against the bright gardens beyond. When she heard them approaching, she wheeled around and hurried past them not bothering to answer their friendly greetings. Instead she stared straight ahead, her mouth compressed in a tight line, and her dark eyes narrowed. Heels tap tap tapped an angry beat across the tile floor until they reached the carpeted gift shop.

"Hmph," Violet said. "Don't she think she's high and mighty."

"Shhh," Catherine cautioned, "She'll hear you."

"What do I care? Who does she think she is puttin' on airs when everyone knows the old goat brought her here and gave her that job as manager of the gift shop cause she's his kept woman.

"That's just rumor." Catherine said coming to Olga Yamnikov's defense. "No one knows much about her, and because she keeps to herself, people tend to invent stories. In fact, he was on that European trip when she was hired."

"Are you tryin' to say I spread false rumors?" Violet was indignant.

Catherine changed the subject which wasn't hard to do with the sight before them. They stared in awe at the transformation of the gardens. Halfway across the lawns in front of the topiary gardens, and bordered by Elmwood's rose gardens, were two large yellow and white striped tents, their sides rolled up to take advantage of the perfect day.

Servers, cooks, and other helpers rushed about. The men were dressed in tights and tunics and the women were in long simple dresses with white aprons and plain white scarves tied behind and under their long hair. Catherine wondered if only long haired girls had been hired or if they were wearing wigs for the occasion.

Stepping through the doors, their senses were assaulted not only by the sight, but also by the smell of the roses covering the long arches creating a floral entrance to the gardens. They strolled across the lawns, and Catherine noticed a few local dignitaries, the board of directors, Augustus Chatterton, his wife, Vera, and Tyler Birchfield were already there.

A sudden scream caused both women to jump, and then they laughed somewhat self-consciously. Behind a bed of fragrant moss roses, they heard the rustling of a peacock as he went into his courting dance. A half dozen peafowl had been brought in earlier this spring in preparation for Chatterton's gala, but they'd only been released several weeks ago after they'd become acclimated. Catherine was always fascinated by the males displaying their trains.

They joined a few guests in the tent where the food would be prepared and served. Long tables were covered with white linen tablecloths, and one long table with silver chafing dishes held the promise of exquisite delicacies. A table in the center held a towering crystal epergne, layered with a rich assortment of fruits creating a masterpiece of design.

"Yummy!" Catherine said. "Look at that display of fruit!"

"Have to be careful," Violet replied. "I can see it all tumblin' down."

Another long table held every kind of drink a guest

could want, and bartenders, also in medieval garb, stood ready and waiting. A few guests stood chatting already with drinks in hand. The smell of burning charcoal permeated the air from the grills outside the tents, where choice filet mignon would be prepared to each guest's preference. The tent flooring was parquet on plywood backing, and each tent pole was camouflaged by lattice work and potted climbing roses. Catherine noticed round tables in the other tent had the same white and light blue tablecloths and centerpieces of yellow roses in silver and crystal vases. Serving girls were setting the tables with fine china with a blue rose design made especially for the event. Crystal goblets, gold plated silverware, and white linen napkins with a blue rose embroidered in each corner completed each place setting.

Fond of folk music, Catherine glanced towards a group of renaissance musicians who were tuning up in the corner. There was a lute player with wild red hair, a woman with a small Saxon harp, a bearded minstrel with something that resembled a guitar, and a tall thin flute player whose glasses were the only thing that didn't fit with the authenticity of their costumes.

Mesmerized Catherine looked around, and quite rare for Violet, even she was speechless. The rational side of Catherine deplored the extravagance, the artificiality of this event, but the romantic side of her was enchanted by the elegance, although she knew it would be short lived, and nothing she'd want on a regular basis. She preferred the simpler things in life, which have their own enchantment.

"Come on," she said to Violet, "we must do our duty as guests."

Catherine took a deep breath and willed herself not to stutter, or glare or do anything to show Augustus Chatterton how angry she was with him. Before she lost her nerve, she headed toward him with Violet at her elbow. He stood between the entrance to the gardens and the tents to greet each visitor as they came.

"Hello, Mr. Chatterton, Mrs. Chatterton," she said with a frozen smile pasted on her face.

Violet echoed her.

"Hello. Perfect day, isn't it? You both look as lovely as roses," Chatterton greeted them.

Catherine, with a mental roll of the eyes, wondered how many times he'd already said those lines today and how many more times he'd say them to all the women who attended. She and Violet each smiled a polite thank you. Mrs. Chatterton gave a brief smile which didn't reach her eyes and murmured something indistinct. Chatterton, still exuding good will while looking beyond them, suggested they go to the bar and get something to drink, effectively dismissing them as unimportant in his world.

"He sure got rid of us fast," Violet murmured as they headed back to the tents.

Relieved she'd gotten through that ordeal, she said, "Oh well, at least we'll get a good meal out of the day."

Violet laughed. "You'd better believe it!"

Catherine looked at the choices offered at the bar then asked for white Zinfandel. Violet looked around in awe and chose the same. Glasses in hand they walked over to one of the pillars of roses, sipping their wine and watching the arrival of new guests. Like thirteen year olds at our first dance, Catherine thought as the corners of her mouth twitched up.

"Poor Mrs. Chatterton," Violet murmured. "She don't look well at all."

Catherine agreed silently. She did look ill or upset about something. It was obvious her smiles and greetings to the guests were forced.

Watching Chatterton greet the guests arriving now in increasing waves, Catherine amused herself by judging the level of each person's importance by the way he greeted them, and how long he held them by his side. She'd tuned out Violet's comments on the women's clothing, and was only vaguely aware when Violet spotted someone she knew and took off, abandoning her for a new set of ears to pour her thoughts and comments into.

As people began to form little socially animated groups, Catherine began to feel ill at ease. Always content with her own company and thoughts, and usually too busy to spend time with others, she now felt increasingly out of place and awkward. Like a black-eyed Susan in an exotic tropical garden with orchids, she mused. She even wished Violet was back and started to look for her. She spied her across the way holding court with several older women about her age, chatting with animated hand motions.

She was trying to decide whether or not to join that group or take a trip to the restroom to hide for a while when a low pleasant voice behind her said, "I'm glad Chatterton didn't insist we dress in medieval costume. I'd certainly feel uncomfortable in tights."

Catherine turned around and laughed up at Tyler Birchfield. "Oh, I don't know about that. You'd look quite nice in tights." Ooops, she thought to herself. She didn't really say that, did she? She rushed on to cover the awkward moment. "The steaks they're starting to grill are making my mouth water. It looks like they might dispense with the boar's head. At least, I certainly hope so, don't you? If he'd really wanted to stay in period, though, the dishes should've been pewter. Of course, I'd probably have to eat on a trencher. You know what trenchers were, don't you?" She heard herself babbling and tried to stop.

Tyler smiled down at her and thought, Whoa! Is the usually serious self-contained Ms. Jewell a little tipsy? He'd never heard her so loquacious before.

She was saved from her own chatter by the entrance of two men with long trumpets draped with ribbons. They blew a loud fanfare which caught the attention of the crowd. Catherine's eyes widened. She looked up at Tyler whose face registered the same look. He glanced down at her and noticed the twinkle in her eyes and the corners of her mouth twitching. He grinned, and she started giggling. Both of them fought for control. Tyler put a hand on her elbow and led her behind the fresh fruit epergne in case Chatterton should see them. It became even harder when she said, "Do you think he'll be called King Augustus before the day is over?" It'd been a long time since Tyler had laughed like that. It felt good.

Finally, controlling their faces by not looking at each other, they followed the crowd through the topiary garden, past the three elephants, the goose, and the dragon topiaries to the entrance of the Blue Garden. When Chatterton was sure everyone was there, he started his speech.

"Ladies, gentlemen, friends, family." He beamed at them all. "There've been many high points in my life. When I made Vera my wife." He smiled down at her. She smiled dutifully, but didn't look at him, Catherine noticed. "When my two children were born." He smiled at Alicia. She didn't smile back. Bradley was not there. "And now I'm announcing a new kind of birth. One also close to my heart, more important than any of my other achievements, except for my family, of course," he added. "I've put many long hours in on this."

A contemptuous snort from behind the largest elephant next to Catherine made her look over that way. Ed stood partly concealed, still in old gardening clothes, as out of place as a burdock in a peony bed. His teeth clamped down tight on the unlit cigar stub. Fury was evident in every line of his body. Disturbed, Catherine looked away.

Chatterton droned on, ". . . but all my work, the loving hours were worth it by the result you see here."

Funny, thought Catherine, except for giving others instructions, she'd never seen him do much with these beloved roses he's talking about. Although maybe he did more in his own private gardens than she was aware of, wherever they are. Not at his house, she knew.

"Ladies and gentlemen come into my garden and meet 'The Augustus Chatterton.'" With a flourish, he motioned them into the Blue Garden.

Eager in their curiosity, the group went through the iron archway covered with 'Casa Blanca' white roses, a 'General Sikorski' clematis and into the Blue Garden. In the very center was the bed that brought many gasps and exclamations from the people who'd come this day to see the blue rose. All the visitors marveled at the pure sky blue color of the buds and the softer blue as the blossom aged, as well as the exquisite form of the flowers. No one seemed to look at the borders of this small perfect garden backed by privet hedges where delphiniums, campanulas, stokesia, iris, lupines, monkshood, lobelia, veronica speedwell, columbine and many other flowers in various shades of blue bloomed in lovely beauty. Silver leafed plants like artemesias as well as many different kinds of hostas and ferns added interest. Throughout the season other blue flowers, annuals as well as perennials, would come and go always creating a new look.

Catherine stood at the edge watching and listening as Chatterton stood beside the bed of roses accepting all compliments and answering questions knowledgeably.

Beside her Tyler Birchfield also watched and reflected on how well Chatterton had done his homework. He probably convinced almost everyone he'd really developed this rose himself.

Slipping away from the crowd, Catherine wandered down the secluded path to the White Garden. She walked slowly down the short flight of stone steps into her favorite garden, enclosed by a six foot stone wall softened by white rhododendrons, white lilacs, and climbing white roses. Only silver leafed or green plants added to the white of the flowers in this garden. Stone benches were invitingly arranged on each side. In the center was a lily pond with white water lilies blooming, and goldfish swimming in and out of their stems. A small stone nymph in the center held a watering can from which water perpetually flowed. She sat down on one of the stone benches near it. The enclosed garden deadened the sounds of the outside world bringing serenity. Even the crowd in the garden only thirty or forty feet away was but a murmur here. She always found the mixture of sun and dappled shade against white blooms relaxing to both her eyes and her spirit. Since the blue roses had arrived from Chatterton's private nursery to the Blue Garden last month, both the Blue and White Gardens, had been closed to the public. Catherine enjoyed the solitude this had brought. Except for an occasional worker, almost no one came here.

A catbird watched her from the dogwood near the steps. It imitated several birds interspersed with an occasional little mewing sound. Suddenly it let out a cry of alarm and flew away. She glanced up and caught a glimpse of someone going back down the path and wondered why they'd not come down, too. With a little sigh, she realized she'd better go back. As she went up the steps, she caught a faint whiff of cigar smoke. Leaning forward, she tried to peer through the branches to see if Ed was on the other side. She couldn't see anything, but noticed a piece of twine tied lower to the trunk of one of the rhododendrons. She wondered why that was there. She'd have to come back to cut it off tomorrow. Otherwise, the twine would eventually girdle and kill the shrub as it grew.

As she went back down the secluded pathway, Chatterton's voice once again assaulted her ears. She walked over and stood by Tyler who was standing alone. He didn't acknowledge her presence, but as she turned to go back to the tents, he also turned and followed her. She was not envious of what Chatterton has, Catherine told herself. She was content with her life and her own little nursery. She aspired to nothing more and didn't want to ever be the center of attention. Then why was she sickened by this? She wondered. A vision of Ed's white rose with a hint of blue at its center, a rose lovingly propagated flashed across her mind. There's something wrong with this world, she thought.

Chapter Six

Tyler and Catherine walked slowly back towards the refreshment tent. "Want something to drink?" he asked. Catherine shook her head. All their earlier high spirits were gone leaving them both silent. She searched her mind for something to say, but he seemed as disinclined to talk as she did so she felt relief when the other guests started trickling back followed by Chatterton.

"Now what everyone has really been waiting for - food!" he boomed out.

Catherine found herself alone once more as Tyler stopped to visit with some people he knew. As he seemed to have no interest in sitting with her, she looked around for a place to sit, preferably by someone she knew or who at least looked congenial. She felt relief when she saw an empty place next to Violet and hurried over to claim it.

Violet smiled as Catherine approached and patted the chair next to her. "There you are," she called out. "I thought you'd abandoned me for someone better lookin'."

Apparently Violet didn't remember she'd left Catherine in the first place. She sat down and glanced at Violet. "Are you enjoying yourself?"

"I am in spite of everythin'," she admitted. "I'm sure glad Ed didn't show up after all."

Catherine didn't say anything.

Violet went on. "So many people have complimented me on my dress. They can't believe I made it myself. It's a complicated pattern, but like I told everyone, I've made all my own clothes since I was a girl. Not all of us was born with a silver spoon in our mouths, I told them. Some of us have to work for a livin'.''

"I don't imagine everyone here is wealthy," Catherine said in a low voice. "There're a lot of journalists and others in the gardening world here who work for their living." She was glad the others at the table were absorbed in their own conversations and didn't seem to hear Violet.

Violet shrugged and changed the subject. "Hmmmm, look at that," she said, licking her lips as serving girls placed salads in front of each guest. "There's even a flower in each salad."

"Nasturtiums," Catherine said.

From then on as course followed course, Violet focused on eating and discussing each dish. "Look at those baby grilled vegetables. Yum! I wonder what herbs are on them. This steak is delicious." she rhapsodized. "Must be a special kind of marinade to get this flavor. What do you suppose it is? Aren't you goin' to eat all yours?" Violet eyed the rest of Catherine's steak. "Wasn't the salmon delicious? I'd like to get the recipe for how they fixed it."

Where in the world does she put it all? Catherine wondered. Maybe she's stuffing some of it in her big straw bag under the table. It was certainly big enough to hold several meals and the plates, too. Catherine smiled to herself and wouldn't have been too surprised if it were true.

Tyler, at a table on the other side of the tent, was still in conversation with the couple he'd stopped to visit. She felt a little disgruntled he'd so quickly forgotten her. Since he'd come to Elmwood, he'd never been more than distantly polite with her until today. In fact, she realized, it was the first time she'd ever seen him smile.

Catherine eyed the dessert tray decorated like a Parisian flower cart. There was a scrumptious looking cake rich with layers of chocolate and cream and oozing with caramel and nuts. A strawberry gateau tempted her, too, but though they all looked delicious, she knew she'd reached her limit. She got up and murmured to Violet she was going to the restroom. So engrossed in deciding which dessert to pick, Violet didn't seem to hear her. As Catherine wove her way through the tables, she noticed Chatterton receiving a note from one of the servers. He opened it, scowled and then crumpled it up, his lips set in an angry line. Who'd dare upset him today? His son's still not here, she remembered and wondered if it was from him.

In the main building, a long line of women waited for the restroom so Catherine went into the gift shop and wandered around looking at the gifts and gardening books. All were much too expensive for her. She noticed Olga Yamnikov wasn't in the shop. She hadn't been at the reception, either. She thought that rather strange because Olga certainly seemed a little closer in class to the guests gathered than Violet, or herself, she admitted fairly. She'd always impressed Catherine as a very cultured and highly intelligent woman. Catherine was intrigued by the mystery she sensed about her. Maybe there was some truth in Violet's assertion. If it were true, she certainly couldn't be at an event with the wife. Maybe she was in the back room or had gone home early with a headache or something. That could be why she seemed so unfriendly. When Catherine noticed the line was shorter, she left the gift shop to take her place.

A short while later, sated by a full meal, the warmth, and a day playing heavy on all her senses, Catherine made her way back across the lawn to the tents. A peacock in the distance screamed. She sighed and wondered how soon she could leave without offending. She looked around for Violet, but didn't see her. Some of the guests had formed into little groups and were wandering around looking at the rose gardens. Catherine was pretty sure Violet wouldn't be with them. Maybe she'd gone to the restroom at the Wisteria Tea Room in the manor house. Even though the

51

tearoom was closed today, the restroom would probably be open.

Catherine noticed a monk walking quickly around the outside hedge of the topiary garden. His cowl covered his head and shadowed his face. Greg Robert crossed her mind briefly before she remembered he was at the dentist's this afternoon. Also, she doubted he'd be here wearing his robe, even if he still had one. She wondered what Chatterton's purpose was of including a monk among the festivities of the day. Could it be because St. Benedict, an early monk in Italy, was said to have planted a rose garden that still survives to this day? And monks are always associated with a love of gardens. Or maybe it's because the Christian church in the Middle Ages always identified the rose with the Virgin Mary and throughout Europe the rose motif appeared in this symbolism in stained glassed windows, illuminated manuscripts, and many other decorations. Catherine had written a graduate paper on the rose and its history once. It'd partly fueled her love of the rose. Or maybe it's a reincarnation of Saint Fiacre, patron saint of all gardeners, she thought whimsically, but she doubted Chatterton had that much imagination or romance in his soul. In fact, she wondered again how a man like him could've developed the blue rose. Although he was concerned about the roses and checked on them almost daily since they'd been brought to Elmwood, most of the work in caring for them had been done by Greg Robert since they'd arrived. She found this incongruous with the sincere and ardent gardener he proclaimed himself to be. He even hired help for the landscaping and gardens around his home.

Now Greg Robert certainly knew a lot about roses. Impressed with his skill and expertise in working with roses, she wondered where he'd picked up his knowledge. It must have been at the monastery before he came to Elmwood. Again she wondered why he'd left.

52

She decided to walk to the Tea Room to look for Violet, but stopped on her way to check on a bed of annuals recently planted. Right now they looked small and puny, but soon they'd fill in all bare spaces and be quite splendid she knew. It was with a sense of relief she finally saw Violet coming down the path tagging along behind several other women.

Trying to suppress a yawn, Catherine asked. "How soon do you think we can leave?

Violet beamed at her. "You youngsters can't keep up with your elders, can you?"

Catherine smiled. "I guess not. Too much food." They turned to go and as they neared the entrance to the topiary garden, there was a piercing scream followed by another and another. A girl in a yellow dress, Alicia, Catherine realized, came running out of the topiary garden and almost collided with her. She grabbed Catherine's arms and cried out, "My dad! My dad! He's in the White Garden! Do something! Do something!"

Followed by the other guests, Catherine ran through the topiary garden, down the walkway to the steps leading down to the White Garden and stopped abruptly.

Augustus Chatterton lay face down at the bottom, his arms outstretched toward the little nymph still serenely holding its watering can oblivious of the horror so near. Embedded deep in his back was a digging fork.

She felt her knees buckle and was grateful for the strong arms that suddenly held her. "Will you be okay for a moment while I check and see if he still needs help?" Tyler asked.

She nodded, and he hurried down the steps and felt for a pulse. With a grim face, he looked up at those watching in horror and said "Someone call the police. He's dead."

Chapter Seven

Sun filtered through the leaves of an ancient Chinese elm outside the window of the old carriage house making interesting shadows and dappling the fat calico cat stretched out in the largest sun spot on the worn wooden floor. She watched the movement of a fly sharing her spot, but was too lazy to do more than watch.

The only other sound besides the fly's intermittent buzzing was the occasional sound of pages being turned by the other occupant in the building, a building whose carriages and horses and old cars had been replaced by rooms filled from floor to ceiling with book shelves full of used books. Special cabinets close to the front desk held first editions. Every corner and even the steps held piles of books. Close to the windows to take advantage of the natural light were comfortable chairs and small tables for the comfort of browsers.

The reading man, completely engrossed in an old copy of *Peddler's Progress* by Odell Shepard, sat at an old wooden table used as a desk. He was John MacDougal, co-proprietor with his mother of Carriage House Books and the Portage Falls police chief. His hair was red, but faded from its once carroty brightness by a liberal dusting of premature gray. His freckles had also dimmed with age, but his eyes, behind often smudged glasses, were still a piercing blue, made even more intense by his light, almost colorless eyelashes.

"Dad!" A younger copy of the man broke the silence

as he opened the screen door and entered. The teenager, tall and gangly with bright red hair, freckles, and those same blue eyes, was what his father once looked like

"Dad," the boy said again in a plaintive tone, "I'm having trouble with the brakes. I can't get the right rear one off, and Lizzy said she'd go to the Dairy Queen and a movie with me tonight, so I've got to get it fixed." He looked at his father with pleading eyes.

"Okay, Josh, I'll have a look at it." With some reluctance John put aside the biography of Bronson Alcott, remembering what it was like being sixteen and having your first car and first love.

"I'm in uniform so I can only advise," he reminded his son as they went out to the old green Chevy jacked up in the parking lot. It was the best Josh could buy with the money he earned working summers at Elmwood Gardens. John waved at an elderly priest, whose thin white hair was sticking up in wisps around his head. He was puttering in his garden adjacent to Our Lady of the Roses Catholic Church just beyond the old stone wall forming the boundary between the church property and Carriage House Books. The wall was crumbling in several areas and no longer useful in keeping anything in or out, but since it was covered with old roses, pink and sweet smelling, it had more charm than a newer wall would.

"Hi Father," he called out. "Your roses are looking nice."

"Thank you, John." Father O'Shawnessy smiled in appreciation of the compliment.

John ended up putting an old quilt down and helping his son pry loose the recalcitrant brake, and then watched as Josh took over. He offered advice on finishing the repair, but only if a question arose. He made sure everything was back on securely, and the brakes had been adjusted properly when Josh finished.

Checking his watch, he headed to the station, but

stopped on his way at the front house, an old Victorian home now a bed and breakfast called The Elms, even though only one elm remained. John's mother, Martha, operated this as well as the bookstore. It had been a rundown apartment house when she'd bought it, but over the years she'd used the rent from the apartments to gradually turn it into a bed and breakfast. Now the only apartment left was the one over the carriage house where John and his son lived. She kept a few private rooms in the back for her personal use as well as the back porch.

John opened the back screen door and called in, "Mom, I'm going back to the station."

"Okay," she called out. She knew now to listen for the bell that rang in the front house when a customer entered the book shop.

An elderly lady in multiple layers of clothes shuffled down the sidewalk in worn blue slippers, pulling a wire cart behind her. Her face had a vacant look as she walked and mumbled to herself. A medium sized brown and black dog of multiple heritages with one drooping ear followed patiently behind.

"Hi, Alma," John greeted her.

Alma Porcase stopped and stared with suspicion at him from faded blue eyes under hooded lids. She worked her toothless mouth but did not answer him. She continued to watch him as he walked on.

He wondered how old she was. It was hard to tell from her appearance. People without teeth always looked much older. He'd bet she was close to eighty if not older and thought as he often did that he should stop out at her house one of these days and check it out. He was sure if he called the Board of Health they'd condemn it, but then where would she go? He hated the thought of going out there or taking steps to have Alma committed. Such a move would probably be a death sentence for the proud and independent woman. And from what he'd heard, she didn't encourage visitors, so even if he went to her house, she wouldn't let him in, he reasoned, thus again he put off taking any steps concerning her.

He walked past the Brogdens' large house next door to the small aged brick building that housed both the post office and the police station. Waving at Mrs. Young, the postmistress inside the post office, he went into the police station next door.

"Hi Chief." Suzy, the young clerk dispatcher on duty, greeted him with a smile. She was glad to have any interruption. She'd been warned about tying up the line with personal calls when she was low on her cell phone minutes, and even the soap opera magazines she was fond of reading could only hold her attention for just so long. With the evangelical fervor of a passionate bibliophile, John tried to interest her in good books, short and easy ones he thought she might enjoy, but as yet he'd not managed to persuade her to read them. Every book he brought in and suggested she read, she'd taken with politeness, thumbed through it, and said with a lack of enthusiasm she'd try it. It always ended up on a shelf, untouched. John, after a few weeks, would quietly and with no comment, return it to his bookstore. He even brought in mysteries thinking that working in a police station might make her want to read some of that genre. Of course, he had to admit, for all the action in this police station, she might as well work at the post office next door. It was a rare day if they got anything more than a traffic accident. Any crime in Portage Falls was usually a breaking and entering, or some vandalism done by teenagers, or once in a while a domestic violence case. He hated those.

He smiled at her. "Quiet day, huh?"

She blew a bubble with her Double Bubble gum and said, "When isn't it?" As if in answer to her flippant remark, the phone rang, and she grabbed it.

"Portage Falls Police." As she listened her eyes

widened, and she even forgot to chew as she glanced at John and said into the phone. "The Chief will be right there."

"There's been a murder at Elmwood Gardens. It's Mr. Chatterton."

"What happened?" John asked as he unlocked a drawer and got his gun out. Embarrassed, he wiped the dust off on his pants, and then strapped it on and grabbed his car keys.

"I don't know. The caller was hysterical."

"Call Tony and tell him to meet me there at once. Oh, and call the county coroner, too." In seconds he was out the door and into the newer of the town's two police cars. With lights and siren on, he headed for Elmwood Gardens.

John was relieved to notice two security guards seemed to be guarding the entrance to one of the garden areas. He assumed that was where the body was located. Groups of people were standing or sitting in either of two large tents. As they stared at him while he walked across the lawns, he felt like he was in a silent movie. He wasn't sure what period it was, though, as he noticed many of the people in medieval garb.

"Nothing been touched?" he asked as he walked up to the guards.

"Nothing," an older grey haired man assured him. "The one fellow checked him to see if he was dead, but he didn't disturb anything. He's right this way." He turned to lead John through the topiary garden and then through the Blue Garden. "I also told everyone they couldn't leave," he went on, "until they've been questioned."

John nodded his approval and said to the younger of the two men, "Would you make sure no one leaves?" The younger guard nodded, and the older guard directed him down a path pressed in by rhododendrons. John paused

58

when he came to the top of the flight of steps leading down to the White Garden and the body. His heart gave a lurch, and he got a sick feeling. This was his first murder in the ten years he'd been police chief, and unlike some members of the profession, who would like to test their skills in solving a murder, he had hoped he'd never have to. Even the bloody and mangled bodies he sometimes had to deal with in automobile accidents had not prepared him for this.

His mind felt fuzzy, disoriented. What should he do first? He tried to remember the steps to take from his criminal justice courses. A soft voice beside him said, "Shit," making it a long drawn out word. With a feeling of relief, he glanced back at his deputy, Tony Montecalvo.

John breathed out a whoosh and replied, "You said it!" Looking around the garden as he went down the four stone steps, he approached the body and knelt on one knee to look closer. Chatterton was lying on his stomach, his head turned to one side. Staring eyes already glazed over assured John he was indeed dead.

"You'd better get the yellow tape from my trunk and rope this off. Oh, and get my camera from the front seat, too, and see if you can get hold of Bill and Pete to help out. We'll need them to comb the area and see what we can find. They can do that while we question the family, guests and everyone else who was here. From the looks of it, that'll take quite a while."

As Tony hurried off, John felt relieved his temporary paralysis seemed to have worn off, and he was sounding like a police officer.

He stood up and looked around again. He only saw one entrance to the garden. He turned to the older security man who stood near.

"Chief MacDougal," he introduced himself.

"George Farmer. I'm with Ace Security out of Cleveland. I've never had to deal with anything like this before, only drunks at receptions and parties. That sort of thing, you know."

John smiled his sympathy at the older man. He understood that, but only asked what had happened and listened as George Farmer, slowly and carefully, trying not to forget anything, enumerated all he had noticed. It hadn't been much. He'd been standing near the entrance to the gardens by the visitor's center while the other guard was in front keeping an eye on the parking lot. He hadn't noticed anything out of order until the girl, Chatterton's daughter, came running and screaming out of the topiary garden.

Tony returned with the yellow tape and asked, "Where do you want me to string it?" His dark eyes kept staring in morbid fascination at the body, garden fork still sticking straight up. John found his eyes returning often, too, but he had a hard time staring for long. He wanted to pull that fork out even though he knew Chatterton no longer felt it. Someone must have had a lot of hatred to kill him that way. He wondered what he'd done to create so much hatred. John tried to cull his memory for what he knew of Chatterton. Very little, he was afraid. The few times he'd met him around town his one impression was of supreme arrogance. They probably hadn't spoken more than a dozen words.

Tony repeated his question about the tape, thinking John hadn't heard him.

John wanted to say, "Hell, I don't know," but instead replied calmly, not showing his confusion all too near the surface, "Let's wait until the coroner gets here, and he's done with what he has to do."

He checked to see how much film he had, then walked slowly and carefully around the body taking pictures from all angles. He'd have to be careful when he sorted the pictures. His niece's eighth grade graduation was last week, and he hadn't used the whole roll. It wouldn't do to accidentally send one of these gruesome pictures to his sister or niece. Tony followed him using his cell phone to get more. Maybe it's time to get a digital camera, John thought.

The wail of an ambulance announced its approach and set the peacocks to screaming. John and Tony both jumped, and George chuckled. "Peacocks. They've been doing that all day. It's probably why no one heard anything."

They were soon joined by a portly middle-aged man with thinning hair in khaki chinos and a knit shirt. Golfing, John surmised. He was followed by two paramedics with a stretcher and a body bag. Walking with care down the steps, he pulled on rubber gloves as he came, staring at the scene.

"Alex Jones," he announced. "What do we have here? Obviously rubbed someone the wrong way."

John grunted his agreement. He knew the coroner by sight and reputation and knew he was both thorough and respected.

Dr. Jones went closer and knelt down on one knee, touched Chatterton's neck, then picked up one hand and dropped it. "Body's still warm, no rigor yet."

"Yes. I haven't started questioning yet, but from what George here tells me, Chatterton was around and quite obvious most of the afternoon."

"Helluva public place to commit a murder," the coroner commented. "Someone took a big chance of being caught." He looked around. "Is there only one entrance?"

"From what I can see," John answered, "there seems to be a crumbling set of steps in that back corner over there, but it doesn't look as if they're ever used."

The coroner continued his cursory examination of the body. "Had to be someone with a fair amount of strength."

"A man you think?" John asked.

"Not necessarily," Jones stated. "A strong woman, or a woman with a lot of anger could probably have done it. Did you get pictures?" When John assured him they had, the coroner carefully pulled the fork from Chatterton's body being careful not to disturb any prints.

John winced. Maybe I should go into another line of work, he thought, but his curiosity was surfacing, and he found his mind forming questions as a certain excitement was taking over.

"Sure is one sharp tool," Jones said. "Wouldn't mind having something like this in my garden. Wonder where you can get one like it?" He set the gardening fork aside and carefully turned Chatterton over and stared at him. He opened his shirt and checked for other wounds.

"Did you check the pockets yet?" he asked.

Startled, John shook his head. He flushed slightly and knelt down beside Jones as the doctor checked Chatterton's pockets and found only a wallet. He pulled a plastic bag from his pocket and placed it inside and handed it to John.

"I've done all I can here," the coroner said as he stood up. "The rest will have to be done at the morgue." He motioned to the two paramedics who came forward and carefully put Chatterton's body in a green vinyl body bag, then strapped him to a gurney.

John turned to watch them depart with the body and noticed Pete Dominic and Bill Johnson, his two part time deputies, watching silently. They came down into the garden to join him. Pete worked at Fortunati Ford as a car salesman, and Bill was the minister of Trinity Evangelical Fellowship Church.

John filled them in then said, "Tony and I are going to start questioning everyone which will take some time. Bill, carefully wrap up the pitch fork. There's a blanket in the trunk of my car. I'll need the fork for prints. Then I want both of you to search every inch of this garden, and check to see if there is anyway anyone could enter besides the obvious way. Any questions? Any comments?" he asked.

Pete shook his head, and Bill bowed his head and said, "The Lord giveth and the Lord taketh away. May he rest in peace."

When he was sure they understood, John turned and headed towards the tents with Tony beside him. "Who did it, Tony?" John asked rhetorically. Tony silently shrugged his shoulders.

Chapter Eight

Catherine noticed Alicia sitting alone, her face in her hands, her body shuddering with sobs. She wondered where Alicia's mother was. As she walked towards her, Alicia looked at Catherine. Dark mascara streaked her cheeks, and her tear-filled hazel eyes looked beseechingly at Catherine. Ellen would be almost her age now, Catherine thought. Her heart softened, and she went to her, sat down beside her, and putting an arm around the slight figure, she murmured soothing sounds the way one does with a child. They didn't know one another well. Catherine thought she was spoiled and self-centered, but in the face of tragedy, there were few barriers.

"No, no, no," Alicia kept moaning over and over.

"Alicia, do you know what happened?" Catherine asked. If Alicia could talk about it maybe it would help her shock, she thought.

With vehemence, Alicia shook her head and now her "no, no, no," was an emphatic denial.

"Did you see anyone?"

Alicia shook her head, still not looking up, but leaning a little more into Catherine for comfort. Soon her crying slowed down to a few hiccupping shudders.

"He wouldn't," she whimpered.

"Who wouldn't?" Catherine asked quietly.

Alicia shook her head again and wouldn't answer.

Two police officers came out of the gardens and walked to the tents. Fortunately, when Chatterton's body had been removed, Alicia, with her head buried in Catherine's shoulder, had not noticed. Catherine knew the taller one was the police chief, John MacDougal. She had seen him around town and had talked briefly with him last winter at Carriage House Books, but she doubted he would remember her. The other, a younger dark-haired man, who walked with a slight swagger, looked vaguely familiar, too, and then she remembered. He was the young man who'd been with Alicia this morning.

"It will be necessary to take statements from everyone. I'm sorry for the inconvenience this may cause, and we'll try to be as quick as we can. No one is to leave until we have taken your statements and contact information," John announced. "Is there anyone at risk of missing a flight?"

The musicians raised their hands.

John nodded at them. "Okay, I'll start with you." He led them to a table near a pillar of roses. "Your name?" he asked a man dressed in medieval garb with long hair and a short trimmed beard.

"I'm David Jones, the leader of this group, The Fourteenth Century Renaissance Band."

Tony wrote it down while John looked with curiosity at Jones' guitar like instrument. "What's that instrument? I don't think I've ever seen anything like it before."

"It's a chitarra batente," he replied.

"I wish the circumstances were different so I could hear you play it," John commented. "Where are all of you from?"

"Boston and thereabouts," David Jones answered.

"How did you happen to get this job?"

"Through our music union. Mr. Chatterton contacted our agent through them, and she handled all the details. In fact, we never talked to him until today."

"Are there just the four of you?"

"Sometimes we have a cello player, but he wasn't able to come, so there are just the four of us here."

John glanced at them and doubted any of them would know anything that'd be helpful, but still he asked. "Were you all together the whole time?"

"Yes, except for two brief twenty minute breaks," a sweet-faced young girl answered.

"Did any of you notice anything out of the ordinary?"

They looked at each other, shrugged and shook their heads. Then the girl spoke up. "I saw a monk."

John glanced at her. "Yes?"

"Well, it's just that he wasn't any of us, and I hadn't noticed one serving or anything. He wasn't there earlier in the afternoon. At least I hadn't noticed him before."

"Did any of the rest of you see him, too?" John asked.

The others shook their heads.

"Where did you see him?"

"Somewhere over there," she motioned vaguely. "He seemed to be hurrying along with his head bowed. Maybe praying."

"Exactly where?" John asked.

She turned and scanned the gardens and then pointed near the garden where Chatterton had been murdered.

"Did you see his face?"

"No, his hood was up."

"About how tall was he?"

She thought for a moment and then shrugged. "I'm not sure. Maybe as tall as David, but I'm sort of guessing."

John looked at David Jones and estimated him a little less than six feet. Of course, she wasn't really sure.

"What time was this?"

"I'm not sure. Let's see. I think we were playing 'In a Garden So Green.' When was that?" She turned to the others.

They all thought a moment, and then the lute player said, "It was two or three songs, maybe four before that girl came out screaming."

"You're flying out tonight?" John asked.

When they told him they had a flight out of Hopkins at ten, he told them to be sure and call if they remembered anything else. Then he dismissed them.

John glanced around, and his eyes stopped on a short balding man in a white apron.

The man caught his eye and walked over, extending his hand. "Mike Kontos, Kontos Katering."

John nodded and briefly shook his hand. After Tony had written down the preliminary information, John asked Mr. Kontos how many he'd employed for the day.

"I have three serving girls and three serving boys as well as two to help with the cooking, and two to serve as bartenders. They're all good kids, college students, except the bartenders, of course, who have worked for me before."

"Did you notice anything unusual?"

"Like what?"

"Anything that didn't seem right."

Mr. Kontos thrust out his bottom lip and shook his head. "Nah, I was too busy to see anything, but what needed to be done."

John thanked him and asked him to contact him if he thought of anything.

The young people working for Mr. Kontos, wide-eyed, serious, and somewhat awestruck at being questioned by police in a murder investigation, produced the same results. Nothing.

"Should we question family next?" Tony asked as he stared at the crying girl.

John's eyes followed Tony's then he looked at Tony with raised brows. "You know her?"

Tony looked uncomfortable, coloring slightly. "Yeah, a little. She's Chatterton's daughter, Alicia."

67

John thought for a moment before he said, "Let's wait until she's a little more composed. Do you know who'd be in charge here under Chatterton?"

"I'm not sure. I don't remember Alicia ever saying."

John looked at the group in the tent and caught the eye of a tall slender man about forty who stood alone. The man walked forward and introduced himself.

"I'm Tyler Birchfield, manager of Elmwood Gardens. I may be able to help you."

"Do you know who killed him?"

"No, no," Tyler denied, shaking his head, "I just meant I could help you with who is employed here, the layout of the gardens and so on."

"How many employees does Elmwood Gardens employ?" John asked.

"Fifty-five," Tyler replied, "although most are seasonal or part time."

"Do they all work in the gardens?"

"Some work in the offices, or the Wisteria Tea Room, or the gift shop."

"I'm sure you can get me a list with names and addresses of all the employees."

Tyler nodded.

"Did you hear or see anything unusual?" John asked.

"No."

"When did you last notice Mr. Chatterton?"

"I'm not sure exactly. I know I glanced at my watch a little after three and wished time would go faster."

"This is not your type of thing?"

"No," Tyler said with a slight grimace.

"Were you here in the tents all afternoon?"

"I went to check on the solar vents in the greenhouse shortly after checking my watch,"

"Is that part of your job as manager?"

"No, but there was a problem earlier, and I wanted to make sure they were working."

"Did you go with anyone?"

"No."

"See anyone or anyone see you?"

Tyler shrugged. "I didn't talk to anyone. I don't know if anyone saw me."

"Were you anywhere near the garden where Chatterton was found."

"No."

"Was Mr. Chatterton your employer?"

"Well, actually it's the whole board. There are five of them, but he's the head of the board."

"Are the other board members here?"

"They were earlier in the afternoon, but I think they're all gone now," he said as he glanced around.

"How long have you worked here?"

"A little over eight months."

"What did you think of him?" John went on.

"I detested him," Tyler admitted with feeling.

John raised his eyebrows slightly and stared at him as he waited for him to go on. After a few moments he did.

"I was only one of many who felt that way. But I wasn't the one who killed him."

John pulled out a handkerchief and taking his glasses off started cleaning them while still watching Birchfield. "Do you know who did?"

Tyler hesitated a moment, and then shook his head.

"But you have some suspicions." John stated as he put his glasses back on.

"Nothing I can really say," Tyler replied.

John waited and when Tyler Birchfield didn't go on, he said, "We'll get back to that later when you've had time to think about it. Who would be right under you?"

"Greg Robert Burns, the head gardener," Tyler said.

"How long has he been here?"

"Eight months."

John gave him a puzzled look. "Both of you have been

69

here just eight months? That seems strange. Was it a restructuring or something?"

Tyler bit his lip. "The former director retired. Whether it was willingly or not, I don't know."

"Where is he now?"

"Florida, I guess. At least that's what I heard. I never met him."

John looked surprised. "No transition period?"

Tyler shook his head.

"That must have been difficult." John commented.

Tyler didn't reply.

"What about the head gardener who's no longer here?"

Tyler hesitated obviously reluctant to say anything. "Ed Flavian went unwillingly," he finally said, "He still comes around almost every day as if he still works here."

"Why was he fired?"

Tyler shrugged. "Chatterton said he was senile and not getting things done."

"What do you think?"

"Well, he's a little odd, I'll admit, but as for senile, I don't know. He certainly knows more about gardening than anyone I've ever met, especially roses." Tyler commented.

"What did Mr. Chatterton say about this Ed Flavian still hanging around?"

Tyler smiled for the first time. He had a nice smile that reached his eyes and changed his whole face. "Ed had a way of disappearing when Chatterton was around so it was only rarely that he spotted him."

"Did no one ever report Flavian's behavior to Chatterton?" John looked incredulous.

"Not to my knowledge," Tyler replied.

"Not even you? You're in charge."

"No." Tyler made no further comment.

"I get the feeling Mr. Chatterton wasn't well liked among the workers here."

Tyler didn't say anything.

John thought awhile. If this Ed Flavian hasn't done anything about the firing in eight months, why would he pick today? It didn't make sense. He probably wouldn't be hanging around on a day like this, but he'd better ask. "Was Ed Flavian here today?"

Tyler looked surprised at the question. "I hardly think so. This wouldn't be anything he'd enjoy. Still," he added with a little twitch at the corners of his mouth, "I wouldn't put it past him to do a little spying out of curiosity."

"Is Greg Robert Burns here today?" John asked. "Does he go by his full name?

Tyler smiled. "Usually, at least we call him Greg Robert although the younger employees call him Mr. Burns. He was here this morning, but left around noon for a dentist's appointment. Most of the workers had the day off. They'll catch up later in the week."

"By the way, I heard there was a monk wandering in the gardens. Who would that be?"

Tyler paused and thought a moment. "No one that I know of."

"You didn't see him?"

"No, not at all." Tyler replied.

"Is Chatterton's family here?"

"I only see his daughter, Alicia. She's the young girl crying."

John nodded an acknowledgement. "What about his wife, and I heard there's a son, too."

"His wife was here for the luncheon and presentation, but I saw her walking toward their house earlier. They live just beyond the gardens." He nodded his head in the direction of the Chatterton home. "His son wasn't here."

"What time did his wife leave?"

Tyler shrugged and replied, "I'm not sure, but I think it was sometime before I went to the greenhouse. I wasn't paying much attention."

"Do you know Mrs. Chatterton well?"

"No. She rarely comes to the gardens."

"Who would you suggest I talk to next that is connected with the gardens?"

"Well, maybe Catherine Jewell, she's our part time plant botanist, or Violet Flavian. She's a hostess in the Wisteria Tea Room. They're both still here," Tyler answered. "I know Greg Robert isn't here unless he's in his cottage. Olga Yamikoff might be around, but I haven't seen her. She wasn't at the luncheon. She's in charge of the gift shop and also the secretary. One of the clerks might be in the gift shop. I'm not sure who's on duty there today."

"This Violet Flavian you mentioned, is she related to the gardener who was fired?"

Tyler nodded. "She's his wife."

John wondered about that but only said, "Thank you for your help. Would you mind sending one of the two women you mentioned over to me?"

Tyler nodded as he rose and then suddenly stopped as he thought of something. "By the way, today's event was being filmed. The photographer is still here. It might be helpful."

"It certainly might," John said looking hopeful. Wouldn't it be great if it focused on who went into and out of the garden at the time of the murder? Then his pessimistic side surfaced. It probably wouldn't show anything of value. Nothing could be that easy. Still one never knew. He looked at the blond woman holding Chatterton's daughter. She must be a close friend of the family. She might know something useful.

Chapter Nine

The guests clustered in subdued groups talking. Gone was all laughter or light hearted chatter. The late afternoon sun added to the anticlimactic feeling. Catherine was glad to notice the caterers had made more coffee and put the leftover desserts and fruit on one table for the captive guests as they went about cleaning up and packing what they could. When they'd done as much as they could, Mr. Kontos sent the young helpers off and stayed on his own to take care of the rest.

It's refreshing to see goodness in the midst of evil, Catherine thought. He certainly won't be paid extra for his time. She watched as the two police officers approached them. The younger one was watching Alicia.

"I'm Chief MacDougal," the older one said, "and this is Officer Montecalvo. We'd like to ask a few questions."

"It was so awful. Who would do that to Daddy?" Alicia said with an uneven voice.

John glanced in surprise at Tony. It seemed maybe he knew Chatterton's daughter a little more than he let on.

Tony avoided John's eye. "I don't know, Alicia, but we'll find out."

John pulled up a chair and Tony did likewise. Leaning forward toward Alicia, John's voice was gentle as he asked, "Miss Chatterton, did you see anyone or anything that would help us find your father's murderer?"

Alicia, her eyes swollen and red, shook her head and said, "No."

"Would you tell me how you happened to find your father's body?"

"I got tired of all the people. There wasn't anyone here my age to talk to so I thought I'd go off by myself. The White Garden has always been my favorite place at Elmwood especially at night. It's rather spooky then, but still beautiful. Anyway, I knew I shouldn't totally leave since Mother had left, and Brad didn't show up at all. Dad was already really mad at me, and I didn't want to make it worse. So I left everyone and went to the garden, and when I got to the top of the steps . . ." She broke off and started to cry again. Catherine put her arm around Alicia again and held her slight body.

John waited a few moments before asking, "Where's your mother?"

Alicia shrugged and mumbled into Catherine's damp shoulder, "Home, I guess."

"Do you know why she left?'

"No, except she didn't want to be here. Maybe she wasn't feeling well."

"I'll take you home," John said, "and we'll talk to your mother. She needs to be told what happened."

"Okay." Alicia sniffed. "Catherine, will you come with me?" she gave her a pleading look.

Catherine shot an inquiring look at Chief MacDougal, and he nodded.

"Sure, I'll come with you," she said.

"Tony, stay here and get statements from everyone I haven't talked to yet. I'll be back in an hour or less to finish the questioning."

"Come on, Miss Chatterton and, umm, Ms. Jewell?" He questioned assuming this was the Catherine Jewell who Tyler Birchfield had mentioned.

He helped the two into the back of the patrol car then left much slower than he'd arrived.

The drive to the Chatterton home was short and when they arrived, Alicia jumped out and hurried up the wide shallow steps leading to a carved oak door. Impatiently she fumbled for her key, unlocked the door, and called for her mother as she entered.

John and Catherine followed her into a large parquet floored foyer dominated by a wide curving staircase. Coming down the staircase was a blond woman, her attractive face marred by a frown.

"What is it, Alicia?" She sounded impatient as she stopped several steps from the bottom and looked down on the three people standing below.

"It's Daddy," Alicia burst out, "He's been murdered." Tears filled her eyes again, but she made no movement toward her mother for comfort.

John watched Mrs. Chatterton. Her face became still, registering no emotion except for a slight flicker in one eye. He wondered if she already knew. She took a deep breath and looked at him.

"What happened?" she asked. Both her voice and face remained impassive.

Looking for any signs of emotion, John watched her face. "I'm sorry to bring bad news, Mrs. Chatterton. Your husband was stabbed in the back at Elmwood."

She frowned and shook her head, then came down the remaining steps. She nodded at a room to the left of the foyer. "Won't you come in and sit down, please." She led them into a large living room and motioned them to the large comfortable furniture in front of a fireplace. She chose a straight backed chair facing them, but somewhat apart.

Catherine's eyes took in the soaring cathedral ceiling, the large windows taking up one wall. She noted the white walls and white couches arranged for conversation on a light area rug with a floral and leaf pattern on warm polished wood floors. Her eyes strayed to the modern art hanging on the walls, the small tables and lamps and unique pieces of sculptures, carvings and other expensive objets d'art; everything looked so perfectly and tastefully decorated. She gave a small sigh as her own haphazardly decorated home floated into her mind.

"Tell me about it," Vera said tonelessly when everyone was seated.

"Your husband was stabbed with a gardening fork," John answered.

"Did anyone see who did it?"

"No." John said and waited.

She sat staring at him, not speaking, waiting for him to go on. Finally, she said with impatience. "Well, tell me what happened."

John told her while Alicia watched her mother's face. Mrs. Chatterton never glanced at her daughter even when she was told it had been Alicia who'd discovered her father.

"What time did you come home?" John asked.

"About one-thirty or two," she replied absently as if her thoughts were elsewhere. "I had a headache so I came home to lie down."

John wondered at the lack of tears. Was it shock, or was she on some kind of medication, or was it a lack of feeling?

"Do you know of any enemies your husband might have had?"

She stared at him without answering his question, and he noticed the clenching of her jaw. Finally, she shook her head and said, "No, of course not. Did you question any of the workers who were brought in today? One of them might've thought he had money. Was he robbed?"

Even Catherine realized she was grasping. I wonder who she thinks it was, she thought.

76

John was thinking the same thing. "Where's your son, Bradley?" he threw out.

"He's with friends out of town," Vera answered quickly.

Too quickly, John thought. He took out a notebook and pen. "Please give me the name and phone number where he can be reached."

"I'm sorry. I don't have it," she blurted out. Her cool demeanor disappeared.

The classic mother tiger defending her young. But why does she seem oblivious of Alicia's suffering, he wondered. Does she suspect her son and not want to give me his number?

Changing course, he asked, "Did anyone notice when you came home?"

Relaxing slightly, she replied "No," sounding calmer now, "Mrs. Winfield had the day off so no one was here."

"You had no contact with anyone after you came home? No phone calls or anything?

She shook her head watching him.

"How did your husband and son get along?" He asked casually.

Immediately the defenses went up again, as palpable as barbed wire in this tastefully elegant room. "Bradley loves his father. Of course, all boys and their fathers have their differences, but they were very close. Bradley's a good son," she added with emphasis.

Catherine noticed Alicia's eyes widen at her mother's speech. Something doesn't sound quite right, she thought. Mrs. Chatterton is laying it on too thick. She glanced at Chief MacDougal to see what he thought, but his face showed no expression as he stared at Mrs. Chatterton without speaking. Catherine tried to remember if she'd ever seen Mr. Chatterton with his son, but she couldn't recall a single time when she had. Of course, she admitted to herself, she don't travel in their circles, and Bradley has never shown an interest in the gardens to her knowledge.

John stood up. "I'll leave you two now. If either of you think of anything that would help, please call me. Mr. Chatterton's body won't be released until after the autopsy. And," he added, "I want to talk to your son as soon as possible, Mrs. Chatterton."

She stared back not answering.

"Any questions?"

She shook her head.

"Come on, Ms. Jewell." Together they left closing the large wooden door behind them.

Car doors slamming, seat belts buckling, mundane noises and actions routine in a world suddenly out of sync. They sat in silence for a moment, each absorbing and trying to make sense of what they'd seen and heard inside.

John put the key into the ignition, then turned to Catherine and quite unprofessionally, said "What do you think?"

"She's one scared lady," Catherine replied and then added in a softer tone, "Poor Alicia."

John nodded in agreement. "You seem to be pretty close to the family."

Startled she stammered, "Not at all. I've only met Alicia and Mrs. Chatterton a few times and only talked with Mr. Chatterton about the gardens and that not very often."

His eyes narrowed. "You and Alicia aren't good friends?" He sounded skeptical.

"No, No," she asserted. "I know it must seem that way, but I had no idea why she was clinging to me. I thought it was because her mother wasn't there, but now I can see that wasn't the case.

John, usually more attuned to books than people, noticed the nervousness in the green eyes staring at him and wondered about it. It was probably just a normal reaction to his uniform, he surmised. "Yes it's obvious she doesn't seem to have a mother she can turn to for comfort."

She sat considering this, her momentary nervousness leaving her, then looked at him puzzled. "I know. It's weird, isn't it?" she said, thinking of her own mother who was always supportive when she needed it, and how she herself would give anything to be able to still comfort her own daughter.

"I wondered about Alicia clinging to me at the Gardens. I mean, we've probably not spoken to one another more than half a dozen times and that superficially. In fact, this morning she came into my shop to buy a plant, and as a person, I was quite invisible to her. So I was surprised when she attached herself to me this afternoon. I feel sorry for her now. She's always seemed like such a shallow girl, but maybe it's all been an act. Maybe she's really been this lonely girl seeking attention all along. I know that sounds like some psychobabble you'd hear on a soap opera or a talk show."

John long ago noticed silence needed to be filled by most people. The longer he remained silent, the more the other person felt compelled to fill the void. When Catherine seemed to run down, he asked, "What was Mr. Chatterton like?"

She made a small face of distaste. "He wasn't a very pleasant man unless it suited his purpose."

"How so?"

"Well," she said, hesitant to speak ill of the dead, but managing to overcome her scruples anyway, "he wasn't a kind man, and didn't seem to care who he hurt. He thought nothing of dressing down an employee in front of anyone."

"And it happened to you, too?"

Catherine flushed, remembering with mortification that morning. As if anyone could keep iris borers at bay, she thought still upset about what he'd said.

"Yes," she answered, but didn't elaborate.

He noted her frown, but let it go for now. "Who else

79

has he offended or hurt?"

"Just about everyone, I'd guess," she said with a slight smile.

"Who in particular that you know of?"

She hesitated, frowning. If she mentioned names it might cast suspicion on them, and she couldn't imagine the murderer could possibly be anyone she knew.

"What about Tyler Birchfield?" he asked when she didn't answer.

"I don't know. I could tell he didn't like him any better than the rest of us did, but I don't know of anything in particular he would've been upset about."

"How well do you know Ed Flavian?"

"He's a fantastic gardener. He knows more than I probably ever will."

"And yet Chatterton fired him," John said.

"It was so unfair." Catherine's tone of voice showed her anger. "There was no reason!"

"Was he bitter about it?"

"Well, yeah, but you can't think he'd murder anyone over it. No way! Ed isn't that kind of guy," she stated with assurance.

"Often a murderer is the last one anyone would suspect. At least it's that way in most mysteries I've read," he said with a smile.

"And I've always read most murders are committed by someone close to the victim," she flashed back.

"So you think it was a member of the family?"

Confused she said, "I didn't say that. I don't know. Couldn't it have been someone who wandered in? Maybe somebody who wanted to rob him for money or drugs or something."

He watched her closely. She was loyal to her friends. He liked that, but it wouldn't help him in an investigation.

"He still had his wallet with money in it."

She shrugged and didn't answer.

"A monk was spotted on the grounds about the time Chatterton was murdered. Did you see him?"

She glanced at him and then away. "Yes, for a few moments."

"Do you have any idea who it could be?

She shrugged and evaded a direct answer. "Well, I've never seen one around Elmwood before." She didn't think Greg Robert was still a monk, condoning her shading of the truth.

John realized she wasn't telling the whole truth but decided to let it go. It seemed Tyler Birchfield was a little evasive about the monk, too, now that he thought about it.

"You probably haven't seen a Renaissance band and medieval servers at Elmwood, either," he said mildly.

"True," she said with a smile, but didn't go on.

"Where were you between three and four?"

"Is that when it happened?" she asked with widened eyes.

"As near as we can make out now."

She thought for a moment. "I'm not sure of every minute, but I was in the visitor's center part of the time waiting in line for the lady's room, and I wandered around the gift shop for a while, then I went looking for Violet because I wanted to leave."

"Who's Violet?"

"She's Ed Flavian's wife. She's a hostess in The Wisteria Tea Room, and helps out sometimes in my nursery, Roses in Thyme. You might have noticed her. She's a tall woman in her sixties with violet hair. She had on a violet flowered dress, too."

John nodded at the description. He thought he remembered seeing someone like that. Tony probably got her statement. "How did she feel about her husband losing his job?"

"She was angry about it, of course. Everyone thought it was a raw deal, but I think she was grateful she still had a job with the gardens even if it's only part time.'

"What do you think of the new head gardener?"

"Greg Robert Burns?" She smiled. "He's just the nicest guy and an excellent gardener, too. Elmwood is lucky to have him. If we can't have Ed, he's the next best thing."

Lucky guy, John thought, to have such a nice woman think so highly of him. And she was nice, he felt. "Is there anything you noticed today unusual or suspicious in any way?" he asked then added, "And please don't worry about being disloyal. It doesn't solve murders. The innocent will have nothing to fear."

She smiled, then sobered as she thought about it before shaking her head. "No," she said frowning as she thought, then suddenly said, "Wait, I saw one of the servers hand Chatterton some kind of paper. He read it, then shoved it in his pocket. He didn't look happy about it, either, now that I think of it, but I don't suppose it was important."

John thought about what she'd said. No paper had been found in his pockets. Had he thrown it away, or had the murderer taken it? He pushed his glasses up with his index finger and turned to start the car. As they pulled out of the circular drive, he said, "If you think of anything more, you will tell me, won't you?"

She nodded. They rode in silence back to Elmwood each deep in their own thoughts.

Chapter Ten

The bell rang announcing a customer. Doris Young, postmistress, nodded her tightly permed gray head at the woman who'd walked in.

"Yes. Yes. I know. Someone's here. I've got to go. I'll call you later when I get home. Love you, too," she said and hung up the phone.

Doris smiled at the tall dark haired woman at the counter. "What can I do for you?"

"I did not know if you would still be open," Olga Yamikoff said. "I would like ten stamps, if you please."

"Sure. Any particular style? Actually, I should have closed ten minutes ago, but it's hard to get off the phone with my mother sometimes." Doris's high pitched nasal voice contrasted sharply with the low, carefully modulated voice of her customer.

"Any kind of first class stamp will do."

"Okay." Doris rummaged in the drawer. "I think these flowered stamps are pretty. You work at the gardens, don't you? You should like these."

Olga nodded as she dug money out of her purse and paid for the stamps. She turned to go, paused and slowly turned back as if she had a sudden afterthought.

"I saw an ambulance go by a while ago. Was there an accident?"

"I don't know. I didn't hear anything. I must've been

in the backroom sorting mail. I always have the radio on so I don't always hear everything. Hold a minute. I'll check and see what happened."

"That will not be necessary," Olga replied.

"No bother. I'm curious, too," Doris said as she dialed a number.

"Ollie, Doris here. Say what do you know about the ambulance that went by a while ago?" She looked at Olga and shrugged. "You haven't heard anything at all? A customer here was curious."

Olga opened her mouth to protest then closed it, embarrassed.

"I'm closing up now, but if you hear anything call me at home." She hung up.

"That was Ollie from Osborne's Funeral Home. He usually knows what's going on. He has a police scanner and listens in pretty much most of the time, but said he just got in. He had a dentist appointment this afternoon. He's having crown work done. That's no fun, believe me."

Olga gave a tight smile and said, "I would not know. Good day." She turned to leave.

"Wait! I'll call the hospital. If my friend, Dora, is working today, she can tell us what's going on."

"That will not be necessary," Olga said over her shoulder.

Doris locked the door behind Olga and watched as she quickly went down the walk and around the corner.

There was no more to talk about. All the small talk had been said. No one was interested in Aunt Aggie's dementia or Uncle Ross's prostate cancer. No one cared to hear that Mark finally got his driver's license after the third try, or that Carol had been accepted at Cornell, and certainly no one was interested in Heather's teething or in the ending of Mathew and Laurie's marriage. The silence wasn't the comfortable silence possible with old friends. Although earlier it wouldn't have seemed possible, even gardening talk about dahlias or peonies or the best way to propagate roses had withered. The small pods of people in groups under the tents were too dispirited to even disband and form new pods. They sat in despondent lethargy, wrapped in their own thoughts as evening shadows heightened the gloom.

Blank faces turned in unison to watch John and Catherine cross the lawn. All eyes held a glimmer of hope their long ordeal would finally end.

Catherine went to Violet, who stared at her with curiosity, while John went to Tony.

"Did you get a statement and contact information from everyone else, Tony?"

"Yes."

"Do you think anyone needs questioned further tonight? Anyone seem overly nervous?"

Tony shook his head.

John sighed then turned to the watching crowd and raised his voice. "We'll call it a night unless anyone has information they think I should know." He waited. When no one responded, he went on. "I'll be contacting some of you over the next few days as I continue my investigation. Any questions?"

There was a general shaking of heads and low murmurs as people gathered purses, car keys, and made a rapid exit toward the parking lot.

John watched them go. "Any ideas, Tony? You've had time to think and watch."

Tony shook his head. "I don't see how it could've been any of these people. They're not the type."

"There's no obvious type. Murders are committed by

the socially elite, too. Not all murderers have tattoos or shifty eyes, Tony. Remember that."

"I know. It's just that . . ." he didn't finish, but John knew what he meant. He felt the same way. The world would be an easier place to live in if people followed a prescribed pattern, fit our little preconceived prejudices, if the good guys always wore white hats and the man with the black hat, or tattoo, or Harley was the bad guy, and little white haired ladies, who raised geraniums, didn't poison their husbands.

"Come on, let's get to the station and go with what we have."

Catherine backed the pickup out carefully and left slowly. She was so exhausted that even though it wasn't yet dark, all she longed for was a hot bath, early bed and the blessed oblivion of sleep. Above all she didn't want to talk to anyone.

Violet had been silent, too, but she kept watching Catherine. "So, that was some excitement, wasn't it?"

Catherine nodded. "Um hm."

"What happened over at the Chatterton home?"

"Not much."

"Well, what was said? How did Mrs. Chatterton act? Do you think she did it?" Violet's mouth was slightly open as she stared at Catherine with an avid look on her face.

Even though Catherine's opinion of Mrs. Chatterton was negative, she felt reluctant to discuss it. "Really not much was said, and I'm sure I'm not supposed to discuss it anyway. I'd imagine there's some law against repeating what I heard." She didn't know of any law, but she wanted to quell Violet's curiosity.

It worked. Violet lapsed into silence. Catherine hoped she hadn't offended her, but Violet said a pleasant good-bye as she slid out of the truck. She seemed in a hurry to get into the house. She's probably eager to tell Ed everything. Or did Ed already know? Catherine wondered.

When John and Tony got to the station, Pete and Bill were waiting.

"Where's the murder weapon?" John asked.

"We carefully wrapped the garden fork and sent it to the State Crime lab," Pete Dominic said. With his neat mustache and slicked back dark hair, he resembled a silent film star.

"Good. You searched the gardens and grounds in the area?"

"Yeah," Pete said. "It looked like someone was hiding in wait in the bushes on the left side of the path going in. The ground was trampled and a couple of twigs were broken. We took pictures."

"Good. Did you get footprints?"

"We tried," Bill Johnson said. "But there weren't any clear ones. The ground's too dry."

John sat thinking. "Do either of you have any ideas? Have you heard anything about him that might give us some idea of who could've killed him?"

Both of them shook their heads.

"He never came in Fortunati's to my knowledge, or the local restaurants, or Star Lanes." Pete chuckled. "Not the bowling type, that's for sure or the Ford type, either."

"It's a terrible thing when evil visits." Bill shook his head in sorrow. His droopy basset hound eyes gave him a perpetual mournful look. "I have a Bible study to lead at eight. You want me to call and get someone else to take over?"

"No, you can both go. Thanks."

John looked through the statements Tony had taken. Only one from a Mrs. Roper, a reporter for Delightful Garden News, reported seeing a monk, but she couldn't give more details. She'd thought he was medium height, but she couldn't tell for sure or his weight either.

"She wasn't more specific?" John asked Tony.

"She said they all look alike in their habits, and he had the hood up so she couldn't see his hair or even his face."

"That seems to be pretty much what the girl in the band said, too." John leaned back in his chair, stretched and yawned. "I'm beat." He closed his eyes.

Tony thought maybe John had fallen asleep. He sat listening to the fan whir and the occasional sounds of a car radio being played a little too loud as it went by. Tony could see the drivers in his mind, their heads moving in time to the beat.

"So tell me about Alicia," John said suddenly into the silence.

Tony started. "Well," he hesitated. "What do you want to know?"

John grinned at Tony well aware of his uneasiness. "How about starting with how you met and how long you've known her."

"We met at Lorenzo's last summer. I was off duty," he asserted before going on. "She'd just graduated from some private college in New England, I can't remember where, and had come home for the summer. She was at loose ends and had too much to drink. Her date was in even worse shape. He was being a total jerk, and she wanted rid of him." He paused trying to decide how much to tell.

John waited until Tony finally took a deep breath and went on.

"Let's just say I got rid of him, and she was grateful

and I took her home. I didn't take advantage of her."

John didn't question how Tony had gotten rid of the unwanted date. Some things were better off unknown. He was sure Tony was telling the truth about his behavior with Alicia. He also didn't ask how Alicia had behaved toward Tony that night. He'd seen interested looks in many a girl's eyes when Tony was near. To Tony's credit, although he was quite aware of his appeal to the opposite sex and tended to swagger a little, he seemed more amused than vain. His manner towards girls, for the most part, was teasingly flirtatious.

"So did you see her again?" John prodded.

"Yeah." With some reluctance he went on. "She called to thank me the next day and suggested we meet at The Pub in Millport. I knew she didn't want me to come to her house and meet her parents. I almost turned her down, but then I thought what the hell. I wasn't seeing anybody then. So I met her."

He stopped again thinking about it. "We sort of dated like that the rest of the summer, always meeting somewhere. She isn't a bad girl, though," he assured John. "It's just that we're from different worlds, and we both knew it couldn't be more even though it wasn't discussed. Toward the end of summer, she said she was going to Columbus to work in one of her father's offices, and we parted friends. That's it."

"And you didn't see her again?

"She called me at Christmas, but I was dating someone then and with work and all, we couldn't find a time good for both of us. Then she called me this morning and asked me to meet her for coffee." Tony sat with a slight frown on his face as he thought of this morning that seemed so long ago now.

"She was obviously upset about something," he went on. "She'd quit her job two months ago and came home, but this was the first she'd called me. She joked and flirted like she did last summer, but somehow it didn't ring true. Something was wrong."

"Do you know what?"

"No, but when I asked her what her father thought about her quitting her job, she said it didn't matter what he thought 'cause she didn't care anymore what he thought. And then she jumped up and said, 'Come on,' and we got in her Porsche and drove all over town. It was almost as if she wanted everyone to see me with her. I've had a real uneasy feeling about it."

"Do you think it's possible she could've killed her father?"

"No." Tony shook his head for emphasis. "I don't see her as a killer at all and especially in the way he was killed."

John waited a while and then said, "I think we both need to sleep on it and maybe we'll come up with some fresh new ideas tomorrow. You go ahead and leave. I'll wait until Joe comes on duty. Oh, by the way. Did you get the video?"

"Yeah. It's on the shelf over there."

John settled more comfortably in his chair after Tony left, but his mind wasn't comfortable. Why did Mrs. Chatterton receive the news of her husband's death so calmly? What was bothering Alicia? Could either of them have the strength or will to kill Chatterton that way? Where was the son? How many people besides Ed Flavian, Tyler Birchfield and Catherine Jewell had a reason to dislike him? Who was the monk?

When Joe Salcone came in for the night shift, John filled him in on what'd happened.

"I was sleeping and missed hearing anything," Joe said. He was retired from a local steel mill and didn't need to work, but after his wife died several years ago, he decided to get a job to help occupy the lonely hours.

"I'm going over the video tonight and look for

anything unusual, although the whole affair was so unusual, I'm not sure what I'll be looking for. Certainly no one was there to film the murder." He sighed as he left the office.

John walked home slower than usual exhausted, but with a mind still churning. A full moon lit up the town, creating shadows on the sidewalk and the lawns. The neighbor's old collie came out to greet him. He patted her absently on the head and mumbled, "Hi, Lassie." She wagged her tail and followed him up the driveway.

A light was still on in his mother's sitting room. He tapped on the back door and within minutes she came to the screen door to unlatch it. They'd never locked their doors when he was growing up, but though the crime rate in Portage Falls was very low, it was still not the world it was before. A truly nefarious person, or even just a larcenous youngster would've laughed at the protection offered by the old wooden screen door.

"You look tired. Cup of tea?" she asked.

"No. I'm not staying long."

They went through to the comfortable sitting room that'd been added beside the kitchen to give his mother a bit of privacy when there were guests in the house. She was still in shorts and T-shirt plus a sweatshirt against the evening chill. She returned to her comfortable chair and curled up in it. The table beside it was piled high with books and magazines, as was the floor beside the chair. A floor lamp flooded her reading area with a soft reading light. She picked up her cup of tea and waited for him to settle.

"Move over, Callie," he said as he nudged the fat calico cat on the couch and settled down with an audible sigh. The cat yawned and started purring, watching him through half closed eyes.

"Did you hear?"

"Only what was on the news. Mr. Chatterton was murdered this afternoon. I saw you on the six o'clock news." She glanced at the clock. "It'll probably be on at eleven o'clock, too."

"There won't be anything new." He told her all he knew so far and then asked, "What do you know of the Chattertons?"

"Not much, I'm afraid. None of them ever came in to buy a book that I can recall. I've seen him around town sometimes, but never talked to him. Same with Mrs. Chatterton. I've seen her at lunch at The Old Mill, and she came into Alice's once looking for something to buy her husband for his birthday. She ended up buying a wooden triptych, I recall. It was quite old and very expensive. I remember Alice commenting on it at the time. It didn't seem anything he would appreciate. I don't see him as religious. Still, who knows? Do you think she could've killed him?"

"Got me," he shrugged. "She seems a cold woman, and I got the impression there was no love lost between them."

"I did hear rumors there might've been something between him and that woman, who either runs the gift shop or is a secretary or something at Elmwood. Olga Yamikoff. She stayed here a few days when she first came to town last winter. She didn't talk much. She's Russian, I think."

He looked at her with interest. "What kind of rumors?"

"I can't remember exactly. Something like they might be lovers or were lovers. I'm trying to remember who said it." She thought for a while and then said. "Oh, I remember. It was Violet Flavian. I saw her at Belle's Diner. She came over and joined Alice and me at lunch when she spotted us. That was a couple of months ago."

"Violet Flavian?"

"Yes. You remember. She worked at Country Gifts before they closed. Now I guess she works at the Wisteria Tea Room at Elmwood. I've also seen her at Roses in Thyme, too."

"I know who you mean," he nodded. "She was there today, but I didn't get around to talking to her. Her husband used to be head gardener at Elmwood, and Chatterton fired him. I'll have to talk to both of them tomorrow."

"I know Ed. He comes in for mysteries and garden books. He's a bit of a curmudgeon, but I like him."

"What do you know about the Chatterton kids?"

"I heard the girl worked for her dad somewhere. I've seen her around town lately during the day so I don't know if she still does. I don't think I've ever seen the boy or didn't know him if I did see him. I don't know anything about him."

"Tyler Birchfield?"

"Who's he?"

"The manager of the gardens. Tall. About forty. Nice looking. He's only been there about eight months. I need to check on his background. He admitted he didn't like Chatterton."

"I imagine there were a lot of people who didn't like him from what I've heard over the years. I think I know who you mean. I think he's been in the shop a couple of times. If he's the one I'm thinking of, he generally buys books about history. True crime stories, too."

John yawned, stretched and stood up "I'm too tired to think straight. You have a full house tonight, don't you?"

She nodded.

"You'd better get to bed, too. Any guests from the Chatterton affair this afternoon?"

"A couple. Not together, though, but friends. They want breakfast at eight."

He kissed her lightly on the forehead and walked out. He knew in spite of his advice, she'd probably stay up for an hour or more at least. She was a night owl. How she got along on such a small amount of sleep, he could never figure out. It must be a holdover from the years when she had to work two jobs to support three kids after she'd

93

become a young widow.

Josh was home, but the lights were out so he must've gone to bed already. He might know something from working at the gardens – something he picked up as scuttlebutt going the rounds as it does in any workplace. Well, it'd wait until morning when he got up. As John went up the outside steps that led to their apartment over the Carriage House, he thought about the video. It sure would be nice if it revealed who the monk was.

She sat in the small sparsely furnished apartment. The only light was from the blinking marquis of the theater across the street. Fred Astaire and Ginger Rogers danced on the billboard in front forever smiling. With the lights off she could ignore the chipped green linoleum floor, the spilled soup only partially cleaned up, the dirty diapers soaking in a pail, the pile of dirty clothes in the corner. What she couldn't ignore was the crying baby. She'd tried putting a pillow over her head, but the piercing screams could still be heard. Walking him didn't help nor had he wanted fed. Day after day it went on. She'd always believed babies slept most of the time. Her baby sure didn't.

Tears streamed down her cheeks in a never ending flow. The baby's crying and her crying were like a terrible perversion of the dance across the street. If only the baby would stop crying, then maybe I could stop crying, too, she thought, and maybe my husband would want to spend more time with me.

Chapter Eleven

Martha pulled the hot, apple cranberry muffins from the oven. The cinnamon apple smell filled the kitchen, and she knew it would drift upstairs and hurry her guests down. She went back to chopping ham, onions and green and red peppers for the western omelet her early guests had requested. She heard them moving around upstairs, and when she heard their steps on the front stairs, she went through the dining room to greet them.

"Good morning. Did you sleep well?"

Ms. Portley, a middle aged editor from The Garden Gnome, assured her she had. Mr. Kinderhook, a tall, thin man from Environmental Gardening Magazine echoed her sentiments.

"Coffee is on the sideboard, both regular and decaf. Would either of you prefer tea?" Martha asked. Both assured her regular coffee was what they needed. "I've set your places on the side veranda through the French doors. Would you take this basket of muffins out and put it on the table?" she asked Mr. Kinderhook who stood closest to her. "Breakfast will be ready in about ten minutes, but if you're extra hungry, you can start with a muffin."

After Mr. Kinderhook took the basket of warm fragrant muffins, Martha hurried back to the kitchen to start the omelets. When each omelet was done and lightly browned to her satisfaction, she pulled plates from the warming oven as well as small sausage links nicely browned. Then she lifted each omelet onto a warm plate, added the sausages, and placed all on a tray with two small crystal fruit dishes filled with freshly cut up fruits. Carefully she carried the tray to the side veranda.

As soon as her guests were served and assured her they needed nothing more at the moment, she fixed herself a cup of coffee and joined them.

"Your garden is lovely," Ms. Portley said, "and how lovely this clematis looks with the roses. 'General Sikorski' isn't it?"

"Yes," Martha nodded pleased with a compliment from a gardening expert.

"What rose is it?" Mr. Kinderhook asked.

"I don't know," Martha said. "It came with the house and always blooms beautifully in June, but unfortunately never again throughout the season."

"One of the antique varieties," he said.

Unable to get yesterday's event out of her mind, Martha blurted out, "That was awful what happened yesterday, wasn't it?"

Ms. Portley shuddered. "I've visited Elmwood many times. It's one of my favorite gardens, but it'll never be quite the same for me again."

"Were you friends with Mr. Chatterton?" Martha asked. Her warm brown eyes were sympathetic.

"Not really. I've only met him twice. Yesterday, of course, and then several years ago when my magazine did an article on Elmwood Gardens," Ms. Portley said.

"What about you?" Martha turned to Mr. Kinderhook.

Mr. Kinderhook looked up from his omelet. "When I was in advertising I dealt with him. We carry ads for Sussex Garden Supplies every month. I've not seen him much since I joined the editorial staff. As for being friends with him, no. I have a feeling he didn't have real friends."

"Are you both gardeners, too?" Martha asked and then laughed at herself. "Well, I mean, just because you write about gardening and work for gardening magazines, I guess it doesn't necessarily mean you go out and muck around in gardens."

Ms. Portley smiled at her. "I can assure you I certainly do muck around in gardens. In fact, if I could afford it, I'd do nothing else."

"Me, too," Mr. Kinderhook assured her. "My area is rhododendrons. I grow other plants, too, but rhodies are my love. I've propagated several new cultivars. Maybe you've heard of 'Sarah's Joy' and 'Angel Abby'? I named them for my daughters."

Martha shook her head. "I don't have much room here to add anything new that's large. The rhododendrons I have are ancient and came with the house like the rose."

"They certainly look healthy," Mr. Kinderhook said.

"Well, I feed them regularly," she said.

"You know," Mr. Kinderhook mused, "I can't imagine Chatterton propagating that true blue rose. It's not that a businessman can't be a gardener, too, but I've had enough contact with him in the past to know a gardener from a non-gardener, and I'd bet my false teeth he wasn't a gardener."

"I've never propagated anything," Martha said. "Just what's involved?"

"For new cultivars, years and years of careful and painstaking work and a real love of plants," he said. "For instance, although many breeders have developed roses they've called blue something or other, in truth they're really a lavender or lilac. Most rose breeders felt that a true blue rose wouldn't happen, but it didn't keep many of them from still trying."

"What would they have to do?" Martha asked.

"Cross pollination between roses time and again until you get what you want. The breeder has to raise many seedlings over and over. I can't see Chatterton being that patient."

"We can thank Gregor Mendel for this," Ms. Portley interjected. "He was an Austrian monk who experimented with peas. Maybe you've heard of him.

Martha shook her head.

"Simplistically," Mr. Kinderhook went on, "a breeder selects plants, in this case roses, with characteristics the breeder wants and continually breeds them, or when developing a new cultivar, cross pollinating two rose types until there are a large number of seedlings running true to what the breeder is looking for. The steps must continue and all the time there's a possibility that the second generation is likely to produce throwbacks to the original pollen parents. Are you following me so far?"

Martha nodded somewhat uncertainly, and Kinderhook went on. "In the case of the Chatterton blue rose, it would be much more complicated with an ancestry of many roses. He didn't show us the pedigree since his patent hasn't been approved yet, but he did apply for it so he had to have submitted the pedigree with the patent."

"And you don't see him doing this?" Martha asked.

Kinderhook shook his head.

"If he did steal it, then who was the breeder?" Ms. Portley wondered.

Kinderhook shrugged. "Beats me. I can't see anyone going to all that work for years and letting someone else get the credit so maybe Chatterton had more to him than I'm giving him credit for."

"Unless the true breeder is dead." said Ms. Portley. "Can you think of anyone it could be?"

"No. At least it's not anyone well known in rose circles."

"More coffee?" Martha asked.

"None for me," Ms. Portley said. "I have a plane to catch."

"I drove, but I've got to get back to write the article, and it's a long drive." Kinderhook added, "You have a lovely establishment here, and breakfast was delicious."

Ms. Portley echoed his sentiments.

After they'd settled their accounts, Martha watched

99

each of them drive off in different directions. It's what she liked about running a B&B, she thought. She met so many interesting people. She hurried to clear the table and prepare for the two couples still upstairs when she heard them starting to stir.

Chapter Twelve

The rain forest section of the conservatory never ceased to fascinate Catherine. This mini ecosystem held tumbling singing waterfalls cascading into small hurrying streams and small pools. Tall tree ferns, banana palms, mahogany trees, bromeliads, and numerous other exotic plants lined the walkways creating a private jungle atmosphere minus the dangers of the real thing. The moist air intensified the rich smells of earth and green vegetation.

She stopped on a bridge and peered down into the dark depths of a still pool and watched colorful fish darting about on pursuits of fishy interests oblivious to the colorful orchids in rock crevices admiring their reflection in the water. No time for dawdling, she chided herself and left the bridge. She followed the paved walkways heading for the bougainvillea near the aviary. Tyler had mentioned it was looking a bit off.

"Hello! Hello! How ya' doin'?" a raspy voice asked.

"Fine," Catherine replied. "And how are you doing?"

"Hello! Hello! How ya' doin"? Awwk!" the voice said again.

Catherine smiled at the bright macaw in the large cage tucked discreetly in a stone cliff with trees and plants partly camouflaging it. "Pete's such a pretty boy," she said.

"Awwk! Pete's such a pretty boy," he replied, cocking his head and watching her closely with one, round, black, button eye.

She laughed at him and moved on. Suddenly the mist machine went on filling the area eerily with a heavy mist.

Drats! There goes what curl I have, she thought. Hurrying down the path and around a corner, she stumbled over someone lying on the path. Letting out a startled yelp, her hand flew to her mouth in the gothic heroine tradition.

"Oops!" the body replied as he got to his knees and sat back on his haunches.

"Tom Rockwell! You scared the devil out of me. What were you doing lying on the ground like that?"

"Sorry," he grinned. "I was checking the valve on the mist machine. It seems to be open a little too much."

Somewhat mollified, she smiled back at the handsome young man, his blond hair as mist dampened as hers. The only difference was that hers hung limply, and his was a mass of springing curls. "Sorry to jump down your throat like that. I guess I'm extra jumpy after yesterday."

"Yeah. It's enough to put the spooks in anybody." He looked at her and his tongue moved inside his cheek as he measured how much she knew. "So what've you heard? Do they have any suspects you know of?"

"I haven't heard anything. The morning news on the radio didn't say anything new."

"Do you think it's anyone we know?"

She shuddered. "Oh, I hope not. I can't imagine it could be anyone I know."

He stared at her without replying.

Catherine suppressed an inward shiver. She was alone with him. What did she really know about him? Stop it, she told herself sternly. You can't start suspecting everyone. But in spite of her inward pep talk, she felt relieved when the door from the desert section opened, and Alicia walked in.

She stared silently at Tom, barely noticing Catherine. "I saw your truck in the lot."

He nodded and said, "Yeah."

Catherine glanced curiously at them. Something a lot thicker than the mist is filling the air, she thought.

"How are you doing, Alicia," she asked.

Alicia looked directly at her for the first time, her eyes sad and haunted. "I feel so, so. . . I don't know, so alone, I guess."

Catherine glanced toward Tom, when he made a little sound, and she noticed a strange look pass over his face.

"I know how awful I felt when my father died," Catherine empathized. "I was only fifteen, and I couldn't imagine life without him." She didn't mention two other deaths that had left her not wanting to live for a long time.

Alicia shook her head impatiently. "This is different. I didn't even like my father," she enunciated carefully.

Catherine didn't know how to reply. "We all have our differences with our parents," she said lamely. Forgive me, Mom, she added to herself, for the lie. "Would you like to go for a cup of coffee?"

Alicia shook her head. She and Tom were talking eye talk again.

Catherine feeling totally unwanted, said with a false cheerfulness, "Well, I'm definitely in need of a cup of coffee so I'm off to the Tea Room. Join me if you change your mind."

She was sure they'd both dismissed her from their minds as she left the steaming rain forest. Well, well, well, she said to herself. So where does Tony fit into this equation?

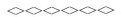

When the door closed behind Catherine, Alicia quickly ran to Tom for comfort. He held her tightly, kissing her dark hair. She cried softly into his denim shirt as they clung together without speaking. Finally, she leaned back a little and looked up at him. "I didn't think you'd be back."

He looked a little shamefaced. "I heard it on the news last night." He didn't add that he hadn't felt sorry. "I didn't know how I could get in touch with you. I laid awake most of the night thinking, and I thought maybe no one knows your father fired me. Maybe if I just showed up, things would go on as before."

She stared intently at him. "Tom, you didn't kill my father, did you?"

"Alicia!" He let her go and stared at her.

She went quickly into his arms again. "I'm sorry, Tommy. I didn't mean it. I'm just so confused. And I won't tell anyone what happened yesterday, either."

He held her close, rubbing her back, his cheek on top of her head, and a small pleased smile played at the corners of his mouth.

Saint Fiacre stared pensively into space pondering the mystery in the gardens. "Don't you have any special powers that can tell us who did it?" Catherine asked him as she stopped on her way to the staff dining room. If he did, he kept it to himself.

Only Greg Robert was in the dining room when Catherine pushed open the door and walked in. He greeted her warmly, and she returned his smile. Helping herself to a cup of coffee, she asked, "Where's Millie this morning?"

"She just went into the main dining room for a minute to check on something. So you had a lot of excitement here yesterday," he said.

She made a face and shook her head. "I can certainly do without that kind of excitement."

Millie came through the swinging door. "Morning Catherine. Got your own coffee, I see. Are you ready for a

104

cinnamon roll?"

"Always," Catherine smiled.

Millie quickly heated one and placed it in front of Catherine. "Did you see Mr. Chatterton's body?" she inquired, her enlarged eyes behind the thick lenses gleaming with morbid interest.

Catherine shuddered inwardly and nodded saying nothing.

Not to be dissuaded, Millie went on. "The news said it was done with a garden fork. Must be something like a pitchfork. That right?"

Again Catherine nodded without speaking.

"Was it in the back? I can't imagine him letting anyone come at him from the front. Was there a lot of blood?"

"Yes. No. I don't know," Catherine replied tersely.

Greg Robert took pity on her obvious unwillingness to discuss the details. "I wondered if the gardens would be closed today."

"I did, too. Have you heard if they are?"

"No. My job doesn't depend on visitors any more than yours. Still I'm not surprised no one called. Have you heard, Millie?"

"No. You'd think someone would let me know so I'd know whether or not to start preparing the lunch specials."

The door opened and Olga Yamikoff walked in glancing around as if looking for someone. Catherine was a little surprised. She'd never seen her in here this early before. She smiled when Olga glanced her way. Olga nodded pleasantly, but didn't speak and sat down at a table near the window.

Millie hurried over with a menu, eager to serve this rare visitor. "Can I get you coffee, Ms. Yamikoff?

Olga smiled. "Please."

What a beautiful smile she has, Catherine thought. It changes her whole face. She wondered why Olga didn't smile more often. Impulsively she said, "Why don't you join us?"

Olga smiled and brought her coffee to their table. "Thank you."

"We were just wondering if the gardens would be open today," Catherine said.

"No. Mr. Birchfield called and said they would be closed until after the funeral."

I could listen to that low voice with that fascinating accent all day, Catherine thought.

"Do you know when the funeral will be?" Greg Robert asked.

She shook her head. "I think the autopsy - is that the word? - needs to be done first."

They glanced up as the door opened again, and Tyler Birchfield entered the room. He glanced in their direction and came over to join them. "Did you hear I've closed the gardens?"

"Yes," Greg Robert answered. "Ms. Yamikoff told us."

"Olga, please," she said.

Tyler glanced over at Millie. "I'm sorry, Millie. I should've called you. I totally forgot you should have been among the first told."

"That's okay. I know you've got so much on your mind with the murder and all."

He turned to the others at the table. "I hated to do it. Some people come from a distance to visit the gardens, and this is a peak time with the roses, but I'm afraid we'd have more curiosity seekers than garden lovers anyway. Besides it would hamper any investigation the police still need to do. They have the topiary and the blue and white gardens secured for now."

"Speaking of roses," Catherine inserted, "Who will get the patent for the blue rose now?"

"I'd imagine the family will," Tyler said.

"I thought maybe he'd have made some arrangements for Elmwood Gardens to have it," Catherine said.

Olga listened intently, not speaking.

"I wonder who'll benefit the most from his will," Millie chimed in, unashamed at eavesdropping on their conversation as she unnecessarily rearranged the sugar bowl, napkin holder, and the salt and pepper shakers on the table next to theirs.

No one answered for a moment, and then Tyler said as he stared into his coffee cup, "I'm sure the police will check that out. I'd imagine it'd be the family again."

"You were all there yesterday," Millie said. "Who do you think did it?"

Greg Robert smiled at the irrepressible Millie. "I wasn't."

Catherine looked at him suddenly remembering the monk she'd seen. "I saw a monk in the gardens yesterday afternoon," she said without thinking.

He looked at her for a moment, then said with firmness. "It wasn't me." He glanced at the wall clock. "I've got work to do. I've wasted too much of the morning as it is." He got up, put some money on the table for Millie and left.

For a moment no one spoke, and then Millie sighed and said "What a hunk of a monk."

They all laughed.

"Is he still a monk?" Catherine asked.

Tyler and Olga both shrugged unknowing or unwilling to say.

Not so Millie. "I don't think so, There was some kind of scandal at the monastery where he was in New York or Kentucky or somewhere. Maybe it was in southern Ohio. I can't remember. It seems the monastery burned down. Something to do with fruitcakes they made. The brandy or something. Someone died I heard."

"Where'd you hear that?" Catherine asked. She felt upset by what she'd just heard.

Millie shrugged becoming evasive. "I don't remember,

but somewhere."

Olga stared intently at Millie. "I would advise you not to spread that around." She frowned. "Gossip is usually a mixture of half-truths or untruths and can cause much damage."

Abashed, Millie blushed and was silent.

With tact Tyler said, "I'd like one of your delicious omelets, Millie. I'm quite hungry this morning after a sleepless night."

"Coming right up," Millie said trying to sound cheerful as she escaped to the sanctuary of her kitchen.

"Excuse me," Olga said suddenly, "but I must go." Laying a few dollars on the table to cover the coffee and tip, she hurried out the door.

Catherine looked at Tyler. He was watching the graceful woman through the window as she hurried across the terrace.

"An interesting woman," he commented.

Catherine silently agreed.

Tyler turned back to her with a smile. "How did you sleep last night?"

"I didn't think I'd sleep at all even though I was exhausted, but I fell asleep almost at once. Unfortunately, I woke up in the middle of the night and couldn't get back to sleep. I kept wondering who could've done it. I keep hoping it was some vagrant or somebody, or at least no one I've ever met."

He smiled in sympathy. "I know. I imagine everyone confronted with murder thinks that. But in a way that would make it worse. If it was an enemy of Chatterton, then you'd be in little or no danger, don't you see?"

"I never thought of it that way." She played with the sugar bowl awhile and then looked up at him. "He wasn't a very nice man, was he?"

"No, he certainly wasn't," Tyler said emphatically.

"Still, a lot of people are unpleasant without getting

killed. I've sure met some."

"It's very possible if you met the murderer, you'd actually find that person much more compatible than you did Mr. Chatterton."

Catherine glanced at him startled. She didn't know how to reply to that. She glanced at her watch. "I'd better look at the hydrangea bed near the lily pond, and then I've got to go. Oh, by the way, I checked the bougainvillea. You're right. It does look a little off. I checked for aphids. I couldn't see anything in particular, but I'll check into it a little more thoroughly and get back to you. It may just need repotted. Anything else you want checked while I'm here?"

"Not that I can think of at the moment," he said turning to the steaming omelet Millie placed in front of him.

"Bye, Millie," Catherine said as she went out the door.

"She's such a nice girl. Cute, too, in her own way. You could do worse," Millie said to Tyler with a nudge at his shoulder and a matchmaking gleam in her eye.

He laughed and said, "Millie, Millie," shaking his head as he did so.

Catherine hurried down the macadam path leading to the lily pond to check the hydrangeas. She glanced at her watch and picked up speed. I shouldn't have taken so long talking. I need to get back to Roses in Thyme so Christy can leave. As she rounded a curve in the path, she saw Olga and Alicia ahead in conversation. Olga was speaking intently to the girl, but Catherine was too far away to hear. Alicia looked distressed and kept shaking her head.

It looks as if she's crying, Catherine thought. When Olga noticed Catherine approaching, she took Alicia's arm and hurried her off down a side path towards the rock garden.

"I wonder what that's all about," Catherine muttered to herself. "Things are getting weirder and weirder".

Chapter Thirteen

A white cat, heading home after a night engaged in cat business, walked purposefully between slanted tombstones in the old cemetery adjoining Our Lady of the Roses Catholic Church. The early morning light gilded the sandstone church further softening walls already gentled by ivy.

John, at the large window overlooking the cemetery, watched without seeing. His mind picked at the problem of Chatterton's murder like fingers picking at a badly tangled skein of yarn. Occasionally he took a sip of coffee from the mug he held, but he no more tasted it then he noticed the masses of pink roses tumbling gaily over the low stone wall separating their yard from the cemetery. His hair was rumpled from a sleepless night and from fingers constantly combing it as if the more he rearranged his hair, the more opportunity there'd be for fresh ideas to enter.

He went over and over those who'd been at the reception. He hadn't noticed anything in the video to help him. Maybe Joe or Tony might pick up on something later, he thought, and wondered about those not been there who might be involved and knew it was also quite possible it could also be someone he wasn't aware of.

It was too early to start background checks on everyone involved, but he decided to go to the station anyway since he couldn't accomplish anything more here.

A stirring in the other room told him his son was awake. Going into the small kitchen, he called, "Josh, I need to talk to you before you get ready to leave for work."

Josh came into the kitchen yawning, fell into the nearest chair and groaned.

As he poured his son a glass of orange juice, John asked, "Did you hear about the Chatterton murder?"

"What!" Josh's eyes widened, and he sat up straighter. "What happened? Who?"

John told him what happened then asked. "So what do you think? Know of anyone in particular who had it in for him?"

Josh shook his head slowly. "Never talked to him. Don't think any of us summer workers have. He doesn't see us when he does come around. We're nobody to him."

"Have you heard anything about the family? His wife? Son? Daughter?"

"I've never met any of 'em, but I've seen his daughter, Alicia. She's hot!" His eyes lit up. After thinking a moment he said. "She was with one of the regular gardeners, the one who works at garden building, rock laying and stuff."

"What's his name?"

"Tom, something or other."

"Were they just having a casual conversation, or did it seem something more?"

Josh scowled as he tried to remember. "More, definitely more. It wasn't anything I could hear, but ya got this feeling, if you know what I mean." John nodded and Josh went on. "I was planting geraniums, and he was laying a stone path for a new bog garden. She came up to him and started talking. I wasn't close enough to hear anything. Next time I glanced up, they'd both disappeared."

"Was that the only time you saw them together?"

"Yeah."

"What do you think of Mr. Birchfield?"

"He's okay. He's the one who hired me. Doesn't say

111

much, but smiles and speaks when he sees me. I like it that he always remembers my name. He's got what you call class. Sorta like Grandma."

John smiled. He knew what Josh meant. Some people had that indefinable something called class, and it wasn't determined by wealth. "Who do you take your daily orders from?"

"Mr. Burns."

"Greg Robert Burns?"

"Yeah."

"What's your opinion of him?"

Josh's smile widened. "He's really cool."

"How so?"

"Well, he's polite when he asks you to do something. It's like you'd be doing him a favor. Know what I mean?" When John nodded, Josh went on. "And he compliments us kids when we do a good job. But when he's ticked about something, he doesn't holler. Sits us down, and kind of leads us into making a suggestion on how it could be better." A smile tugged at the corner of Josh's mouth. "Then acts all happy 'cause you've come up with this really cool idea."

John smiled at Josh. "How long did it take you to figure out what he was doing?"

Josh grinned. "When I heard him doin' the same thing with others. I think it's pretty neat the way he does it."

"Better than yelling and ridiculing, I'd say." John was glad his son's first job experience was a good one.

"You're working today, aren't you?"

"Yeah. I'd better get a move on. It's not that Mr. Burns ever says anything, but none of us want to disappoint him. He seems to care about us kids, ya know? Like he thought my car was great. He asked all kinds of questions about it."

John smiled. "Keep your eyes and ears open today. You'll be my unofficial deputy."

"Yeah, sure thing!"

"How'd your date go last night? Any trouble with the brakes?"

"Brakes seemed fine. I had a good time," Josh said omitting any details as he headed to the bathroom for his morning shower.

John rinsed out his cup and Josh's juice glass, picked up the video and headed down the stairs for the station. He waved to his mom, standing at her kitchen window starting breakfast preparations, as he crossed the graveled parking area in front of Carriage House Books. She smiled and waved back. A wren suddenly burst forth in exuberant song above his head. He smiled at it and went on, feeling just a little better.

"Morning, Joe," John greeted Joe Salcone. "Anything new?"

Joe yawned and rubbed a hand over his bald head. "Nope, not even a fender bender, and not even Mrs. Puckett calling to report a peeping Tom again."

"Tony not in yet?" John asked then added, "He worked late last night."

"Same as you," Joe commented.

"Yeah, well it comes with the job. When you're a big time police chief, there's a lot more responsibility." A smile twitched at the corners of his mouth.

"How late did you stay awake thinking about this?"

"Whadda ya think?"

"Any ideas?"

John frowned. "Not really. It's too soon to have any yet. Have you thought of anything?"

"I don't know anything about him or the family. They were way out of my league. Did you watch the video?"

"Yeah, but I didn't see anything but people, flowers and Chatterton making his pompous speech. I didn't think there'd be anything, but it helped me get familiar with faces at least. You working today?" Joe worked part time at Better Home Improvement in Millport.

113

"No, not today."

"Why don't you leave? I couldn't sleep so I thought I'd come in early. No sense in both of us staying until Tony and Suzy come in. Do you think you'd have time to watch the video at home? You might see something I missed."

Joe nodded and reached for it. "I'll do that. What're you doing today?"

"I'm running background checks on everyone at Elmwood and the family, although I'm not very optimistic about anything turning up. And I'll go talk to the head gardener who was fired last fall. I understand he was pretty upset about it."

"Ed Flavian?"

"Yes. You know him?"

"Yeah. He comes in Belle's sometimes in the winter months when things are slow. Seems like an okay guy."

"Did you ever hear him talk about getting fired?"

"I remember once. There were a bunch of guys sitting around, and Ed was grumbling about it. I don't remember exactly what was said. I know that the feelings were all decidedly anti-Chatterton that day, even from those who didn't know him. I remember someone saying 'What goes round comes round. His day'll come.'"

"Are you stopping for breakfast at Belle's this morning?

Joe nodded. "As usual."

"Keep your ears open."

"Will do."

After Joe left, John took the notes he'd made in the night and sat down at the computer. He glanced at his watch. Almost seven.

When Tony came in, he found John hunched over the computer he fervently hated, frowning as he laboriously pecked out words with one finger.

Tony grinned. He loved computers and he had no difficulty whizzing through the internet and finding information both useful and totally unrelated to police business. It amused him to see John's obvious antipathy towards "Big Brother" as John disparagingly called the computer. Tony enjoyed spiking his conversation with computer-speak to watch a bewildered look flickering in John's eyes when he did. But because Tony liked and admired John, those tweaking times weren't often.

"How's it goin', Chief?" Tony's voice was cheerful.

John pushed his chair back from the computer and swiveled around. "Damn machine," he muttered. "Here's a list of people I want background checks on. I've checked the few I did."

Tony looked at the sheet of paper John handed him and gave a low whistle. "That's a long list."

"Who do I leave out? There are a lot of people who work for Elmwood, and there were a lot of guests there yesterday. I didn't even add the part time summer help to the list or the special workers brought in for the day. If this first list doesn't turn anything up, we'll have to dig further. Of course, even if nothing raises a red flag, it still doesn't mean the murderer is not someone on the list."

John stood up, stretched, and reached for the patrol car keys lying on the desk. "Oh, contact Sussex Garden Supplies. Find out if anyone from there was at Elmwood yesterday. Also, find out everything you can about the business; who's in charge, their financial situation, and so on. I've heard he's involved in other businesses, too. Find out what you can."

"You think it might be business related?" Tony asked.

"It's always possible, but somehow I doubt it. The M.O. is all wrong. Still we need to check all avenues."

"Where're you goin' first?"

"Out to talk with the previous head gardener, Ed Flavian."

John waved at Suzy, who was pulling into a parking place in her little Honda Civic, as he climbed into the patrol car. She cheerfully waved back, her mouth working furiously at a fresh wad of gum.

He turned north and headed out Main Street. On both sides the mostly clapboard houses of early Western Reserve architecture squatted solidly, their roots going as deep and as far back as the old maples sheltering them. As he passed Roses in Thyme, he glanced at the small garden center with curiosity. He'd been favorably impressed with the owner.

As he passed over Willow Creek Bridge, he noticed Maggie Fiest weeding. He slowed, called out a greeting and waved. She waved back. He liked Maggie. She was a regular customer at Carriage House Books. They'd had many literary discussions over the years, often agreeing, and sometimes disagreeing on the relative merits of a certain book or author.

Just past Anderson's farm he turned left onto Anderson Road and soon came to Raspberry Lane, a horseshoe road beginning and ending on Anderson with a small allotment of mostly slab homes. He remembered when he'd been a young boy and old man Anderson had sold this section of his farm to a developer. At the time John had been upset about having a part of the land he freely roamed developed. He realized now Mr. Anderson did what he thought fair. He'd divided the money from the land sale with two of his children, who weren't interested in farming. The rest of the farm he'd deeded to the son who wanted to farm the land that'd been in the family for over a hundred years. Gary Anderson must be close to sixty now, John guessed. Still going strong, though. He had two sons who also loved the land. He noticed one of the boys on a tractor mowing. He waved and the man in the straw hat waved back. Mark or Matt? He couldn't tell from this distance. He inhaled a deep breath through the open car window. Nothing smells sweeter than new mown hay, he thought.

A sizable portion of the farm still surrounded the allotment. Over the years what had once looked like a flat

Monopoly board with little rectangular houses all alike sitting on a large green tablecloth had changed. Trees and shrubs planted by new owners years ago, grew and now gave it a settled look. Each owner had added his or her own identity, not only with trees and shrubs, but by adding garages, decks, rooms and gardens so unless you looked closely, you didn't notice how they all came from only two different house plans.

As he drove slowly down Raspberry Lane looking for house numbers, he guessed the Flavian house would be the one just before the road curved. He was right, but a garbage truck blocked their drive. Alma Porcase came down the sidewalk towards his patrol car pulling her wire cart behind her, now full to overflowing. A flowered silk scarf covered all but a few wisps of gray hair, its red and yellow floral colors the only bright note in her faded beige or gray outfit consisting of her usual multiple layers of clothes. Behind her followed her black and tan dog looking just as raggedy as Alma. She must be on her way home, he thought. She lived down a short gravel road across from the first entrance to Raspberry Lane called Dump Road because years ago the town dump had been located there. A few houses were at the beginning of the road, but just past the old dump site, it turned into a dirt lane going through a woods. At the end of this lane lay Alma's house.

"Hi, Alma," he called out.

She stared at him and mumbled something.

"What?" He raised his voice. "I can't hear you over the garbage truck."

"I want you to find my baby," she said louder. "I been asking you for years. Some cop you are," she retorted with distain.

"I'm sorry. I'm still looking," he said placating her.

"Humph," she snorted and moved on down the road.

When she'd first started asking John about her baby, he'd checked into her history and found she'd lost a baby to some sickness more than fifty years ago. It was buried in the Portage Falls Cemetery. She'd had two other children who'd grown up and moved away. One had died in the Korean War, and he didn't know what'd happened to the other one. He remembered stories of Old Man Porcase. He'd been a mean abusive husband and father who'd drank himself to death more than twenty years ago. In those days the police pretty much steered clear of domestic violence. John hated those cases more than anything, too.

The garbage truck moved on, and he pulled into the driveway. Violet Flavian watched from the front window. As he strode up the sidewalk, she opened the door.

"When're you goin' to do somethin' about that woman? She's got no business rummagin' in people's garbage," Violet greeted him with a scowl.

Somewhat taken aback, John said, "Oh, she's harmless enough. Most people don't seem to mind."

Violet ushered him in and changed the subject suddenly becoming friendly and smiling. "I guess you're here to question me about what I saw."

John noted the change and wondered which most accurately represented the real Violet Flavian. Probably the first, he guessed. "Did you see anything?"

"I'm not sure. Oh, do sit down. Would you like some coffee or tea?" she offered, a gracious hostess.

"No, thank you. I just had breakfast." He said as he looked around for a firm chair to sit on. The overstuffed lavender flowered furniture looked like a trap hard to escape from. He chose the only straight backed chair he could find, a dainty little petit point one he perched on gingerly.

"Now," he said getting out notebook and pen, "What do you think you might've seen that was important?"

She sat on the arm of a couch and smoothed her skirt, patterned in large purple flowers, down over her knees and frowned in concentration. "I'm not sure if it's important.

That foreign woman, Olga Yamikoff, was starin' at Mr. Chatterton when Catherine, that's Catherine Jewell, when we came in, and if looks could kill, he would've dropped dead then and there," she said emphatically. "Just ask Catherine if I'm not right."

"Do you know why she, um, seemed angry with him?"

"Probably a lover's quarrel," she surmised sounding smug.

"There was something between them?"

"Well, a little bird told me that. Besides, why else would someone like her come to this little town to work? And I saw them arguin' right after she got here. That tells you they knew each other from before."

"What were they saying?"

"Oh, I couldn't hear. They were too far away."

But I'll bet you sure tried awfully hard to hear, he thought. "Did you see anything else, anyone who looked like they didn't belong there?"

"Not that I can think of."

"Some people reported seeing a monk."

"Yes, but well, it was a medieval feast and all."

"But no one hired him to be part of the festivities as far as I can find out."

"The head gardener used to be a monk," she volunteered. "It could've been him."

John looked up with interest. "You're talking about Mr. Burns?"

"Yes. He was with some monastery. Out of state, I think, but I forget where. He was involved in some scandal. Someone died, I heard."

"I'll check on it. Anything else?"

"No, but I'm glad if I was any help." She got up and started towards the front door.

"I'd like to talk to your husband now."

"He wasn't there," she blurted out. "He wouldn't know anythin'."

"Where is he?"

"In the back yard. Where else?" Her face folded into a frown as she turned and led the way to the back door.

John noticed the difference between Ed Flavian's living area and Violet's, and found he vastly preferred Ed's section. He noted with approval the piles of books stacked around here and there. Without even meeting him yet, his impression of Ed jumped several notches. He knew there wouldn't be scientific data supporting his feelings that readers were less apt to commit a violent crime than a nonreader. Some detective you are, he chided himself as his eyes caressed the old books lining several shelves. His attention was drawn next to the lovely garden outside, a mass of vibrant blooming flowers, and the slightly stoop shouldered man at the back of the garden turning compost with a pitchfork. He turned the heavy pile with ease from one bin to another.

John stepped out the door and walked slowly to the working man, stopping to smell the roses along the way.

"Mr. Flavian?" John said as he approached.

Ed turned around and stared, his shrewd blue eyes alert and intelligent under grizzled brows.

"Chief MacDougal," he acknowledged.

"You've been in the book store." John realized he'd seen him several times there as well as in Belle's Diner. "I've never had the chance to meet you formally."

Ed's smile was dry. "I've had a little more time on my hands lately to come into town."

"So I've heard. Can we sit down?"

"Over here." Ed put his pitchfork into a bucket of sand before leading him to a picnic table under a maple tree near the garden shed

"Why did you do that?" John asked curiously.

"There's oil in the sand. It keeps the tines from rusting, and they're always sharp. I do that with all my tools."

"Mr. Chatterton sold top quality garden tools, I hear."

"Yep, he did. Some tools it don't matter a whole lot if you buy a cheaper variety. Only yuppie gardeners think they have to pay big bucks for garden gloves and such, but for other tools it pays to get the best, and they need to be kept that way if you have to slice through hard soil."

"I understand leaving Elmwood Gardens was not your choice," John said as tactfully as possible.

"I was fired, you mean," he spat out with contempt. "Call a spade a spade."

"Why were you fired?"

Ed put an unlit cigar stub in his mouth and chewed on it while he thought of an answer. "Let's just say we didn't see eye to eye."

"About what?" John persisted.

"He thought I was too old."

"Is that the only reason?"

Ed stared at John then looked away and shrugged. "That's what he said."

"Forget what he said. What was the real reason?"

Ed shook his head. "A lot of people think sixty-five is old. Do you?"

"Not particularly," John smiled. "Do you?"

"Hell, no! I can outwork men half my age. And out think 'em, too."

I'll bet he could, John thought. He realized Ed had led him away from the question he'd asked but decided to drop it. "Were you at the Gardens yesterday?"

"Yeah," Ed admitted. "I watched the shindig from behind the shrubs by the topiary garden."

"Did anyone see you?"

Ed shrugged. "Not that I know of. I think Catherine, Catherine Jewell, might have suspected or got a glimpse. She's a smart one, that girl is."

"Did you see who killed Mr. Chatterton?"

"No, I left before he was killed."

"How do you know when he was killed?"

"Violet told me. Apparently they'd all sort of talked over when he'd last been seen, and when he'd been found."

John nodded an acknowledgement. "Did anyone see you somewhere else during this time?"

"You mean do I have an alibi? No. I walked home the way I came through the woods and fields. It's not far."

"What did you personally think of Mr. Chatterton?"

Ed gave a short laugh. "You've gotta be kidding. I couldn't stand the man. Never could. Not from the first day he came."

"When was that?"

"About fifteen years ago, I guess."

"Why didn't you like him? I mean before he fired you."

Ed looked around at his gardens as he searched for words. His face gentled as his gaze lingered on his roses. He looked at John wondering if he could possibly understand. Something there must've reassured him maybe John could because finally he said. "A true gardener has a lifelong love affair with his garden, with plants. As Emerson said, 'Nature is the symbol of spirit.' Now Chatterton, he was in it for show; to impress only. Do you understand?"

John nodded and thought of his books. He felt the same way about them. He thought, How lucky the person who has such a passion. Or was it always lucky? Could it become an obsession? When was the fine line between passion and obsession crossed?

"Did you kill him?" he asked quietly.

Ed smiled. "No, but I sure as hell am not sorry he's dead."

Everyone was gone now. They all said the baby looked just like its father. She knew what they were thinking. They thought maybe she lied. That the baby wasn't really his. Well, it was his, alright. He'd looked so proud when everyone said it and cooed and ahhed over the baby. But that hadn't kept him here.

"Just goin' out for a quick one," he'd said. That was over an hour ago.

The baby started whimpering again.

"Oh God, Baby. Please don't cry. I'm so tired. I just want to sleep, and sleep, and sleep."

But the baby's whimpering grew more and more insistent until its cry became wails.

Chapter Fourteen

Catherine sat back on her haunches, ran a hand through her short sun frosted hair, and surveyed the area she'd just weeded with satisfaction. Her tabby cat strolled over and flopped down then rolled over stomach up, inviting a belly rub.

"Okay, Lily," Catherine smiled, "but just a short belly rub. I have lots of weeding yet to do." The cat half closed her eyes in bliss. The Jody Belle daylily is too short to go behind the irises, Catherine thought as she rubbed Lily's stomach. Maybe the Amethyst Crown would look better. The perennial garden, between Roses in Thyme and her house, not only satisfied her personal gardening needs, but was also a good advertisement for the nursery. Many customers seeing a flowering display in a garden wanted the same for their own.

"That's enough, Lilly. I need to mulch now." Getting to her feet, she started lightly spreading fine mulch around Sweet Williams and delphiniums. The sound of crunching gravel announced a potential customer. Turning, she saw a Portage Falls patrol car.

"Good morning," John MacDougal said as he got out. He glanced at his watch. "Yes, I guess it is still morning. Your garden is looking nice."

"Thanks." She walked towards him. "It still needs a lot of work, though."

"According to my mom, gardeners are never totally satisfied."

"Maybe that's what makes gardening America's number one hobby. It's such a challenge. Are you here as a customer or a police officer?"

"How about friend."

She raised her eyebrows, and he grinned at her. "I guess it is police business."

"Let's sit down where it's cooler." She led him into a lattice covered area attached to the shop. It was at least ten degrees cooler there with vines climbing up and over it pleasantly shading the area from the noonday sun. In the green filtered light, it had an almost underwater feel. She motioned him to a seat at the wrought iron table and asked, "Would you like some iced tea or lemonade?"

"That sounds good, if it's no bother."

"Of course not. Which do you want, or would you prefer coffee?"

"Iced tea."

"Lemon? Sugar?"

"A little lemon, please."

She left and hurried down the short path to the side door of her house.

He looked around as he waited for her. He liked the floor of old bricks and wondered if she'd laid them herself. The potted and hanging plants, as well as a small stone fountain splashing water, created a cool and pleasant place to sit. It's amazing how much she's done in the short time she's had this place, he thought. He hadn't been here for several years, not since Mr. Crafton owned it. It certainly didn't look this nice when he had it. In fact, even though it was close, he knew his mother had always gone to a nursery in Millport for her gardening needs since she claimed Mr. Crafton seldom had anything she wanted.

"Thank you," he said as she came back with two tall glasses of iced tea on a tray and a small plate of cookies. He eyed the cookies.

"You reminded me it's getting close to lunch,"

Catherine said referring to the cookies as she took one. "Chocolate chip, my favorite. Violet brought them a couple of days ago, but they're still good."

"Did you enjoy the Celia Thaxter book, *An Island Garden*, you bought last winter?" He asked as he helped himself to a cookie. Breakfast had been a long time ago for him, too.

She gave him a broad smile. "You remembered that?"

He grinned. "I usually remember books better than people, I'm sorry to say. I knew you looked familiar last night, but couldn't place you until later."

"I loved the book," she enthused. "Her writing is a little more effusive than the garden books of today, but I enjoyed her quaint way of describing the world around her, and I found much of her garden hints helpful even today. I'd love to go to Appledore Island. I've read her original garden has been restored."

"Do you read much besides garden books?"

She laughed. "Yes, of course, although in the spring and summer, unfortunately, I don't have as much time for reading as I'd like."

"I can't see why not," he said shaking his head with a smile and looking around at all the work she'd done.

"I like biographies and a good mystery, although since I started living alone, I don't read any that are too scary," she admitted, "and I'm working through a list of 'One Hundred Books Everyone Should Read.' It's a list put together from a survey of English professors."

He laughed. "How many of them have you read?"

She rolled her eyes and made a rueful face. "Not too many, I'm afraid. Last winter I read *Middlemarch* by George Elliot. I enjoyed that."

"You've done so much with this place," he said changing the subject. "You've had it a year now, haven't you?"

"A year and two months to be exact, and I want to do

126

so much more." She looked around and her eyes took on a dreamy look.

"Like what?"

"For starters, I want another greenhouse or even two. I want to extend my herb selection. And then I want to eventually clear the field behind the place and start raising my own roses, daylilies and hostas. Maybe eventually I might get into the mail order business, too, but right now I have to worry about making the payments on this place and keeping my truck going. It's almost done for."

"You are ambitious! I admire people with dreams and goals. Are you going to fit a family into that schedule someday?"

All the lightness left her. She smiled a tight smile that didn't reach her eyes and shook her head slightly. She looked towards the door and said in a flat voice, "No."

He wondered at the abrupt change in her, but decided not to pursue it. In fact, he was slightly embarrassed. He realized he'd overstepped the bounds of good taste to ask a personal question like that and quickly changed the subject.

"I just talked to Violet and Ed Flavian." He reached for another cookie, then looked at her as he bit into the cookie and chewed. "Why didn't you tell me Greg Robert Burns was a monk once, or maybe still is?"

She colored, disconcerted and slightly embarrassed as if she'd been caught doing something wrong. "I don't know. I guess I didn't think of it," she stammered.

He took off his glasses and started polishing them. He watched her and waited for her to go on before putting them back on and adjusting them.

"No, I did think of it," she said sounding defiant as she looked directly at him, "but I didn't want to make him look guilty or anything because he's just about the nicest person anyone could meet, and he'd never ever hurt anybody or anything."

"Are you in love with him?" he asked quietly. He

paused a moment. That could be too personal, too, but he reassured himself it was in the line of police questioning.

She looked startled. "No, it's nothing at all like that. He's a nice person, and I value his friendship."

John let it drop. "Ed Flavian admits he was at Elmwood yesterday. He thinks you saw him. Did you?"

"Yes," she admitted.

"You neglected to tell me that, too."

She said nothing as she watched a lemon slice turn in her iced tea while she gently shook it.

"I assume it's misguided loyalty and not deliberate obstruction."

She shot him a challenging look. "What's wrong with loyalty?"

"Nothing, but it doesn't help solve murders."

"They had nothing to do with it," she said with assurance.

"Ed Flavian has a pretty good motive. I don't know about the Burns guy, but a monk's habit with a hood does make a pretty good disguise."

He got to his feet, and she followed him to the door without speaking. Before leaving, he turned to her and said, "Please don't keep anything suspicious from me again. You seem to know everyone involved. If you notice anything that doesn't seem quite right, or anything that would help, call me."

She nodded, but didn't answer.

He looked at her for a long moment, then got in his car and backed out slowly.

"Shoot!" Catherine muttered. She'd accidentally pulled another young Shirley poppy as she was weeding. After Chief MacDougal left, she had a hard time keeping her mind on what she was doing. Finally she decided to call it quits, and got to her feet, gathered up her weed bucket, trowel, gloves and kneeling mat and walked to the compost area to dump the almost full bucket of weeds. After putting everything away, she stood indecisively staring into space. Then with a deep breath, she made up her mind.

"Christy," she called as she went looking for her behind the greenhouse. Christy was watering the potted hostas and ferns arrayed down an aisle of heavy black plastic under the dappled shade of locust trees. "I'm going to the Flavians' for a bit. Keep an eye out for customers, will you?" I'll make sure I'm back in time for you to leave."

"Okay," she said.

"If you want, I'll run you home when I get back."

"Thanks, but I can take the path behind Mrs. Fiest's house through the woods and fields. It's not far, and besides, I want to see if I can find Snowball. He didn't come home last night." Her brown eyes looked worried.

"Cats are like that in the summer time," Catherine said. "I know Lily is, but when winter comes, she doesn't want to put one foot out the door."

"Maybe you can ask Mr. Flavian if he's seen him. Sometimes Snowball likes to sleep in his garden shed. Mr. Flavian doesn't mind. Says he keeps the mouse population in check."

"I'll do that. Be back soon." She paused to wash her hands and knees, grabbed keys and purse and left.

She wondered what she'd say as she drove the short distance to Violet and Ed's house. She couldn't think of a reason for a visit in the middle of the day, but it didn't seem to matter.

Violet greeted her with as much friendly warmth as if she were a regular and much valued visitor by folding Catherine into her purple bosom with a big hug of welcome. "I just got back from grocery shopping at Millport. Would you like something to eat?"

129

Catherine noticed they were finishing a late lunch. "No, thank you. I already ate." Actually she hadn't except for the few cookies because she'd been too upset to think of lunch.

"Get the gal a cup of coffee and a piece of your strawberry-rhubarb pie. No one makes a better strawberry-rhubarb pie than Violet," Ed claimed.

Catherine's stomach rumbled at the mention of food, so she sat down and gratefully accepted the pie and hot coffee in a mug covered with wood violets.

"Cream? Sugar?" Violet inquired.

"A little milk or cream. Whatever." Catherine took a bite of the pie. "Ummm. You're right. This is wonderful," she said chewing with pleasure.

They discussed what they thought were the best cultivars of rhubarb, and what soil was best, and so on until Ed, always perceptive, said, "Well, Missy, what brings you here besides the pie? I'm sure you didn't smell that pie all the way over to your place."

Catherine shrugged as she searched for something plausible to say. The truth was she wasn't sure herself why she was here. Reassurance, she guessed. Reassurance these people she considered friends weren't involved in the murder. She looked at Ed and gave him a sheepish smile. "Chief MacDougal stopped in a while ago."

"Did he tell you he thinks I did Chatterton in?" A small smile twitched at the corners of his mouth.

Catherine grinned back relieved to see Ed looking unworried. "Not exactly, but he did mention you had a motive."

"Maybe in his eyes I did, but though I certainly didn't like being fired at my age, it's not the end of the world, and I certainly wouldn't kill over it. With my Social Security and a few odd jobs here and there, I can make enough for Violet and me to get by on."

Catherine smiled feeling better. "That's what I told

him, sort of; at least I told him you'd never kill anyone." She glanced at Violet for affirmation. Instead she caught Violet staring at Ed, a faraway look on her face.

When she realized Catherine was looking at her, she nodded, smiled and brushed one well-manicured hand over her lavender tinted hair, "Of course, Ed wouldn't hurt anybody," she agreed. "He won't even kill snakes or chipmunks in the garden."

"Snakes are beneficial, and chipmunks don't do enough harm to kill them." Ed claimed repeating an old argument.

"He wondered why I hadn't mentioned seeing you at the gardens."

"Why didn't you?"

"I don't know. I guess because it would sort of seem like pointing a finger at you. I knew you couldn't do anything like that."

"I'm glad you feel that way," Ed said.

"I think they should look at his business," Catherine said. "It seems to me that most murders are probably committed over passion, revenge or greed." She paused. "I guess that's not original thinking, is it?"

"No, but it's probably the truth," he said.

"I think they should look at the family," Violet said. "If he was foolin' around, his wife might've killed him."

"Do you really think a woman could've done that?" Catherine asked. "I can't see a woman being that strong."

"If he was lying on the ground maybe they could," Ed interjected.

"That's silly," Violet commented. "Why would he just be lyin' on the ground?"

"What if he tripped and fell down those steps," Catherine said.

"And the murderer just happened to have the fork?" Ed sounded skeptical. "That seems pretty farfetched. He couldn't have picked a better tool for it, though. Those gardening forks by Sussex are the strongest and sharpest ones going."

"Could the murderer have snuck up behind him and pushed him, and then jumped down the steps and stabbed him?" Catherine went on theorizing.

"I suppose so," Ed admitted.

"The twine! The twine!" Catherine exclaimed. "Before this happened, I noticed twine tied around one of the rhododendrons. I was going to go back the next day and untie it before it girdled the bush, but I forgot. At the time I couldn't figure why anyone would've done such a thing, but now I see. It was used to trip him. That has to be it."

Ed nodded. "You could have something there."

"Then Mrs. Chatterton, or his son or daughter could've done it," Violet said.

"I suppose it's possible," Ed said. "I can't really see the girl doing it, though. She's just a bit of a thing."

"You're just like any man. Can't look beyond a pretty face. She rides horses," Violet said, "and you have to be strong to do that."

Ed ignored her. "You know, I saw the Chatterton boy's black jeep parked in the parking lot of the Township Park behind Elmwood when I was going home yesterday. I thought it was kind of funny he wasn't celebrating with his father, but I've heard they never did get along."

"Did you tell Chief MacDougal?" Catherine asked.

"I didn't think of it. Maybe I should, though."

"I should probably tell him about the twine, too. That could be important."

They sat in silence thinking over the possibilities that had been raised. Then Catherine stood up. "I've got to get back to the shop now. Christy has to leave soon. Oh, that reminds me. Have you seen her cat, Snowball? He didn't come home last night, and she's worried."

Ed laughed. "He got locked up in my shed last night. I didn't know he was there when I closed up. He came out

132

complaining this morning when I opened the shed. He's a wanderer, that cat is. He likes to visit me."

"I'll tell Christy. She'll be relieved. Cats are a nuisance sometimes, but I enjoy mine."

"I can't abide the cat hairs and kitty litter. That's why I never wanted one," Violet said. "Or dogs, either. I have so many valuables, I'd be afraid they'd break somethin'."

Catherine could see that happening in Violet's part of the house as she gingerly picked her way through the overcrowded living room holding her purse carefully so it wouldn't swing. Even so, she managed to brush against a small glass topped pedestal table and started it rocking. Violet clutched at a ceramic figurine of a Victorian lady in a full-skirted lavender ball gown and rescued it just in time.

Amidst apologies and reassurances no harm was done, Catherine made her escape and breathed a sigh of relief when the door finally closed behind her.

Chapter Fifteen

The shadowy interior of Our Lady of the Roses brought welcome relief from the hot afternoon sun. Father Patrick O'Shawnessy slipped in through the side door from his garden for a moment of quiet meditation. He paused for a few moments to inhale the fragrance of varnished pews, hymnals, candles and flowers and then genuflected before the side altar holding the tabernacle. After offering a brief prayer, he walked down the carpeted aisle between age darkened oak pews highlighted in jeweled tones from the sun streaming through stained glass windows. As his eyes became accustomed to the dim light, he noticed a bundle of rags lying on a pew underneath the largest of the stained glass windows, the one depicting Our Lady of the Roses. The patron saint, clothed in a cobalt blue gown and surrounded by pink and red roses, looked down with a mixture of serenity and compassion on her lovely face at the old woman lying so still.

Stretched out on the floor near the old woman, lay a shaggy brown and black dog with nose on paws keeping watch over her and her cart full of odd shaped bags and bundles.

Father Pat sighed. He'd told Alma time and again the dog was not allowed in the church. Alma always assured him it wouldn't happen again, but she either forgot or chose to ignore his request. He was inclined to think it was the latter.

"Hello, Ralph," he said softly to the dog. Ralph didn't raise his head from his paws and didn't look up, either, but thumped his tail in acknowledgement of the greeting.

Smart dog, Father Pat thought. He knows he's not supposed to be here, and he's apologetic about it.

He sat down near Alma to quietly pray. His thin, white hair, once blond, still had a touch of yellow, causing it to glow as the light shining through the gold halo above the Blessed Mother's head touched it. Inside the church all sounds from the outside world were muffled, creating a world of serenity and peace. Father Pat loved this old modified gothic church, brown sandstone barely visible through the ivy covering it. He thought of the flying buttresses and high interior arches as an offering of architectural prayer to God. His gaze moved upward to the arched ceiling with a painting of the Assumption of Our Blessed Mother assisted by a bevy of angels. He hoped no future committee or pastor would want to see that beautiful painting painted over in the name of modernization.

Father Pat, long past the age of retirement, had offered to postpone retirement if he could stay here with this church. Since there was always a shortage of priests, the bishop had agreed.

Sometimes he wondered about the Chatterton family of long ago, who were responsible for this church. Originally it'd been a small wooden church called St. Mark's, but the Chattertons offered to finance most of the building of the new church, a grand church, if the name would be changed to Our Lady of the Roses. Apparently there'd been no objections to the name change, at least none Father Pat had heard of, but that was long before his time.

They'd brought in an English architect and had it built in the style of a church in some long forgotten English village where the Chattertons had originally come from. He couldn't remember where exactly. The beautiful stained glass windows had been made there, too, and carefully shipped to America along with the artisan who lovingly, carefully pieced them together and put them in place. What a lot of money that must have been, he thought.

135

He pondered the age old question. Should money be spent on magnificent structures to praise God, or to feed the poor instead? It seemed even more pertinent now as Alma lay quietly sleeping, swathed in rags, in this beautiful tribute to a Higher Being.

"What do you pray for?"

He glanced down at Alma and saw her half closed eyes watching him. She was curled childlike with her hands under her cheek. A bandana was tied around her wispy gray hair and under her chin. Remembering the custom of women and girls always covering their heads in church, he wondered idly if she'd ever been a Catholic.

"What for or why?" he asked with a smile.

"What for not why. What could a priest want? Money? Women?" Her mostly toothless mouth twitched in what could've been a smile.

He thought for a moment. "Mostly I pray for others, for people with their problems."

"Doesn't work, does it," she said.

"We don't always see God's ways," he replied. "Sometimes we can see our prayers answered, and it reinforces our belief. Sometimes we have to trust God hears and has a larger plan we're not aware of. Do you pray, Alma?"

She stared pensively at the Blessed Mother and then said so quietly he could barely hear her, "I used to, but it never seemed to work." She looked at him then. "Do you ever think God will let me find my baby?"

He felt that old pain as he laid his hand gently on the frail shoulder and said simply, "Yes, he will. You can be sure of that."

She sighed deeply and sat up. Ralph lifted his head, his brown eyes attentive.

"Where did you go today?" Father Pat asked. "And did you get anything good?" Alma wouldn't take handouts from anyone. In her own way she was proud and refused what she called charity. Rummaging in dumpsters and garbage cans was different in her eyes. Father Pat often left things carefully wrapped in his trash can for her. He suspected other people did, too.

"I did Main Street early this morning. I got half a bag of dog food from the can where that collie lives. I guess he didn't like it. Then I got some good stuff out on Raspberry Lane. I got a pretty plate with only a little chip out of it, and some apples that were just a little soft on one side. Make good applesauce, they will. And would you believe someone threw out a perfectly good robe? It'll keep me warm this winter."

He smiled wondering who the kind soul was who gave that to her. Most people gave their leftover clothes to Good Will or the Salvation Army so that had to be intended for her, just like the wool blanket he'd caught Martha MacDougal putting in her trash can last fall.

"Me and Ralph better get going. Ralph's gonna eat well tonight with that dog food, ain't ya, Ralph."

The dog smiled and wagged his tail.

Father Pat walked her to the large, carved, wooden, front doors and escorted her down the steps as if she were the richest and most socially important person of his parish. It wasn't an act with him. He genuinely cared for others, especially the needy ones, and who in this town was needier than Alma? He would've liked to drive her home, but he knew she'd refuse.

He stood watching her frail and shuffling form with the old, white, too large tennis shoes on her feet, until she was out of sight around the corner. A feeling of great sadness for Alma and all the poor lost souls of the world came over him, and even the sight of his beloved roses when he returned to the garden, couldn't lift his spirits.

Hush little baby
Don't say a word
Papa's gonna buy
You a mockingbird

She sat in the darkened room rocking the quiet baby. The blinking lights from across the street tinted their faces a garish red and green.

And if that mockingbird
Don't sing,
Papa's gonna buy
You a diamond ring.

She rocked back and forth, back and forth, and crooned to the baby in her arms. Her headache was gone now. In a trancelike state, she rocked on even after the marquis lights across the street were turned off, unaware of the blue lips of her limp baby.

Chapter Sixteen

The lunch crowd at Belle's Diner seemed busier than usual judging by the cars parked up and down the street. Someone had even parked in John's space with the "Reserved for Police Chief" sign. Normally even-tempered, today John was in no mood for such blatant law breaking. Sticking his head in the door first to make sure it wasn't anyone on important business, he took time to write out a ticket and put it on the windshield with an extra snap of the windshield wiper for good measure to make sure it stayed.

"Where's Tony," he asked Suzy.

She popped a big bubble. "Went to Belle's for a bite a few minutes ago."

"Did he leave any messages?"

"Yeah, there's some faxes and a note for you on your desk."

"Anything else new?" he asked as he checked the faxes and Tony's message.

"A ton of reporters called," she answered with relish. It was obvious she was enjoying the unusual excitement.

He picked up the faxes to take with him. "I'm going home to grab a sandwich. Have Tony wait or call me if something comes up."

"Okay," she said as she went back to her soap opera magazine.

John crossed the street dodging a few cars. He knew what the main topic of conversation would be in the diner. Maybe Tony will pick up something, he thought. If he got a chance, he'd stop in later when things got quiet and talk to Belle. She knew everything going on in this town.

Over a cheese and salami sandwich and a cup of coffee, John read the faxes and Tony's note. He gave a silent whistle as he read the information on Greg Robert Burns. Glancing at the clock, he rinsed his cup and hurried back to the station. He was eager to talk to Tony and glad to see he was back.

"Some interesting stuff here," he greeted Tony waving the papers in his hand.

"Yeah, I'll say."

"Come in the office." John closed the door behind them noticing Suzy's disappointed face as he did so. He didn't want to hurt her feelings, but the information on the faxes shouldn't be town gossip. He wasn't sure Suzy, nice if a bit ditzy, was as discreet as she should be. He wondered briefly if she'd already read them.

"Did you see the Burns guy set fire to St. Boniface's monastery where he came from? Some guy died in the fire. One of the monks." Tony's dark eyes radiated excitement.

John bit his lip, frowning. "Yes. I found out from Mrs. Flavian he is, or was a monk." He wondered if it had anything to do with Catherine's enigmatic reply to his question. "The report said it was an accident."

"Then why do you suppose he left? Do you think there's some question about it?"

"I don't know. It'll be something to check out. Anything come through on Olga Yamikoff? Mrs. Flavian seems to think there was something between Chatterton and the Yamikoff woman."

"No, not yet. Only Birchfield, Burns and that little bit on the Chatterton family so far."

"I see Birchfield was a professor at Cuyahoga Valley Eastern College. He left two years ago. I don't see anything on what he was doing between then and when he was hired at Elmwood last fall," John said. "Nothing much of interest on the Chatterton family, either." He glanced through the papers again and then tilted back in his chair thinking.

"Check on the former manager of Elmwood, too. You'll have to find out what his name is. He left about the same time Ed Flavian did. That seems a little strange. Also, get the address of Sussex Garden Supplies. I'll need to check that angle, too. Did you get hold of his lawyer?"

"I called and the receptionist at Silvernail, Ketchem and Silvernail said Mr. Silvernail Sr. would call back this evening. He's out of town and won't be in till late this afternoon. It seems he's the only one who handles Chatterton's affairs," Tony said.

"Did you hear anything interesting at Belle's?"

"Everyone was talking about it and asking me questions, but no one seems to know anything. Lots of opinions, though."

"Like what?"

"Well, some thought it was the foreign woman, others thought it was probably the wife, either that or a jealous husband," Tony grinned.

"Anyone have any reason to believe that?"

"Nah. They just seemed to be shootin' off at the mouth."

John sighed. "There'll probably be a lot of that. I'd better get out to Elmwood now before people start thinking I'm not doing my job." He pushed back his chair and got up. "Pete and Bill still out there?"

"Far as I know. They haven't come back yet."

"I'll see if they found anything. I doubt it though."

Suzy was painting her long fake nails in alternating colors of aqua and purple when he walked out. John chuckled shaking his head, "Suzy, this place would be so dull without you."

She held one hand out admiring her artwork. "Kinda neat, don't cha think?" She looked at him for confirmation.

He smiled. "Um, they certainly are unique."

"That's what I think," she said with a nod of satisfaction then glanced from the corner of her eye at Tony lounging and grinning in the doorway of John's office.

"Hey, MacDougal!" the big voice boomed out from across the commons.

John turned and smiled at the large husky woman matching the voice as she came striding toward him. She was dressed in her usual uniform of jeans, plaid shirt, work boots and Cleveland Indians' ball cap.

"Hi, Mayor. What's up?" he asked as she approached.

"It's not what's up with me. What's up with this murder? What are you doing about it?"

"Mostly talking to people right now."

"Hell of a thing." She shook her head. "We can't have this sort of stuff going on in our town, you know," she said glaring at him.

He nodded in agreement. In spite of her blunt manner, John liked Mayor Winifred Partridge, usually called Mayor or Fred. Apparently most of the people in the town felt the same way because she'd run unopposed for more than fifteen years now.

"Guess it couldn't be helped." She took off her cap and ran her hand through short cropped gray hair. "Got any ideas who could've done it?"

"Not now," John admitted. "He wasn't well liked, I'm finding out, but that isn't a sufficient reason for murder."

"Hell no," she agreed. "There are lots of people I can't stand, but I don't go about bumping them off. Well, keep me informed. I have to get back to mowing." With that she abruptly turned and strode back to the tractor she used to mow the commons. She wasn't only Mayor, but general grounds keeper, did snow plowing, and handled any other job she thought needed done about town.

142

John smiled at her retreating back and thought how hard it was to believe she was once his math teacher. He got into his cruiser and headed for Elmwood Gardens.

"Well don't that beat all get out!" the paunchy man in plaid Bermuda shorts said. His golf hat announced "I'm retired, this is as dressed up as I get." Standing in front of a RV at least thirty feet long with California license plates, he frowned as he read the sign in front of Elmwood Gardens stating the gardens were closed.

"Does it say why or when they'll open again?" a feminine voice from inside queried.

"Says they'll be open on Monday, but we can't hang around that long. Hell of a note," he grumbled.

John gave a slight tap to his horn since they were blocking the entrance.

The man turned around startled and then hurried to climb back into the road monster before pulling into the empty parking lot to turn around.

John pulled up to the locked gates, and a young man on duty opened them so he could pull through while the couple in the RV gawked.

The tents, tables, and everything else from yesterday's gathering had been taken down leaving the lawn only slightly trampled. Parking his squad car in the shade of a large maple near the topiary garden, he went in search of Pete and Bill and found them sitting on a bench in the garden where Chatterton had been found.

"Find anything?"

Both of them shook their heads. "Nothing that seems to mean anything," Bill said. "A few candy and gum wrappers and a few cigarette butts, but they could've been thrown down anytime by anybody."

"Did you collect them? I'd imagine the gardens were thoroughly cleaned before the big reception yesterday."

"Yeah. We picked them up wearing gloves and put them in a plastic bag," Pete replied.

"Probably won't amount to anything," John admitted, "but we'd be remiss in not checking it out. Did you check the garbage cans for that note that was handed to Chatterton?"

"Yeah. Messy job but nothing," Bill said.

"You supervised the tearing down of the tents and stuff, too, I see."

"Yeah, they just left," Pete tried to suppress a yawn.

"As soon as you take the yellow tape down, you can go. I don't see any purpose in either of you staying here any longer. Did you talk to anyone today?"

"Nope. No one came anywhere near us," Pete said.

"You haven't had lunch yet, have you?"

"No, but it sure sounds good." Bill, always hungry, answered quickly.

John smiled. "How about going to Belle's for lunch and picking up what you can in the way of scuttlebutt. Talk to Belle and see what she's heard. Tony was there, but she was pretty busy with the lunch crowd. She might have more time to talk now. Let's meet at five back at the station and go over what we've learned."

They agreed and quickly left. John looked around at the small sunken garden. Sunlight and shadows patterned the soft shades of greens and white. Water in the fountain gurgled and splashed. A sweet scent permeated the air from the white roses tumbling over the stone walls. The whole effect was one of serenity and peace, John thought. Even the gruesome murder doesn't quite take that away, and yet as he turned to go in his mind's eye the body of Chatterton, garden fork still in his back, was clearly visible lying at the foot of the mossy stone steps leading in and out of the garden, and in spite of himself, he felt an inward shudder.

John went in search of Greg Robert Burns. He tried his cottage first and then went to the staff lunch room, stopping on the way in to look at the statue of a saint in a stone alcove near the entrance. Saint Francis, he surmised, but on looking closer, he noted the name Saint Fiacre. Never heard of him. Looks secretive, he thought.

Lunch was over in the staff lunch room, and Millie was cleaning up. Dishes finished, she was wiping the counters before leaving. She looked up at John with inquisitive eyes when he entered.

"Can I help you?"

"I'm looking for Mr. Burns."

"I think he's working in the vegetable garden."

John looked around. "You keep a clean place here."

"You won't find any dirt here or in the Tea Room, either." She was pleased he'd noticed.

"Would you like a cup of coffee?"

"That would be nice." He pulled out a chair and sat down with a sigh. "It's been a long day. Have you worked here long?"

"Seventeen years," she said with a touch of pride. She put coffee and cream on the table and sat down opposite him.

He shook his head. "You've seen a lot of people come and go." He added cream to the mug before taking a gulp of hot coffee.

"I sure have. I can tell you, I've seen it all. You just wouldn't believe the things I've seen."

"I'll bet you're a real student of human nature."

She looked at him uncertainly, but saw only a look of friendliness on his face so she went on. "Some people think they're so much better than anybody else, but they got to answer nature's call like anybody else. In the long run, they ain't no different when all's been said and done."

John nodded. "Yeah, I know what you mean. I imagine

145

everyone who works here in the gardens is pretty nice, though. Maybe you know my mom, Martha MacDougal?"

"I might know her to see her," Millie said, "but I can't place the name."

"Anyway, she always says, 'If they're a gardener, they're a good person,'" he laughed.

"I don't know about that. I don't do much more than plant a few geraniums and petunias. I like to cook." She thought a few moments. "That's not really true, though."

"How so?"

"Well, I don't like to speak ill of the dead, and I'm not much of one to gossip, but Mr. Chatterton was a gardener, and he wasn't nice, no way."

"I think a lot of people felt that way. Why didn't you like him?"

"He was snooty. Just like his wife. They don't even see ya. It's as if you're no more than a piece of furniture or something."

"What about the Chatterton kids? Are they snooty, too?"

"I've never seen much of the boy. The girl only comes in when Tom, one of the gardeners, is in here. She don't have eyes for nobody but him."

"Chatterton must've had some friends. Did they ever come in with him?"

"Sometimes he'd bring people into the Tea Room, and they'd talk and laugh, but I don't think they were really friends. I think it was just business or something."

"From what I've gathered, everyone else around here gets along pretty well, am I right?"

"Yeah, it's a pretty good bunch of people," she agreed.

"When Ed Flavian was fired did anyone take sides and not cooperate with the new head gardener?"

"Not that I know of. That was a raw deal Ed got, but no one seemed to blame Mr. Burns. He's really a decent sort."

"What happened to the manager of the Gardens before Mr. Birchfield?" John asked.

"Mr. Mansfield? He retired. Went to Florida, I heard."

"No problems there that you heard of?"

"No, but he didn't seem hardly old enough. Only sixty, I think. That's younger than me. Still maybe he saved his money. One never knows."

"You didn't work yesterday, did you?"

"Only in the morning for the staff. We all left around noon before the doin's."

"Well, I'd better get going." He got up slowly and stretched. "Which way to the vegetable gardens?"

"When you leave, follow the path towards the back and then turn left. You can't miss them." she directed.

He seems like a nice young man, Millie thought as she watched him from the window. Good looking, too. Nice build with those shoulders. Not much of a policeman, though. Too nice. He didn't write anything down, and he didn't even check to see if she had an alibi, either.

A small brown bird perched on the fence near the man hoeing the corn. John watched the man at work. He noted the longer brown hair tied back with a red bandana, the full beard, the strong muscles showing beneath a sweat-stained blue work shirt. The man spoke to the small bird, "Are you hoping I stir something up, Phoebe?" before noticing John. He leaned on his hoe and watched John approaching him.

John looked around the garden, noticed tender young sprouts soon to be lush vegetables and admired the neatness and order, and the hard work that'd gone into it. His eyes roved over young cabbages planted in a row in front of a feathery row of carrots. Behind that, young beans were already climbing vigorously up a wooden bean frame. He thought of Mr. McGregor's garden and half expected to see Peter Rabbit come hopping out. With a smile on his face as he imagined it, he walked up to the man leaning on his hoe.

"John MacDougal." He held out his hand. "And you must be Mr. Burns."

Greg Robert Burns shook his hand firmly, as a warm smile lit his face, crinkling the laugh lines around his eyes. "Greg Robert," he said. "Let's go sit down out of the sun."

John followed him to the edge of the garden to a grape arbor with benches under it. "The garden looks wonderful. It makes me want to go out behind my place and start digging."

Greg Robert laughed. "Unless you're prepared for a lifelong, love hate relationship, you'd better not even start."

"What's that leafy plant with the colorful stocks," John asked.

"Bright Lights Swiss Chard."

"I like the red flowers planted by it."

"Red celosia. It's companion planting. In this case the flowers are purely ornamental, but the dill planted by the cabbage is to deter cabbage worms. Chamomile and sage will do the same thing."

John felt himself warming to this man and could understand the respect he'd garnered from all those he'd met who spoke so highly of him. "I need to ask you some questions."

Greg Robert nodded.

"The fork that killed Chatterton. Could it have come from here?"

"I don't know. We have four of them. We can check to see if any are missing." He turned and started for the tool shed. "Of course, I know one of the gardeners has one," he said over his shoulder, "and sometimes the young part-timers forget and leave tools out."

As they stepped into the building, John looked around. Tools were neatly hanging from hooks on the walls and smaller ones as well as gloves in cubbies or bins.

Greg Robert led him to where two garden forks were

hanging. He nodded at the empty hooks. "Two are out. One is accounted for."

"How long has the other one been gone?"

Greg Robert shrugged. "I don't really know. I don't inventory every evening, although I usually look to see if there are any empty hooks at night, but I'll admit, I don't always do it, and I didn't look this morning, either. When I gave out assignments this morning, I told the kid who needed it to get it."

"Is the shed kept locked?"

"Not in the day time, but I lock it at night."

"Always?"

Greg Robert looked sheepish. "Well, sometimes I may forget, but that rarely happens."

"Were you here yesterday when Chatterton was murdered?"

Greg Robert shook his head. "No, I had a dentist appointment at eleven, and then stopped for lunch in Millport. After that I did some shopping for groceries before coming back."

"What time did you get back?"

He shrugged watching John intently now. "I'm not sure. I rarely wear a watch and don't pay much attention to time. Probably around four o'clock or so, I'd say, from the position of the sun, and the amount of time I was gone."

"Anybody see you around three?"

"I don't think so." All traces of a smile were gone now. "Um, Alma Porcase, but she doesn't wear a watch, either, and doesn't have much sense of time. I stopped to visit her before I came home."

John looked at him curiously. "I didn't think Alma ever had visitors. She's not very friendly as a rule, at least to men."

Greg Robert smiled again. "She makes an exception in my case, I guess. Her dog was sickly several months ago. Somehow she knew I had an extensive knowledge of herbs and thought I might be able to help him."

"And did you?"

"You see him still following her around, don't you? He had a bad case of worms. I gave him a dose of wormwood, and it helped."

"Did you learn about herbs and their healing properties in the monastery? John watched him closely.

Greg Robert stared at John before nodding. "Yes."

"Why did you leave the monastery?"

He stared out over the garden as a look of sadness came over his face. "For personal reasons," he said so softly John could barely hear him.

"A monk was seen on the grounds about the time Chatterton was killed."

A startled look appeared on Greg Robert's face. "It must've been somebody Mr. Chatterton hired to act the part."

"No. We checked. Was it you?"

"Absolutely not. I told you I wasn't here then."

"Do you have a monk's robe?"

"Yes. It's in the back of my closet. I haven't worn it since I left the monastery last year."

"Would you mind showing me?"

"Of course not. This way."

A subdued and quiet Greg Robert led the way to the small stone gardener's cottage. He opened the screen door and led John in.

"You never lock up?" John asked.

A smile flitted across Greg Robert's face. "Why should I? Look around you. What's to steal?"

John looked around at the simple furnishings in the small room with bare white walls and wood floors. The only items in the room were a plain brown couch badly worn, a small table with a reading lamp beside the couch, books on the floor and in a small bookcase, a faded throw rug, and a crucifix on the wall. He could see the kitchen was just as sparse with only a small table, two chairs, a stove and a refrigerator. He followed Greg Robert into the only bedroom. A single bed with a blue and white quilt, a nightstand with a small lamp and clock, a Bible, and another crucifix over the bed made this room as simple as the other two rooms. Greg Robert went to his closet that held only a few items of clothes and a cardboard box on a shelf. He reached into the back of the closet and then bent down to feel on the floor. Turning around and coming out, he faced John with a look of bewilderment on his face. "It's gone," he said.

Chapter Seventeen

It wasn't until she was carding the gate at the entrance and the large wrought iron gates were swinging open that Catherine remembered a flashlight. Maybe there's one under the seat, she thought, but she hadn't touched it since last year. She hoped it still worked.

She drove slowly up the drive. Everything seemed strange in the dark. The large trees silhouetted against a darkening sky tossed their leaves in anticipation of a storm. Even though rain was needed, she hoped it would wait until she got home.

All evening that twine had nagged at her. Maybe the police already found it, she thought. Maybe it's not even important. But she knew it was. The twine wasn't an old half rotten one that'd been there a long time. Once she'd picked up the phone to call Chief MacDougal, but then put it back down. What if it was gone? What if he brushed it off as unimportant? Finally, she decided to go check to see if the twine was still there before calling him. After she'd made the decision to go, a last minute customer came, who couldn't make up his mind on what he wanted. He browsed slowly up and down the aisles while Catherine tried not to show her impatience. He finally settle for one delphinium and stayed on to chat about nothing important, ignoring the fact the shop's closing time was a half hour ago.

She was turning the key in the lock as the last customer slowly drove away when the phone rang. Catherine always had a hard time letting a phone ring so she hurried to unlock the door and grabbed the phone.

"I was just about to hang up," Maggie said on the other

end.

"I was just on my way out."

"Oh, I'm sorry. I won't keep you long," Maggie apologized.

But as so often happens between friends, a two minute call turned into fifteen as Maggie told her what was new with her boyfriend, a Marine in Iraq. They kept in touch almost daily through e-mail or Skyp. "I'd better let you go," Maggie finally said.

"Okay. I'll see you."

But before Catherine could hang up, Maggie said, "Oh, I forgot what I really called about. I told you I have to pick up my aunt at the airport tomorrow, but what I wanted to ask you was if you'd take my place on the Mobile Van tomorrow. I only have one person to pick up."

"What time?"

"Around noon. Alma Porcase has a doctor's appointment. It shouldn't take too long."

"That'll be okay. Christy will be here, and it's not quite as busy right now as it was last month and at the beginning of this month."

"Thanks. You know where to pick up the van and where Alma lives, don't you?"

"Yes." Catherine assured her and jotted down the note before again locking up and finally leaving.

Pulling into a space between Tyler's white Lumina and Greg Robert's truck, she noticed lights shining on the overgrown shrubbery surrounding the gardener's cottage. As she climbed out, she turned her flashlight on to test it. A faint beam showed no more than two or three feet in front of her. She grimaced and turned it off to conserve the weak batteries. She hoped it would be enough to find what she needed.

Faint somber strains of music came from the upstairs apartment in Chatterton Manor where Tyler lived. She wondered if it was a CD, or he was playing the piano.

Someone had told her he was an accomplished pianist. Who told me? Probably Millie. She seems to know a lot about everyone, she thought.

Catherine cut down a short path leading from the work area and past Greg Robert's cottage. The faint smell of decaying vegetation from the compost bins hung in the warm slightly humid air. The breeze from the incoming storm seemed to be staying in the treetops. She darted through light patches cast on the path from Greg Robert's kitchen window and glanced in curiously as she passed, but she didn't see him. No sounds came from his open windows.

Quickly she slipped through a gap the staff often used in the hedges surrounding the topiary garden. She walked between the dragon and the duck and glanced at the topiaries, now grotesque dark shapes against a moonless sky. Nothing seemed familiar. For a moment she hesitated wanting to run back to the safety of her truck or Greg Robert's cottage. Stop it. Stop being so spooked, she told herself. She checked this garden at least once a week, and had been here yesterday. But her self-admonitions didn't work, especially when she heard something rustling on the other side of the hedge separating the Blue Garden from the Topiary Garden.

Cautiously, she went through another slim opening and peered around the Blue Garden before going all the way through the hedge. The nodding heads of the pale blue 'Augustus Chatterton' roses were like ghostly disembodied faces watching. The cry of a nighthawk startled her for a moment. She looked around and couldn't see anything moving. My imagination certainly is overactive tonight, she thought. Maybe it was a raccoon I heard, and tried not to think of the recent rash of warnings about rabid raccoons.

Picking up speed she moved down the rows between the blue roses towards the entrance to the White Garden. Again she thought she heard a noise and stopped to listen, but heard nothing unusual.

Catherine ducked around the hedge of old shrub roses to reach the entrance to the White Garden. One waving branch grabbed her and clung to her T-shirt with its thorns. She managed to disentangle herself before entering the path leading to the White Garden. Because it was enclosed in old rhododendrons, the path was devoid of any light. Catherine clicked on her flashlight. The weak beam barely made a dent in the dark tunnel and then suddenly went out as she took a few steps forward. She shook it, and it came back on. She moved forward a little faster wanting to accomplish her errand before the light went out again.

"I think it was about here," Catherine muttered wanting to hear a voice, even her own, against the oppressive darkness. Squatting down she shined the light along the trunks of the shrubs. A little ahead to the right she thought she saw what she was looking for. She moved toward it, bent low, and peered closely. Yes! She said to herself. There it is. She got down and crawled in, but as she reached the shrub with the twine, her light suddenly went out again and no amount of shaking it and tapping it against the ground worked. She laid it down and in the dark felt for the twine and the knot. She worked for some minutes on it, but it was too tight to pick apart and undo. Maybe she shouldn't do this, anyway. It could be evidence, she thought. As she started to back out, she felt something furry rub against her bare leg. She let out a yelp and scrambled out and to her feet, her heart pounding. In the dark a few feet away, she saw a white shape watching her.

"Oh," she breathed out a little moan, "Bonnie Charlie! You scared me. I thought you were a raccoon."

The cat walked over and rubbed against her legs purring. She squatted down in the dark and stroked him feeling relief not only because he wasn't a wild animal, but because he was a warm and friendly creature. Somehow, in spite of his small size, he made all the bogeymen disappear.

At least he did until he stiffened and stopped purring, and in the dark she could see his white head turned alertly toward the White Garden. Had the cat seen the murder yesterday? She wondered.

Catherine didn't wait to find out what the cat saw or heard. She leaped to her feet and dashed down the path running into the stiff branches on each side of the narrow path. She flew back through the Blue Garden and into the Topiary Garden. In Catherine's imagination she felt the murderer's hands grabbing her from behind. She darted between the dark and sinister topiary forms toward the opening. The three gnomes watched her frightened dash. Or were there four now? In the dark she couldn't find the gap in the hedge. Frantically she felt up and down where she thought it should be. A sudden clap of thunder made her cry out in alarm. Finally, she found the opening and slipped through. She decided to go down the walk to her left and to the driveway instead of behind Greg Robert's cottage and the work area.

With heart beating, she glanced behind her and seeing nothing, slowed to a fast walk to catch her breath. She was looking over her shoulder again when someone in front of her grabbed her arms. She screamed.

"Catherine, what are you doing here?" Tyler asked as he let go of her arms.

She looked up at him unable to speak.

"I saw your truck in the parking lot and decided to see what was going on. I'd just stepped around the hedge when you came running into me like the topiaries had turned into demons." He gave a little chuckle. "Now you're looking at me as if you think I'm a demon, too."

She could see the quizzical look on his face from the faint light of the cottage ahead.

"You startled me. I . . . I just wanted to check on something . . . the blue roses looked off," she mumbled with a small attempt at a smile.

156

"In the dark?"

She could see his eyebrows raised. "I was afraid I'd forget tomorrow," she offered as a weak excuse. "I had a flashlight, but it went out, and I accidentally dropped it."

He didn't answer immediately, but glanced at Greg Robert's cottage and then back at her. "Let me see you to your truck."

He thought she was meeting Greg Robert, she realized, but for some reason she couldn't explain even to herself, she didn't want to tell him the real reason she was here.

"Looks like it's going to rain," he commented as they walked to her truck.

"Yes. We sure could use it." Comments on the weather over, they walked on in silence.

When they got to the parking area, he waited as she tried to start the truck which groaned and grumbled before finally roaring to life, and he continued to watch as she backed out and drove slowly down the drive. He wondered why she really was there as he watched her retreating tail lights until they were gone.

Chapter Eighteen

Tonight Richardson's biography of Emerson couldn't hold John's attention. He'd reread the same paragraph on the start of The Transcendental Club three times before he gave up. Instead he stared into space as he went over today's questioning of those involved in the Chatterton murder, or at least the ones he'd been able to get to.

He thought of his return trip to the Chatterton home this afternoon and his conversation with Mrs. Chatterton. She'd just returned from playing tennis and yet every hair was in place and her tennis whites were as neat and unwrinkled as if she'd just put them on. She made no excuse for playing tennis on the day after her husband's death. John surmised not much would keep her from her prescribed daily schedule.

She'd been polite, showing little emotion until he'd asked about her son, Bradley. He remembered the spark of agitation she'd had a hard time concealing. She still claimed she didn't know the friend's last name where he was staying. It was Rich something, she thought. Her eyes had been evasive when he'd asked what town. Cincinnati, she'd thought, or somewhere close to it. She'd still claimed she couldn't think of anyone who would kill her husband.

"He was strong-willed and outspoken," she'd admitted. "I know a lot of people didn't care for him, but I can't think of anyone who hated him that much."

Her eyes had become hostile when he'd asked "How

well do you know Olga Yamikoff?"

"Not well. She's an employee of Elmwood," she'd emphasized 'employee.'

He'd mentally treaded water. "Did your husband know Ms. Yamikoff before she came to the gardens?"

"I have no idea," Her eyes and tone had made him think of blue ice.

He'd decided to drop that line of questioning. "Did your daughter work for your husband?"

"She worked for Sussex last winter."

"Why did she leave?"

"You'll have to ask her."

Then she'd stood up. "Now if that's all, I have things to attend to," she'd said effectively dismissing him as she'd led him to the door.

Earlier before leaving Elmwood Gardens to talk to Mrs. Chatterton, he'd gone in the front entrance of the Chatterton Manor House. He'd looked with admiration at the polished wooden floors partially covered with Persian rugs; their colors muted with age yet still rich. A wide mahogany staircase swept up from the main foyer. It'd been years since he'd taken the time to visit The Manor House. It still looked much the same.

To the left were the offices of Elmwood Gardens. He asked for Olga Yamikoff and the woman in charge directed him to her office at the Visitor Center. "I think she's left for lunch, though." She took his message asking Ms. Yamikoff to call. But, either she'd not returned, or she'd chosen to ignore the message.

"Is Tyler Birchfield in?" He'd asked next.

"Not right now. I think he went over to the greenhouse. Do you want him to call, too?" the woman had asked him politely.

"Not necessary. I'll get hold of him later."

Before leaving, John wandered into what'd once been the drawing room now partially roped off with a thick red velvet cord. Faded wallpaper with large pink and red cabbage roses decorated the walls. At the windows red brocade drapes with gold tie-backs dimmed the room.

Stiff furniture furthered the museum look. In front of the horsehair sofa was a table with an open book and a pair of wire-rimmed glasses. Even that touch, as if the owner had just stepped out, didn't make the room look lived in. John liked antiques, he'd grown up with them, but he preferred what was comfortable rather than stiffly formal. Especially a couch and chairs in a room where one sat to read.

Over the fireplace, in a heavily ornate gold frame, hung a portrait of the first Augustus Chatterton, who'd had this house built. John gazed in curiosity at this ancestor who amazingly resembled the murder victim, he thought. After watching the video of yesterday's reception at Elmwood Gardens several times, he was acutely aware of the resemblance. There was the same slightly pugnacious jaw, the heavy eyebrows over shrewd eyes. The video hadn't shown anything out of the ordinary that John could see if you discounted the whole reception being out of the ordinary with its medieval theme. He'd looked in vain for the monk that had been reported.

All this thinking made John hungry. He went to the kitchen, flipped on the overhead light, and started rummaging in the refrigerator. He pulled out a leftover pork chop and the remains of a salad. Both were two days old, but he was too hungry to care about freshness.

Where is the Chatterton kid, he wondered as he sliced a hunk of Italian bread and generously slathered it with butter.

Something's strange about that, he thought. Is Vera Chatterton upset because she doesn't know where he is or because she suspects him? He poured a large glass of milk and carried everything to the kitchen table. It's funny Greg Robert Burn's habit just happened to disappear. Is he telling the truth or does he know where it is? John

160

wondered as he gnawed on the cold pork chop. He supposed someone could've stolen it from his closet since according to him, he never locks his door. It would have to be someone who knew he was a monk and had the robe. There's something likable about the guy. John thought. He could see why Josh and Catherine Jewell responded with such warmth when speaking of him. He speared a piece of broccoli from the salad and chewed thoughtfully. He couldn't let feelings rule. Besides there was some mystery about why he'd left the monastery. Maybe he should take a trip there, he thought. He guessed it would be about three hours away or maybe four.

He wondered about Ed Flavian. He seemed a bit of a curmudgeon. John smiled thinking of him. Damn! He liked him, too. You're not going to be much good at solving this murder if you like all the suspects, he told himself.

Ed and his wife were certainly poles apart. He always wondered about marriages like that. What was the glue that held them together when other marriages with couples having much more in common often failed? He thought about their wedding photo in a silver frame that had been on the table beside him in their living room. She'd been a tall, big-boned, blonde girl in a blue dress with a small veil on her head. He'd noticed a shy wistful look in her blue eyes. Surreptitiously he'd studied the woman before him and could see nothing of the shy girl in the photograph. A much younger Ed, slightly shorter than his wife, had stared back soberly at the camera, his dark hair combed neatly and greased to lay flat.

The phone ringing startled John out of his reverie. He hurried to grab it before it woke Josh, and immediately recognized the low pleasant voice on the other end.

"Chief MacDougal?"

"Yes?"

"This is Catherine Jewell. I hate to disturb you so late, but you said to call if I remembered anything."

"That's fine. I was still up. What is it?"

Catherine explained about the twine and her trip to find it. Then she added hesitantly, "I guess I shouldn't have tampered with it in the first place since it was evidence." She didn't mention her fear or the fact that she'd heard something or of meeting Tyler Birchfield.

John rubbed his chin thinking. If he was upset that she'd possibly compromised some evidence, he didn't say. "You think someone could've used the twine to trip Chatterton then?"

"I'd thought that, but tonight it looked too short to go across the path, but I could've sworn yesterday there was quite a bit of it, although I guess I can't really be sure."

"Why'd you go on your own instead of telling me first?"

"I wanted to make sure what I saw would've worked the way I thought it might before I called and sent you on a wild goose chase."

"Don't ever worry about that. Often the most inconsequential things can have great importance." He could remember some detective in a mystery novel saying that once. He only hoped it was true, and he could do as well as those literary detectives. He sighed inwardly. "Could you meet me in the gardens early tomorrow and show me where it is?"

I'm usually there by six-thirty or seven at the latest. I spend a few hours checking things before opening my nursery at nine."

"How about if I meet you at seven by The Topiary Gardens?"

"That's good. I'll be there."

"See you tomorrow," John said and hung up.

He sat thinking. A long twine could answer the question of how a man of Chatterton's bulk and size could've been at a disadvantage, and would've made it easier for a murderer. He supposed it might've even have made it possible for a woman to do it.

He finally stood up, stretched and yawned, and started for his bedroom when the phone rang again.

"Yes?" he said into the phone as he snatched it up.

"Joe here. Ran into something kind of funny. I checked the parking lot at the Township Park and there's a Jeep parked there. It was there last night, too. Same spot. I don't think it's been moved. I saw it around eight last night and never got around to checking back later."

"Did you run a license check?"

"Yeah, and this is what's really funny. It belongs to Bradley Chatterton."

John let out a low whistle. "You see anything inside?"

"The back seat's piled with stuff, and it's all covered with a blanket so I can't tell what it is. I made sure I didn't touch the car in case something's happened to the kid. Didn't want to disturb any prints."

"Good thinking! I'll be there as soon as I get hold of Karl the Keyman."

John pulled into the parking lot. At least it hasn't started raining, he thought, as distant lightning flashed across the sky. Joe was sitting in his patrol car and got out when John arrived.

"Let's dust it before Karl gets here," John said after he walked around it and checked inside with a large light.

"Yeah. I thought that's what we'd do."

They'd just finished lifting prints when head lights signaled the arrival of Karl. A short slightly rotund man with an elfin look leaped out of his van. He reached in the back and got his tool kit before coming over. "Hi, ya," he greeted with a puckish smile on his freckled face. "This'll cost you extra, you know."

"Yeah, yeah, Karl, we know," John smiled.

Within moments Karl worked his magic, and the door

163

was open. Reluctantly John leaned into the back seat as Joe shined his light in the window. Both were afraid of what they might find. John lifted the blanket revealing a pile of clothes, and then gingerly he moved the clothes on top to reveal what lay underneath. Joe held the light steady. There were a keyboard, speakers, wires, and other equipment but not, as John was relieved to see, a body.

"This doesn't look good. Why would a kid, even a rich kid, just leave a car like this?"

Joe shook his head. "Sure doesn't seem right."

"Check out the prints," John said, "and also check the inside, too. Make sure it's dusted thoroughly. I'm going to the Chatterton home now."

The house was dark except for landscape lights and a light beside the door, but shortly after John pressed the doorbell a light came on in the foyer, and a face peeped out a side window.

"Chief MacDougal," John announced through the door showing his badge.

He could hear a lock turning and then the heavy door was opened by an older woman in a flowered housecoat and old green slippers. Her gray hair was tousled and her eyes alarmed.

"Who is it, Harriet?" Vera inquired from the top of the stairs.

"It's the police, Ma'am."

Vera came down the stairs frowning, worry showing on her face. She held her blue silk robe tightly around her. "That will be all, Harriet," she dismissed the housekeeper.

Harriet, now more curious than alarmed, left with reluctance. Probably to listen behind a door, John guessed.

"I don't mean to alarm you, Mrs. Chatterton, but we've found your son's Jeep in the parking lot at the Township Park. It's been there since yesterday. Have you heard from him since we last talked?"

Vera shook her head, her face expressionless. "What

164

does that mean? Why would he leave his car?"

"He probably left it and went with a friend," John said in a reassuring tone, although he could see no outward signs of worry on her face, only a cool composure.

"But why on earth would he leave it?" Vera asked again sounding bewildered. Faint signs of worry were now appearing in her eyes.

John realized she either really didn't know where her son was, or she was a very good actress. "I don't know, but we'll check it out. Nothing much was in the glove compartment, but in the back there was a keyboard, speakers, and clothes. Does that sound normal?"

"My son is a musician. He plays in several bands," she answered in a monotone.

"Could he be with one of the bands now?"

She shrugged. "I suppose he could be."

"But you don't know?" John prodded.

Vera snapped back. "No. My son is an adult now. I'm not a clinging mother checking up on his whereabouts."

Obviously not a close family, John thought. He couldn't imagine Josh taking off like that without a word even when he became nineteen, and he couldn't imagine not worrying if he ever did disappear. He kept his thoughts to himself. "Can you think of anything he might've had in the Jeep that would be missing?"

There was a pause as Vera thought about it. "He has a Martin guitar he cares a lot about. It's quite expensive. That must be with him. I can't think of anything else."

John thanked her and told her he'd let her know if he heard of anything about her son. She nodded and showed him to the door without another word.

He drove home yawning. The rain had started, and the windshield wipers were hypnotic. He longed for bed, but knew there'd not be many hours of sleep this night. The refrain "And miles to go before I sleep, and miles to go before I sleep." kept running through his head

165

Chapter Nineteen

The gardens glistened as the sun tiptoed in and smiled at the flowers fresh from their night-time shower. Catherine stopped to admire an intricate dew sparkled spider web draped between two Canterbury bells. As of yet no insect marred its pristine beauty. It would be some kind of orb-weaver, she surmised. She leaned down to check and found a small black and white spider. Someday, she told herself, she'd make a study of spiders so she could identify them.

A glance at her watch hurried Catherine down the path toward the topiary garden. How benign and friendly the gardens seemed today. What a difference a little sunlight can make, she thought. She saw the police chief leaning against the brick gatepost leading into the topiary garden. He was smiling as he watched her approach. She smiled, too, glad there seemed to be no hard feelings over yesterday's differences.

"You're early," she greeted him.

"But not as early as you. You must be one of those people whose feet are running the moment they hit the floor in the morning."

She laughed. "Not quite, but I do function best in the morning, especially after that first cup of coffee. What about you?"

He smiled back at her. He liked her wide humorous mouth and the laugh lines at the corners of her eyes. He surmised the sadness he'd seen in her eyes yesterday was something unusual with her. Again he wondered about it. Maybe it was a recently ended love affair? "I'm best in the mornings, too, or late at night when most of the world is asleep. Afternoons are my low point."

"Me, too. I really have to push myself after lunch until I can get over that slump. I'd like to see siestas become the vogue in this country."

He laughed in agreement then sobered. "You'd better show me the twine."

"Okay. It's this way." She turned and led him past the Topiary Garden and into the Blue Garden. They walked without talking past the 'Augustus Chatterton' roses still roped off. John glanced at them wondering why they'd generated so much interest. He'd seen other roses that were More impressive that those. Today they seemed to have lost some of their rich blue coloring and were now merely a pale tint of blue. When they reached the walkway to the White Garden, Catherine said over her shoulder, "It's this way," as she led him down the shadowed path. Some of her uneasy feelings from the night before returned, and she was glad of John's presence behind her. She stopped a few feet short of the steps down to the White Garden and knelt down.

John squatted down as she pulled aside a branch and said, "It's back in there."

"Where?" he asked looking closely.

She looked again feeling bewildered. Panic flooded over her. Quickly she lay down and wiggled under the bushes. "But it was there!" she exclaimed. She turned her head and saw he'd crawled in beside her.

"Which bush?" His voice was calm.

Catherine glanced at the ones near her. They looked different in the daylight. "That one I think." She pointed to one.

He squirmed past her and examined it. "The bark is slightly scuffed." He examined it closer. "It looks like there's a slight nick, too. Maybe where a knife cut the twine."

She breathed a sigh of relief that he believed her. "I

left my flashlight under here, too, but I don't see it now."

He glanced around then looked over his shoulder at her, "Why would you leave your flashlight?"

She flushed and gave a small embarrassed laugh. "The batteries gave out and something brushed against my leg. Believe me I was out of here pretty fast."

With their faces close under the shrubs, he could see the freckles where a stray sunbeam touched her nose. For a moment he had an impulse to kiss her, but discretion won out. He smiled and said, "Did you see what it was?"

"It was Bonnie Charlie, Greg Robert's cat."

"And you say the twine was here last night?"

"Yes, but like I said, it seemed shorter."

He backed out and she followed. Sitting back on his haunches, he stared thoughtfully towards the steps.

She watched him, unwilling to intrude on his thoughts.

"I suppose the killer could've reached in and cut off as much twine as he could reach without crawling under the shrubbery," he thought out loud. "Time would have been a problem. He wouldn't want to risk being caught crawling under the bushes."

"Then why take it out now?"

"Maybe it was their first opportunity. Maybe the murderer realized you knew about it and wanted to remove the evidence," he said as he looked at her. "Maybe they hoped if you did tell me, without the twine I wouldn't believe you."

"But you do believe me, don't you?"

He smiled at her serious face. "Yes. Even if there wasn't a mark on the trunk, I'd believe you."

She smiled at him pleased.

"Now," he said getting up and reaching for her hand to help her, "I'm going to try a little experiment. Are you willing to help?"

She nodded and curiously watched as he pulled some twine out of his pocket similar to the twine that had been there, she noticed.

"Is this like the twine you saw?"

"Close. That might be a little thinner and it's green. What I saw was grayish tan. Do you always carry twine in your pocket?"

He laughed. "No, but you said you thought the twine seemed shorter than what you'd originally seen, so I brought enough to work with. I'm going to tie it to the same shrub and bring it across the path like this," he said as he worked. "Now, I can see a little opening in the bushes on the opposite side here. I want you to hide in there, and when I walk down the path, you're to pull on the twine and try to trip me."

They tried it twice, but she either pulled too soon or too late. Finally, on the third try she timed it just right. As John hurried down the path, as he imagined Chatterton would've done, he stumbled and fell forward. Horrified, she rushed out and saw him sprawled at the bottom of the steps. The image of Chatterton flashed through her mind.

"Are you all right?" she called out, a worried frown on her face.

He got up slowly and grinned up at her before brushing himself off. "It worked," he said with enthusiasm. "Now we can be pretty sure how a man the size of Chatterton could be caught off guard."

Catherine glanced around the White Garden relieved to see in spite of what'd happened here two days ago, the garden was still serene and beautiful. The stone cherub still emptied water from its jug untroubled by falling bodies. Maybe in time she wouldn't think of the horror, but only appreciate the beauty. She turned back to John. "It seems an iffy way to plan a murder. Look how long it took me to trip you up."

He nodded. "You're right. I suppose he figured if he didn't trip him, he could still push Chatterton down the steps and then stab him."

169

She bit her bottom lip as she thought about it. "It would be harder, though."

"How so?"

"Well, the fork was probably hidden in the shrubs, right?"

He nodded.

"So all the murderer would have to do after he tripped him was to grab the fork and follow, but if he pushed him, he couldn't do it with the fork in his hand so he'd have to step back into the shrubs to grab it and that would take extra time."

John looked amused. "Would you be interested in a job as a part time detective along with all your other jobs? You're good and you're right."

She grinned at him shaking her head.

"I need to get back. I really appreciate your help and the information. I was only half kidding about the job offer, you know. There are no job openings now, but if there were . . ." his voice trailed off.

"I'm glad I could help. I've never pretended to be a killer before," she laughed.

"You did a good job." He made a rueful face as he brushed dirt off his pants and hands.

"Did you get hurt?" she asked again.

"Nah, I'm tough," he said with a lopsided grin. He was careful, though, not to show her his right knee was starting to ache as he walked away.

"By the way," he said turning around, "what time does Ms. Yamikoff get here?"

Catherine shrugged. "Around eight, I think."

John glanced at his watch. "It's almost that time now so I think I'll wait." He turned around and walked a little slower than usual toward the Visitor Center.

Saint Fiacre smiled an enigmatic smile today. "What's so funny?" Catherine asked him as she went by on her way for coffee.

"Morning, Millie," she called out with a lilt to her voice.

"Be right with you," Millie answered from the kitchen.

Catherine helped herself to a cup of coffee and sat down near a window. She liked looking out over the perennial gardens behind the manor house. The constant change from week to week or even day to day made perennial gardens so exciting. She saw Olga pulling in to park her Volvo next to Tyler's car. Good, Catherine thought. Chief MacDougal, John, won't have to wait too long.

Olga started down the drive towards the visitor center. Guess she's not coming in for coffee today, Catherine thought. But suddenly Olga stopped and turned facing back the way she'd come. In a few moments, Tyler came up to her. Catherine could see him speaking to her. She couldn't hear what he was saying even though the window was open, but it looked intense. Olga shook her head negatively several times. He said something more. She shook her head again then turned and hurried down the drive. Tyler watched her out of sight, a slight frown on his face, before he turned to go back toward the garden sheds.

Curious, Catherine wished she could've heard what they said. If they'd been closer, she might've been able to read the expressions on their faces. She glanced up startled when Millie spoke behind her. She hadn't heard her approach.

"Looks like a romance blooming there."

Catherine shrugged.

Millie went on. "I think it'd be a good match. They're both classy people. Have you ever heard Mr. Birchfield play the piano?"

Catherine nodded. "Yes."

"Oh, if I could only play like that." Millie sighed. "I've been taking lessons for two years and I can't get past 'Fur Elise.' Mrs. Crow, my piano teacher, keeps telling me my timing is off."

Catherine turned and stared at her wide eyed. She'd never before hinted at musical aspirations. "I didn't know you even had a piano or that you played."

"It's an old upright I bought several years ago. I've always wanted to play one, but I've never had the chance, and when I saw it at a garage sale for a really good price I could afford, well, I bought it. Middle D and a lower B stick, and the piano tuner says the sound board is cracked so it sounds kinda dead in the middle. It'd be too much money to replace it so I just deal with it. Besides it took too much work to get it upstairs to my apartment as it was." She shrugged and changed the subject.

"I got some good cream cheese Danishes in. Want to try one?"

"Sounds delicious. Where's everyone else today?"

"Don't know. You're the first in this morning, and even you're late."

"I know. I'll have to eat and run." She didn't tell Millie why she was late.

Millie brought Catherine the Danish, fixed herself a cup of coffee and sat down. "With the Tea Room closed there isn't much to do."

"Do you know when it's going to open again?"

"The funeral's tomorrow so I think they'll probably open Sunday. At least that's what Mr. Birchfield said. Are you going'?"

Catherine nodded with her mouth full of cheese Danish.

Millie went on. "I need to get a dress. I called Violet to see if she wanted to go to Walmart, but she said she didn't need a dress. Her an' Ed are going' to do something today. Never knew her to pass up a shopping trip."

Catherine smiled her acknowledgement of Violet's love of shopping. Her home was an example of that.

Millie looked out the window. "Look! There she goes again," she said as she watched Alicia hurrying down a path. "Guess I know where she's going'. Her and Tom got a thing going'. I'm surprised he's still here."

"Why?" Catherine asked, torn between fueling Millie's gossip and her own curiosity. At least Olga wasn't here today, she thought.

"Old Man Chatterton wasn't happy about it, I can tell you," Millie said. "Fact is, I heard him shouting at Tom the morning he was killed. I was taking some garbage out to the compost area. Saw Alicia running away, an' I heard him shout 'You're fired!' I hurried back inside with the garbage cause I didn't want anyone to see me."

Catherine felt unsettled by this. "Did you tell anyone?"

"No. Truth to tell I forgot about it 'til I saw Alicia high-tailing it to meet him. Don't seem right somehow, her dad dead and all. Seems she should respect his wishes."

"You don't think Tom could've killed him, do you?"

"Nah! I've known him and his family for ages. They go to my church. He's been working here since high school. Goes to college. He's a smart boy. Going places, too. Mark my word."

Catherine looked at her watch and jumped up. "I've got to run. I need to stop and get cat food at the Mini Mart before I open up. See you, Millie," she said as she hurried out the door.

Chapter Twenty

The Cottage Garden

July 7 and 8
A two day seminar in planning and designing
your own cottage garden with Elmwood Garden's
horticulturist, Catherine Jewell.

Ms. Jewell will teach the course using illustrated
handouts, lectures, guided plant walks handouts.
The seminar will include a workshop where students
design their own gardens with Ms. Jewell's help.
The fee will also include a luncheon in the Wisteria
Tea Room on day two.

Fee: $75.00. Course limited to 20.
Advance reservations required.

Contact: Elmwood Gardens
Olga Yamikoff
P.O. Box 364
Portage Falls, Ohio 44134-6636
Phone 330-335-9205

John read the flyer on the bulletin board in the visitor
center while he waited for Ms. Yamikoff to finish a phone
call.

WHAT'S EATING YOUR PLANTS?
July 23

Follow Detective Jewell with your magnifying glass
in hand to take a close look at plants and plant
damage. (Yes, even Elmwood Gardens has these
nasty critters lurking about.)

"May I help you?" a pleasant low voice with a slight
accent said from behind him.

John turned. Olga Yamikoff stood near him. She was
slender and almost as tall as he was. Her dark hair pulled
back in a French twist emphasized her high cheekbones.
She wore a long sleeved dark leotard top with a flowing,
ankle length skirt in a Georgia O'Keefe print. On her feet
were soft ballet style slippers.

She looked at him, not saying anything more, but there
was a gleam of humor in her dark almond shaped eyes.
Such was her air of poise and sophistication that John
found himself feeling awkward.

"Chief John MacDougal," he said abruptly when he
realized he'd been staring at her for too long. He held out
his hand then wondered if she'd think it inappropriate of a
police officer.

A small smile lurked at the corner of her mouth, but
she graciously took his hand in hers. She had a surprisingly
strong grip for such a slender hand, John thought.

"Please come over and sit down." Moving with a
dancer's grace, she led the way to comfortable chairs
secluded from the main lobby. John sat down somewhat
mesmerized.

"You must be here to talk about the murder," she said
taking the initiative.

"Yes," he said, still at a loss for words. "Umm, you're
rather new to Elmwood Gardens, aren't you?"

"Yes. Four months."

John waited a moment. When she didn't go on, he asked. "How did you happen to hear about this position? I mean, you're not from around here, are you?"

"No, I am not. I read about the job in a gardening magazine." Her eyes never left his face.

"Oh, you're a gardener, too." He was trying to understand this strange and slightly exotic woman, at least by Portage Fall's standards.

"No." She gave a slight shrug. "I just happened to pick it up in a waiting room." Again she didn't elaborate, but sat waiting for him to go on.

"Where did you live before coming to Portage Falls?"

"New York City."

"Were you a receptionist or a manager of a gift shop there, too?"

"No." He waited, but she didn't go on. After some moments she lifted her chin and looked at him. "I was a teacher of dance."

He stroked his chin. Why am I surprised? He thought. Everything about her speaks of dancing, classical dancing. She intrigued him. "Why'd you give it up?"

She stared for a moment at her long slender hands with pink tipped nails and then looked up at him. "Can we leave it at personal reasons?"

He shrugged. "I've heard rumors you and Chatterton were lovers." He was reluctant to confront her with the rumor, but at the same time hoped to shake her poise and find out why she'd really came to this small town.

She made a little moue' of distaste. "Oh, rumors!" Her face showed contempt. "I have often heard small towns are full of rumors."

He didn't bother to defend small towns. For all their good points, he was well aware of this negative aspect of small town living. He waited, realizing she still hadn't told him whether or not there was any truth in these rumors.

She stared outside at the sunny lawn like a green sea with islands of shade from large trees. She was frowning slightly and seemed to have forgotten his existence. Finally she turned to him and looked directly into his eyes. "No, we were not lovers as the town thinks. He was my husband."

John felt his eyes widen in surprise. "Your husband?"

"Oh, not for many years now." She breathed a small sigh as she made a decision. "I do not know how it is here, but in the country in which I was born, the police always know everything. Perhaps it is best I tell you my story and save you the time of digging." Her lips curved up into a small smile, and he smiled back.

"You have a kind face. Perhaps you will understand why I did the things I did.

I was born in Kiev, in the Ukraine," she said, starting at the beginning. "From my earliest years I showed a talent for the dance. At quite a young age, I was accepted into the Soviet School of Dance and eventually danced at the Bolshoi Theater. Dancing became my whole life.

"On a tour of this country more than twenty-five years ago now, another ballerina and I daringly slipped away from our chaperones and attended an American party. My friend had met a rich American back stage, and he had invited her. She talked me into going with her as she did not want to go alone." Olga smiled in reminiscence of her long ago adventure.

"At the party I met a handsome and most forceful young man, Augustus Chatterton. He was not rich then, but he liked to be with rich people.

"Do you believe in love at first sight?" she suddenly asked John.

Caught up in her story, he was taken off guard by the question. "I don't know," he stammered. "I suppose it could happen."

"But it has never happened to you?"

"No," he said, but then a laughing face with freckles suddenly appeared in his mind.

"Well, it happened to me and Gus. Already I was becoming dissatisfied with the Russian Ballet and the lack of freedom, both artistic and otherwise. My parents were dead. I had been born to them late in their life. It did not take too much persuasion to leave the party with Gus.

"I won't go into all the details of my defection. It was most difficult and frightening. The Russia of those years did not take kindly to acts of betrayal, and I feared for my life." Her mobile face expressed the anguish she'd experienced in making her decision to defect.

"After I had been granted asylum, and the paperwork for my citizenship in this country had been applied for, Gus and I were married quietly by a Justice of the Peace. Although we were in love, that first year was difficult. So many cultural differences," she said shaking her head. "I missed my dancing most dreadfully, and I think Gus began to feel I was a burden to him. And," she raised her hands and shoulders in a philosophical shrug. "we really had nothing in common beyond the physical attraction.

"About a year later I tried out for and was accepted by a local ballet company. I was ecstatic even though it was much less than what I had done before. Still, I always give my best."

He believed her. There was a certain quality about her, determination for lack of a better word that described her. He waited patiently for her to go on as she paused lost in recollections.

"It was not many months later that I became with child." A look of sadness passed over her face. "Like some men, Gus found my body unattractive as the baby grew, so now we did not even have physical attraction. Also, I was most ill through much of this time. It was a painful time both physically and emotionally for me.

"Gus had started a new business with financial backing

from one of his wealthy friends and was working many long hours. I missed my dance."

She became brusque then, reluctant to show any semblance of self-pity. "The baby was born. I found a good nursemaid and went back to the dance. I worked hard, and then an offer was made from a big and well-known dance company. I went to Gus so excited about the offer, and he told me to go, but the baby must be left behind." She shook her head. Pain showed on her face. "Oh, the bitter fights and arguments, but," she shrugged, resignation showing in the droop of her shoulders, "in the end I had no choice."

She looked at John for some glimmer of understanding. "The dance was my life. Without it I would be but an empty shell. That he could not understand. Unless I was willing to give over our baby completely to him, he threatened to see my citizenship in this country would not be completed. I would be sent back to Russia, never to see my baby again, and most certain to be sentenced to many years in the Gulag, if not death."

"But he couldn't do that," John said.

She shrugged, "Probably not, but I was young and naive to the ways of this country. In Russia many men have that kind of power.

"So I kissed my baby good-bye and went to New York. His lawyer had me sign a paper giving up all rights." She did not tell of her pain, but John could read it in her eyes.

"So you danced," he said gently.

"Yes," she smiled and then sobered. "For four years I danced, danced as I never danced before."

"And then," he prodded when she paused for a long time as if reluctant to go on. "And then the KGB caught up with me," she said with a heavy sigh. "A bullet in the knee as I was leaving by the stage door after a performance. There was no proof of who it was, of course, but I knew. I was an example to future defectors. So no more dance," she said with a shrug and a half smile. He knew only years had healed that emotional wound.

"When my knee had been replaced and healed enough, I became a teacher of dance." She did not tell of the years of therapy and despair before she became a teacher. "Eventually I opened my own studio. And I am good," she said lifting her chin.

John didn't doubt her assertion. "Did Chatterton know about the attack on you?"

"No." She shook her head. "I chose not to let him know."

A very proud and independent woman. John wondered if Chatterton knew even if she didn't tell him.

"So what made you take this job?"

She smiled at him. "I really did see it in the back of a magazine in a waiting room. It just sort of jumped out at me, and I said to myself, 'Why not!' I wrote and applied for the job, and Mr. Birchfield called me. I came for an interview and got the job. Of course, it was some weeks before Gus found out," she added with an impish look in her eyes.

"Why did you give up your dance studio for this job?" He thought he knew.

"I wanted to see my daughter. Besides," she added with a smile, "I did not completely give up my studio. I have some excellent people who are in charge."

"And your daughter is?"

"Alicia, of course."

"Does she know?"

She nodded. "Yes I told her shortly after I came, but not before I had a chance to make her acquaintance, and we had built up a sort of friendship."

"How did she react?"

Olga beamed. "At first she was shocked, of course, but then she was happy. She had never felt loved by Vera." Olga frowned. "How could anyone be cold to such a child as Alicia? But it created many problems between Alicia and Gus. She hated him for what he had done."

"Hated him?"

She looked at him startled into awareness of what he might deduce from her comment.

"Yes," she snapped, "but not enough to kill him. She only hated him with the emotionalism of youth. I could not say this with such assurance if it had not been some months since she has known. The first sense of betrayal has long passed."

"And what were your feelings about him?"

"Contempt. Animosity. Some anger. But not hatred. That was worn away by time and hard work many years ago."

"What did he say when he found out you were here?"

"Oh, he was angry. But he no longer had power over me." She smiled in memory of her small triumph. "I told him if he got rid of me I would let others know about what had happened. Gus always liked to be important and save the face, you know? So he had to put up with me here. It wouldn't do for people to know he had abandoned me and taken my child from me."

He had to ask. "Where were you between three and four yesterday?"

"I had walked to my apartment in town to lie down for a while. I had a headache."

He rubbed his temple. Another headache. Must be common with Chatterton wives. "Anyone see you?"

She smiled and shook her head. "Not a soul that I know of."

John watched her face for a moment, not speaking. She's either not worried because she's innocent, or not worried because she knows there's no proof she killed him.

He rose to go. "Thank you for your time," he said, and then paused. "Do you know of anyone who could've killed your ex-husband?"

She frowned slightly. "No."

Olga watched him as he walked to the door. He turned to glance back. She was still watching him.

As he got into his car and buckled his seat belt, the fragrance of her perfume remained with him, and he still felt the essence of her as he put his car in gear and drove away.

He stood watching her as she rocked and crooned to the limp baby. The harsh overhead light made the scene before him even more horrid.

Hush little baby
Don't say a word.
Papa's gonna buy
You a mockingbird.

"Why are you looking at me like that? Why are you crying? See how quiet and good our baby is? Someone's at the door. Hurry and open it before they wake the baby up."

And if that mockingbird
Don't sing
Papa's gonna buy
You a diamond ring.

Chapter Twenty-One

It was as she slowed down to enter the rutted lane, a tunnel like lane dense with overhanging trees, that she heard the howling. It was like nothing she'd ever heard before. The pain-filled sound wailed on and on and put Catherine on edge. She gripped the wheel a little tighter. If I believed in demons, I'm sure that's what they'd sound like. The isolation added to her unease. It'd been at least a half mile back to the gravel part of Dump Road, and the only two houses on the road were near the beginning. At least a mile, she guessed.

Low hanging tree branches smothered in wild grape vines brushed the top of the bright red Portage Falls Mobile Van. "What a long way Alma walks each day," she said aloud to drown out the mournful sound getting louder and louder. She was tempted to roll up the windows, but the air conditioning in the van wasn't working.

At the end of the lane, she pulled into a clearing. Squatting in the middle and surrounded by overgrown shrubs and drooping spruce trees sat a house that years ago had lost any paint it might've once had. Blank windows, at least the few visible through the overgrown yews, watched her malevolently. The howling became louder and occasionally interspersed with frantic frenzied barking.

Catherine hesitated getting out. What's wrong with the dog? She wondered. Would it bite? Could it be Alma's dog? He'd never seemed anything but patient and gentle as he followed Alma on her rounds.

"Alma!" she called out several times through the open van window and tapped the horn lightly a few times. There was no answer, but now the dog started to whine. With an increasing feeling of unease, she got out of the van and started up a walk made of old boards. A movement in the tall weeds near the walk startled her. She caught a glimpse of a large black snake slithering away. Apparently it had been sunning itself on the warm boards.

"Alma!" Catherine called out again. The dog became strangely silent, waiting. The silence seemed even more ominous than the dog's barking and howling. Had it found a way out? Was it crazed and now stalking her? She heard a noise from the side of the house as if something was moving away. It sounded larger and more purposeful than a dog or cat.

"Alma?" She cried out a little louder. A piercing shriek from a blue jay in a spruce tree nearby caused her to jump, but there was no other sound.

Going up to the porch, she stepped over a missing second step and knocked on the old wooden door. A gray lace curtain obscured the interior. The dog started its whining again and then erupted once more into mournful wails. Catherine shuddered. It's enough to curdle your blood, she thought. Where can Alma be? I don't think she ever leaves her dog. She sidestepped several rotting floor boards and cupped both hands around her face to see through a dirty glass window into the dim interior. She could see piles of debris; bags, boxes, and more clutter of unidentifiable objects. There were a few pieces of furniture mixed in with the junk. In a far corner in darker shadows was a cot or a day bed. She couldn't be sure which. It looked like piles of clothes or rumpled blankets on it. She looked closer straining to see when suddenly something hit the window. She leaped back in alarm almost falling through the rotted floor boards. The dog scratched and howled at the window.

Catherine hesitated not knowing what to do. Was Alma in there sick or hurt? Was the door locked? Would the dog attack if she opened the door? She went back down the rotting steps staying to the sides that seemed a little more secure and followed a narrow path leading through weeds around the house. At the far end of an open area behind the house was a gray and rotting outhouse.

"Alma?" Catherine shouted. Could she be in there? She stared but didn't want to intrude if Alma was. She turned and looked at the back of the house. A little more sunshine reached this part of the house. Fading purple iris beside the back steps were threatened to be overrun by invasive mint. Carefully she went up the porch steps. A wooden kitchen chair sat on the porch as well as a few pots of plants dying or already dead. She looked through the window in the door, but could only see a wall and the edge of a refrigerator. The dog appeared and barked at her. She tried the door gingerly. The knob turned, but she was afraid to go in.

Going back down the steps, she glanced at the outhouse. She shivered with a feeling someone was watching her from the decrepit building. Almost racing around the side of the house to the van, Catherine jumped in and rolled up the windows leaving only a crack and locked the doors. Normally she wasn't a nervous Nelly, but this isolated place made her jittery, and she wasn't sure it was just because of the murder two days ago. She dug out her cell phone and relayed a message and her cell phone number to Suzy then sat waiting, gnawing her thumb, feeling agitated. I should be doing something, she thought.

The phone jingled. "Yes!" She visibly relaxed when she heard the calm reassuring voice on the other end.

"Catherine, I'm on my way now," John said. "What seems to be the problem?"

She told him then added, "I was afraid to go in."

"You did right. You can't be sure about a dog defending its place. Just hold tight. I'm turning onto Dump Road now."

186

She hung up, but didn't get out of the locked van until she saw the patrol car come out of the tunnel of trees and park behind her.

John smiled at her then turned serious as he led the way to the porch. "Let's see what's wrong." He took a big step over the missing second step and tread gingerly around the rotting floor boards on the porch.

"Alma," he called out rattling the doorknob. The dog started another frenzied round of barking. "It's okay, Ralph, it's okay." He turned the knob and slowly opened the door, his hand on his gun in case the dog attacked.

The dog leaped at the door forcing it open suddenly and burst through, a wiggling, whining, barking bundle of shaggy black and brown fur.

"What's wrong, Ralph?" John bent slightly to pet the agitated dog. The dog whimpered. Straightening up, John opened the door and walked in with Catherine at his heels.

The stench was overwhelming, a mixture of unwashed clothes, mildewed newspapers, rotting food, human excrement and the acid putrid smell of vomit. Catherine opened her mouth to breath and looked around her at the piles of litter. Empty boxes and grocery bags lay on top of old clothes, newspapers, magazines, crockery, jars, aluminum cans and a wide variety of assorted clutter Alma had collected on her daily journeys into the village.

She heard John's sharp intake of breath and leaned to one side to look around him and see what he was looking at. Her eyes widened in alarm. On the cot under a pile of clothes, one arm hung over the edge.

He walked to the bed and pulled aside a brown wool blanket partially covering the head, exposing Alma's face with lifeless staring eyes. Even in death there was a look of pain on her face and a trickle of what was probably vomit dried at the corner of her mouth.

The dog came up to Alma whining and gently scratched at her still body.

John picked up the outstretched arm then laid it back down. "I'll go call for the coroner," he said in a choking voice and quickly walked to the door as a feeling of nausea washed over him. Catherine followed on his heels, not feeling too well herself.

Out in the fresh air, the feeling of nausea both were experiencing subsided, but John was still unsure whether or not he'd be able to hold down his breakfast.

"The coroner?" Catherine questioned as she followed him to the patrol car.

"Yes. Whenever there's an unattended death of unknown cause, the coroner has to be notified."

"You don't think, though . . ." she stopped at the enormity of the sudden thought.

He shrugged as he got into the patrol car and picked up the phone. "She was old, but she always seemed spry enough. Why were you here?" he asked glancing up at her and pausing in the dialing of a number.

"I'm taking over for Maggie Fiest today on the Mobile Van. I was taking her to a doctor's appointment in Millport."

"Was she having a problem?"

"I don't know. I'll give you the doctor's name and address. It's on the routing sheet." She hurried to the van to get the information while John placed his call to the coroner. He took the number she handed him and called the doctor.

"Arthritis," he said to Catherine. "Her doctor said she was in excellent health for her age. She was eighty-three. Would you believe it?" He stared in thought at the house. "I'm going back in to look around."

Torn between curiosity and revulsion, curiosity won out and Catherine followed.

Together they explored the downstairs of the house careful not to touch anything; John from a policeman's point of view of not destroying evidence and Catherine

188

from a sense of fastidiousness. Something she never felt when grubbing about in the good clean dirt of the earth.

She wouldn't have won any "Good Housekeeping" awards," John remarked as he looked around the kitchen.

"Martha Stewart, she was not," Catherine agreed.

On the table and counters were dirty dishes caked and crusted with rotted and molding food. The old electric stove, once porcelain white, was now yellow and brown with layers of splattered and spilled grease. A cast iron skillet held congealed grease. In the sink was a pan of soaking dishes, the water gray and full of bits of food and floating grease. A gray rag was draped over the edge.

"It looks like she tried to wash dishes. I can't understand how anyone could let a place get this bad." She made a mental note to start cleaning out the piles of magazines, newspapers, junk mail and other clutter that seemed to be accumulating in her home.

"Mental illness, partly," John said. "Also, no one throws soap in a dumpster or garbage can. I don't suppose anyone thought of it even though many people put other things in for her."

"People put things in garbage cans for her?" Catherine was surprised.

John smiled. "Yes. It's sort of an open secret. Alma was too proud to take what she called charity, but she'd take things from garbage cans or dumpsters since people were throwing it out anyway." His smile faded as regret filled him. He thought of her wandering the streets with only a dog for company. "I should've done something about her. I often asked myself if she'd be better off in a nursing home, but I always felt the answer was no. Maybe I was just taking the easy way out."

"Were you ever here before?"

"Only as far as the yard. Alma didn't take kindly to visitors. She felt we were out to rob her. My mom stopped fairly often, but no matter how many times she came, she wasn't invited in. Of course, Alma seemed to have welcomed Greg Robert Burns." He wondered about that.

"She did?" Catherine's eyes widened.

"Seems he helped her dog a few months ago, so she thought he was okay."

"He does have a way with him." Catherine smiled a fond smile. "Do you think she'd have stayed in a nursing home if you had taken her?"

John shook his head. "I doubt very much she would've stayed without restraints and mind-numbing drugs."

"Then you did the best thing leaving her to live the way she wanted."

"I guess, but I'll always wonder if I should've done more to help her."

Catherine stared at the kitchen window. On the sill was a jelly jar with wilted plants. She walked over to look closer at them. It looked like Alma's attempt at adding a little bit of beauty to her home. "Four leaf clovers." She spread the dried leaves apart with her fingers.

John swallowed. An incredible sorrow almost overwhelmed him. "It didn't work, did it?"

Hearing the pain in his voice, she glanced at him. "I don't know. Maybe she avoided a lot of bad things we'll never know about." She realized the guilt and sorrow he was feeling for someone he'd known all his life, "and she won't suffer anymore."

A sudden feeling of anger at herself washed over her. How could she mouth the very platitudes she'd heard so often from well-meaning people who'd tried to console her when death had taken her husband and child? She'd hated those empty words. She closed her eyes. Oh, David, Ellie. How could I trivialize anyone's death this way? John's voice brought her back.

He was standing by the table. "Looks like her supper." A plate of half-eaten macaroni and cheese sat there as well as a Styrofoam container with the remains of something yellow and white. A cup with dregs of weak tea completed the meal.

"Not much of a dinner," Catherine said as she put her own pain aside. She'd had years of practice at this.

They returned to the main room. Both of them avoided looking at Alma with her staring lifeless eyes. A green stuffed chair with a ripped cushion and one spring sticking out was placed close to a pot-bellied stove that seemed to be the sole source of winter heat. A few logs and sticks were in a wooden box next to the stove. One front window had drapes once blue, but now faded to a shade more gray than blue. Tattered dingy lace curtains hung at the other window. A bare light bulb hanging down from the ceiling was the only source of light. The few odd tables were cluttered with old magazines and knickknacks; a once colorful grinning clown chipped and peeling, a flowered vase with a large crack down it, a ceramic cardinal, faded red with a missing beak, among many other things. On one of the tables was a pretty little vase with raised purple violets on it. One of the violets had been broken off.

"This looks like it could have been Violet's," she said.

John glanced at it. "I saw a plate in the kitchen that was once my mom's."

Catherine walked over to a fireplace. Filled with leaves and debris, it obviously no longer worked. On the mantle photographs were lined up in old frames. She looked at a family photograph of people from long ago. She wondered if they were Alma's parents. They were a dour faced group. Even the youngsters stared without a glimmer of a smile. There was another picture of a young man in uniform. She looked at him closer.

"Alma had a son who went off to war," John said at her elbow. "I think it was the Korean War, but I'm not sure."

She picked up a picture of a baby in a carriage outside under the trees. The baby was smiling. "Do you think this

191

is the same son?"

John shrugged. "Maybe, or maybe the baby who died."

He walked over to a door leading out of the main room and opened it. Inside there was even more clutter thrown around. Most of the boxes and bags had been emptied of their contents and dumped haphazardly. "I wonder why she threw everything all over."

"Especially since she does have all these boxes and bags to put things in."

"Unless," John said stopping to consider.

Catherine waited for him to finish what he was going to say and then prodded. "Unless?"

"Unless someone was looking for something."

"But what could Alma have that anyone wanted?"

"I can't imagine."

The sound of car doors slamming announced new arrivals. John and Catherine went through the main room to the door. Tony was coming through the tall grass and just getting out of another car was Dr. Jones.

"Long time no see," Dr. Jones called out and chuckled. "What's with Portage Falls all of a sudden? Is this some sort of plot to keep me off the golf course?"

John's smile was tight. "In here. Be careful. The porch boards are rotting."

"Not too safe for someone my size, I'd say," Alex Jones said acknowledging his well-fed frame.

Tony stepped aside to let Dr. Jones go first. Catherine heard Tony gasp and hold his breath for a moment as he came in, and she realized she and John had somehow become acclimated to the smell inside the house.

Dr. Jones took a cursory glance at the squalor then set about to examine Alma. "Probably died sometime in the night. Can't be much more accurate than that right now. Do you know of any medical problems?"

"I talked to her doctor. According to him, she was in good health except for arthritis."

"Hmm. She might've aspirated on her own vomit. Could be food poisoning." He looked around. "Certainly looks like a prime breeding ground for salmonella or botulism."

"Could it be an unnatural death?" John inquired.

Dr. Jones looked up at him in surprise. "As in murder? Always possible. Why would you think that, though?"

John looked slowly around the room again. "The mess. I know Alma collected daily, but it seems to me her stuff would be stacked somewhat neatly or kept in boxes so she could find things. Look around. Catherine and I both noticed everything has been thrown haphazardly about as if someone was looking for something." Tony and Dr. Jones both looked around. With his eyebrows raised, Dr. Jones said, "You could be right, but I can't imagine what anyone would want. Could be she was searching for something to take, antacids or something. Of course, some people think a lot of old people hide money. I don't see any signs on her body of a blunt trauma. She wasn't beaten, and there are no signs of puncture or gunshot wounds. That's what'd be associated with a crime perpetrated by the type looking for something to steal."

He glanced towards the door. "The ambulance is here. I'll finish the examination at the morgue. Got pictures yet?"

Startled, John said. "No. Tony, get the camera from my car and get pictures."

Relieved to get out of the house, Tony hurried out, leaping down from the porch. In a few moments he returned. Everyone moved back as he went about getting pictures.

"Make sure you get pictures of each room from all angles, especially the kitchen," John said. "I want to check the upstairs while you're doing this."

Using a rag, he opened the door to the second floor. Narrow wooden steps led up to the shadowy upstairs. Curious, Catherine followed. Upstairs narrow aisles led

193

between boxes and stacks of newspapers. Cobwebs hung from the ceiling and draped the windows as eerie curtains.

"See what I mean?" John asked.

"Yes," Catherine said catching his point at once. "Her clutter is organized, such as it is."

"No one's been up here in a long time."

"No footprints in the dust." She said pleased with herself for noticing.

"Good observation, Nancy," John said with a slight grin.

"Elementary, Dear Watson," Catherine grinned back mixing up her literary characters. She sobered as she heard the noise downstairs signifying Alma was being removed, a reminder of the horrors below. "Do you really think she was murdered?"

"I don't want to think so, but there's a bad feel here."

Catherine shuddered and silently agreed with him.

He turned to go down the stairs, and she followed carefully behind on the steep and narrow steps.

Tony stood to one side watching as the paramedics carefully carried the gurney with Alma through the door.

Dr. Jones was placing Alma's last meal in a plastic bag. "I'll check her stomach and check this, too. Macaroni and cheese. Yum! Lemon meringue pie," he said sniffing slightly at the Styrofoam container. "Tea. I'll have to get a container for this."

"They'll need to be dusted in case anything suspicious shows up," John said.

"Yes, you're right. I'll have that done right away."

"Tony, I want both doors pad-locked until we get the results of the autopsy."

"You really think the old lady was done in?" he asked with eyebrows raised.

John shook his head. "I don't know, but I don't want to leave the house open to anyone who may come along. I'll wait here until you get back. Go to Howie's and put it on the account."

Soon everyone left except Catherine and John. He started around the side of the house.

"I remember hearing a noise," Catherine said

John looked at her. "What kind of noise? When?"

"It was when I came. It wasn't much. Like something or someone moving around the house there." She pointed towards the east side of the house.

John walked to where she'd indicated noticing the well-worn path leading around the house. Catherine followed. I'm beginning to feel like Tonto or Robin, she thought, always in the shadow of the Great Man, but to be honest, she admitted, he doesn't act like a Great Man.

He followed the path Catherine had followed earlier, and as she'd also done earlier, he stopped to survey the area for a while. Then he headed down the path to the outhouse stopping midway. The tall grass here showed evidence of something recently cutting through it and into the woods.

"So someone was there watching." A shiver went through her.

"Not necessarily. This could be from yesterday. Could've been Alma or even the dog. Either one might've gone into the woods for some reason or maybe a deer." He turned almost bumping into Catherine rooted to her spot staring at the broken weeds, and smiled down at her. "It's probably nothing but an overactive imagination. We have the 'haunted house' spooks, I think," acknowledging they both were feeling uneasy. "It's the setting. Perfect for a ghost story or scary mystery."

"I hope you're right, and that's all it is." She glanced down at the shaggy brown and black dog watching them mournfully. "What'll we do with the dog?"

"I'll take him to the animal shelter, for now."

After Tony returned with the padlocks, John left him to his task, and he walked with Catherine to their vehicles. With only a little encouragement, Ralph jumped into the

195

back of the cruiser. As Catherine followed John back down the shadowy tunnel of trees, she glanced uneasily into the back seat of the van. In her imagination, she felt eyes watching her. She shivered again and was glad when the van came out of the shadows and into the sunshine.

Chapter Twenty-two

Catherine inched along pulling sour grass, digging up long-rooted tenacious dandelions by the score, and uprooting creeping ground ivy wending its ubiquitous way through the sidewalk garden connecting Roses in Thyme with her house. There's too much to do, she lamented, and too little time to do everything that needs done. Still, when she sat back on her heels and looked at the area she'd weeded, she felt a sense of satisfaction as she saw a weed free section of garden.

The tall blue delphinium spikes looked especially nice this year. No crown rot, no mildew, no pests or diseases at all, she thought with pleasure. She liked the pinks and roses of the dianthus in front of the delphiniums.

For brief periods the weeding occupied her mind, soothed her, but always the nagging thought returned. What if someone had killed Alma?

She'd just started towards the compost pile with another full bucket of weeds when the phone started ringing. Putting her bucket down, she ran to the house to answer. She glanced at the kitchen clock as she grabbed the wall phone by the refrigerator. Seven-thirty! No wonder I'm feeling hungry, she thought. She hadn't eaten since eleven o'clock that morning. She answered on the sixth ring, thinking about what she could fix in a hurry.

"No, I was weeding, Greg, but I'm calling it quits for the day anyway." She opened the fridge and pulled out eggs as she listened.

"I'll see if I can get to it after I check the blue roses tomorrow. I noticed this morning they were looking slightly off. The leaves are starting to wilt." She leaned over to open a bottom cupboard and pulled out a small skillet.

"I'm nervous about borers. I want a closer look and I'll probably do some pruning. They were treated with systemic, weren't they?" She opened the fridge again for milk and butter.

"I thought so. Well, some of those little buggers can be pretty persistent." She walked to the sink, took a flowered mug from the dish drainer, filled it with water and put it in the microwave, setting the timer for two minutes.

"Yeah, I agree it'd be terrible if we lost any of them." She put butter in the skillet and turned the burner on.

"Listen, how about if I run out and look at those pines tonight." She cracked two eggs into a cup and whipped them with a fork.

"No, it's no bother. You say it's that new grove planted several years ago beyond Swan Lake?" She added some water and continued beating. When the butter started to sizzle, she poured the mixture in.

"Could be a lot of things. Maybe sawflies. Can't tell till I check." She went to the toaster and popped two pieces of wheat bread in and pushed the lever down. The microwave beeped. Taking the hot water out, she added a rounded spoon of instant coffee.

"Just let me grab a bite to eat, and then I'll run over. See you later." She hung up, grabbed a plate from the cupboard and scraped the eggs onto it, and started to eat her hasty supper. She stood at the kitchen counter looking out the window towards the nursery, and thought about what she might do with the garden by the corner. She wasn't quite satisfied with the Johnson Blue cranesbill there. It had a tendency to cover the other plants.

The phone rang again. Catherine swallowed a bite of toast, and grabbed the phone. She smiled when she heard her mother's voice, "Hi, Mom! What's up?"

She listened with a small smile on her face. "Yes. It was upsetting." Her mother's voice made her feel everything was under control, that she was loved and there was someone who could make everything all right. At least most of the time. "No, I'm okay." She reassured her mother and filled her in on just enough details to satisfy her mother's curiosity, but not enough to alarm her which meant she was careful to avoid all mention of Alma. There was no sense in causing her mother any sleepless nights of worry.

She'd just hung up the phone and took another two bites when it rang again. "Boy am I popular today," she muttered in resignation as she answered the phone, but the voice on the other end caused her face to widen into a broad smile.

"Grandma, how nice to hear from you." She held the receiver slightly away from her ear as her grandmother's voice trilled out loud enough for Lily to prick her ears and look up.

"Your grandfather was worried and wanted to know if you were all right."

"Now, Kit. You know it was you who's been worried," her grandfather's gravelly voice came over the line. She could picture him on the extension in his office/den at the old roll top desk piled high with papers.

"That's not true, Homer."

"Is so. You been trying to call all afternoon and evening ever since you read about the murder in the paper. Then you kept fussing 'cause you didn't get any answer."

"Well, maybe, but you kept fussing, too. Did you get a hold of her yet?" Her grandmother said, mimicking her husband's voice.

Catherine grinned. They argued like this from morning

to night, but she knew how deeply they cared for one another. It showed in the looks they exchanged, the little touches when they thought no one was looking, the fussing grandma did over grandpa's creature comforts, and the uneasiness grandpa showed when grandma was away.

Finally Catherine broke into their argument. "I don't know why no one answered earlier. Maybe Christy was watering plants when I was gone and didn't hear. I've been out in the garden all evening. I might've been in the back part. Mom just called, too. Like I told her, there's nothing to worry about. Whoever had it in for Mr. Chatterton isn't interested in me."

"Well what if it's some homicidal maniac?" Her grandmother's concern showed in her voice.

"Now, Kit," her grandfather jumped in. "You've been watching too many crime shows."

"Well, it happens. It's a good world, but there are ill who are on it."

Catherine smiled. Her grandmother lived by proverbs. "Now Grandma, our worse misfortunes are those which never befall us." How often she'd heard those words the summers she'd spent on her grandparents' farm while growing up.

Her grandfather's rusty chuckle came over the line. "She's got you there, Kit!"

"You can both stop worrying," Catherine said. "This is a little town. I'm quite safe here."

"How's the business doing?" her grandfather asked.

Happily she launched in on an update of what was going on, and soon fifteen minutes went by before she realized it.

"I've got to go," she said with regret. "I promised the head gardener at Elmwood I'd look at some pines infested with something."

"Kind of late, isn't it?" her grandfather questioned.

"Not if I hurry. I'll try to call this weekend if I get a

minute." And with that they had to be content. A warm loving feeling remained for a good while after she'd hung up. It'd been a long day, and she thought wistfully of a shower and a good book or gardening magazine.

Catherine looked at her cold meal congealing on the plate and made a face. It didn't look appetizing anymore. She scraped what was left into a container for the compost pile then put the dishes to soak in soapy water. Before leaving, she washed her dirty knees, then grabbed her keys and hurried out the door. "I don't want to be caught there after dark again," she muttered then added "Good Hildegard," as the truck started right up. "Maybe that mechanic is a pessimist. You've been good the last two days."

But evening shadows were already starting to sneak their way into the gardens as she parked next to Greg Robert's and Tyler's vehicles. She knocked on Greg Robert's cottage door, and after waiting impatiently for a few minutes, she decided he'd already gone on. She debated whether or not to drive to the lake and then decided the exercise would be good and started off at a brisk walk down the black topped drive leading past the vegetable gardens towards Swan Lake.

As she neared the lake, she took the left fork to go through a grove of mixed hardwood and hemlocks that lead eventually to the new pine plantation on a hill overlooking the lake. The path through the grove was pleasant with the smell of hemlock giving a north woods feeling. She could see the lake through breaks in the underbrush and trees. The fallen pine needles muffled the sound of her footsteps. Several little chickadees flew close landing on branches near her as they inquisitively checked her out and called out their trademark song.

A cabin here on the shore of this lake would be perfect, she thought not for the first time. This place always enchanted her.

A loud splash from the lake startled her. Beavers? She wondered. Curious, she took a small side trail down to the lake to look. The sun had already set, and the sky was reflected in pinks, golds, and reds on the smooth surface. Cat tails and marsh grasses grew close to shore as well as water lilies. Maybe it was a big snapper, she thought. A large dark shadow floating in the water about forty feet further caught her eye. Her heart gave a lurch as it floated eerily in the water resembling a body. She pushed through the underbrush suddenly desperate to get to it. When she reached the point closest to it, she could see a large brown garment floating, but she couldn't tell if anyone was in it. Without pausing she waded in reaching for it.

Suddenly her head exploded with pain, and she fell forward. As the water closed over her, she panicked and grabbed for anything that would hold her up, but the flimsy water plants seemed to be pulling her down instead of helping. Gasping she swallowed a mouthful of water as she tried to hold onto consciousness. Then she relaxed as David's face floated into her fading consciousness followed by Ellie's face beside his. They were smiling and shaking their heads no.

Just as she started to lose conscience, hands grabbed her. She fought to get away and surfaced coughing and choking still fighting. She couldn't tell if she was fighting to save her life or to return to David and Ellie.

"It's okay. It's okay." she heard as everything went dark. She was dimly aware of being carried ashore and laid down.

"What's going on?" a brusque voice asked.

"It's Catherine. I found her thrashing around in the lake." Catherine recognized Greg Robert's voice.

"Is she alright?" the other anxious voice came closer.

Catherine cautiously opened her eyes and looked into Ed Flavian's concerned face.

"What were you doing in the lake, Missy?" Ed asked.

"The brown robe," she croaked.

"Robe?" Ed's brows drew together.

"In the lake," she nodded slightly then grimaced as pain shot through her head again.

"What robe?" Greg Robert asked.

"I heard a splash. When I checked I saw something brown floating. When I got closer, it looked like a robe. I thought it might be someone."

Greg Robert hurried to the lake with Ed following. Their eyes searched the water.

"There's something." Ed pointed at a darker shadow floating further out.

Greg Robert plunged in and as the water deepened, he started swimming until he grabbed the brown shadow and towed it in. Catherine saw him pulling a heavy brown garment with a rope partially tied to it trailing behind and watched him drop it on the shore. He glanced at her and then looked at Ed. "It's my habit."

As the two men stared at each other without speaking, Catherine felt the unspoken questions and answers passing between them.

She tried to get up and groaned. Both men turned and came back to her.

"My head," she moaned.

"What happened to your head?" Greg Robert asked.

"I don't know," she gritted out. "It felt like something hit my head when I went in."

Greg Robert carefully felt the back of her head and located a swelling. "What a goose egg! There doesn't seem to be any blood, though. Let's get you up to the house. Can you walk or should I get my truck?"

"I'll walk," she said sounding braver than she felt. She didn't really want to do anything causing movement.

After they'd walked a short distance, he noticed the pain on her face. "I think you'd better sit on this bench. Ed will stay with you while I go get my truck."

As he jogged off, she closed her eyes grateful she wouldn't have to walk further after all. She shivered in her wet clothes as the evening darkened.

"Here, Missy." Ed took off his flannel shirt and draped it around her shoulders.

"Did you see who hit you?"

"No. I didn't even hear anyone."

Ed sat quietly beside her. She found his presence reassuring. He's such a kind man, she thought. She heard the sound of Greg Robert's truck, and in a few moments his headlights swept over them. Carefully he helped her into the front seat.

"Just a minute. I'll be right back." He hurried back down the path returning shortly with the dripping robe and threw it in the back of his truck.

"Do you want a ride home?" he asked Ed.

"No. I'll go back the way I came." He turned and soon only the white blur of his T shirt could be seen on the path into the woods.

Greg Robert climbed in and with care backed into the first place he could turn around.

"I think I'd better take you to the hospital and have you checked."

"No. I'll be all right."

"Are you sure? That was quite a whack you got."

"I'll be fine." she repeated. She wasn't sure of that, but her hospitalization was minimal, and she couldn't afford a medical bill right now. She'd wait and see how she felt in the morning.

He drove cautiously, aware that movement hurt, and parked next to her truck. His face showed his concern as he helped her out. "You're coming in, and we're calling the police."

She didn't argue and let him lead her into his cottage. "Go in and get out of those wet clothes. You can wear something dry of mine." From his closet he pulled out a clean pair of jeans and a flannel shirt. Gratefully she took them. Ed's shirt was now as wet as her clothes.

As she washed some of the mud off her face and arms and changed into dry clothes, she heard Greg Robert on the phone. When she came out, she saw him in the kitchen and heard the cheerful sound of a tea kettle whistling.

Catherine sat down on the plain brown couch and found it surprisingly comfortable. She put her head back, closed her eyes, and felt she could fall asleep here and never move again.

"Here," Greg Robert said in a low soothing voice.

She opened her eyes and saw a hot mug of tea being held out to her. With gratitude she accepted and cupped the hot mug in both hands sniffing the fragrance.

"Hmmm," she said appreciatively as she took a sip. "This tastes different than anything I've tasted before. What is it?"

"It's my own special blend of herbs with some comfrey. I also added a little splash of something extra to warm you up because you're shivering," he said as he watched her. Then he went to the kitchen and came back with an ice pack. "Put this on your head. It should help."

She took it and leaning against the back of the couch, she placed it on the lump. She felt strangely shy sitting here in his clothes with him watching her. She noticed he'd changed into dry clothes, too. Before the silence lengthened too awkwardly, headlights swept across the wall as a car pulled up, and a car door slammed.

Chapter Twenty-three

"I've been thinking about this perp." Tony leaned back teetering on two chair legs.

John, writing at his desk, peered at Tony over his glasses. "Perp?"

"Yeah, you know. The guy who killed Chatterton."

"Yeah, I know." The corners of John's mouth twitched.

"I was thinking. Had to be someone who worked at the gardens."

"What makes you think that?"

"Well, who else would use a garden fork or know where those things are kept?"

"You've got a point." John conceded.

"So that sort of narrows it down to the Burns guy, Birchfield or Ed Flavian."

"There're a lot more workers at the Gardens than that."

"Yeah, but it's got to be someone with a motive."

"True," John agreed.

"And I don't think it could be a bopper."

"Bopper?"

"Yeah, you know, a hit man. They wouldn't pick a public place like that, and they'd use a piece to do him."

"Piece." John nodded.

"Somehow I don't see it as a junk deal, either," Tony went on.

"Junk?"

"Yeah, you know, drugs."

"Oh . . . drugs. No, I agree. I don't see Chatterton involved with drugs, and drug dealers have more direct ways to waste someone," John added straight faced.

"Well, someone was definitely pushed out of shape unless it was some kind of kook."

"Pushed out of shape, angry." John nodded.

"And then I thought maybe Chatterton stumbled onto some scam and had to be silenced."

"Any idea what kind of scam?"

"No. I thought if we do a little digging something'll turn up. Like the torch job of Burns."

"Torch job?" John raised his eyebrows.

"Yeah. That abbey where he used to live. Burned. Did he torch it intentionally? Did Chatterton find out about it?"

"I talked to the abbot last night," John said.

"You did? You didn't tell me." Tony sounded miffed.

"Sorry. Forgot. Things've been going down so fast I've had trouble getting a handle on this deal, especially since no one has a rap sheet. And I didn't want this Burns guy to get a bum rap if he's innocent. It'd be too easy for someone to hang it on him." His face showed no expression, but there was a suspicious glint of a twinkle in his eye.

"Well, what'd he say?" Tony prodded.

John sobered. "The abbot spoke highly of Greg Robert Burns. Said he'd tried to talk him into staying. It seems some of the brothers were making fruit cakes – they sell them – and a candle ignited the brandy. The fire spread and one entire wing was damaged. One of the monks was badly burned and died."

"Sounds like murder to me."

Ignoring him, John went on. "According to the abbot, Greg Robert was a hero. He extinguished the flames on the other monk's robe and got burned, too."

"How bad?"

"His hands and legs, he said, but I guess he healed okay."

"Why'd he leave then?"

John shrugged. "The abbot said it was Brother Burns who spilled the brandy near the candle causing the fire."

"Could've been arson."

"There was an investigation. Apparently there was no suspicion it was anything but an accident." John reached for the phone that started ringing.

After a few terse words, John hurried to the door. Ralph raised his head and rose to follow. "Stay boy." John said to the dog as he rushed through the door.

"Want me to go with you?" Tony asked.

"No, stay here," John called back without stopping.

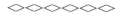

Catherine's eyes went to the door when she heard a car door slamming. The screen door opened abruptly as John came in without knocking. He stood there staring at her not saying anything for several moments as he took in the wet muddy hair, a streak of mud still on one cheek bone, and the outsized clothes on her slender frame.

He took a deep breath. "What happened?" His teeth were clenched as he stared at her.

She looked up at him and suddenly felt like crying. Neither Ed's nor Greg Roberts' solicitousness had brought on feelings of self-pity, but now John sounding so angry caused tears to well up in her eyes and threaten to spill over.

Greg Robert glanced at her and noticed the tears. He offered John a chair. When they'd both sat down, he told John what he knew allowing Catherine time to regain her composure.

John kept glancing at Catherine. "Why were you out there alone in the dark?" He said in a clipped abrupt manner.

208

"It wasn't dark when I went," she shot back angry at his tone of voice and manner.

"What made you go out there alone before dark then?" He asked between gritted teeth aware he wasn't handling this well, but unable to stop.

Greg Robert watched them both without interrupting.

"My job doesn't have set hours. I needed to check the pines on the far side of the lake." She glared at him, her tears gone now.

"Did you see or hear anything before the splash?"

"No."

"What about after you went in?"

"No."

"How did you happen to be there?" He turned to Greg Robert.

Catherine sat sipping the pungent and strangely soothing concoction Greg Robert had brewed for her. Her headache started fading away, and she began to feel light headed as if she were floating away from her body. It was a pleasant sensation. As if in a dream, she heard him answer John's question.

"When I came back from checking the greenhouse, I saw Catherine's truck and figured she'd gone to the pine grove so I followed her."

"How did you know that's where she'd gone?" John was scowling.

"Because we'd been talking about it on the phone shortly before." He spoke calmly as if unaware of John's anger. "When I heard splashing, I ran and pulled her out. Ed came along, and she told us about the robe she'd seen, and I pulled it out."

"Robe?"

"Actually, it was my habit, and no, I have no idea how it got in the lake."

Catherine drained the large mug, hiccupped and giggled.

209

John looked at her, his eyes suspicious.

The corners of Greg Robert's mouth twitched. "I'll get the robe for you." He went out to his truck and returned in moments with the wet habit. "There's a rope tied around it. It might've had a rock tied to it that came loose."

John pulled his eyes away from Catherine, who had a vague smile on her face, and he looked at the sodden robe. "I'll take it with me. Are you sure it was yours?"

"I think so. I haven't seen it since it disappeared. There probably aren't too many of these around so it's probably mine."

"I'm going home," Catherine announced as she got up holding onto the edge of the couch for balance. She staggered a little when she let loose.

"What's wrong?" Alarmed, John jumped up to help her. "Concussion do you think?"

Greg Robert grinned. "Drunk, I'd say. I might've put too much brandy to warm her up in the herbal tea mixture she was drinking."

Catherine dozed in the front seat of the patrol car as John drove her home in silence. He knew this wasn't the time to question her. He waited patiently while she rooted in her purse for her keys, and took them from her gently when she had trouble getting the key into the keyhole. To his surprise he found the door unlocked. "The door wasn't locked," he said.

She shrugged and said, "Oh, well."

He shook his head. "Oh, Catherine."

He reached in, found the light switch, and flooded the kitchen with bright light. "I'll check things out," he said as he walked in.

"No. It's okay. I'm okay. Everything's okay." she said enunciating each word with care. Suddenly all she wanted was a hot shower and her soft comfortable bed.

"I'm not sure a doctor shouldn't see you." He felt uncertain about leaving her.

"No," she said with as much firmness as she could muster. "I'll be fine tomorrow. I'm just awfully tired tonight."

John stared at her for a moment then said, "Good night. Make sure this door's locked." He waited until he heard the lock click. When he thought she wouldn't hear, he reached out and checked to see if it really was locked. He returned to his car still uneasy and stood by it until he saw a light go on upstairs in what he assumed was the bathroom. Through the open window he heard the sounds of a shower. Only then did he get in and slowly drive away still disturbed.

Catherine stood under the hot water long after the shampoo had been rinsed out and not a trace of mud remained. She relived her near drowning and the feelings David and Ellie must've had that night when their car had gone into the river. Tears mingled with the water. Their faces, when they'd appeared earlier were so loving. "Did you come to save me?" she murmured. She'd wanted to join them, but apparently it wasn't to be. "Someday, Dear Ones," she whispered. Lethargy set in and she lacked the energy to get out. Finally she forced herself to leave the shower and toweled herself dry, wincing when she toweled her hair and hit the growing lump.

Slipping into a terry cloth robe hanging on the back of the bathroom door, she went down the hall to her bedroom, turned on the bedside lamp and turned down the covers. The bed looked inviting with its garden of roses. As she turned to put the decorator bed pillows on the wicker rocker, she noticed the smashed baby's head on the floor.

Catherine inhaled sharply and fell to her knees. "Why? Why?" she cried as she took the baby's head in her hands.

One china blue eye stared at her sightlessly in the badly cracked face. A little smile still remained on the small, red, rosebud mouth. She got up and went to the chair holding the slashed and ripped body of the doll. Her grandmother's, the doll meant to be her daughter's one day. Stuffing oozed out and the doll's pretty blue dress was in shreds.

She felt violated. Someone had been in her house, her bedroom. Someone had invaded her personal place of safety, of comfort. Trembling, she went to the phone unable to take her eyes from the mutilated doll.

"Maggie." Her voice trembled. "May I spend the night? Will you come and get me right away?"

Wrapping the comforter from the bed around her, she went downstairs to wait at the back door for her friend.

Chapter Twenty-four

A blue jay family invaded the feeder scattering the purple finches enjoying their breakfast and a cheerful conversation. Four young blue jays, almost as large as their parents, perched on the handles of a red wooden wheelbarrow and flapped their wings. With open mouths they squawked and begged their parents to feed them. The beleaguered parents, also hungry, quickly ate throwing unwanted seed on the ground as they searched for sunflower seeds.

Catherine watched in amusement as the youngsters became more vociferous in their bid for attention. Finally one of the parents, probably the mother, Catherine thought, flew down and pushed a seed or two down the gullet of the closest one. She did this for each one until they sat sated and quiet.

"Good morning. I didn't hear you get up," Maggie said. "I see you found the clothes I put out for you."

"Yes, thanks. It's good we're about the same size. I'd hate to walk home in just a T-shirt and comforter," Catherine laughed.

Maggie tilted her head to one side. "You're taller and thinner, but with shorts and a T-shirt it doesn't really matter. Coffee?"

"Sounds wonderful," Catherine said as she got up and followed Maggie from the small breakfast room to the kitchen and perched on her favorite stool at the counter.

She loved this old kitchen with its original wood floors partially covered with rag rugs and with warm rich cherry cupboards. She leaned over and sniffed at a big blue bowl of yellow roses.

"How'd you sleep?" Maggie inquired as she filled the coffee maker with water and measured the coffee.

"Better than I thought I would."

"You were falling asleep talking to me." Maggie smiled at her. "Bagel? Eggs? Toast? Anything else?"

"Yes."

"Yes what?"

"All of the above," Catherine laughed. "I'm starved. I barely ate any supper last night. No, I'll have whatever you're having."

"I've been up since six painting so I'm quite hungry, too. Let's have a big country breakfast. You can scramble the eggs."

While working together, Catherine asked, "Is that what the roses are for?"

"Roses?"

"Your painting. Were you painting them?"

"Yes, but I thought I'd bring them in here to enjoy until I'm ready to get back to it. Have you thought anymore about who could've smashed your doll?"

"I thought until I fell asleep and as soon as I woke up this morning, but I haven't the slightest idea."

"Any chance it could've been your cat?"

"No, not at all. Even if she were a mischievous cat, she couldn't have done that much damage. I thought maybe some kids, but why just the doll?" Catherine frowned.

"And you said nothing else was broken or missing?"

Catherine shrugged. "I didn't look much. I just wanted out of there."

"Who can blame you after the night and day you had. How's your head, by the way?"

"Sore when I touch it or comb my hair, but at least I

214

don't have a headache any more. That is as long as I don't shake my head."

"Things are really getting weird in this town." Maggie spread cream cheese on the bagels. "Let's carry our plates to the breakfast room. I love watching the birds at the feeder."

"I was enjoying a family of blue jays when you came in. Someday I'd like to have a big window like this by my kitchen table so I can watch the birds." Catherine said before going back to Maggie's comment. "Do you think these things are connected?"

"Who knows?" Maggie shrugged. "We haven't had a murder in this town since Mrs. Porter shot her husband. That was when I was still a kid. I think it was ruled self-defense."

"John thinks maybe Alma was poisoned."

"John MacDougal?"

"Yes," Catherine wasn't sure she should be saying anything, but needed to talk to someone.

"Poisoned!" Maggie said shaking her head in disbelief. "Who'd hurt Alma? If she did die of poisoning, it was probably food poisoning."

"Yeah, you're right. I guess after Chatterton's death I'm imagining things."

Maggie looked at her thinking about what she'd said. "But John must've thought this, too, or you wouldn't have said anything. Why? What would make either of you think that?"

Catherine decided she'd better not say any more about it so she shrugged and said, "Nothing really. The house just seemed old and spooky."

"It certainly does. I've never been in it. If I had to pick Alma up, she always met me in her driveway. I don't think anyone's ever been in her house."

"Ten o'clock!" Catherine exclaimed glancing at a wall clock. "Is that the right time?"

215

Maggie nodded.

"I've got to get ready for Mr. Chatterton's funeral." She got up in a hurry and started carrying her dishes to the kitchen.

"What time's the funeral?" Maggie asked. "Leave the dishes. I'll get them later."

"Eleven."

"Aren't they having it kind of soon? What about the autopsy?"

Catherine shrugged as she put her dishes in the sink. "I guess they rushed the autopsy. Maybe rich people can do that, and maybe it's because the cause of death was pretty obvious."

"I'll run you home," Maggie reached for her keys.

"No. I can walk it. It's just a short way."

"You sure? I can come in and check things out for you."

"No," Catherine repeated. "Thanks for your concern, but no. Everything will be fine." She hurried out the door with a "thanks for everything." She jogged down the drive, but soon slowed down to a walk as jogging caused her head to ache.

Relieved to see her truck parked in front of the shop, she wondered who'd returned it and how they'd started it. She was the only one with keys.

In spite of her confident words to Maggie, she was nervous about going into her house, but as she toured it room by room, she was glad to see nothing else was damaged or disturbed. With sadness and anger, she picked up the doll and all its pieces, put them in a plastic bag and put the bag into an old trunk at the foot of her bed. I'll take her to a doll hospital as soon as I get the time, she told herself and hoped her grandmother's doll wasn't beyond repair.

In a rush she slipped into a dark skirt and an ivory colored silk blouse, and then searched through a dresser

216

drawer looking for a pair of panty hose without a run. On the fifth try, she finally found a pair. She added a little makeup and green eye shadow, a touch of coral lipstick which went well with her summer tan, and brushed her short hair. When she was done she stepped back from the full length mirror to survey the results. "Not bad." She smiled at herself in the mirror.

Hurrying, Catherine arrived somewhat out of breath. The parking lot was full so she had to park two blocks away. She slipped into a little niche along the back wall between the rack of votive candles before the statue of The Blessed Mother and Howie Turner, the proprietor of Turner's Hardware. She smiled her thanks at him as he squeezed a little closer to Mr. Walters, on his other side to make room for her. She smelled the odor of pipe tobacco and Old Spice. Both men were of ample girth and wore suits that looked decades old. Probably only used for weddings and funerals, she thought. Curious, she looked for people in the pews she'd know. She spied a frothy violet tulle hat and knew that must be Violet even before Violet turned her head. Next to her was Millie's bright auburn head. Even with her curls piled high, Millie's head did not come much above Violet's shoulder. Both were craning their necks looking around with avid curious eyes and then nudging each other and pointing in what they considered a discreet manner as they spotted someone they recognized. Ed didn't seem to be here.

Hopefully a little more discreet than Violet and Millie, Catherine continued looking around. She saw the Elmwood Gardens contingent sitting together; Tyler, Greg Robert and Olga several rows back from Violet and Millie. The rest of the Elmwood Garden workers sat in the last two rows. Most of them looked ill at ease.

Catherine's eyes strayed to people lining the walls, unable to get seats, and caught John staring at her from the far side. He looked different in a sport jacket and tie instead of his uniform. He gave her a slight smile. She returned it then looked away flustered and embarrassed as she thought of her less than sober behavior the night before.

The organist playing a Bach fugue was joined by Our Lady of the Roses choir for the opening hymn, "*Morning has Broken*." She recognized the voice of Irene Masters, the choir director and lead vocalist. With the choir as cue, Augustus Chatterton's family filed in. Vera Chatterton, looking exceedingly svelte in a black designer dress, was accompanied by a tall, handsome, white haired man who held her elbow. They were trailed by a somber faced Alicia staring straight ahead. She wore a long flowing dark silk skirt and a silk blouse to match in a flowered pattern.

Catherine glanced at Tom Rockwell and saw his eyes following Alicia as she walked down the aisle. She also noticed Alicia's brother wasn't with them.

"*Praise with elation, Praise ev'ry morning, God's recreation of the new day.*" The voices in the church rang out. Catherine wondered who'd chosen this song. It was one of her favorites, but didn't seem appropriately funereal. Of course, she thought, it could be a new day for Mr. Chatterton. Or she thought somewhat irreverently, a new day for Vera Chatterton. He couldn't have been an easy person to live with. She sang along with the congregation. Howie Turner glanced down at her and raised his voice to effectively drown her out.

As soon as the family was seated, the funeral procession started. An altar boy carried the large crucifix slowly down the aisle, followed by Father O'Shawnessy and Deacon Mike. They were followed by two more altar boys. At the end of the procession, six pall bearers pushed the casket draped in white with a large spray of red roses almost covering the top. Catherine wondered why an

218

arrangement using the blue roses hadn't been made.

Prayers were said by the casket and incense from the incense burner waved until the smell permeated the church. Catherine watched somberly. The smells, the ritual brought bittersweet memories. It reminded her of the church she'd gone to when she still lived at home, but it also reminded her of David's and Ellie's funeral. Tears pricked her eyes, and she forced her mind away from that other funeral and instead concentrated on this funeral Mass. She remained attentive for a while, but soon her mind started wandering over recent events. On her mind and probably the minds of just about everyone else here was who killed Chatterton? She also wondered if Alma was poisoned, and who threw Greg Roberts' habit in the pond and hit her on the head last night? Who came into her house and smashed her doll? Was any of this connected or were they isolated incidents?

Her eyes wandered over the crowd. Could it be someone here? She glanced at John and noticed him watching the crowd, his face intent as his eyes roved. He was thinking the same things she was, she realized. He's standing on the side not because he came late, but because he has a better view of who's here. She noticed Tony on the other side of the church also standing and watching.

The eulogy was very brief and contained more words of scripture than reminiscences of Chatterton's life. She saw Alicia's slim shoulders shaking, but Mrs. Chatterton sat motionless throughout.

The Mass ended with *Amazing Grace*, a hymn that always brought tears to Catherine's eyes. Before the casket and family left, Mr. Osborne, the funeral director, announced the burial would be private, but there would be a luncheon in The Wisteria Tea Room at Chatterton Manor at Elmwood Gardens. Everyone was invited. They were to go there directly, and the family would join them after a brief service at the cemetery.

All eyes watched as Vera, composed and dry-eyed,

walked back up the aisle staring straight ahead. The tall white-haired man again walked by her side. As before, Alicia tagged behind, her eyes swollen and red as she dabbed at them with a tissue. An elderly couple and a middle aged woman followed behind. That seemed to be the whole family.

Once the family departed, Catherine merged with the crowd flowing out the door. Friends greeted friends and although the conversation was muted, the somberness of the service lifted with the absence of the family.

"How's the head this morning?" she heard from close behind her. She turned her head and looked up into John's eyes.

She smiled. "Fine," she lied, or at least partially lied. If she didn't touch the lump or shake her head too fast, she felt fine. He worked his way up beside her.

"Did you bring my truck back?"

He nodded. "I thought you might need it."

"How'd you do it without keys?"

"There're ways," he said smiling. "By the way, you need to have it looked at as soon as possible. I don't like a sound I heard in the engine."

Catherine grimaced and said, "I will."

They found themselves outside on the sidewalk. He seemed reluctant to let her go. "Are you going to the Chatterton Manor?" he asked.

"Yes. Are you?"

He nodded. "Where are you parked?"

"A couple of blocks down the street."

He turned and walked with her. "I'm worried about what happened to you last night. I have one of my deputies out there looking for a club or stick that could've been used," he said when they were out of earshot of others. "Do you have any idea who it could've been?"

She shook her head slightly. "No. I've thought and thought and I just . . ." she shook her head again. "No."

He walked along frowning. "You were probably just a casual victim, someone who happened along, and the person who threw in the habit was afraid you saw something. I'm sure they think if you saw anything you've already told what you know so you won't be a threat. You haven't had any strange phone calls or anything, have you?"

She didn't answer. She probably should tell him about the doll, but somehow it was painful to talk about it, as if something obscene and dirty had touched her life.

"What happened?" he asked stopping and taking her arm to stop her.

She looked up at him troubled. "When I got home last night and after my shower, I found my grandmother's antique doll smashed in my bedroom."

He took in a sharp breath. "Why didn't you call me?" he blurted out frowning.

She shrugged. "I just . . ." she started and then couldn't go on. How could she explain the feelings she had?

He waited for her to continue and when she didn't, he asked in a calmer tone of voice. "What did you do with the doll?"

"I picked it up and put it in a bag."

"We'll go to your house before we go to Elmwood. I want to look at it. I'll follow you."

He walked her to her truck without saying anything more. A car horn sounded and Catherine looked up to see a lavender encased arm waving. Both Millie and Violet were craning their necks to watch John and Catherine. Even from a distance she could feel their intense curiosity. She gasped as Violet's car almost hit a parked car, but just in time she righted her car and proceeded down the street.

Catherine laughed. "You almost had a ticket to write."

John laughed, too, and the stiffness between them disappeared.

John made Catherine go in careful detail over each step in finding the doll and where it had been and prodded her into thinking if she'd noticed anything else. He pointed to a mark on the bedpost that had probably been made by the doll's head.

When he'd finished questioning her, he said. "I want to take the doll with me," He looked around the room with its antique bed and dresser, the flowered wallpaper and lace curtains at open windows letting in the soft June day. He noticed two pictures on the nightstand beside the bed. One was of a smiling man and the other of a young girl with a smile like Catherine's. He wanted to look closer, but his attention was brought back to Catherine when she spoke.

"I probably shouldn't have touched it."

He shrugged. "Your prints would've been on it anyway. There's probably not much chance of finding any identifiable prints." He turned and headed downstairs.

As she followed him, she asked, "What did you do with the habit?"

There was a lot of white cat or dog hairs embedded in it that even the dunking in the pond didn't get rid of."

"Greg Robert has a white cat so that's understandable. He said he thought the habit was his, didn't he?"

"Yes. I went back and talked to him for quite a while after I took you home."

"You don't really think he did it, do you?"

He turned at the bottom of the steps and looked up at her. "I don't know. I don't like to think so, but so far what little evidence there is could lead to him."

Catherine followed him to the kitchen. "But what motive could he have?"

John shrugged. "What motive does anyone have? Money? Revenge? If it's revenge, it could be your friend, Ed."

"Money. Greg Robert certainly doesn't seem interested in that. What about Mrs. Chatterton? And who was that good looking white-haired man with her?"

"That was the family lawyer, Edwin Silvernail."

"They looked tight," she commented, eager to direct his attention away from people she cared about. "It could have been a murder of passion."

Aware of what she was doing, his lips quirked up. "I'll look into it."

"Have you heard any more about Alma?"

"No. It's too soon for all the tests to be done. Hopefully the results will be in by next week or even in the next few days, with any luck."

"I'm hoping it was natural causes. Did you take Ralph to the animal shelter?"

"Not yet. I haven't had time. We'd better leave." He paused and looked at her. "You know it might be good if Ralph came here to stay with you for a while."

"No. Lily wouldn't like that."

"He'd be some protection."

"No." Catherine grabbed her purse and keys and led the way to the back door. A large fly buzzed against the screen door trying to get out.

. *"I heard a Fly buzz - when I died,"* she quoted Emily Dickinson.

"I imagine Chatterton is *'Safe in [his] Alabaster Chamber'* by now," John quoted back.

Catherine looked up at him startled then smiled and said, "I think it's a case of: *"Better to go down dignified / With boughten friendship at your side / Than none at all./ Provide, Provide!* She glanced at him with an impish look.

"The boast of heraldry, the pomp of pow'r, / And all that beauty, all that wealth e'er gave, / Awaits alike th' inevitable hour. / The paths of glory lead but to the grave. John quoted solemnly with a straight face.

Catherine laughed, delighted. "I think you've bested

me in poems of death for now. So much for Poetry 101."
And my preoccupation with death and dying after David
and Ellie died, she added to herself. She hurried down the
path to her truck calling out over her shoulder, *"but beware,
I'll 'not go gentle into that good night.'"*

Chapter Twenty-five

Cars lined the drive leading to Chatterton Manor. Catherine passed them hoping to find an opening in the staff parking lot and was relieved to find a place. On her way to the Wisteria Tea Room, she stopped for a moment at Saint Fiacre's statue. He seemed sorrowful today, as if he knew of the tragic events happening lately. She said a silent prayer to him that the murderer would soon be found and all would be well again at Elmwood Gardens.

Passing the door to the staff dining room, she went to the main terrace. Wisteria covered a sturdy iron arbor arched over the flag stoned terrace. The effect towards the end of May was breathtaking as clusters of lavender flowers hung down, filling the air with fragrance. Those visitors afraid of bees were limited to eating indoors. For those intrepid enough to take their chances, luncheon was a delight to all the senses. She made it a point to eat on the terrace often when wisteria was in bloom, and as far as the bees went, Catherine found them far more interested in the flowers than the people eating below.

"Hey, Catherine," Greg Robert greeted her. Although he'd removed his tie and loosened the top two buttons of his light blue shirt, to Catherine's eyes he still seemed unnatural in a sports jacket and dress slacks. It must be the beard and shoulder length hair, she thought. They seemed to go more with jeans and work shirt. He was alone, a glass of wine in his hand.

She smiled and walked over glancing around as she went. "Quite a crowd."

He nodded. "Just getting here?"

"Uh huh. I had to go home for a few moments after the funeral."

"Are you okay today?" He looked concerned. .

"Yes. I want to thank you for all you did for me last night."

"Forget it. I'm just glad I happened to be nearby. How's the head?"

"A little sore and a headache. Maybe that's partly a hangover?" She gave him a stern look.

He laughed. "It warmed you up."

"It did that!"

"Come and get something to eat and drink. If I know you, even a crack on the head hasn't diminished your appetite."

She gave him a playful punch on the arm. "You're right. Who did the cooking today? I saw Millie at the funeral."

"They brought in some caterers, I guess, or maybe it was the Women's Guild from the church."

They wound their way through tables, each stopping to greet people they knew so it was a while before they got inside to where the buffet line was. Catherine hadn't realized how hungry she was until she went down the table taking helpings of everything.

"This looks good. I wonder what it is?" she said.

"I'd say it's salmon croquettes."

"Oooh, I'm impressed." She looked at him wide-eyed.

He laughed. "Cooking is an interest of mine. I worked as a chef once."

"A man of many talents," she said with a grin, but more impressed than her teasing let on.

She chose coffee rather than wine or punch. As all the tables on the terrace were filled, they settled for a table in a corner of the Tea Room near the kitchen, a little apart from other tables. Large potted plants next to it created an illusion of privacy, but still allowed them a view of other people.

"I thought Father O'Shawnessy gave a nice eulogy," Catherine said, "but it seemed heavy on scripture and light on his life."

"Probably because he wasn't active in the church, and Father O'Shawnessy barely knew him. Any details of his life would have come from the family."

"I guess his wife didn't give him much to go on then. I wonder if his son called or came home."

Greg Robert shrugged. "I wouldn't know. I haven't seen him. Have you thought anymore about who could've hit you? Do you remember anything at all?"

She slowly shook her head. "Nope. I haven't the foggiest idea. Did you get some of this salad? It's delicious."

"Seven layer salad. Yes, I got some. Chief MacDougal took some cat hairs from Bonnie Prince Charlie last night. His royal highness objected most vociferously."

"I'll bet he did," she laughed. "Funny I didn't hear that going on."

"He came back after taking you home. I think I'm his main suspect," he said staring at her, an unfathomable look in his eyes.

"Well, he'd better look in another direction."

"Thank you for your trust," he said with a slight smile. "Actually, I could've been trying to drown you before Ed came along, so then I tried to make it look like I was saving you."

"Is that what MacDougal thinks?"

He nodded. "At least he considers it a possibility."

"But that's ridiculous," she said emphatically.

He cocked his head looking at her. "Is it?"

She stared at him, mouth slightly open before deciding

227

he was joking even though his face didn't show it. "Yes, it is," but she didn't sound quite so emphatic now.

"Did you hear about Alma?" she asked.

"Yes. Chief MacDougal told me last night."

"It was so heartbreaking."

"He also thought she might've been poisoned."

She stared at him and wondered how much John told him, "The place was so dirty it's a wonder she didn't get food poisoning before."

He watched her face gauging how much she knew, then decided to drop the topic. "More coffee?"

She glanced in her cup. "Yes, but I can get it."

"I want to check the dessert table. You save our spot, and I'll get enough for both of us."

"Sounds good." She continued eating and wondered what it'd feel like being under suspicion. Not too good, she thought. We've got to find the real murderer. That thought brought her up short. We? She stopped chewing. We? Well, why not, she told herself. She could dig around, too, and keep her eyes open. Greg Robert needed all the help he could get. Unless the murderer was found, he'd always live with some people wondering. But why him? Certainly there were others with real motives.

Her eyes strayed around the dining room and lighted on the table occupied by Vera Chatterton, Edwin Silvernail, the elderly couple, and the middle-aged woman who'd been at the funeral with her. She noticed Alicia wasn't with them.

"All alone?" a voice inquired brightly.

Catherine turned her head and smiled up at Violet. "For the moment."

"How's your head?" Violet inquired as she sat down in the chair opposite Catherine. "Ed told me you bumped it pretty hard on a branch last night and fell into the lake."

Catherine paused then said lightly, "Okay. It's a little tender, but I'm pretty hard headed."

228

"Where's that charmin' Chief MacDougal you were so chummy with by the church?" Her smile was coy and her eyes glinted with curiosity.

Catherine shrugged. "I don't know. I haven't seen him since I left."

"It looked to be a pretty serious conversation."

Catherine felt a twinge of annoyance. She knew Violet fed on gossip, friendly and otherwise. Although she didn't approve of gossip in general, she had to admit almost everyone was curious about others, so generally she tended to overlook this propensity of Violet's, but now that she was the target, she didn't like it.

"It looked like more than it was," she said as she scraped the last of the Greek potato salad from her plate. Hurry back, Greg Robert, she said to herself.

"I didn't realize you were friends."

Catherine shrugged and looked around hoping to catch someone else's eye. Finally, she changed the conversation. "Where's Ed?"

"Oh, he wouldn't come to this," Violet said. "He didn't like Chatterton at all."

"I hardly think there're many here who did."

"Yeah, but Ed's different. If he don't like ya, he don't like ya, dead or alive. 'Sides it'd take more than this to get him to dress up. His only suit must be more'n twenty-five years old. It's what he'll be buried in.

"I wonder who those folks are with the widow," Violet went on.

Catherine shrugged. "I don't know."

"Probably some relatives. That white-haired man's awful distinguished lookin' and pretty darned handsome, too. He sure is payin' a lot of attention to the widow. Look at the way she's smilin' at him. Wouldn't be surprised somethin's goin' on there. Oh, there's Mrs. Warner. I've gotta go have a word with her." Violet got up with alacrity and with a friendly tap on Catherine's shoulder, she was off on another hunting expedition for facts, half-truths or outright fabrications. Catherine wasn't sure if it mattered to Violet.

"Do you mind if another woman alone sits down?" a low amused voice asked. "You seem to have a private little niche here where you can observe the comings and goings while being alone."

Catherine glanced up with a smile. "Of course I don't mind, Olga. Greg Robert went to get some desert for us, but I suspect he's been waylaid. I'm sure he'll bring more than enough for all three of us."

"Oh, I won't be wanting any. It will take some time to get back in shape after this brief hiatus as it is."

"Back in shape!" Catherine said. "But your shape is already so beautiful."

"Thank you," Olga said. "I was not fishing for compliments. I am a dancer and every spare ounce is felt. You don't look surprised. Perhaps you already knew?"

"No, it's just that your looks, your way of moving, everything about you says a dancer, a classical dancer."

"You move gracefully, too. Did you ever study dance?"

Embarrassed, Catherine laughed. "When I was a kid, I wanted to be a ballerina. I twirled all the time, but after a year of lessons, I gave it up for baseball." She felt pleased with the compliment, but figured it was spoken more in kindness than truth.

"You speak as if you might be leaving soon."

"My mission has been accomplished so it is time I go back to New York and my dance studio," Olga replied. "I have already turned in my resignation. Now I merely wait for a replacement to be hired and trained."

"May I join you?" Tyler Birchfield asked as he pulled up a chair from another table.

"Yes," they both said as they moved their chairs to make room. As she looked up from untangling her chair leg from another chair at an empty table behind her, Catherine intercepted a long intent look passing between them. Hmmm, what have we here? She wondered to herself and then felt sheepish and berated herself for being no different than Violet and Millie, if a little more subtle about it.

"Quite a crowd, isn't there?" Tyler commented.

"You would think he was much admired," Olga replied with a Mona Lisa smile.

"Oh, I think it's much more an occasion of curiosity, don't you?"

"Or maybe duty," Catherine said, thinking of her own reason.

"Yes, definitely that. At least for those of us who worked for him," Tyler admitted.

"Olga tells me she's leaving," Catherine blurted out the thought uppermost on her mind.

"Yes," Tyler answered as he stared hard at Olga, while she looked around the room and refused to meet his eyes.

"Excuse me," Olga said, "There is Alicia. I want a word with her." She left them to hurry out to the terrace where Alicia stood by the steps with Tom.

Tyler's eyes followed her, an inscrutable look on his face. He seemed to have forgotten Catherine. She felt awkward. It was obvious she'd brought up a touchy subject. As the silence stretched on, she searched for a topic to smooth things over.

"Who do you suppose will take Chatterton's place on the Board of Trustees?"

"There's some speculation Mrs. Chatterton will want to fill his position," Tyler said.

"Mrs. Chatterton! I wasn't aware she had any interest in the gardens."

"It was just something several of the board members suggested. As far as I know, she hasn't been asked yet."

"Where did you work before you came here?" Catherine hoped she wasn't being presumptuous in asking him.

For a while he didn't answer. "I was a professor of botany at Cuyahoga Valley Eastern College and a research botanist there." He paused for such a long time as he played with a spoon that Catherine thought he'd say no more about it. Finally he sighed and looked up at her. "I was working on research for a new herbicide being touted by its backers as better and safer than anything on the market today. It was said to be ecologically sound. Completely harmless to any living thing except the plants targeted with a rapid breakdown in composition."

"And was it?"

"No. There was strong evidence the residuals of this herbicide lasted quite a long time, and it was carcinogenic."

"What happened?"

He looked at her with a twisted smile. "I didn't have tenure and my contract wasn't renewed with the college. I was relieved of my duties in the lab and all my work was kept."

"But that can't happen!" She was indignant about the unfairness of it.

"It can and does sometimes when there's a lot of money invested in a new product and when the investor is not overly scrupulous."

"But who?" She was shocked and angry for him.

"You want a name or a company?"

She shrugged.

"Chatterton."

Her mouth fell open. "But . . . but you were working for him here. I don't understand."

His face was sad. "Since I started this, I guess I'd better tell you my story." He stared into space for a moment as if searching for words and then began slowly.

"I loved my job. I loved working with the students, especially those students who had enthusiasm for the field. I imagine you were that kind of student." His lips twisted up briefly.

She smiled remembering her passion for botany that Professor Higgins had inspired.

"I also loved the lab work. The research. It was a challenge, and a mystery to be solved," he went on talking directly to her.

She nodded, remembering the hours spent in lab work in college, the thrill of identifying microbes under a microscope. For a while she'd considered a career in some sort of research.

Tyler looked down and started playing with the silverware arranging and rearranging it into different patterns, before taking a deep breath and continuing. "After months of searching for a new position, I gave up. Every promising lead ended when my references were checked."

Catherine shook her head in commiseration, but could find no adequate comment to make. It all seemed so unfair. It didn't seem to matter to Tyler whether she responded or not. She got the feeling he'd not been able to talk about it before and needed to release what had been dammed up for so long.

"When my savings were used up, I moved in with my father." Again he paused for a long while.

"How did you find out it was Chatterton behind all this?" Catherine asked.

"There were little clues pointing to it. I couldn't be completely sure, but I never really doubted it."

"Then how could you work for him?"

"I couldn't find a job anywhere in my field, and I couldn't stay a burden for my father. He's elderly and his income and savings aren't much. When Chatterton contacted me, at first I felt an incredible rage, but I was also curious. We met in his office here at Chatterton Manor. I knew he was the one who'd blackballed me in my profession. I wanted to have it out with him. To tell him I knew. When he offered me the job, I was so furious, I could've killed him right then." He stopped, lost in memory.

"And?" Catherine finally prodded.

He gave her an intent look. "I decided two could play the game. I came with the intent of finding out all I could to stop him. It would've been better, of course, if I could've been hired by Greener Safer Earth, his company making the product, but my goal was to bring Chatterton down in some way and stop that product from being released on the market."

"Some kind of revenge." Catherine nodded. "I don't blame you."

"Yes, but the strange thing is even though I detested Chatterton, I felt no real sense of satisfaction in his death," he admitted. "It's as if healing had already begun by just working for Elmwood Gardens. But I still need to stop the herbicide from being marketed. I've been busy at that through the EPA and other environmental groups, and I am making headway."

Catherine almost asked him if he'd killed Chatterton, but lacked the nerve, not from fear but because she didn't want to break this beginning thread of friendship. Also, she wasn't sure she'd blame him if he had killed Chatterton. The thought unsettled her. She wondered at it and felt a little guilty.

"Did you think I wasn't coming back?" Greg Robert plopped a plate of assorted cookies on the table and carefully set a cup of coffee in front on her. He pulled up the chair Olga had vacated earlier.

Catherine smiled and looked the plate over sticking the tip of her tongue out in anticipation. "I figured you were waylaid by someone or couldn't figure out what cookies to pick," she answered him. "This looks good." She picked up a fancy cookie, rich with chocolate and nuts.

"Yes, I was. Waylaid, that is." Greg Robert was grinning, his eyes twinkling.

234

"What?" Her curiosity was aroused by his manner.

"Oh, someone wanted to know if I'd marry them."

"Someone proposed to you?" Incredulous, her mouth dropped open.

"No, no," he said then cocked his head. "Wait a minute. Am I so undesirable no one would consider that?" he teased.

"No, I didn't mean it that way. I just . . ." she broke off not knowing how to end it.

Tyler smiled at the two of them as Greg Robert went on. "No. Someone wanted to know if I could perform a marriage."

"Can you?" Catherine asked.

He didn't answer her directly. "I told them they should seek counseling and see their own parish priest."

"Who was it?" Tyler asked, a thoughtful look on his face

"I'll let the young folks announce their engagement themselves when they're ready," Greg Robert replied.

Catherine felt someone watching her and looked up to see John standing by the door leading to the front of the Manor House. He was trying to get her attention. Excusing herself, she went to him.

"My cell phone is dead. I guess the battery needs recharged. I didn't come in a patrol car. Where's a phone I can use in private?"

"Come with me." She led him into the main hall, past the museum rooms, and up the wide front stairs. Most of the upstairs bedrooms were part of the museum, open for display, but several were offices. "I'd let you use mine, but I forgot it," she said over her shoulder. It happened all too often with her.

"This should be unlocked." It was. "Do you want me to leave?"

He shook his head and dialed the station number.

"John here. You called." He listened for a moment.

"Okay. What's that number?" He dialed again.

"John MacDougal here." He picked up a pencil and scribbled on a tablet laying there.

"That was fast." He stared out the window as he listened. "You're sure?"

Catherine watched his face trying to read what was being discussed.

He shook his head. "Doesn't look good, does it."

"Thanks for rushing it through."

John replaced the receiver and sat in thought for a moment. "Alma was poisoned," he said looking at her.

She plopped down on a chair. "Poisoned," she breathed out. "So our bad feelings yesterday were more than an overactive imagination?"

"Yes. It was arsenic in the lemon meringue pie."

"Where would someone get that?"

"Dr. Jones said it's an active ingredient in a particularly strong ant poison."

"Wouldn't she taste it?"

"He said a combination of the lemon and the fact that the elderly have a decreased sense of taste would make it relatively easy to administer it that way."

Catherine shuddered. "Were the two murders connected, do you think?"

"I think so. But how? There has to be something Alma knew. By the way. I talked to the BCI a while ago. An old college chum of mine works in the lab. There were two different kinds of white cat hairs on the robe, and one wasn't from Greg Robert's cat. Different texture and length. Said he'd run a DNA test to make sure, but he was pretty sure just from studying it under the microscope."

"I knew it couldn't be Greg Robert," Catherine said.

"Doesn't totally rule him out." Come on." He started for the door, "I want to go back to Alma's house."

As they turned to leave, they heard a door close and looked at each other, then hurried into the hall. All the doors, except for the rooms on display, were closed. In a moment they heard the beginnings of a Beethoven Sonata from the third floor apartment as Tyler began to play softly. From behind a door nearby, they heard water running.

"Where does that door lead to?" John whispered motioning to a door further down.

"It leads to the kitchens. It was a servants' entrance. Wait. I want to use the bathroom up here," she said, curious to see who was in there.

"I'm going down the back steps. I'll meet you at my car." He left as Catherine waited.

Soon the bathroom door opened, and Violet came out. "Hi," she said with a smile. "You caught me. I hate to use the public restrooms downstairs. I always sneak up here to use this one when I'm working. Guess you do the same thing, huh?"

Catherine half smiled, nodded and went in closing the door behind her. Had Violet been eavesdropping? She certainly wouldn't put it past her. Or had Tyler been listening outside the door? Or someone else?

Chapter Twenty-Six

John stood by his car waiting. "Did anyone go through the kitchen?" she asked as she came up to him.

He nodded. "Yes, but no one could say who it was. One of the kitchen help saw someone out of the corner of her eye, but didn't pay much attention. She kind of thought it was a man. I didn't see anyone when I came out. Did you see who was in the bathroom?"

"It was Violet Flavian."

"Would she be the kind to eavesdrop?"

Catherine rolled her eyes. "Would she ever! She's one of the nosiest people I know."

John smiled at her then glanced over her head. "It seems Mr. Burns is interested in our conversation, too. He's watching from his window."

Catherine resisted the urge to turn her head and simply shrugged although she found it a little disquieting.

"I want to go back to Alma's house and look around some more. Would you go with me? You might notice something I'd miss."

"Let me take my truck home. You can pick me up there since it's on the way."

As Catherine drove down the drive, she glanced into the topiary garden and was surprised to see Alicia and Tom embracing. She'd suspected something before, but now they seemed to be quite open about their feelings. She thought of Millie's comment about Chatterton firing Tom the morning of the reception and felt uneasy. Maybe she should tell John about it.

As she pulled out of Elmwood's parking lot, she glanced at her gas gage. Oops! She'd better stop at the Mini Mart before she got stranded.

After filling up, she went in to pay. She grabbed a loaf of bread and stood in line behind Alice Wetherby, owner of Alice's Antiques. Miss Wetherby slowly counted out all her change to pay for her bread and milk. Catherine was tempted to pay for it herself as the woman kept digging in her purse for more coins, but as impatient as she was, she didn't want to be rude.

"I know I've got some more change in here. Problem is I've got everything but the kitchen sink in here, too" Miss Wetherby said. "Ahh, here's a dime." She held it out to the patient clerk and went back to digging in her capacious purse. "I dropped in all the change Doris gave me when I bought stamps this morning. Here's another nickel. Not a wooden one, either," she chuckled. "Oh, here's a penny. I always say a penny saved is a penny earned."

"You hear from Brad?" a voice behind Catherine asked.

"Yeah. He called yesterday," another voice answered.

Catherine glanced up at a round security mirror overlooking the cash register area and saw two young men. Both had long hair. The blond one had hair pulled back into a pony tail, and had numerous earrings in one ear. The other one had long, curly, brown hair with a bandana controlling its unruliness, jeans with the knees out and a denim vest.

"Did he say where he was?" the blond asked.

"Nah. Said he had some thinkin' to do. Said it was probably better if he stayed away," answered Denim Vest.

"Does he know about his old man?" Blondie asked.

"Yeah, but he didn't want to rap about it." Denim Vest replied.

"Can't believe he ditched his wheels and all."

Catherine was listening so intently she was unaware Miss Wetherby had left, and the clerk was waiting for her to pay.

"Sorry," Catherine muttered. "Ten dollars on pump four and the bread."

"That'll be twelve nineteen."

Catherine paid and left, resisting the urge to start quizzing the boys. However, she did note the car and license plate number of the only unattended car at the pumps. Maybe it would be of some use to John.

He was pulling in as Catherine approached her place. She was relieved to see he hadn't been kept waiting. Never one to patiently wait herself, she assumed most people felt the same.

"I was worried you'd be waiting." She hurried up to his car. "I had to stop for gas."

"I stopped to get Ralph, and I never mind waiting. I usually have a book with me, or use the time to think."

She climbed in the front seat. "Hi, Ralph," she greeted the dog in the back. He grinned and thumped his tail.

"I've got to tell you what I overheard at the Mini Mart," she said as she fastened her seat belt. She blurted out the conversation verbatim as he pulled out onto the road and headed toward Alma's. "And I got their license number and make of car," she ended with a triumphant flourish as she produced the slip of paper.

"Good for you!" He gave her a pleased smile. "I'll check this out later. Interesting. I've been wondering if the Chatterton kid had met with foul play. Sounds like maybe not, if they're talking about him and not someone else."

"How many kids would ditch their cars around here, especially a nice one like they implied it was?"

240

"You've got a point."

Ralph started whining as they turned down the road leading to Alma's house. He leaned forward, his ears alert.

"Poor fellow," John said. "He's been good, but sad. I can tell he misses Alma."

"How old do you think he is?"

"I think Alma got him about six years ago. He was probably close to a year old. A stray. He showed up in town and started hanging around, and always seemed to disappear when the dog warden showed up. Then he started following Alma. From then on they were inseparable."

As they got closer to the house, Ralph paced anxiously back and forth on the back seat. His whining became continuous, interspersed with excited little yelps.

As soon as John stopped and opened his door, Ralph leaped over the seat and raced to the front of the house and then around back, his nose to the ground searching.

John and Catherine followed him. "I had the house padlocked. We'd better use the back door. The porch is a little safer," John said as he searched through his keys.

When they came around the house, they stopped in dismay. The window of the back door was completely smashed out, and an old chair was placed under it. Ralph had already leaped through the broken window and was searching the house.

"I probably should've had the windows boarded up. I never thought about that."

"Kids, you think?"

"Could be, but I doubt it. No one's ever bothered her to my knowledge, and who even knew she'd died?"

"Except the murderer," Catherine said.

"Yeah," John breathed out on a long sigh. "Let's go in. I'll unlock the door, though. We don't need to climb through the window. Try not to touch anything. We'll have to check for fingerprints, but I'll bet there won't be any except Alma's."

Together they went in and walked around looking. Nothing seemed to be disturbed in the kitchen, but in the main room almost all the garbage bags were emptied into a pile on the floor.

"Somebody was looking for something, and it looks like they found what they were looking for." John looked grim.

"How can you tell?"

"There are still a dozen or so bags not dumped so whatever it was the intruder wanted, when it was found they obviously left. Probably in a hurry in case someone came back."

"Yeah, I see what you mean," she said. "Unless . . ."

"Unless what?"

"Unless we disturbed whoever it was, and they took off."

"You've got a point. It's possible."

She shivered inwardly and was glad she wasn't alone. The house gave her the willies.

John glanced into the spare room. "It looks pretty much the same as yesterday.

Catherine looked around trying to see something that might be important, but the incredible mess, even worse than yesterday's horror, seemed overwhelming.

Ralph was nosing a brown rag near Alma's bed and whimpering. She walked over to check and almost gagged from the smell. Dried vomit caked a burlap sack. She started to turn away then something caught her eye. "John, come here," she called.

She pointed when he came. "That burlap sack seems to have white hairs, maybe cat hair on it. Ralph has no white hair on him. Did Alma have a cat?"

"Not that I know of." He thought for a while. "I think I'll have it checked. It could be the monk's robe was stored in the burlap sack or at least came from the same place."

Carefully he picked it up by one corner and put it in a black plastic garbage bag after he'd dumped its contents.

"You're making a bigger mess," Catherine chided.

He smiled slightly. "The empty ones have been touched by the intruder. Whoever it was probably wore gloves, but just in case, I don't want to touch anything that might have fingerprints on it."

Ralph accepted Alma was not in the house or the immediate vicinity, and he lay beside her bed, his nose on his paws with a sorrowful look on his face.

"Poor Ralph," Catherine said and squatted down to pet him. His tail thumped feebly, but he didn't raise his head.

"He's barely eating for me," John said looking down at the two of them.

"The window will have to be boarded up until I can get a crew in Monday to sift through everything. We'd better go. Come on, Ralph," John called.

For a moment it looked like he wouldn't obey, but then got up and followed them slowly. He stopped halfway to the car and looked back, before turning and following them, his head low. He climbed into the back seat and laid down, his nose on his paws again.

"It almost makes me want to cry," Catherine said as she felt her eyes prickling.

"I know. I've felt incredibly sad for him, too."

John called in an order for the window to be boarded up. "Sort of like locking the barn door after the horse has run off," he said. Heading back down the lane, they both sat in silence intent on their own thoughts.

As John pulled into Roses in Thyme's parking lot, his thoughts were on Catherine. Probably asking her to go with him tomorrow wasn't very professional, he thought, but he was worried about her, especially after what had happened last night. It seemed like she'd attracted the murderer's attention for some reason.

He turned to her. "Are you always open on Sundays?"

"I am until the end of August."

"Could you get someone to mind the shop tomorrow and go on a day trip with me?"

"I suppose so," she said slowly, thinking of who she'd ask. Maggie and Christy each watched it for a half day today. She hated to ask them for tomorrow, too. Maybe Violet? She usually didn't want to do Sundays.

"Where would we be going?"

"Saint Boniface's Monastery. It's about three hours from here."

Her eyes widened. "Is that where Greg Robert was?"

He nodded watching her.

"You still think he may be guilty?" She searched his face for some clue to his thoughts.

"Not necessarily, but I'd feel better if I knew a more about him, his background, who he is. The key to his guilt or innocence may lie there."

"I'll call you later if I'm able to find someone," she said as she got out. She knew Greg Robert couldn't be guilty, and felt a little guilty about being a party in checking him out, but truth to tell, she was curious about him, too.

"Look how quiet he's sleeping in the box. He looks so pretty against the white satin. Poor baby. You're so cold," she said as she leaned over the baby and tugged the white blanket up closer to his chin.

The soft pink torchiere helped cover up the gray pallor of the still baby. People filed by offering words of sympathy she didn't hear.

> *And if that diamond ring*
> *Turns brass,*
> *Papa's gonna buy*
> *You a lookin' glass.*

Chapter Twenty-Seven

Catherine took the old, plaid, flannel shirt down from the line and sniffed it. She loved the smell of clothes hung out to dry in the sun. They had a fresh sweet aroma better than anything that could be added to a dryer. She folded it neatly to return it with her thanks.

On her way to Ed and Violet's house, she honked and waved at Maggie mowing her lawn. Not for her a riding mower even though she had a sizable lawn. Maggie claimed it was good exercise pushing a mower.

She pulled into the Flavians' driveway and went up the neat sidewalk edged with purple, lavender and white petunias. As she waited for Violet to answer the doorbell, she looked out over the neighborhood. Christy's little sister, two houses down, was riding her pink bicycle up and down a cement driveway while Christy's white cat lay on the front stoop watching the child, its eyes half closed. Further down the street, Catherine saw a stout middle-aged man on a riding mower on his little bit of lawn. She grinned, thinking of Maggie.

Catherine was just about to go around to the back when she heard the inside door open. She turned and was surprised to see Ed. She smiled. "I brought your shirt back. Where's Violet? I thought she was the official greeter in this house," she teased.

"She's not feeling well. Come on in."

"Oh, I don't want to bother you if Violet's sick."

"No bother," he mumbled as he turned to go back through the house. "She won't hear us. We'll take some iced tea out back."

Catherine followed him through the quiet house and into the kitchen. She laid his shirt on a chair and put her purse and keys on top of it.

"Sugar? Lemon?" he asked as he took a large pitcher of iced tea from the refrigerator.

"A little lemon, please."

He poured two tall glasses, added a slice of lemon to each and put the pitcher back. "We'll go out back. Too nice to stay inside."

"It certainly is." She felt uneasy. Ed seemed strange this evening. There was no twinkle in his eye, no hint of a smile. She felt like she was intruding even though he'd asked her in.

They went out to the picnic table under a large sugar maple.

"Hear it was a pretty fancy funeral luncheon," he said.

"It was that. There were a lot of people there, too."

Ed was silent staring into space. She couldn't tell if he was thinking about the funeral or had only mentioned it to make conversation. She looked around the garden, so lovely, so neat.

"Your garden is so perfect," she said feeling a little envy.

"Should be. I don't have much else to do with my time." He stared at his garden with no look of pleasure on his face.

Catherine didn't know what to say so she changed the subject. "Look at that clematis growing up your shed. That is truly magnificent. Is it Nelly Moser?"

"Yep."

She got up to examine it closer and then wandered to his rose bed stopping to examine and smell each one. "I like the raised beds for your roses. It certainly helps the drainage."

"Violet says they remind her of graves."

"Oh, I don't think so. Or at least I never would've thought of that. Here's the rose I noticed the other day. In this light, the buds almost look as blue as Chatterton's. Not when they're opened, though." She stood looking at it and a sudden realization filled her. She turned to Ed wide eyed. "The Chatterton Rose!"

Ed looked at her, but didn't speak.

"It was your rose. You propagated it." She stared at him in bewilderment.

He turned away and walked through his gardens. She followed. "Why, Ed? Why did you let him steal it?"

He turned on her, anger and misery in his face. "Drop it, Missy," he said curtly. "I want nothing more said about it, now or ever."

"Okay," she said, and then not knowing what else to say she said, "I'd better go now. I was gone all day so I have lots to do yet before dark." She was babbling now in her nervousness.

He nodded, went to his lawn swing, and sat down and stared at his garden, ignoring her.

She took her glass inside, picked up her purse from the kitchen chair and started toward the living room. There was no sound except the soft whirring of the overhead kitchen fan and a ticking clock.

On a sudden impulse, Catherine tiptoed down the thick, lavender, plush carpet of the hall leading to the bedrooms. The door to Violet's bedroom was closed. Softly Catherine turned the handle and peeked in. The shades had been drawn and the room was in semi-darkness. She could see Violet lying on her bed on top of the covers. Catherine saw she was still in the clothes she had worn today.

"Violet?" she inquired in a low voice. There was no movement. Heart beating rapidly, she crept closer. "Violet?" she said again. When there was still no answer,

Catherine reached out and touched Violet's arm. It was warm and slightly clammy. She stared at Violet's chest and detected a slow steady rise and fall.

Suddenly she was aware of someone behind her and turned around. Ed's eyes bored into hers. "I think you'd better go."

Flustered and feeling guilty, she stammered, "I wanted to see if I could do anything for Violet."

"You can't. She's taken a sleeping pill and will sleep until tomorrow."

Catherine turned and hurried out. "Good-bye," she said over her shoulder as she went out the door. Ed didn't answer and closed the door firmly behind her.

When she got home, the light on her answering machine was blinking. She punched the play back button and listened as John's voice came into the room loud and clear.

"Got your message that you couldn't find anyone for tomorrow. It's all taken care of. My mom said she'd be delighted. She means it, too. She's the gardener in the family and is excited about doing this. She'll be there around eight o'clock to go over the ropes with you. Said she'd take her pay in perennials. After you've filled her in, come to my place, and we'll leave from here. See you tomorrow."

Catherine clicked off the machine. She wanted to talk to him about Ed and Violet, but decided to wait until she saw him. Just the sound of his voice on the answering machine reassured and calmed her. As she locked up the house, she found herself eagerly looking forward to tomorrow. It'd been such a long time since she'd gone anywhere further than the immediate vicinity of Portage Falls. She went upstairs to look through her wardrobe. Just what should I wear to visit a monastery? She wondered.

Chapter Twenty-eight

Strolling through his garden before nine o'clock mass, Father O'Shawnessy waved at Catherine as she parked her truck next to John's car and got out. She waved back, feeling a little guilty about missing Mass. She stopped to admire the pink roses blanketing the stone fence between Carriage House Books and Our Lady of the Roses Cemetery before climbing the outside steps leading to the apartment over the bookstore.

John opened the door before she knocked.

"Hi," he said smiling. "Did you get my mom all clued in?"

"Yes. The shop doesn't open until ten today, but she said she'd use the time to get familiar with the place. I like your mom. She's so pleasant and didn't make me feel like I was imposing."

John looked pleased. "That's my little Italian mama."

"Italian?"

"Martha Maria Maggiano MacDougal. Come in for a moment. I want to tell Josh I'm leaving. He's getting ready for work."

Josh, hearing voices, came out before John could get him.

"Hi." He looked at Catherine with curiosity.

"Hi," Catherine smiled. "I've seen you around the gardens."

"Yeah, I've seen you, too."

"Do you like the work?"

He shrugged. "Yeah, kind of. It's a good summer job,

and the people are nice."

"We're going now, Josh. Grandma's watching Ms. Jewel's shop if you need her for anything. We probably won't be back until six o'clock or so," John interrupted.

"See ya," Josh said as John held the door for Catherine. "Have fun," he called after them as they went down the steps.

"I told you, it's police business," John called back over his shoulder.

"Yeah, I know," Josh answered through the screen door. They didn't turn around to see the ear-splitting grin on his freckled face.

As they drove out of town on this perfect June morning, Catherine breathed a sigh of contentment.

"What's that all about?" John glanced at her with a smile.

"I haven't been away for so long, so business or not, I'm really looking forward to this."

John's smile widened. "Me, too."

They rode along for some miles in mutual contentment talking about inconsequential things. It wasn't until they got on the interstate that she thought of her visit with Ed.

"Oh, my goodness! I forgot!"

John glanced at her.

"I visited Ed and Violet last night, and it was disturbing."

"What happened?"

Catherine told him what had happened. "Do you think we should check on Violet?"

"We can't without a better reason than that. Do you really feel he's harmed her?"

"I don't know. I wouldn't think so, but it seemed so weird. He acted so strange. And I forgot to tell you about the roses."

"Roses?"

"Yes, blue roses. You know that was the whole deal

251

about Chatterton's big reception."

John nodded.

"Well, I'd noticed some roses at Ed's last week that seemed to have the faintest blush of blue. Last night a few of the buds had a definite tint of blue, and then it dawned on me. Of course," she said, stopping for a moment.

"Yes?" John glanced at her.

"The Chatterton Rose. It was really Ed's."

"Did you say anything to him?"

"Yes. Yes, I did."

"Did he admit it?"

"Not really, but he didn't deny it, either. Just sort of told me to butt out of what didn't concern me."

John let out a slow whistle. "So you think Chatterton stole the rose Ed had developed?"

"It looks that way. It certainly makes more sense that Ed, a master gardener, had propagated the rose rather than Chatterton, who was a rather indifferent gardener, I'd say."

"If that's true, and I agree with you it sounds plausible, why would Ed let it go?"

Catherine shook her head. "It doesn't make sense."

"If he got it patented, would he have made a lot of money?"

"Oh, I'd imagine, plus a lot of fame in the horticultural world. But I can't figure out why he'd let Chatterton take credit for his rose."

"I can think of two reasons why. A large amount of money or some kind of pressure. Blackmail, if you will," he said.

"I don't think a lot of money means much to Ed, and whatever could Chatterton know that he could use to blackmail Ed?"

"What about Violet?"

"She'd probably like the money, but why wait until Chatterton already had it? I can't see anyone blackmailing her, can you?"

John shook his head. "I can't imagine where she'd put anything else in that house if she did have more money for a spending spree. Getting back to the rose. Ed and Homer Mansfield, the former director, left about the same time. Ed was let go, but in spite of his grumbling, he didn't seem to fight it."

"No. He didn't to my knowledge," Catherine said.

"We checked Mr. Mansfield. He didn't have much to say about it. Claimed he wanted to retire to the south, but there was a sizable amount of money deposited to his account. Much more than the severance or retirement pay for him entered into Elmwood's books."

"So Chatterton wanted to get rid of anyone who knew the rose wasn't his?"

"It looks that way," John said. "It looks like he paid off Mansfield, but fired Ed. What kept Ed from saying anything?"

"Do you think he's paying Ed something?"

"Could be. That would rule him out as a suspect if he is. Any money being paid would stop with Chatterton's death. Do you think Violet knew about the rose?"

"I don't know. Somehow I think not. She still works at The Wisteria Tea Room and has no interest in gardening. I don't think Ed and her talk much, to tell you the truth."

"Where were the roses raised?"

"I don't know. They were brought in last month from a private garden somewhere."

"When we get back, I'll check it out and check the Flavians' background, too. They've been in town for as long as I can remember, and I've never heard anything against them."

"Maybe Chatterton threatened to fight dirty like he did with Tyler Birchfield, and Ed didn't want to go through all that." Catherine surmised.

"What about Birchfield?" John glanced quickly at her.

"Oh, I don't know. I shouldn't tell you what was told

in confidence. It's not right."

"Catherine," John said through his teeth, "We're not talking idle gossip here. If you know something that might help me, spill it."

"Chatterton was responsible for Tyler losing his last job and his not getting another one for a really long time," she blurted out all in one breath.

John stared at her, wide eyed, his mouth open.

"Watch out!" Catherine said alarmed.

He turned back to the road and righted his car that'd been drifting off the highway.

"Okay, okay." he said dragging the words out, and to do him credit, with only a little bit of sarcasm, "Would you fill me in with a few more details, please?"

She told him Tyler's story, feeling guilty about her betrayal of a confidence.

He let out another low whistle. "That certainly gives him a good motive and with no more of an alibi than Ed."

"Why wouldn't he have killed him sooner or in a less obvious manner? You know, some night or something. At least in a more isolated spot."

"Poetic justice? At the moment of his glory? Ill-gotten glory, true, but to Chatterton, from what I've heard, how he got it wouldn't matter to him."

"That reminds me," she said, "it's kind of strange, but the leaves of the blue roses were looking a little yellow the other day. Kind of wilted, in fact. I was going to mention it to Greg Robert and check them again, but with all that's been going on, I forgot. If we get back in time, I should run over and look."

They rode on in silence for a while with the interstate mesmerizing them with its monotony, and each of them digesting the possibilities that had arisen. Finally, John broke the silence. "Did you have breakfast?"

"A bagel about six-thirty."

"We're about an hour away yet. Let's stop for coffee

and something to eat. I didn't eat much, either."

They pulled off the interstate and into a Bob Evans. Coffee sounded good to her, and when she smelled the food, she realized she was, in fact, quite hungry.

"I want everything," she said as she scanned the menu, but settled for corn meal mush and sausages. It was something she rarely fixed for herself. John ordered French toast and bacon.

As if in mutual agreement, they dropped all talk about the Chatterton murder for the time being.

"So tell me. You know I'm a half breed, Irish Italian. What about you?"

Catherine laughed. "I'm a mutt like Ralph, a mixture of Polish, Slovak, Scotch-Irish, English and Welsh."

"They always say mutts are better than pure breeds," John grinned.

She smiled. "You're not married, are you?" Catherine asked though she knew he wasn't.

"Nope. Josh and I bach it."

"What happened to your wife?" She wasn't sure about asking such a personal question.

John didn't seem to mind. "She didn't like small town life, so she left Josh and me for the bright lights of New York City."

"How long ago?"

"When Josh was two. It's been fourteen years now."

"Only two!" She couldn't imagine a mother leaving her child. "Does she ever see him?"

"Oh, at first she'd come back to see him once in a while. She couldn't keep him there. She's an actress and works odd hours. Because he was so young and her visits so infrequent, he always looked at her as a stranger and didn't want much to do with her. Mothering isn't her bag."

"How sad." Compassion showed on her face.

"Not for us." He sounded defensive. "We're doing just fine. Josh is a neat kid, and any mothering he needed growing up, he got from his grandmother."

"I meant for her. She's missed out on so much."

"Yes, she has, but it was her choice. We'd better get back on the road," he said, effectively cutting off any more conversation about his ex-wife.

As they were pulling out onto the interstate, he asked, "What about you? Have you ever been married?"

Catherine stared straight ahead, nodded and said, "Yes."

He glanced at her. When she didn't say anymore, he prodded. "And?"

"David and my daughter, Ellie, both died ten years ago."

Damn! John thought. No wonder there's so often a shadow in her eyes, eyes that should be laughing with those laugh lines she has. "What happened?"

She stared straight ahead, then swallowed and said so low he had to strain to hear her, "A storm came up suddenly. David was bringing Ellie home from a softball game, and they went off the road into the river. They both drowned." She was afraid to look at him as she fought tears. Maggie was the only other person in Portage Falls who knew her story.

John felt a lump rise in his throat. He glanced at her profile again and reached over to squeeze the hands she was twisting in her lap. "That must have been hell for you."

Her lips trembled, and she tried to smile. "I'm okay. Really, I am. It's just hard when I tell people who don't already know. It comes back fresh all over again." She didn't tell him of her visitation from them the other night, how the near drowning caused her to relive that terrible night. It wasn't something she wanted to share. Maybe he'd think she was a little mental.

They rode in silence for a while. Catherine tried to regain her composure and bring the outing back to the light hearted trip it'd been. John, full of sympathy and curiosity, was hesitant about asking any more questions.

They passed an old station wagon with hundreds of bumper stickers covering every available spot. An old man clutched the wheel creeping along at forty miles an hour. The inside was piled high with junk, and a big hound dog sat on the front seat watching the world go by.

Catherine chuckled. "He's sure making a statement, isn't he?"

John laughed in relief as well as humor. He found it hard to deal with the grief of others; to know what to say.

"Oh," Catherine suddenly remembered. "Did you know Olga Yamikoff turned in her resignation?"

"You are full of information. No, I didn't know it."

"She said her mission was accomplished."

He smiled. "And you think that mission may be the murder of Chatterton."

"Well, I don't know. Maybe," she said flustered. "Violet thought she was a mistress or ex-mistress of Chatterton's."

"Ex-wife, and her mission was to tell Alicia she was her mother."

"What!?"

"Yes, she was Chatterton's first wife and gave their baby to Chatterton to raise."

"How could she?" Catherine forgot for a moment John's wife had done the same thing. Olga seemed different than what she imagined John's wife was like.

"She was a young girl, a dancer from Russia, who'd defected. She was unaware of her rights and intimidated by Chatterton. As we're finding out, he was quite ruthless in his methods of getting what he wanted."

"How did Alicia feel about it?"

"According to Olga, happy. She'd never felt loved by Vera."

"Yeah, I can believe that. She does seem a cold fish," she said. "I wonder how Vera Chatterton felt about an ex-wife showing up?"

"I'm not sure she cared that much. A cleaning woman, who worked for the Chattertons until last fall, thought there was something going on between Vera and Edwin Silvernail. She wouldn't be clearer about it, and I didn't press her."

"Violet thought so, too. She's quick to pick up on things like that."

"Gives her a motive, too, doesn't it?"

"Could a woman have committed the murder?" She wondered.

"The tines on that garden fork were as sharp as stilettos."

She shuddered. "I thought women stuck to poison or guns."

He smiled. "You read too many mysteries. Actually, you're right, but nothing is an absolute in murder. 'Lizzie Borden took an ax, gave her mother forty whacks.'"

"A lot of people think she got a bum rap. Then what about Alicia?"

"What about her?"

"Well, I imagine she was really upset when she found out what her father had done."

"I don't know. I'm sure she was, and it's probably why she quit working for him. But murder? Somehow I doubt it. She seemed upset about her father's death. I'm not sure she's that good an actress."

"What about her boyfriend?" Catherine asked.

"Boyfriend?" He thought of Tony.

"Tom Rockwell. He works at the gardens. Millie heard Chatterton fire him that morning, but he showed up the next day as if nothing had happened."

"Catherine! What else are you keeping from me?"

"It's not that I'm keeping things from you. I tell you as I think of them."

John shook his head. "Maybe I ought to put you on the

258

payroll. You've given me more leads this morning than I've turned up in the last four days. Okay, tell me more about this Tom and Alicia thing."

"Well, I've noticed looks and things, but it's been much more obvious in the last few days. Millie just told me Friday morning, and said he's a nice boy. His family goes to her church. He always seemed nice to me, too."

John's lips twitched. "Another suspect you like." He thought about it for a while. "Family's always the first to be suspected. There's still the kid, Bradley."

"Did you find anything more about him?"

He shook his head. "I talked to the kid you overheard. He said Bradley needed to get away to think for a while. Claims he didn't know where he was, but said he'd have him get in touch with me if he heard from him."

They drove on in silence, until John pushed play on the CD player. Simon and Garfunkel's voices singing "Scarborough Fair" filled the car. Catherine smiled at John and joined in with "*Parsley, sage, rosemary and thyme. Remember me to one who lives there, he once was a true love of mine.*"

John glanced over at her and bit his lip trying not to laugh at her slightly out of tune rendition of the song.

"We're almost there," he said as he took an exit without the usual clutter of restaurants and gas stations - nothing but fields and a sign pointing to Bigley one way and Wolf's Glen the other.

Catherine started to feel uncomfortable about the upcoming visit. What if they learned something about Greg Robert that changed her good opinion of him? Even if they didn't, and she was pretty sure they wouldn't, it still could change their friendship if he discovered she was part of checking up on his background.

259

Chapter Twenty-nine

They drove through rolling farmland then crossed a small river, and turned right onto a gravel road. Forests pressed in on both sides making it seem a single lane as it twisted and turned ever climbing until they finally came out of the forest on top of a hill. Straight ahead stood a walled mansion made of massive stone blocks with large wings extending out on each side.

Catherine's eyes widened. "Look at the view! You can see for miles and miles from up here. Oh, and look at that building! It looks like a castle."

Radiating out from St. Boniface's Monastery were orchards, gardens and pastures with sheep and red and white cows grazing. From the south side of the building stretched an orchard enclosed by a low stone wall. She guessed there must be close to ten acres of pruned apple and peach trees. The view covered miles of rolling fields, woods and a meandering river to distant blue hills. Everywhere their eyes traveled, they saw neatly maintained grounds.

They pulled into a parking lot in front of the monastery. Large wooden doors stood wide open inviting them into a charming courtyard.

"Look at the carvings on that door!" Catherine's mouth hung open. "They're incredible!"

John's eyes roamed over the door. "You wouldn't find anything like that today. Few people could afford to hire a craftsman to do that these days."

"Oh," Catherine let out a long ecstatic sigh as she looked through the gates. "Look at the herb garden! Oh, I could die for a garden like that."

In the middle of the court yard a large herb garden was arranged in an old English knot design. Roses of every color lined the stone walls.

"Fig trees, too! Usually they don't do well this far north. It must be because they're sheltered here."

John smiled at her enthusiasm, but understood it. He was impressed, too.

Catherine's eyes lingered on every aspect of the garden as they went to the front door. In keeping with the nature of the house, the door was heavy, darkly stained oak with large black hinges and a gothic style door handle. John rang the bell. Far within a deep tone sounded. Soon a tall thin monk in a rough brown habit opened the door. His jowls sagged, and melancholy brown eyes sunk in folds of skin gave him a hound dog look.

"We're here to see Brother Jude" John said. "He's expecting us."

The monk nodded and with only a slight movement of his mouth that might've been a smile, said "Follow me."

They followed his Nike Swoosh as he led them down a dark passageway, his tennis shoes moved without sound on the stone floors. In thin wall alcoves, candles in sconces were lit even in the daytime to alleviate some of the gloom. Coming to an open door, he motioned them into a small room. "Please wait here," he told them then left.

John and Catherine perched on the edges of straight backed, plain, wooden chairs. Two narrow windows held leaded mullioned glass set into the thick stone walls. Except for the chairs they sat on, a crucifix on a wall, an oak table and a lamp, the room was bare of furnishings.

"Mission furniture," Catherine whispered.

John looked at her raising his eyebrows.

"The furniture in here. It's mission style."

"Oh." He shrugged.

In a few moments the monk reappeared. "The abbot will see you." He turned and went back down the hall without checking to see if they followed.

John and Catherine leaped up and hurried out to see him gliding swiftly down the hall. They followed as fast as they could without running. Catherine was glad she'd worn sandals with her taupe skirt and white blouse instead of heels.

He stopped outside another heavy oak door and nodded towards it. John glanced at him then knocked on the door.

"Come in," a deep voice boomed out.

John opened the door and ushered Catherine in before him. Standing there with a wide smile of welcome was a short, rotund, elderly monk with dark hair showing very little gray. His blue eyes sparkled. He, too, was dressed in the order's brown habit.

"Welcome." His voice was much larger, fuller and deeper than his short size would suggest. "You must be Chief MacDougal, and this is?"

"Catherine Jewell," John said holding out his hand. Brother Jude shook it and then offered his hand to Catherine. She shook it surprised by his youthful manner and vigor.

"Sit down," Brother Jude said. The wooden chairs in his office were more intricately carved and had red velvet cushions. His desk was a long wooden table. All the stone walls were softened by bookcases filled with books, their bindings faded with wear and age except for a row of Andrew Greeley paperbacks.

"I'm not sure I can help you anymore than I could over the phone."

"My problem is I have too many suspects. I'm trying to eliminate some," John admitted.

"I would think you could eliminate Brother Greg

262

Robert. He is not a violent man."

"The person who murdered Mr. Chatterton wore his monk's robe, and I understand he was connected with the death of a monk here."

"I thought I made it clear over the phone the death of Brother Giles was an accident." All traces of a smile left his face. "What did he say when you asked him about his robe?"

"He claims someone must have taken it from his cottage."

"Then you must accept that as the truth and look elsewhere."

"Tell me about him," John said.

Brother Jude sat back in his chair, put his fingers together to form a steeple and thought for a moment. "Brother Greg Robert started his life as an activist." His lips held a faint smile. "First as a campus activist and then an activist on the streets of New York City. Like many young men and women he thought if he fought hard enough, he could change the ways of the world. He fought against drugs, disease and homelessness. Eventually he burned out. It all seemed so hopeless. He came to us a little over fifteen years ago, depressed, questioning God, questioning himself. We took him in and put him to work in the gardens. In time, God and the gardens healed him, and he asked to become one of us. We all prayed with him and for him for many months to make sure this was really his calling. I became convinced it was, and I've never regretted my decision to accept him as one of us."

"Then why did he leave?" John asked.

"Through hard work, Saint Boniface's is self-supporting. Just barely, though, I might add. You may have noticed the orchards."

They both nodded.

"Beyond that we have an area where we grow grapes. We sell fruit. We grow all our own vegetables as well as keeping chickens, sheep and a few cows. We make wine and peach brandy to sell. Some of our brothers make simple furniture, bookcases, tables and such that are sold in nearby towns. And we also make and sell fruitcakes for Christmas."

He paused lost in thought while they waited. Finally, he went on. "Brother Greg Robert and Brother Giles were making fruit cakes one evening, and the brandy caught on fire. In only moments the fire spread in the kitchen. Brother Giles caught his habit on fire while trying to extinguish the flames. Brother Greg Robert dragged him out into the snow and was able to put it out, but Brother Giles had been badly burned over much of his body. Brother Greg Robert's hands were burned in the effort, too. After many weeks in the hospital and after much suffering, Brother Giles died. The kitchen and left wing were badly burned, too. Brother Greg Robert never forgave himself for what happened. That's why he left a place he loved, but he hasn't forgotten us. He sends money every month and sometimes a little note with it."

"But why?" Catherine's brows gathered together. "Why would he blame himself?"

Brother Jude looked at her, and his face showed the sadness he still felt. "Because the two of them had been helping themselves to the brandy as they made the fruit cakes, they were not as careful as they would've been if they'd saved all the brandy for the fruit cakes."

"Oh." She felt an immense sorrow for the tormented Greg Robert.

"Thank you, Brother Jude. I think all my questions have been answered," John said as he rose to his feet. "Thank you for your time."

"Will you stay for diurnum? It's almost noon so will you also break bread with us?"

John glanced at Catherine. She smiled, nodded and turned to Brother Jude. "We'd like that very much. Thank you."

He led them to a chapel with stained glass windows like precious jewels set into the gray stone walls. They sat in pews at the back and within moments a dozen monks filed in and took their places in front. Soon their voices echoed through the chapel in beautiful Gregorian chants, a noonday prayer to the Lord.

Catherine and John sat with mouths slightly opened, mesmerized and then disappointed when the monks ended their musical prayers and filed out as silently as they'd entered.

Brother Jude beckoned from the door. When they joined him, Catherine remained speechless deep in reflection.

"This way for lunch." He led them into a room with one very long trestle table and benches on each side. They were directed to sit at the end of one bench.

Lunch was the brothers' biggest meal of the day, Brother Jude informed them. Each place held a plain white crockery plate and a mug. A large pot of soup was at the end of the table, and one of the brothers ladled soup into white crockery bowls and passed them down each side of the table until everyone had a bowl of steaming hot vegetable soup. Then all bowed their heads in prayer led by Brother Jude's deep baritone voice. When grace was completed, crusty, sweet-smelling slices of bread piled high in baskets was passed, while jugs of milk and crocks of fresh butter were placed on the table within easy reach of everyone.

Lunch was a merry meal. The monks talked, laughed and enjoyed John and Catherine's company, asking them many questions and answering theirs freely.

After lunch, Brother Jude showed them about the grounds and answered more of their questions. As they drove away, he stood in the parking lot waving good-bye.

"What a wonderful place." Her smile felt like it would

split her face.

John smiled at her. "It almost makes me want to join them."

"They have everything there they need; a dairy, chickens, gardens. It's so self-contained."

"It's certainly impressive."

"I can't get over the building, either."

"Labor was cheap when it was built, and there weren't taxes at the time, so the industrialist, who originally built it, didn't pay nearly what it would cost to build a comparable building today," John said. "Also, he probably wasn't too scrupulous about how he raised his money. He paid his men low wages and built it at their expense."

"I'm glad the granddaughter who inherited it left it to the Brothers."

John nodded his head in agreement.

"One thing was accomplished," she said, "You can't possibly think Greg Robert is guilty, anymore."

"It doesn't look that way. I didn't want to believe it, either, but I felt it should be checked out. And it was a nice drive, wasn't it?" His eyes crinkled in a smile.

"It's been a wonderful day," she agreed smiling back at him.

Chapter Thirty

Dear Catherine,

Everything went well. I enjoyed myself thoroughly. Mrs. Muster couldn't make up her mind between The Pilgrim or Graham Thomas. I convinced her she should have both. I certainly couldn't help her make up her mind! Both are so lovely. Wish I had room for more roses. Mr. Darby, the old crank, came in complaining that a rose he bought last year died. Couldn't remember the name. I sent him away with a bug in his ear. You don't need customers like that!!

And now about my pay for having such fun. I see you have a few Digitalis x mentonensis tucked away in the back green house. Were you saving them for anyone? If not, I'd love a couple of them. Or if they're not available, there's a lovely little dianthus out there, too. I think it's called Kaleidoscope. Such choices!!

Call me anytime,
Love, Martha

Catherine smiled as she read the note, although she made a small face of alarm when she read the part about Mr. Darby, before shrugging. He must not be a regular customer since she couldn't place him. She was relieved John's mother had seemed to enjoy herself.

She went through the shop and out back, touching flowers lightly as she passed smiling and humming. It had been an enjoyable day and the pleasant feelings remained.

Turning on the hose, she started watering the ferns and hostas. As she worked her way down one side of the nursery and then back up the other, she mulled in her mind the visit to the monastery and their discussion of the murders. When the mosquitoes became too persistent, she gave up on the watering, locked the shop and escaped to the house.

"Lily! Kitty! Kitty! Come in now," she called before going in. The tabby cat came running and demanded to be let in as Catherine turned the key to open the door.

"Just a minute, Lily. Be patient." She flipped on the kitchen light. It wasn't quite dark yet, but it would be soon, and the inside was shadowed. She still didn't feel as safe as she had before the incident the other night.

After Lily was fed, she prepared a cup of tea and dug into her cookie tin for some cookies to go with it. They'd stopped for supper on the way home, but now that seemed hours ago.

Juggling the tea, a plate of cookies, and a mystery, she went into the living room and curled up in a corner of the couch. Pushing her hair off her face, she opened the book to the spot where she'd last stopped, prepared to spend a pleasant evening. Slipping out the birthday card from her mother she used as a book mark, she was reminded of Violet by the bouquet of violets on the front of the card. She probably should call and see how she was, she thought, but it was with reluctance she picked up the phone and dialed. Something was strange there, and it made her uneasy.

After the second ring, she heard Ed's gruff voice. "Ed here."

"I was just calling to see how Violet is." She felt uncomfortable speaking with him.

"She's fine." His voice was brusque.

"Could I talk to her?"

"She's not here right now. She's out walking."

Catherine hesitated a moment. "Okay. Tell her I called." She hung up, a frown on her face. "That's strange," she murmured. "I never knew Violet did any walking, and it's almost dark." It increased her feelings of apprehension. Something was wrong. She wondered if she should call John. Yesterday she'd have been reluctant to send out alarm bells over what could be nothing, but after today, she was more confident he'd listen to her uneasy feelings and seriously consider them.

She pulled the phone book out from under the couch, looked up his number and dialed it. The phone rang and rang before she hung up. His answering machine must be off. Maybe he's at the station, she thought. She was a little more reluctant to call him there, but before she lost her nerve, she dialed that number.

"Portage Falls Police," a voice answered.

"Is Chief MacDougal in?"

"No, I haven't seen him all day. He called in about three hours ago, though."

"This is Catherine Jewell. If he comes in will you have him call?"

"Will do," the voice said and hung up.

She chewed on her lip. Maybe he's over at his mom's or just went to the store. I'll try later if he doesn't call. She tried to read but found it hard to concentrate. Lily jumped up and settled down next to her and started to give herself a bath.

The ringing phone startled her. She grabbed it before it could ring again. "Hello?"

"Catherine, Ed said you called," Violet sounded out of breath.

"I called to see how you were feeling. I stopped last night, and Ed said you weren't well." She didn't mention she'd tiptoed into her room and found her in a deep stupor.

"Oh," Violet laughed, "just a headache. I'm fine now."

"Ed said you were out walking?"

"Yes. I thought it was about time I started exercising a little to take a few pounds off. It's cooler in the evening."

"Yes, it is. Well, I'm glad you're all right. I was a little worried about you." Catherine felt awkward now.

"Aren't you sweet to be concerned. I'm just fine. Never better," Violet reiterated. "If that's all you wanted, I'll let you go. Bye-bye," she said and hung up before Catherine had time to say good-bye.

"I guess I worried for nothing," Catherine said to Lily, who grooming done, was curled up next to her purring. But she still felt uneasy. Why did Violet all of a sudden start walking? Of course, people had to start things sometime. Maybe like she said, she'd put on a few extra pounds. She'd certainly eaten a lot of food at Wednesday's reception. She opened her book and started to read, but couldn't keep her mind on it. Instead she kept thinking of Ed and Violet. She still couldn't imagine Ed as a violent man, but he'd seemed so distant, so cold yesterday. She went over what she and John had discussed today. Those cat hairs on the burlap sack could be important. Two white cats. "Christy's white cat!" she exclaimed. It'd been locked in Ed's gardening shed. The burlap sack must've come from there, but why would it have the fur from Greg Robert's robe? "Unless," she said, "Greg Robert's robe was in the burlap sack."

Lily looked up and meowed. Catherine absently started stroking her as she continued thinking out loud. "Okay, let's say the robe was in the burlap bag in Ed's potting shed. Who put it there? It would have to be Ed or Violet." She shook her head. "Not Ed. No. He's been such a good and kind friend since I came to Portage Falls." Her mind pictured his smiling blue eyes and how he always called her Missy. He almost treats me like a daughter, she thought.

"Okay," she spoke out loud again. "Probably just about everybody at the gardens knew Greg Robert had been a monk. I doubt the Chatterton family did, though. None of them seemed interested in the gardens. I don't see Tyler or Olga doing this. Maybe Chatterton, but not Alma." She sat in silence for a while staring at the clock without seeing it. "The burlap sack and probably the robe, too, were most likely in Ed's potting shed," she muttered. "Since I don't want to think Ed could do such a thing, it sort of leaves Violet." Catherine scowled and ran her fingers through her hair. She hated to think it could be her. She always got along with Violet. After all, Violet helped out in her store, and could Violet have the strength to kill Chatterton, or the nerve?

Catherine stood up and went to the kitchen to make another cup of tea. While she waited for the water to boil, she thought. Ed's always wandering around at the gardens. He has a path from his place to the back of Elmwood. Could he have been the one to hit her when she went in the lake to get the robe out? Again Catherine shook her head. She still didn't want to think Ed would hurt her. Could it have been Violet? But why? It didn't make sense.

Her thoughts went to the robe again as she put a tea bag into the cup of boiling water. The people who saw the monk thought he was of average height or maybe a little taller. Ed was short, shorter than Violet. Of course, she thought, it would be a little hard to judge height from a distance especially with the cowl up. Catherine started to focus on Violet now. She could've gotten the robe anytime when she left the Wisteria Tea Room. It would've been a little risky, but it could be done. If it were Violet, where would she have hidden it until that day, or did she take it with her the day of the reception?

"Violet's big straw bag!" She said aloud. "That's how

she could've got it there and out. If she was the one," she added. She supposed it could be rolled up and fit down into the bag. She had an old beach bag somewhere, she thought. She could roll up her robe to see if it could be done.

"Okay, Lily." Catherine was excited now. "I've figured out how Violet could've gotten the robe out of Greg Robert's cottage and to the reception. Now when could she have set up the murder weapon and twine? That doesn't seem like something Violet would do. Ed? No. We're going to stick with Violet for now." She took a sip of the hot tea as she thought.

She's probably absorbed more gardening lore over the years than she talks about. She's certainly seen Ed out in his garden working with the fork. For all Catherine knew, she could've asked him questions pretending a sudden interest in his work and gardening. Catherine thought about that. It was possible she supposed. If it had to be one of them, she preferred to think it was Violet.

"And," she went on out loud now, "she could've gone over to the garden some night when Ed was gone or in his back room reading or even in bed. It's not very far to the gardens by Ed's path. Or could they have worked together?" She shook her head. "No, not Ed." She refused to consider him as the murderer.

Catherine picked up Lily and leaned back. "Now we have to get to Alma. That murder makes me feel much sadder. It was probably because Alma took the robe in the burlap sack out of the garbage can, don't you think, Lily?"

The cat purred. but didn't open her eyes even when she heard her name. "That would've been easier for Violet. I imagine there's arsenic in the potting shed." Catherine still refused to think of Ed.

And then there's my antique doll, she thought. Was it connected? Maybe. That still upset her and made her feel threatened. She looked at the dark windows uncovered by drapes. Black against the night. Was anyone watching her?

Her eyes went to the clock. Almost ten. She decided to call John to discuss her thoughts. Since he wasn't at the station or he would've called, he was probably home, she reasoned.

After only a few rings, the phone was picked up. "Yeah?" Josh answered.

"Josh, this is Catherine. Is your dad there?"

"No, isn't he with you? Duh! I guess not, or you wouldn't be calling, would you? I don't know where he is. His car's gone. I just got in fifteen minutes ago. You want him to call you?"

"Yes, please, if it's not too late."

"Okay. See ya," he said as he rang off.

She sat thinking, wondering where he was, but after a few moments she sighed and picked up the book again. Maybe he's with a friend having coffee or a beer. After all, I don't know him well enough to know if this is normal or not. Maybe he's a night owl and goes out a lot.

With that she settled into her book and tried to read, but between her thoughts of the murder and her day with John, she couldn't concentrate. At eleven o'clock, she stood up, stretched, yawned and then went around turning out lights before going to bed. I guess if he did come home, he decided it was too late to call, she reasoned feeling disappointed.

In the night she woke to thunder, lightning and heavy rain. She got up to check windows, closing the ones with rain coming in. When she crawled back into bed and pulled the covers up around her shoulders, she paused to think, as she always did in inclement weather, of the poor souls unprotected from severe weather and not blessed with a warm bed as she was, and said a little prayer for them.

She thought of John and with a sudden feeling of panic, she realized she was starting to care for him. No. She wouldn't allow it. Never again would she take a chance of caring for someone beyond friendship. That said, she turned over and punched her pillow before settling down to sleep, but it was a long time coming. In spite of her resolution, her thoughts kept going back to him. She tried to think of David, but John's face kept appearing instead.

Chapter Thirty-one

It'd been days since John had found time to read the Emerson biography. Stretched out in his recliner after a long day driving and now with his feet up and a cup of coffee beside him, he let out a small sigh of contentment. Books were good anytime, he thought, but they were like a delicious dessert when they came at the end of a full day. Josh was out somewhere so there was no sound of his music or the TV. Evening sounds filtered through the open window. Next door the Brogden's young granddaughters were under the spruce tree between their properties. He could hear the murmur of their voices without distinguishing the words. Birds in the Chinese elm outside the window discussed their day as they settled in.

His thoughts strayed from the written words to his day with Catherine, and his face relaxed into a smile as he thought of the pleasant trip and their conversations. It seemed hard to believe that less than a week ago he only knew her by sight. He wasn't ready yet to pursue thoughts beyond their beginning friendship, but even that much left him with a warm feeling.

He thought of the tragedy in her life and marveled at the courage she had to not only keep going, but also accomplish so much. His mom had the same kind of courage when she'd been widowed so young. He wondered if it would be harder to raise three kids alone like his mom, or to be left childless in addition to being widowed. He couldn't imagine either.

From Catherine his thoughts went to Greg Robert. He was relieved he was a suspect who could probably be eliminated. And now where did he go? In his mind he reviewed the remaining suspects. Unless it was someone other than those they'd discussed today. That was always possible, of course.

Picking up the notebook beside his chair, he turned to each suspect, jotting down the new information he'd learned today. The trouble was, he thought, there were too many suspects. And how did Alma tie in? He didn't know how, but he felt in some way she did. Two murders in this quiet little town in two days had to be more than a coincidence.

He wondered if she'd said anything to Father O'Shawnessy the last day she visited him. Maybe something Father Pat forgot. He sat up, slipped on his sneakers, and headed for the rectory taking the short cut over the wall and through the cemetery.

Father Pat greeted him with a warm smile. "Welcome. You're just in time to share a little blackberry wine and some rhubarb pie Mrs. Brozinski made for me."

"Lucky man," John grinned, "to have so many women catering to your needs."

Father Pat nodded. "Yes, I am fortunate. The women of this parish always see to my culinary needs." He patted his comfortable stomach.

"I want to ask you some questions about Alma."

"Come on in." Father Pat showed him into his study, a small cluttered room. He moved a pile of newspapers from a brown leather chair with a crack in the seat showing its stuffing to make room for him. John was no stranger to this study. Father Pat was a well-read scholar who loved discussing thoughts and philosophies on a wide range of topics, and John spent many an enjoyable evening with the elderly priest.

"Could you repeat everything Alma said that last day?"

"Hmmm," Father Pat said, pulling on his left ear. "Let's see." He thought for a while then told him what the general flow of the conversation had been and of the sadness of it.

"Did she tell of anything she'd seen, or anyone, or anything strange?"

"She was happy about some dog food she'd found. People put things out for her, you know."

"Yes, I know." John thought of the lemon pie. Had someone put that out just for her? "Anything else?"

"There was a chipped plate. And she was pleased about a perfectly good robe she found. Couldn't believe anyone would throw it out."

John mulled these items over in his mind. There'd been dog food at her house. One chipped plate looked pretty much like another. The robe. A niggling thought occurred. "Did she say what the robe looked like?" He leaned forward.

"No. Do you think it's important?"

John rubbed his bottom lip. "I don't know, but what if she was talking about a monk's habit?"

Father Pat stared at John. "And that would mean?"

He told him about a monk being seen at the gardens. Father Pat made no comment, but sat watching him, waiting. John smiled. "It was probably Greg Robert's habit, but it doesn't look like he was wearing it from what I've found out so far."

Father Pat relaxed and breathed a sigh. "Good. I like that young man."

"Did Alma say where she'd been that day?"

Father Pat thought for a while. "I think she said Main Street. She was on her way home."

"I know it was garbage day on Main Street. I saw a garbage truck on Raspberry Lane, too. In fact, I saw her

277

there. I forgot about that. I don't think she went up to houses to forage. I've never noticed her doing that. Of course, there are dumpsters in town. She checked those out regularly."

"If anyone wanted to get rid of something incriminating, I don't know if they'd come into town to do it. Unless it was someone who lived in town."

"True, but so far none of the suspects I have live in town. Well, thanks for your help, Father," John got to his feet.

"It's a terrible thing." Father Pat shook his head. "Portage Falls has its share of pettiness, dishonesty and prejudice, but it never seemed to harbor evil."

John agreed. As he walked back across the cemetery, he thought about the robe. It could be important. If it's an old chenille robe, then that's not why Alma was killed, but if she found Greg Robert's habit, then someone went to drastic lengths to get it back so Alma couldn't tell where she found it.

It was important to know if Alma found a night robe or Greg Robert's habit, John decided. He didn't remember any robe, but it could be in one of the bags. He knew there'd be no sleep for him that night unless he checked her house. He thought of letting Joe know where he was going, but then decided to just go. It wouldn't take him more than twenty to thirty minutes, he figured. He also decided against taking Ralph. It seemed to upset the poor dog to go there. John got his spare car key from under the stone frog by the outside water spigot. Not too original, but crime had never been much of a problem here. And besides, who'd try to rob the police chief? Within moments, he was heading out Main Street toward Alma's house as the evening shadows lengthened.

As he drove down the rutted lane trying to avoid the worst holes, the trees overhead blocked out what daylight remained creating an ominous feeling. He felt relieved

278

when he finally pulled into the clearing by Alma's house. Someone was standing in the shadows as he pulled closer to the house. Then he recognized Violet and scowled. What in the hell was she doing here?

Taking the keys to the padlocked back door from his glove compartment, he climbed out and walked towards her.

"I'm so glad you came," she called in a relieved tone of voice. "There's a cat down in the cistern. I can hear it crying, but I don't know how to get it out. I was just going to run home and get Ed, but maybe you can do something about it."

"I'll see what I can do." He returned to his car to grab a flashlight. "What're you doing back here this late in the evening?" he asked when he returned.

"I like to walk in the evenings when it's cooler. I don't have to worry about traffic on this lane. Usually I don't come this far. Lucky I did tonight or the poor little cat might've drowned."

"That's funny. I'm sure the stone cover wasn't off yesterday, or I would've noticed it." He leaned over and shined a light down into the cistern. The light glared off water about eight or nine feet down. Clinging with front paws to a brick jutting out a few inches, a white cat mewed piteously.

"Can you see anything?" Violet inquired at his shoulder.

John straightened up. "Yes. There's a white cat down there."

"Oh, poor kitty," Violet crooned. "We've got to get him out."

"He's too far down for me to reach."

"Maybe if you put a branch down? Or maybe we could tie some sheets together and lower them down so it could climb up them," Violet suggested eager to be of help.

"It's worth a try." He glanced around for a long stick

279

and not seeing any close at hand, he unlocked the back door and went inside to pull down one of the drapes from the front window.

Violet was standing at the back door as he came back. She was looking around in obvious disgust. "I can't see how anyone could live like this." Her voice was full of scorn. John shrugged and together they returned to the cistern.

"We'll see if this'll work." He leaned into the cistern and dropped one end of the drape down toward the cat while holding onto the other end. "Come on, Kitty. Grab hold. It's not quite long enough," he said stretching further.

With a sudden lurching of his heart, he felt his legs lifted, propelling him forward. Wildly flailing his arms and legs, and grasping for a hold on the smooth wet bricks lining the cistern, he felt himself falling. He hit the cold water hard. Twisting and turning he was able to right himself and came out of the water gasping for breath. With a strong feeling of unbelief, he looked up.

"Violet!" he called out. A face appeared for a moment, a dark outline against the fading sky, and then he heard a scraping sound as the stone cover was slowly shoved back into place leaving total darkness.

"Violet!" he screamed again. The sound echoed off the walls reverberating with chilling finality. In a few moments he heard the sound of a car starting up and driving away. In despair he realized it was his car.

Chapter Thirty-two

"Get off my head, cat," John said as he plucked the furry feline from his scalp and placed it back on his shoulder. The cat muttered a complaint into John's ear.

"Too bad, cat. You're at least drier than I am."

The rumble of thunder made him nervous. Right now the water was chest high. He wasn't sure what a heavy rain would do. He suspected the water level would rise, and wondered how long he'd been down here. In the pitch black of his watery prison, time had become amorphous, lacking definition. What seemed like hours and hours to him might be much less.

He'd given up trying to find cracks or crevices in the smooth, slimy, brick wall. Except for one uneven brick about chest high the cat had been clinging to with front paws before the arrival of John, who'd given it a more secure and drier resting place, there were no others John could find within reach. He'd tried to use that brick out-cropping to gain a toe hold, but it hadn't worked, and the attempt only landed the two of them back in the water with a big splash and a swelling bruise on his forehead.

So John stood trapped in this watery cistern roughly four feet in diameter and tried not to let the words 'watery grave' take hold in his mind. To keep his thoughts off those dreaded words, the cold and his weariness, he'd alternately recited poetry, sang songs, and talked to the cat.

It was strange, he thought, that the only poems he

seemed to remember dealt with death. *"Because I could not stop for death, it kindly stopped for me"* kept running through his mind. He paused occasionally to listen for human sounds without and wondered when he'd be missed. Would anyone ever find him here? He thought with despair of his car gone thus leaving no clue to his whereabouts.

"Why were you thrown in the well, cat?" he asked.

"Mrrp," the cat responded.

"I'd wager it's because you're the cat whose hairs are on Greg Robert's habit. Right?"

"Mrrrow," the cat answered trying to get more comfortable on John's shoulder.

"Now the question is whose cat are you? Your hair is too long to be Greg Robert's cat. I don't think Violet and Ed have a cat so why would Violet throw you in?" John wondered aloud.

The cat, strangely enough, started to purr.

"Well, I certainly am glad one of us is comfortable," he said sarcastically.

"Of course," he went on, "maybe it wasn't Violet who threw you in and then pushed me in." He still found it hard to believe a woman in her sixties, even a large woman, could have dispatched him with such ease.

The sudden muffled sound of rain on the stone cover caused his heart to constrict. It was hard enough with his feet on this semi-solid rock bottom now covered with thick mushy and slimy sediment. He wasn't sure how long he could last if he was forced to tread water, especially with a heavy cat on his shoulder. "You certainly are a fat cat," he complained.

"Maybe it was someone else, and maybe they kidnapped Violet, or maybe they hit her on the head and knocked her out or worse," he theorized, but he knew that was far-fetched and the villain in this piece must be Violet. But why? For the hundredth time, he wondered why she would do something like this. It had to be either she was the murderer or she was protecting the murderer. "And if she's protecting the murderer," he said out loud, "then it could only be Ed." He thought of what Catherine had told him about the blue rose.

"Cat, if you're not Ed and Violet's cat, why'd she want to get rid of you? It has to do with the cat hairs on the robe. I'm sure now Violet overheard me talking to Catherine about it yesterday." Or was it the day before? Was it Monday yet? He wondered.

The cat tried once more to perch on higher ground; John's head.

"No, you don't. Ouch! Get those claws in, or I'll drown you myself."

"Errow," grumped the cat.

"I wish I could ask Catherine whose cat you are. She'd probably know. Could you be a neighbor's cat that sleeps in Ed's garden shed? That could be it. I'll bet he has the ant poison that killed Alma, too. Or did. I'd wager that's disappeared by now."

John stopped his monologue and sneezed. The sound reverberated off the stone walls and startled the cat causing it to dig its claws into John's shoulder.

"Dammit!" he yelled which only alarmed the cat more and caused it to dig even deeper. With extreme care while gritting his teeth in silence, John disengaged the claws from his skin. It was in this temporary silence he became aware of another and frightening sound; a trickle of water running into the cistern from somewhere above his head.

Chapter Thirty-three

The phone chimed in with the alarm clock creating a raucous duet. Confused and alarmed Catherine reached first for the phone.

"Hello?"

"Catherine, this is Josh," said a hesitant voice.

Catherine rolled over in bed to the other side and smacked the alarm button. "Yes, Josh." A feeling of dread hit her.

"Have you heard from my dad?" She could tell by the hesitant tone of his voice, he was embarrassed about calling her.

"No. Not since we got back about six. You mean he hasn't been home?"

"No, and it's not like him. He hasn't reported into the station either. I checked."

"Oh, wow." Trying to reassure him, she said, "He probably had car trouble or something."

"Tony said he'd go out looking. I thought I would, too, but he wanted me to stay close in case Dad called or came home."

"It must be hard waiting," she commiserated through her own feelings of dread.

"Yeah, it is, I woke up half an hour ago, and saw the kitchen light I'd left on for him was still on, and he wasn't in his room."

"Would you like me to come over and wait with you?"

"Would you? I don't want to worry Grandma, but it's hard waiting alone." His voice seemed younger now.

She thought Martha would probably be stronger than both of them but said, "I'll be right over."

Catherine pulled on shorts and a T shirt, washed her face, brushed her teeth and hair, said a little prayer her truck would start this morning and was out the door in less than ten minutes. After a few feeble attempts, the engine roared to life, and she headed down Main Street to John's hoping he either was already there, or Josh would've heard from him by the time she got there. She was glad to see the storm in the night had passed. There were still some heavy clouds, and the radio predicted more storms coming, but she hoped the forecast was wrong, the wind would blow the clouds away, and the day would clear up.

She pulled in next to Josh's car and got out, glancing toward the Bed and Breakfast as she did. Martha was standing at the window. Catherine gave her a slight smile and wave before hurrying up the outside steps of Carriage House Books. Josh stood on the landing waiting for her.

"Anything new?" she asked.

He shook his head and turned to go inside. "I sure appreciate you coming," he said and swallowed. "Would you like a cup of coffee?"

"Sure. I didn't take time for any." Giving him something to do would help him as much as the coffee would taste good to her.

Ralph got up from the rug in front of the kitchen sink and walked over to greet her. "I see you still have him."

"Yeah." Josh gave a weak grin. "Dad said he's been too busy to take him to the animal shelter, but I don't know."

Catherine leaned down to pet the dog as Josh turned away to get a cup from the cupboard.

"Dad left his keys on the end table and his wallet, too," Josh said as he filled a cup with water. He stopped. "Do you mind instant?"

"No. It's what I drink at home mostly." She glanced at

the table by the recliner and saw John's keys, wallet, a half cup of coffee with film on it, and an open book face down ready to be picked up again. Her heart constricted. Stop it, she told herself. He's okay.

"How'd he start his car?" She started wandering around the room.

"He keeps a spare key hidden outside. I checked. It's gone."

Catherine stopped at a large window facing the parking lot for the bookstore and across to Martha's bed and breakfast. A few rather neglected plants sat on the windowsill. She walked to an overflowing bookcase and read some of the titles; *The Complete Poems of Emily Dickinson, New England Summer, Best Stories of Sarah Orne Jewett, The Murder Room, The Street Lawyer.* Next her eyes went to the pictures on top. She picked up one of a younger John with Josh when he was about eight. Josh had on a baseball suit and both were beaming. There was another one of Josh in his Cub Scout uniform. She picked up another of John and a young dark haired woman holding a baby. This must be his ex-wife, she thought.

"That's my mom." Josh stood beside her with a cup of coffee.

"I thought it might be. She's very pretty." She put the picture back and took the coffee he offered.

"I guess. I haven't seen her in at least ten years." He shrugged sounding matter-of-fact.

She carried her cup to a round oak table. Josh paced for a while before sitting down on another chair, but within moments he jumped up again, filled another cup with water, put it in the microwave and sat back down.

"This is good," Catherine said as she took a sip.

"Thanks." The conversation died. Some company I am, she thought, as she tried to think of something encouraging to say without it being a lie or sounding too light and unfeeling. Her feet started fidgeting. A need to leave and start looking for John was building in her, but she hated to leave Josh alone.

"Did you ask your grandmother if she knew where your dad had gone?"

Josh's eyes widened. "No. He wouldn't have told her without leaving a note for me, too."

A tap at the door caused Josh to jump up, but Martha was in before he took a step.

"Okay, what's going on?"

Josh looked guilty and stammered, "Nothing."

"Tell her Josh," Catherine said.

"It's Dad. He's missing," Josh blurted out, his voice quivering. The microwave beeped, and he rushed to get the cup keeping his back to them until he regained his composure.

Martha looked at Catherine, and she quietly told her all she knew.

"Is anyone looking for him?"

Catherine glanced at Josh's back. When he turned around, his eyes were moist, but he seemed to have regained his composure. "Tony is, and Joe stayed over at the station to listen for calls until Suzy gets in.

"Josh called me to see if I'd heard from his dad, or if he'd told me anything yesterday about where he might be going," Catherine explained in answer to Martha's unasked question. "I offered to come over and wait with him until his dad gets back."

"I didn't want to worry you," Josh said as he stood by the microwave.

"Thank you for your concern, honey, but you must know I'd want to know," Martha said.

As Josh stood silently, the phone rang. He stared at it afraid to answer. Martha reached for it and answered.

"Hello." She listened without comment then asked. "Do you have people out looking?" She nodded. "Please keep us informed, either here or over at my place," she said before hanging up.

"John's car was found at the park. He's not in it."

They both stared at her trying to figure out what that could mean.

"Do they think he went somewhere with someone else? Josh asked.

Martha shrugged. "I don't think they have any idea. They're checking the car for finger prints."

Catherine's heart sank. "Could he have gone into the woods? Maybe went through to Elmwood Gardens?" She thought of the lake and her near escape and shuddered.

Martha shrugged again, worry plain on her face. "I don't know. I'm sure they're checking on every possibility. Tony called Joe, Pete and Bill in. Suzy's in now to answer the phone." She glanced at her watch. "I've got to fix breakfast for my guests. I'll be back as soon as I can hurry them on their way." She turned and left, little left of the spry energetic woman who'd cared for Catherine's shop yesterday.

"Do you think Dad . . . do you think Dad found the murderer?"

Catherine took a deep steadying breath. That thought had been in her mind, too. "I suppose it's possible."

"He sure is the best dad in the world," Josh blurted out.

Catherine felt her eyes prick. "I believe that, and he's lucky to have a son like you, too. He told me that yesterday."

Josh lips quivered in an attempt at a smile. "We're really tight, you know."

"Yeah, I know." She swallowed.

Josh jumped up and grabbed his keys. "I'm going out to find him. I've got to do something."

Catherine whose feet had been tapping said, "Me, too. We'd better decide where each of us will go so we don't cover the same territory."

They both started for the door when Martha returned.

"Fortunately my guests decided they'd rather get on the road than eat breakfast. They were downstairs drinking a cup of coffee and just left. That doesn't happen very often, but I must say I'm glad it did today. I didn't feel like making small talk. Here're the apple oatmeal muffins they passed up." She put a basket on the table, with a red checked cloth in it keeping the muffins warm. The smell was comforting, reassuring, a smell that said, "There, there, all will be well."

"Thanks, Grandma, but Catherine and I are going out to look for Dad."

"I understand. I want to go, too. Where are you going?"

"Josh, why don't you go to the gardens," Catherine said. "You're familiar with them. I'd start with the woods near the lake. You might get some of the other workers to help, too. Comb the whole gardens."

Josh nodded as Catherine went on. "I'll start searching out my way and beyond."

"I'll go the other way on the back roads towards Millport," Martha said.

A knock at the screen door caused them all to pause in alarm as Tony walked in. Fear was on each face.

Tony shook his head. "It's as if he just vanished into thin air. The car has no prints on the steering wheel or the door handles on the driver's side, but there are some on the passenger's side that aren't John's."

"Those are probably mine," Catherine said. "I was with him yesterday."

"It looks like his car was stolen and abandoned there. His cell phone was on the front seat. The good news is there doesn't seem to be any blood stains in the car."

Catherine's heart constricted. John couldn't have just wandered off. He'd have taken his phone to call home. He was either lying hurt in a ditch somewhere or someplace, kidnapped, or worse. That Josh and Martha were thinking

289

the same thing was plain on their faces.

"I've got to go find him," Josh blurted out.

"You probably should stay here in case he calls," Tony said.

"No." His voice rose. "I've got to go look for him. I can't just stay here." He tore out the door, and they could hear him leaping down the steps two at a time.

"We're all heading out to look," Catherine said. "We feel we need to be doing something to find him."

Tony's hands at his side opened and closed. "I understand. I feel the same way. Just check in at the station every so often. I'd better get back to the search now." He didn't want to admit he didn't have any idea where to look. As he turned to go, he wished he could be more optimistic, but it didn't seem good.

As Catherine and Martha prepared to leave, Ralph whined at the door. "I'll take him with me," Catherine said.

"Okay." Martha nodded as she closed the door behind her and followed Catherine down the steps.

Ralph jumped willingly into the front seat of her truck. As Catherine pulled out, turning left towards her home, a flash of lightning streaked across the sky. Another storm was moving in.

"What I really need to know," she said out loud when she passed her place, "is where to look." She drove past Maggie's house, driving slowly and looking into ditches as she went before turning left onto Anderson Road.

Ralph started whining and barking as they passed Dump Road. On a sudden impulse, Catherine backed up and turned onto the road leading to Alma's house. She glanced into her rear view mirror and could see the Flavians' house down Raspberry Lane where the road curved. His truck and her car were both parked in their drive. She slowed down when the road turned into the muddy lane. The sky darkened even more and thunder rumbled. This lane could turn into a real quagmire, she thought. Already there were numerous puddles from last night's rain.

A huge roll of thunder announced her arrival in the clearing by Alma's house. Catherine stared at the gray dismal house. Its blank windows, illuminated in the near dark by flashes of lightning, seemed to stare back at her malevolently. Large drops of rain started exploding against the windshield. In spite of Ralph's whining, she hesitated. The house looked threatening, like a house from every spooky movie she'd ever seen. The combination of the old house along with the bolts of lightning electrifying the air, strongly tempted Catherine to turn and leave. Why would John be here? There's only one in a million chances of that, she rationalized.

"No matter," she said firmly to Ralph, "I need to check to satisfy myself he's not here." But she decided against turning the engine off. The last thing she needed now was to be stranded back here, she reasoned as she opened the door and slipped out. Ralph leaped after her, happy to be home. Another loud crack of thunder caused her to jump as she closed the truck door. Making a mad dash for shelter, she sprinted after Ralph, around the house, and up onto the back porch where she stopped in alarm. The back door stood open. She knew John locked it Saturday night. A voice in her head said, "Run! Run back to the truck. Go for help." But another voice argued with the first voice. "No. John may be in there. He may need help and minutes may count." She wished she'd remembered her cell phone.

With muscles tense and ready for flight, she walked into the kitchen illuminated only by faint gray light through dirty windows, the open back door and flashes of lightning. Her eyes darted around. It seemed the same with piles of dirty dishes and the dead flowers and four leaf clovers in the jelly jar on the windowsill. She wondered about the muddy footprints on the linoleum. Were they there before? She couldn't remember. With all the filth would she have noticed?

She went into the front room where shadows and gloom were even murkier, and noticed old drapes on one window had been yanked down, but the gray tattered lace curtains still hung at the other window. The windows were so dirty that even without drapes at the one window, it didn't help alleviate the gloom.

"John?" Catherine called out. Her voice seemed strange even to herself. She felt like she was in a grade B horror movie, in which evil waited behind every door. In what felt like slow motion, she went through the room checking behind chairs, under piles of clothes, and she even checked under the cot. Every part of her body was tensed and in flight mode. A scrabbling sound in the next room caused her to jump. She wanted to turn and run for the back door, but forced herself to go to the door where she heard the noise and pushed it open wider. Ralph was in there sniffing around. She breathed a sigh of relief. Good old Ralph! She felt a little safer.

"See anything, Ralph?" Her voice seemed loud even to herself. Ralph, intent on his own investigation, ignored her. As in the first room, she checked under piles of clothes in case John was lying bound and gagged under any of them. She refused to think of other possibilities.

"Let's go upstairs and check."

Opening the door, she peered up the dark stairs. "I wish I'd thought to get a flashlight," she said to Ralph as he came up behind her. The sound of her own voice and Ralph's presence helped her courage. Slowly, feeling each step with her feet as she went, Catherine worked her way up toward the lighter gray shadows at the top. She remembered the upstairs was divided into two rooms. Dark shapes against the gloom took on evil forms in the half light. She turned to look around, and let out a small, choked, terrified scream as she spied a human form standing near the window. Another flash of lightning revealed it as a dressmaker's dummy. She closed her eyes, took in a deep breath and released it.

"Let's get busy and check this out, Ralph," she said a little louder to scare away the spooks. It was as she was opening an old leather trunk that she thought she heard a door close downstairs. She froze and saw Ralph, his ears pricked, staring at the stairs, too.

A sudden impulse made her call out loudly. "It's about time you got here, Tony and Bill. What took you so long?" She listened intently. Were those footsteps leaving? With rain beating against the roof, it was hard to hear.

"Maybe the back door blew shut," she said to Ralph. "That's probably what it was."

He glanced at her, and then ignoring what was or wasn't downstairs, started his own investigation.

In the semi-dark, she couldn't see what was in the trunk. Gathering up what little courage she had, she reached in to feel inside, hoping she wasn't disturbing any mice or worse. But the trunk held only old clothes, and she closed its lid grateful for small favors.

Ralph scratched at the door to the other room. Catherine, in a hurry to be out of there, opened it and went in. Boxes and bags were stacked everywhere. Quickly she went through checking anywhere someone could be hidden. When they were both satisfied, she said, "Let's go, Ralph."

As Catherine started down the stairs, she was again overcome with a feeling of something menacing lying in wait. She wished she had another way out. She wondered how good a guard dog Ralph was? She had a feeling he wasn't very good, but didn't want to dwell on that thought.

Glancing around the main room, she hurried to the kitchen. The back door was closed.

"The wind must've blown it shut," she said to Ralph. He gave a little yip from the other room. "Come on. I know you want to stay, but you can't," she said eager to be gone. He came to her, but stopped and looked back. She pushed at the back door, swollen from the rain. It wouldn't open creating a feeling of panic in her. With her shoulder and a hard push, it suddenly flew open propelling her out onto the porch.

"Come on, Ralph." When he reluctantly came, she closed the door. Looking through the rain at the shed, she said, "Let's check that out and then we'll go." She hurried down the steps and into the pouring rain. She didn't look back to see a shadow at the kitchen window.

Chapter Thirty-four

The cold water on his face and the cat's claws in his scalp trying to keep its balance brought John awake, sputtering. For a moment he fought to orient himself. The water was now slightly over his shoulders. He had dozed off leaning against the wall and been dreaming of Catherine. Her voice, her sweet voice, seemed so real. He could hear rain faintly on the stone cover again.

"Come on, Ralph," he heard faintly. This was no dream, he realized.

"Catherine!" he screamed. "Help me!"

"Where are you?"

"Mrow!" the cat howled plaintively.

"Shut up cat! Down here. In the cistern," he shouted.

In a few moments he heard the heavy stone being pushed back with a grinding sound, and a slow sliver of light appeared, gradually growing larger until the stone cover fell with a thud on the other side. Catherine's outline appeared against the gray sky.

"John?" She peered into the deep shadows, seeing only a white blur.

"Down here," he called back, choked with emotion. "Please get something so I can get out. I'm about ten feet down."

"I'll be right back. Hold on." She straightened up and stood for a moment, thinking about what to get. Maybe there was a ladder in the shed. She hurried off to check, but hadn't gone more than a few feet when Violet appeared from around the corner of the house.

She stood watching Catherine. Her wet purple sweat pants and lavender knit top clung to her form, and her lavender tinted hair hung down in wet strings. Black mascara streaked down her face and bright red lipstick, smeared on with an unsteady hand, made her face look like pictures Catherine had seen of Indians on the warpath. Behind water streaked glasses, her eyes stared as if in a trance.

"Violet!" Catherine exclaimed, forgetting her suspicions in the night, "I'm so glad to see you. John's down in the cistern. I need help getting him out."

"I wish you hadn't come." Her voice sounded sad. "I always liked you."

Catherine looked puzzled. "What do you mean?"

"Catherine!" John screamed. "Get away! Run! She's the murderer!"

The words echoed, mingling with the rain, and now she remembered what she'd decided in the night. She stared at Violet in horror as the words sunk in. When Violet brought her hand forward, Catherine saw the large knife. She must've gotten it from the kitchen, Catherine thought, still mesmerized by what was taking place.

"No, Violet," she said, still not willing to believe, still thinking she could reason with her.

"Why did you have to meddle? I wouldn't have hurt you if you'd just minded your own business." She spoke as if she were trying to reason with a child. Then with a sudden move, she brought the knife up and lunged at Catherine.

Catherine leaped aside, and Violet came at her again. She was surprised at how quickly Violet moved. Desperately she looked around for some weapon. She may be younger, but Violet was much larger, taller and heavier.

When Violet came at her a third time, Catherine

dodged and grabbed a half rotted two by four lying near the path. It was about five feet long making it unwieldy for Catherine, but it was the only thing close enough to grab.

Violet stood warily watching. "Now Catherine, you know you won't use that. I just want you to be able to join your boyfriend. That should make you both happy." Her mouth opened in a hideous parody of a smile.

Again Violet lunged at her. Catherine swung the two by four. The weight and momentum of the board, knocked her off balance, but she felt satisfaction in knowing the board had at least hit Violet a glancing blow.

With a scream of rage, Violet wheeled around before Catherine regained her balance and came at her, knife upraised and swiped at her, and she felt the knife cut into the back of her shoulder.

After a moment's sharp pain, Catherine ceased noticing it as fear and anger took over. She raised the two by four and brought it down on Violet. It glanced off her head and knocked her glasses off. Violet's face contorted with fury. She rushed at Catherine, swinging the knife wildly.

Again Catherine dodged, and swung the two by four hitting Violet's right shoulder, causing her to drop the knife. Instead of reaching to pick it up, she lunged at Catherine, grabbing the other end of the board.

Together they both grimly held on to opposite ends trying to wrest it away from the other. Violet managed to pull Catherine forward a few steps. Catherine gritted her teeth. She didn't know how long she could hold on.

As Violet, with almost super human strength, gave another hard pull, Catherine, forced forward a few more steps, tripped over the dog, who'd come between them. Catherine's hold loosened as she fell forward. She looked up in time to see Violet bringing the raised board down and rolled away just before the board hit the ground. Catherine frantically scrambled and lunged forward, grabbing onto

Violet's legs and hung on, trying to bring her down.

Violet dropped the board and started beating on Catherine's head and shoulders with her fists as Catherine hung on grimly, pulling and shoving with her shoulders until Violet finally lost her balance and fell backwards. Catherine tried to scramble away and get to her feet before Violet could, but Violet twisted around and grabbed one of Catherine's ankles, and jerked hard, bringing Catherine back down before she'd completely stood up.

Ralph sat watching and whining. At first he thought it was a game. Somewhere in his mind, there was a dim memory of boys wrestling in which he, as a puppy, had joined in, but he didn't remember big sticks being involved.

Now he was convinced it wasn't a game, but he didn't know what to do. The younger woman had stepped on him and tripped over him, so he'd retreated to a safer distance. Both women seemed determined to hurt the other. The younger one had been nice to him, but he remembered the older one from his walks with his own person, and while she never talked to him, she'd never done anything unkind to him, and her smell was on many things his person brought home. And she'd been in the house only moments ago.

He went over to check the dropped knife and picked it up taking it back to where he'd been sitting out of reach of the women. It belonged to his person. Ralph continued to watch the two women now rolling on the ground in the mud. He gave a tentative little bark, politely asking them to stop this nonsense and get out of the rain. They ignored him.

Catherine felt herself passing out as Violet straddled her middle with her hands around Catherine's neck squeezing. She heard Violet muttering some words about the sheriff and a baby. She tried pulling Violet's hands away, clawing at her face, but it was as if Violet could feel no pain, as if she was no longer human.

As Catherine twisted and turned trying to break Violet's hold, she heard John's voice calling her name. That, combined with unexpected help from elsewhere, gave her the impetus needed to throw Violet off just as Ralph decided this had gone on long enough and leaped on Violet's back and growled. That was just enough to loosen Violet's hold, and with a last desperate burst of energy, Catherine twisted her body enough to knock Violet off. She leaped up, grabbed the two by four, and with an effort born of desperation, raised it and brought it down with all her remaining strength on Violet's head as Violet was struggling to her feet.

Violet sprawled flat and didn't move. Catherine stood breathing heavily, staring at Violet, watching, but she still didn't move.

Slowly Catherine walked to the cistern and leaned on the edge. "John," she said breathing hard and out of breath, "I think I just killed Violet."

He stood there, water almost to his chin, tears streaming down his face, unable to speak.

"John?" she called out alarmed.

"I hear you," he choked out.

. "I'll get you out. Just hold on a little longer."

There was no ladder in the shed. She went into the house and started knotting sheets, blouses, nightgowns, slacks, anything from the floor looking reasonably sturdy and easy to tie until she had a makeshift rope about twenty feet long. Picking it up, she hurried outside and tied one end to the closest tree a few feet from the cistern.

"John, I'm dropping down a makeshift rope," she called out as she lowered it. She leaned back in surprise as a white furry creature flew up the knotted clothes and raced off with Ralph in eager pursuit.

"What was that?!"

"Don't ask," John muttered as he grabbed hold and slowly, stiffly, started pulling himself up. Catherine waited, eager to see him, and when he grabbed hold of the edge of the cistern, she reached under his arms and pulled, helping him the rest of the way out. They both fell to the ground and lay there staring at each other.

"You are the most beautiful person in the world," he said as he stared at Catherine's mud streaked face and hair.

She grinned at him, well aware of what she must look like, and at the same time filled with overwhelming joy because he was alive and well. "You're pretty gorgeous yourself."

Both of them lay there too tired to move, oblivious of the rain, until the sound of a truck revving up brought them back to where they were. They sat up in time to see Catherine's truck back up, hit a tree, turn around and come toward them. They leaped up and started for the corner of the house. The truck swerved and went bouncing down the lane at top speed with Violet at the wheel.

"My truck!" Catherine wailed.

"You left your keys in it."

"Yes, but . . ."

John smiled. Who was he to lecture? They stood listening to the sound of the truck fading away.

"It looks like we've got some walking to do," he said. "Guess we'd better get started."

"Yes." She sighed deeply, then looking at him asked, "Why is your face all scratched?"

He grimaced. "I take it you've never been a perch for a cat who's afraid of water."

"Oh, no," she said with wide eyes, and then her lips started to twitch as the image of John with a cat on his head flashed through her mind. The giggles started next, born of exhaustion and relief as well as humor, and soon the giggles escalated to complete doubled over laughter.

John tried to act offended, but soon he was chuckling, too.

"I'm certainly not getting much sympathy from you,"

he complained.

She hiccupped, and he grabbed her hand. "Come on. I'd say we both need a hot bath." He yawned and added, "And a bed, but before that, I have a murderer to catch."

They started walking. Fortunately the rain had let up.

"Tell me," Catherine said, as they skirted the first puddle, "however did you get down in that cistern?"

"Would you believe an old lady pushed me in?"

Catherine shuddered. "If that old lady is Violet, I can. I can't believe how strong she is."

"Your shoulder! Your back is all bloody."

"Violet had a knife."

" Let me check." John carefully pulled up her shirt and looked at the wound. "You may need some stitches, but the bleeding seems to have stopped."

"Tell me more," Catherine said as they started out again.

John explained what'd happened. Catherine no longer felt like laughing. Her eyes were full of sympathy.

He smiled down at her. "But it was all worth it to have the brave lady riding up on her white charger to rescue me."

She smiled back. "Ralph helped. He jumped on Violet just when I was about to breathe my last." She touched her throat where bruises were already beginning to show.

"It sounded like a terrible battle. My heart was in my throat," John admitted. "I felt so helpless."

"I guess I didn't do too badly considering I've never been in a fight in my life, but please," she looked up at him, her face serious, "don't put me in that situation again. I don't like fighting."

His laugh was rueful, "I don't like fighting, either, so I'll do my best to see neither one of us get into another situation like that again."

They walked on in silence with Ralph close at their heels. The first euphoria of rescue had worn off, and now an overwhelming fatigue settled on both.

Catherine broke the silence. "You know Violet said a strange thing as she was choking me. She said, 'The sheriff took my baby away, and you helped him. Now you'll both pay for it.'"

"The woman's deranged."

"Do you think it just happened, or she's always been like that, and I just never noticed? Last night I started to wonder, but I still couldn't quite believe she could be a murderer." She paused before adding, "Until today."

John shook his head. "I don't know, but we'll have to get her before she kills again."

Both of them thought of how close they'd come to being victims three and four.

As they came out of the lane and started down the gravel road, they saw a highway patrol vehicle fly by on the highway with siren wailing, lights flashing. They both picked up speed and hurried down this short stretch of road. As they approached the highway, a Portage Falls patrol car flew by with lights flashing and siren wailing, too. As it passed Dump Road, it screeched to a halt, skidding slightly on the rain slick pavement. With a sudden squeal, the car backed up and slammed to a stop. A dumbfounded Tony leaped out. "John!" he stammered. "Catherine!"

They smiled at him. "Could you give us a ride?" John asked. "We're kind of tuckered out and a mite bit wet, too."

When they were settled in the back with Ralph at their feet, John asked. "Where were you off to? What's up?"

Tony glanced at them in the rear view mirror. "Bad accident. Truck apparently traveling at high speed on these wet roads missed a curve and hit a tree. The license plate shows the truck is registered to one Catherine Jewell."

They looked at each other and then stared ahead not saying anything. In a few moments they reached the accident scene and climbed out.

The highway patrolman glanced curiously at John and

Catherine, taking in their wet, muddy and battered appearances, then turned to Tony. "Ambulance is on its way, but it's too late. I think the woman died instantly. We'll need to notify next of kin. It's registered to a Catherine Jewell."

Catherine leaned against John and started to cry.

"The driver is Violet Flavian," John said as he held Catherine. "Tony, you'll have to tell Ed. Have him meet the ambulance at the hospital. I'll talk to him later."

They both looked surprised. "She borrowed the truck," he said by way of explanation. "We'll wait in the patrol car until you're done here, Tony."

John held Catherine as she cried. Finally, she straightened up and wiped her eyes and nose on her shirt sleeve. "I keep thinking of how she used to be so cheerful and full of life. I don't want to think of her the way she was today, and how she is now."

"Then don't. Violet was sick. Try and remember her as she was before. Poor Ed. I wonder if he knew."

"I think he might have suspected, but like me, he didn't want to believe it just like I didn't want to believe it was Ed or Greg Robert. Why did you say Violet borrowed my truck?"

"If Violet acted alone, and I think she did, then the case is closed. It will have to come out, of course, so the people of Portage Falls can rest easier, but maybe I can protect Ed from it becoming headline news, at least as much as possible."

"Do you think it was suicide?" She said in a small voice.

"How can we know?"

Chapter Thirty-five

The statue of Saint Fiacre had a peaceful look this morning as he stared over the gardens. Catherine paused, and with a little smile, murmured "Thank you."

"Hi, Catherine," Millie called out when Catherine walked in. "Glad to see you back. I heard you got hurt on Monday."

"Yes, clumsy me. I tripped and fell against a rake and cut my shoulder."

"How many stitches?" Millie's eyes behind thick lenses magnified her curious look.

"Only ten and the doctor said there probably won't be a scar. So what's new over the past few days?"

"You heard about Violet, of course." She shook her head. "Ed's so shook up he didn't even have calling hours. I heard she was in pretty bad shape. They couldn't have an open casket anyway. Never seems a proper burial and all if you can't view the body."

"I'm sorry, Millie. I know you were good friends," she said sympathetically, even though Millie didn't seem too grieved. It would probably hit her later. She found the horror of that day already starting to recede a little, but knew it would always be with her and not disappear like the wound on her shoulder would. She hoped the nightmares would cease, too.

"Yes. I'll certainly miss her," Millie said and sniffed. Catherine realized for all her casual conversation, she was missing her friend. Why'd she have your truck?"

"She borrowed it." She knew everything would come out in the next few days, and hoped Millie would forgive her for not telling the truth, but she didn't want to talk about it now.

"Did ya hear the Chatterton kid came home?" Millie asked.

"No. Did he? Where was he?"

"Well, get this. Seems he's not gonna stay home. He don't want his old man's money, either. Can you believe that? From what I heard, he says he wants to make it on his own as a musician." Millie shook her head in disbelief.

Catherine wanted to say good for him, but decided it wasn't worth offending Millie. She'd worked hard all her life and naturally couldn't understand anyone refusing an easier life.

"I imagine his mother was glad to see him."

"Yeah, I'm sure, but ya never know with her. From what I can see, she don't show her feelings much. Did ya hear Alicia and Tom are engaged now?" Millie went on.

"I thought something was going on there."

"Some folks think he's only marrying her for her money, but not me. He's a good boy, and it wasn't him chasing her."

"Have they found someone to take Olga's place yet?"

"Not that I know of. Wasn't that something her being Alicia's mother?" In wonderment, Millie shook her red head her beehive swaying. "Sounds like a movie to me."

The door opened and Greg Robert walked in. "Hey, Catherine," he called out. "How you doing? Understand you got hurt."

"Yes, clumsy me." She told him the same story she'd told Millie, but from the gleam in his eye and slight smile, she was sure he didn't believe her. She wondered if he knew the truth.

"Where's your coffee and cinnamon roll?" he asked with eyebrows raised.

"Oh, I'm sorry!" Millie exclaimed jumping up. "We got to talking and I forgot."

"I'd like one, too."

She brought them two cups of coffee, and then put two cinnamon rolls in the microwave.

"I checked on the raspberries," Catherine said. "They're coming along nicely."

"The grapes are looking good, too," he said. "Now if only the raccoons don't raid them as soon as they get ripe, there ought to be enough for a lot of homemade grape jam."

"Isn't there something you can do about them?" she asked.

"Live trapping, I guess, but that just transfers the problem elsewhere. I thought I'd try spraying with a mixture made with hot peppers. I've heard it works."

Millie placed two hot cinnamon rolls in front of them. "I've got to set up the dining room now. Do you need anything else before I go?"

They assured her they were fine. "You've talked to John," she said when Millie left.

He smiled and nodded. "You've had a rough few days, haven't you?"

"I guess, but not as bad as John. I'll be glad to get back to gardening. It's easier and safer." She took a bite of the cinnamon roll oozing sugary syrup and wiped a drip off her chin.

"I heard you visited Saint Boniface's."

"Yes." She looked at him to see if he was offended, but he was smiling. "Oh, Greg Robert, it's so beautiful! I was so impressed, and Brother Jude and everyone were so nice to us." All the superlatives she could use didn't seem enough to cover her feelings about St. Boniface's.

"I'm pleased you like my home," he said quietly.

She stared at him. "You mean?"

"Yes, I'm going home."

"Oh, I'm going to miss you, but you must think it's the right thing for you."

He nodded. "I've enjoyed Elmwood and the people here, but it's time I went back where I belong."

"When will you be leaving?"

"Tomorrow."

"Tomorrow! But they need to find someone to take your place, and that'll take time."

"No, it won't, dear Catherine. Ed will be back where he rightfully belongs."

"Ed!"

"Yes, Ed. The two of you will work very well together. I'm glad I was able to see you before I left," he said as he stood up, "and thanks for always having faith in me."

She walked out with him. "That was easy. I never doubted your goodness. Would you've left without saying good-bye if I hadn't come back today?" she asked feeling hurt.

He smiled down at her. "No, I would've found you."

"What about Saint Fiacre?" she asked as they passed the statue.

"He's happy here, and I think Elmwood needs him. I'm leaving Bonnie Prince Charlie, too. Ed will move into my cottage when he's ready. The board, at Tyler's suggestion, agreed to give him a life time lease for a dollar a year. He'll take care of Charlie."

"I'm going to miss you." She felt tears start in her eyes.

"And I'll miss you, Catherine," he said as he hugged her long and tight, "but you'll come and visit me, won't you? I'd really like that."

"I'd like that, too." But she knew it wouldn't be the same.

He tapped her lightly on the nose, then wheeled about and hurried off.

Catherine watched him go until he turned the corner and was lost to sight. She swallowed the lump in her throat then walked down to the rose gardens. It was time she got back to work.

Her eyes registered dismay as she stared at the blue

roses, or what'd once been the blue roses. The leaves were withered and dead, and the roses remaining drooped, faded and colorless.

"It's for the best, Missy," Ed's gruff voice said as he stepped through the hedge from the topiary garden.

"Did you?"

"No. It wasn't me," he said simply, and she knew it must've been Violet. She'd probably sprayed them with an herbicide.

She took a deep breath and turned to him. "Ed, I'm so sorry about Violet, and I'm glad you're back here where you belong."

"Thank you. I'm sorry for the grief she caused you." His eyes showed his misery.

"It wasn't your fault. Violet was sick, and you couldn't help that."

"Let's go sit down."

They walked over to a bench under a spreading beech.

"I feel it's my fault," he said after they'd sat for a while. "You see, I knew she was getting worse, and I didn't want to admit it."

"That's understandable."

"It all goes back to when we got married. It was one of those kinds of marriages, and I felt trapped. I'd had a year of college and was home for the summer working in the coal mine office. I had such dreams of getting out of that little coal mining town and making something of myself. Then I met Violet. She was only eighteen and so pretty. Well, she got pregnant, we got married, and it ended all dreams of college and making something of myself. I had a wife and kid to support now. Violet cried all the time and so did the baby. The apartment was small, always dirty. Violet didn't do anything once the baby was born. From what I've read since, I know now Violet suffered from postpartum depression, but at the time I didn't know that. I resented her and the loss of my dreams. I went out every evening with buddies drinking just to get away."

Catherine listened with sympathy. She'd seen some of her high school friends trapped in such a situation.

"One evening when I came home," Ed continued, "the baby was dead. Violet sat rocking and singing to him. She refused to believe he was dead. Even after the baby was in his coffin, she sang and talked to him as if he were alive. The doctor and I both believed Violet smothered the baby to quiet him. He was colicky and cried all the time. I should've stayed home and helped care for him. I've never forgiven myself for it, you know."

Catherine's heart ached for both of them. She placed a hand on Ed's gnarled rough hand lying on his knee.

"Violet had a complete breakdown and went into a mental hospital for a year. When she came out, I brought her north. Too many people gossiping and thinking our son died an unnatural death. Even our relatives were cold towards her. I thought it better to get her away.

I got a job in a steel mill, and we rented an apartment in the city. I missed the country, though. Eventually, we bought the house on Raspberry Lane. It wasn't quite country, but close to it with fields all around. It was all we could afford. That was almost thirty years ago now. Then there was a long strike at the mill. I found a job at Elmwood and loved it so much I didn't want to leave when the strike ended. At first Violet was against it. It was a lot less money. She liked having money to buy pretty things, but finally she saw it'd be better for me, so she went along with it and got a job at a gift shop in town. It was good for her to get out of the house and meet people. We never had any more kids, you know. Eventually I got the job as head gardener."

"How long ago was that?"

"Oh about twenty-five years ago. Something like that. I don't keep track." He continued on with his story about Violet. She listened and rubbed his hand knowing he needed to get it out.

"When Violet was in her early forties, she had another bad spell, and went away again for treatment. I told people she was taking care of her sick mother. When she came back everything was fine again."

"What happened this time?" Catherine asked.

"It was the blue roses. Violet never paid much attention to what I was doing. She wasn't interested in gardening, you know. Somehow Chatterton found out about the roses and wanted them. He offered me a large sum of money if I'd let him take credit for them and keep quiet about being the propagator. He knew I'd never talked about them to anyone."

"Why didn't you ever speak of them?"

"Violet wasn't interested, and I've never had many friends outside of the gardens, and even here we're too busy to talk much. Besides, it's best to keep such things to yourself until they're ready to be patented. Do you understand?"

Catherine nodded.

"Chatterton wanted those roses, but I wouldn't sell. So he hired a private eye to dig into my past and found out about our baby."

Anger filled Catherine. "So he blackmailed you."

Ed shrugged. "I guess you could say that. I didn't care for myself, but I didn't want Violet hurt. She set such store about looking good, always liked to imagine herself as being better than common folks." He laughed slightly. "I was a real trial to her."

Catherine thought, but didn't say, Violet had real quality in Ed and was blind not to have recognized it.

"So how did Violet find out what Chatterton had done?" She asked, assuming that was the reason for Violet killing him.

"She started to piece things together. She may have acted flighty sometimes, but she was shrewd. One night she

310

flat out asked me. I was feeling depressed over losing the head gardener's job and admitted it."

"What'd she say?"

"Oh, she ranted and raved, but didn't want anyone to find out about the baby, although she never talked about that. Sometimes I honestly think she completely forgot the night of our baby's death and didn't believe she was responsible. Maybe she couldn't have lived with herself if she'd accepted the truth."

Catherine thought of her smashed doll and wondered.

"When Chatterton was murdered, I worried, but I didn't see how she could do it, and I didn't want to believe she was capable of anything like that."

"I can understand that."

"I couldn't see any connection to Alma, either. I thought it was a normal death. But then when you almost drowned." His voice trailed off as he thought of the horror of that night. "I followed Violet. She was carrying something, a brown bundle in her arms. It seemed strange. Then I lost her in the woods. I was quite a distance behind because I didn't want her to see me. You understand I still didn't think she'd done it, but I was getting suspicious. I was pretty sure Greg Robert hadn't hit you, but I didn't want to think Violet did it. She always liked you."

Catherine squeezed his hand. "I really believe she did."

"I drugged her the night you came, you know."

"I thought so," Catherine smiled. "I was beginning to wonder if you were the murderer."

Ed didn't smile. "She was talking strange, and by now I was becoming more and more convinced it was her. I drugged her that night, but when she got up in the morning, she seemed so normal I started doubting my suspicions.

When you called, she'd left a note saying she'd gone for a walk. I was frantic and didn't know where to look. She came home after dark, unnaturally cheerful and laughing. She was so strange and wouldn't take any medication. I sat up all night watching her. She seemed to be sleeping okay. I fell asleep as the sun was coming up and didn't wake up until ten. She was gone again." He stopped as he relived his fear and worry.

"How awful for you," Catherine murmured.

"You know what's really awful?" he said, pain showing in every line of his face.

"What?"

"I'm relieved she died," he whispered. "Maybe now she's at peace with our son."

Catherine wiped her eyes, and leaned forward to put her arms around him. "Oh, Ed. I'm sure you're right. You did everything you could for her, but she couldn't forgive herself."

She sat back. "I'm so glad you're back here. There's healing in work, and there's healing in gardening."

He nodded. "I'll get you a new truck, too."

"No, my insurance will cover it."

"No, please let me, or at least let me add to the amount the insurance gives you to get a better truck," he insisted.

She smiled mistily at him. "I guess I can't turn down an offer like that." She heard her grandfather's voice say: "Never turn down a gift offered in good faith. It offends and hurts the giver. Graciously accepting a gift is a kindness to the giver. It helps them feel good about their gift and themselves."

"Have you told all this to John MacDougal?"

"Yes. He came over yesterday, and we talked. We can't figure out how Violet got Chatterton to leave the reception and meet her there alone. Probably she sent him a note and said something threatening about announcing who the real propagator of the rose was. He had the patent, and he could've blustered and lied, but I imagine people would've always wondered."

"It does sound plausible, and people already wondered about him and the rose."

312

"Chief MacDougal wishes it could all be quiet for my sake, but it isn't possible. Said he'd do what he could to down play it to the press. He's a nice guy."

"He certainly is," Catherine affirmed.

"I've offered to pay for Alma's funeral and gravestone. He said that'd be nice, and said if Alma's kid was still alive, he didn't seem to care for her."

"She did seem to live a lonely sad life."

He nodded, and they sat in silence before Catherine asked. "Are you selling your house?"

"Yes, eventually but not right away. I don't want to live there anymore without Violet. I've got the gardener's cottage here, and that's enough for me."

"What are we going to do about those dead roses?"

"Dig them up and burn them."

"What about the ones at your house?"

"If you mean the blue ones coming along, maybe they should be destroyed, too."

"Oh, you can't do that," Catherine protested.

"You can have them then."

"I'll take them, but I'll expect you to come over and tend them. And maybe someday you'll be ready to apply for a patent."

He shrugged. "We'll see," but he didn't seem too interested.

"The cat in the well with John. It was Christy's cat, wasn't it?"

"Yes. It sleeps in my shed a lot on the burlap sacks I have stored there."

She wondered about the lemon pie, but decided not to ask. John probably already had.

"My ride is here already, and I've barely done any work this morning. I'll probably get fired," she said in mock seriousness.

"Not if I have anything to say about it," Ed said gruffly.

She leaned forward and kissed his cheek.

"Go on," he said embarrassed. "Your ride is waiting for you. Either that or you're in some kind of trouble."

Catherine laughed and hurried off to get in the Portage Falls police cruiser waiting to take her home.

About the Author

Gloria Alden lives on a small farm in northeast Ohio in the area of the fictional town of Portage Falls. She has two ponies, a few hens, two barn cats, two house cats, two African ring-neck doves, a canary and her companion, a collie named Maggie. She's a retired elementary school teacher with an MA in English. In addition to writing, Gloria is an avid gardener which is why she chose a gardening theme for her books.

In addition to *The Blue Rose,* her debut novel, Gloria has four short stories and numerous poems published. The second book in The Catherine Jewell Mystery Series, *Daylilies for Emily's Garden* will be out in the spring of 2013.

She is a member of Sisters in Crime, The Guppies, a subgroup of Sisters in Crime and the Cleveland chapter of Sisters in Crime as well as being a long time member of The Trumbull County Writers Group.

If you enjoyed *The Blue Rose,* you'll want to read another Catherine Jewell mystery – *Daylilies for Emily's Garden* will be coming out early spring, 2013. Following is a sneak peak at the first chapter.

CHAPTER ONE

Emily Dickenson is dead. Emily Dickenson is dead. The refrain kept repeating itself in Catherine Jewell's head as she drove down Main Street in Portage Falls. It was the title of a mystery she'd read years ago. She wondered why it suddenly popped into her head now. She pulled into an open spot near Belle's Diner. *"Because I could not stop for death / It kindly stopped for me."* Stop it, she told herself as she got out of her truck. What's with the death thing this morning? She wondered.

Once inside the diner, she shed all morbid thoughts as she looked around for her friend. A smile lit up her face when she spied her, and she hurried to Maggie Fiest.

"Been waiting long?" She slipped into the booth.

"Nope. Just got here."

"Did you run this morning?"

Maggie nodded. "Seven miles. I'm starved."

"I've got something to tell you," Catherine said leaning forward and pumping her fists in the air over the table. The natural laugh lines around her eyes became even more pronounced, as her smile reached its limits. "I might get a job redoing the gardens at the Llewelyn estate."

"Really? Great. Look at your menu so we can order. Then you can tell me all about it."

Catherine picked up her menu and then set it aside. "I know what I want. I'm so excited about the possibility of getting it. You've lived here a long time. What do you know about her?"

"She raises pugs," Maggie said, "or at least she used to."

"What're they?" Belle asked, interrupting Catherine and Maggie's conversation as she came to take their orders.

"Dogs," Maggie answered, "a small breed."

"Never heard of 'em. Is that how she makes her living, or is it a hobby?"

"Hobby, I'm sure," Maggie said straight-faced.

"Who're we talking about?" Belle inquired next.

Ignoring the amused snort that came from her luncheon partner, Maggie answered, "Emily Llewellyn."

"Oh, her! You girls know her?"

They both shook their heads.

"Me, neither. Never came in here. Probably thinks she's too good. Probably eats at The Mill. She's some kind of author, ain't she?"

Catherine and Maggie both nodded.

"Are you girls ready to order yet?"

"I'll have the tuna salad on rye," Catherine said, "and could I have a salad instead of french fries?"

"Uh huh, but you sure don't have to watch your weight so I don't know why you don't take the fries. And you?" She turned to Maggie.

"I'll have the tuna salad on rye, too, but I'll have the french fries that come with it, even though I probably shouldn't."

"You young girls! Always worryin' about your weight when you're skinny as snakes, the both of you. I'll be back to give you refills on coffee as soon as I give your orders to Henry." She headed for the kitchen. Her ample girth in the blue uniform straining at the seams showed she didn't worry about fatty foods and cholesterol.

"You certainly found that hanging basket of fake geraniums fascinating," Maggie said.

Catherine chuckled. "I was afraid I was going to laugh out loud."

Maggie shook her head. "What a character!"

"I don't think I've ever seen her husband."

"He never comes out of the kitchen, at least not until they close up. Maybe not even then," Maggie added with a

317

wicked gleam in her eye. "I think I come in here because I like being referred to as a girl," she went on. "When one's approaching thirty, it sounds pretty good."

"When you're forty, it sounds even better."

Maggie grinned as she pulled shoulder length brown hair back from her face and refastened the clip at the nape of her neck. "You look like you're still in your twenties."

"Yeah, right!" Catherine laughed. "Actually, I'm quite comfortable with my age."

They stopped talking as Belle came to fill their coffee cups.

"Now, tell me more about this new job," Maggie said after Belle left. "It sounds exciting. Imagine working for Emily Llewellyn!"

"I don't have the job yet." Catherine erased the smile, but her lips still quivered at the corners.

"Oh, you'll get the job. I'm sure of it."

Catherine's repressed smile burst forth for a moment before she sobered again, although now her toes started tapping replacing the smile. "I've never read anything she wrote, but I've always been fascinated by the old Llewellyn Mansion. I think it's because of the high hedges that give a passerby teasing glimpses. It's never enough, and because of that, it fires the imagination. Have you ever been on the grounds?"

"No, but I know what you mean. I've always wished I could see more of it. Maybe you can hire me to do some work for you," Maggie grinned.

"She writes historical romances," she continued. "Quite a lot of them. I'd never read any until she moved to town a few years ago. I was curious so I found a used one at Carriage House Books."

"Any good?"

Maggie shrugged. "I guess if you like that kind of thing. I don't particularly care for quivering bosoms and rippling muscles, but the writing seemed good. She's apparently also a respected scholar of Emily Dickinson. According to John, she's had quite a few literary criticisms published and a biography, too."

"That's too weird!" Catherine interrupted. "On the way here the refrain 'Emily Dickenson is dead' kept running through my brain."

Maggie shrugged. "Well, as far as I know she's still alive. Emily Llewellyn, I mean, not Emily Dickenson. Did she come to your shop, or did she call you?"

"She called, or rather her secretary, Charles McKee called."

"What exactly does she want done?"

"He said they want the original gardens restored. I imagine it'll be quite an undertaking, but exciting, too." Catherine's eyes sparkled.

"Anyone else bidding on the job?"

"I'm sure there's probably others. He said they'd heard good things about my work, and Miss Llewellyn wanted me to put in a bid. Maybe they talked to Tyler at Elmwood Gardens or maybe the Catchpole family. Remember I did a job for the older Mrs. Catchpole last summer, and then her son and his wife wanted work done, too. It's the only garden designing I've done since I came to town."

"Nice going! I knew you'd go places. Will you be able to do it all yourself? It'll probably be a lot bigger than what you did for the Catchpole's."

"I haven't seen it yet. I'll know more after I've seen the gardens this evening. He said there were fountains and pools to be redone and walkways, too, in addition to the gardens. I'm going to talk to Tom at Elmwood and see if he wants to moonlight and help me with some of the rock construction, if I get the job."

"Here's your lunch, girls," Belle said as she slapped plates down on the table. "Anything else I can get ya?"

They both shook their heads.

For a while Catherine and Maggie ate without talking.

Both had put in a full morning of work; Maggie Fiest, in her studio painting before running, and Catherine at Elmwood Gardens where she was a part time botanist, and then at her nursery, Roses in Thyme, repotting perennials.

"Have you ever seen Miss Llewellyn?" Catherine asked as she picked up her mug to take a sip of coffee.

"No, I don't think so, except I saw her in her garden once when I was riding my bike, but that was a couple of years ago. I've heard her secretary/companion does all the shopping. I used to see her on talk shows sometimes."

"Really? I never have, but then I don't seem to have time to watch much TV."

"I don't, either, but sometimes when I get home from school I'm too tired to think so I turn on the TV to sit and stare mindlessly at something for a while before I can get up and run. She was pretty much a regular on a lot of different talk shows for a while. She was a hoot! Funny, witty and with those outlandish hats she always wore, a real character," Maggie remembered.

"She never married?"

"I heard she did. Some rich guy much older than she was. He died a few years later. At least I think that's what I heard, and she took her maiden name back."

"Was she related to the original owners of the Llewellyn Mansion?"

"It was her aunt, Miss Lucretia Llewellyn. How's that for a name! She was an eccentric character. Always wore black, and had a handyman who drove her everywhere in an old black car. Kept it real shiny. His wife was her housekeeper. It was a household straight out of a gothic novel." Maggie chuckled.

"That was before I came."

"Yeah. She died about ten years ago. The house was empty until Miss Llewellyn came."

"When was that?"

"About four years ago, I think. Funny thing now that I

think about it. I heard somewhere Emily Llewellyn always wears white. Eccentricity must be a family trait."

"And no one ever sees her?" Catherine inquired. Her eyes widened and her mouth slightly opened as curiosity grew about this possible new client of hers.

"I'm sure people do. It's just I've never seen her around. For all I know, she could be quite active in town. I doubt she's the type who'd come to Belle's Diner." Maggie grinned.

Catherine smiled her agreement.

"Anything else?" Bell inquired as she came up to clear away their dishes.

"Nothing for me," Maggie replied.

"Me, either," Catherine echoed.

"I'll total your checks then. Say, did you hear about the mayor over in Blackburn being investigated by the state? Ain't that somethin'? Bet there's some crooked politician connected with that highway that's comin' around our town, too." She pursed her lips and nodded her head several times. "That highway no one wanted. I always said you can't trust no politician."

"That's not true," Maggie said. "For instance, you can't tell me Mayor Partridge is not a totally honest person."

"Yeah, well her. She don't seem like no politician. Anyway, seems someone in the Mayor's office got nervous and snitched in return for immunity accordin' to the noon news."

"Must have been a Blackburnian warbler," Maggie said straight-faced.

Both Belle and Catherine stared blankly at her, and Maggie laughed. "I can tell you two aren't bird watchers. A blackburnian warbler is a bird."

They both still stared at her. Maggie shook her head and rolled her eyes. "Someone who snitches is said to sing."

"Oh!" Catherine said and laughed.

Belle still looked a little confused, but laughed politely.

The two friends paid their bill, and said good-bye at the door.

"Come back soon, real soon," Belle called after them as they left.

Catherine headed for her truck smiling. Emily Dickson is not dead.

Made in the USA
Charleston, SC
27 January 2016